THEIR OWN GAME

by
Duncan James

PublishAmerica
Baltimore

© 2005 by Brian Goodfellow.

All rights reserved. No part of this book may be reproduced, stored in a retrieval system, or transmitted in any form or by any means without the prior written permission of the publishers, except by a reviewer who may quote brief passages in a review to be printed in a newspaper, magazine, or journal.

First printing

ISBN: 1-4137-9615-X
PUBLISHED BY PUBLISHAMERICA, LLLP
www.publishamerica.com
Baltimore

Printed in the United States of America

Chapter One
THE FIRST TO FALL

Major Bill Clayton, dressed in civvies, leant against the bookstall in the main concourse of Belfast's International airport, going through the motions of selecting something to read. From where he stood, he had a good view of Martin McFosters, surrounded by journalists in front of the check-in desk, briefing them before he left. One of Clayton's men was among the press corps, tape recorder in hand, listening intently.

Clayton and his opposite numbers in Special Branch liked to keep an eye on McFosters, but didn't usually bother to see him off on his travels. They knew that this trip was to be something rather different, though. Not that McFosters had any idea. Clayton looked across to his police colleague, sipping coffee from a polystyrene cup. The coffee was awful: it usually was, but he, too, had a good view of McFosters. No one seemed to notice that there were more than usual armed police milling around.

McFosters was off to do more talking. Off to America, which remained the main source of cash for the Republicans, as it had been since before the troubles began. A large part of America, and not just the Irish-Americans, shared the Nationalist view that the British should quit Northern Ireland and their oppressive rule, and that the two halves of the island should be united once again into a single community.

From time to time, influential voices in the States had sought to bring pressure on Westminster, and on Dublin, in an effort to bring this about. It has to be said, too, that influential voices in the States were not averse to putting pressure on McFosters from time to time either, and this visit was likely to be one of those occasions.

His briefing finally finished, Martin McFosters turned to pass through the check-in desk. Clayton and his colleagues glanced briefly at one another in acknowledgement that their role at the airport was over, and made their separate ways towards the car park and their offices. There were calls to be made, but on secure phones, not mobiles. They were too easy to intercept.

McFosters passed through immigration, suffered the indignities of baggage and personal security searches, and made his way to the first class lounge. He was alone this time. It had been made clear to him previously, in the nicest possible way, of course, that Stateside fund-raising efforts were not designed to allow him and half a dozen of his top people to swan around the world in luxury. So this time he went alone. But he insisted on traveling first class, just the same. He was, after all, President of Sinn Fein, and an elected member of both the European and the British Parliaments. And he had previously been invited across, not just to attend and speak at fund-raising dinners, but also to meet senior senators from both houses, and even, once, to meet the President of the United States himself. So first class it was—both his own financial people and the generous American donors had at least agreed upon that.

But he still didn't like the Boeing 747, not even the new, stretched version. Comfortable perhaps, especially in the upper cabin, but the food was predictable, the movies generally boring, and the whole journey just that bit too long, what with the lengthy check-in procedures and all. And there was a limit to how much free champagne even he could sensibly consume.

He didn't really like flying at all, to be honest. He wished he could persuade his people that he should travel via London for a change, but he knew it wasn't even worth thinking about, even though their coffers were swollen with more cash than they would ever need, short of all-out war. They wouldn't even let him save time going by Concorde when that was in service. But he couldn't afford not to go when invited, although he had to admit that the excitement of visiting America after so many years of isolation had gone. This was the third time in as many months that he'd made the dreary journey to update sympathetic senators on the latest twists and turns of the British government. They were keen to know what progress was being made, and found it hard to believe that, after all the apparently positive, if slow, movement there had been through the peace process, things now appeared to be stalled again.

For years, the President of Sinn Fein and his immediate lieutenants had been isolated from mainstream politics, not least because of their association with, and in some cases, parallel membership of, the IRA. Martin McFosters was not alone in this. The leadership of the political wings of the Protestant paramilitaries were in the same boat. Those who supported terrorism were never likely to be taken seriously by the political parties who existed because of the ballot box, rather than because of the bullet and the bomb.

Slowly, though, that had changed. Now, with power sharing in Northern Ireland, McFosters and others had a voice. Their power-base was reinforced by the ballot box as well. To some extent, they had been able to quell the violence through a series of cease-fires, which had been more or less maintained. They had undertaken to use their influence over the IRA, which they had always claimed was not born of a direct link, to work towards "decommissioning" stockpiles of weapons, through an independent body which was actually powerless to do anything except talk. Protestants and Catholics alike had dragged their feet over this, and other issues, and both sides of the political divide also had to deal with militant members who still believed that violence, rather than talking, was more likely to bring progress.

But talking there still was, and plenty of it. And there was violence, too, in spite of the many concessions that had been made in the continuing effort to bring peace to the troubled province. Rather too much violence, in fact. McFosters had to admit that it was making his life more difficult than he would have wished.

This visit was about money. He must make sure he kept up the pressure for the continued flow of funds, and make sure, too, that those whose political support might be wavering, understood that nothing could be achieved, in peace or war, without very substantial amounts of cash. Certainly more than could be raised through the normal methods on the Irish side of the Atlantic. Protection rackets, drugs, prostitution, crime and so on had their value, but the US dollar was available in much greater quantities than they could ever raise, through the huge and influential Irish American population.

It had certainly always been readily available in seemingly endless sums in the past, although there had been one incident, very recently, when urgently needed cash had not been transferred with the usual speed. At one time, a clerk in the branch of the Manhattan State Bank, where several million dollars was held anonymously, had even claimed that the account had been closed. Of course, it hadn't, but several attempts had to be made at other US banks before the required sum was eventually put together and moved to one of their many accounts in Ireland. A cock-up somewhere that would eventually be sorted out, but if anything, it had proved that McFosters' oft proposed and always rejected idea that some of their huge wealth should be invested, had been ill advised. Cash in a bank was like notes under the mattress - quickly and easily available.

The States had always been the main source of cash for the Republican movement, ostensibly to keep Sinn Fein's political efforts alive, although only the most naive would pretend that the steady flow of dollars had not also gone towards buying arms and keeping the IRA going as well. And they were still there, and still needed cash support. Weapons that, in theory at least, had been put beyond use by the decommissioning process, had to be replaced, and those remaining, stored and maintained. NORAID understood this, although for some inexplicable reason, parts of the US administration appeared not to. They believed that their support of Sinn Fein was bolstering the Republican's political efforts, and that was what this visit was all about - American support for the Republican dream of unification.

But he would find it difficult to explain to his Senate supporters that there was, in reality, no longer a peace process at all. His friends in the real IRA had seen to that. The shock of the first devastating bomb in London's Docklands was followed quickly by the assassination of a Cabinet Minister and then bloodshed at Twickenham during the England v. Wales six nations game. Political dialogue over many months and years had not taken things forward as fast as some had hoped and others had wanted, so the militant hot-heads had decided to put a little pressure on things to help the talks along.

It had put the nationalist cause back on the front pages of the world's press, all right, but somehow it wasn't quite having the effect they had all hoped for, any more than it had in the past. Impact, yes. Results—well, perhaps it was a bit early for the changes in attitude to materialise. More time, and more incidents, then we'll see. McFosters was not himself convinced, and he knew that friendly senators weren't either, so this could be one of his more difficult visits. Perhaps it was as well he was on his own, although he could see that a bit of support in the few days ahead might very well be welcome.

***

Somehow, Martin McFosters survived the journey. The menu was the same as last week, and he wouldn't mind a quid for every time he'd seen *The Hunt for Red October*. Sean Connery as a Russian submarine captain with a Scottish accent was the only faintly entertaining thing about the whole film. But he'd never heard of any of the others, so he'd half watched it again, and pretended to doze, between glasses, to prevent neighbours from getting too chatty.

Now he ambled with the crowds towards the immigration desk at Washington's sprawling Dulles International airport, with his mind almost in neutral. Not because of the free drink, of course. It had already been a long and tiring day, and in any case, he knew automatically where to go and what to do. There was no novelty in it for him any more.

Eventually he got to the head of the queue - inevitably, the others had moved quicker than the one he'd chosen to join. He shoved his passport towards the immigration officer, as he had done so often before. The man smiled, took it, glanced at it, looked up, and turned to his hidden computer screen. His fingers moved deftly across the keyboard, although, an Irish-American himself, Clint thought he recognised the passport's owner. The computer confirmed McFosters identity, and flashed up special instructions, in red. This often happened with VIPs or semi-VIPs.

"You're expected," said Clint, looking up. "There's a guy waiting for you outside."

"There always is," said McFosters, wondering who it would be this time.

Clint squinted again at the passport. This was one they'd been waiting for all right, and although he'd been told to hang on to it, it looked OK to him.

"I need to get this checked out," he said, waving the passport towards McFosters. "You go through, and this will catch up with you later. I guess we know where you're staying."

They should do, thought McFosters, *they made the booking. Probably the Sheraton again.* He hoped so, anyway. Very comfortable that was.

But he was uneasy. He never liked being parted from his passport, even if he was being treated like a VIP.

"I'll hang on to it, if you don't mind," he said, holding out his hand to take it back.

"Sorry," said Clint, "orders." And he waived vaguely towards the computer monitor in his cubicle, as if that explained everything.

"Why can't you check it out now, while I wait?" demanded McFosters.

"Because I can't, that's why," said Clint, getting annoyed. "Just relax. We know who you are and where you're staying, and we'll get it back to you as soon as we can, OK?"

McFosters thought it probably was OK after all, nodded, and went through. If the worse came to the worse, he had another passport at home—and an Irish one, too, just in case of emergencies. But they were both forgeries. Good ones mind, but forgeries none the less. He always preferred to use the real thing when on legitimate business, even if it was a British one. Anyway, he was tired, and was looking forward to a hot shower and a decent meal. The man smiled again, as he headed for baggage reclaim and customs.

"You needn't bother with that this time, Mr. McFosters," said a voice.

It belonged to a tall, crew-cut man in a loose fitting raincoat. McFosters had never been met 'air-side' before - always after customs. The man did not introduce himself, but they shook hands.

"Sorry about the passport," said the man. "Don't worry about it—just red tape, or another survey or some damned thing. I'll see you get it back. Anyway, we can skip customs. We'll find your bag and have it taken to your hotel, along with the passport. I've got a car for you right outside. You're booked in to the Sheraton—they say you like it there."

"Yes I do," said McFosters.

This was different. McFosters grinned his thanks. Perhaps, after all, people were beginning to take him and his cause seriously again on this side of the Atlantic, if not the other.

"Personally," said the man, "personally, I prefer motels. They're clean, cheap, and don't ask too many questions about who you're with. Know what I mean?" he said with a wink.

McFosters followed his escort, down long, dimly lit corridors, through the customs administration offices—almost empty at this time of night—and out on to one of the myriad of small internal roads that carved the airport into a small town. They got into the waiting limo, and drove off in silence.

***

Clint had had a lousy day. Let's face it, a Jumbo full of Colombians is always trouble. More for customs than for immigration, he had to admit, but trouble enough. They always got them first. There were always long lists of 'prohibiteds' and 'wanteds,' and it was up to him and his buddies on the other desks to spot them before they got through to customs. But he didn't envy their job, either. The thought of having to body search some of the drifters he'd seen come through the airport made his flesh creep.

He was tired. This was always the worse shift, anyway. Every damned aircraft from every damned country in the world trying to get in before the night restrictions.

And too many new names and faces to look out for were added to the lists and the mug shots every shift. Mostly drug runners, he guessed, but Irish, too. And Arabs. Muslims all looked alike to him, same as the Chinese.

It might not be the best job in the States, but Clint did his best not to let anyone slip through.

He'd spotted McFosters, hadn't he? So he reckoned he'd earned his beer. That's what he'd planned for tonight, and he was looking forward to it. A quiet beer or three on the way home, and then watching the ball game on video, if the damned thing had worked, which sometimes it didn't. He must get it fixed.

Clint headed for the staff parking lot, down long, dimly lit corridors, past the customs administrative offices, which were mostly empty at this time of night.

Somehow, he didn't hear the car, or see it, until it was too late. There was no one else about as he had stepped into the narrow road, just about where McFosters had gotten into the limo.

Apart from the car, three things struck him as his head smashed into the tarmac. The damned car had no lights on, it was going too fast, and he should have looked, anyway.

He was dead on arrival at the hospital.

***

Bill Minton was in the Oval Office, going through the motions of working late, when the Chief of Staff, Colin Carlucci strode in, without knocking. This was why Minton was really there—waiting news. The President's executive secretary disappeared fast, without being asked. Laura Billings knew the signs, and knew something was afoot.

Minton sat, grim faced, his stomach churning, and looked up. This was it. It had started. Probably the biggest gamble of his political life. This would be bigger than Watergate, the Gulf War, Bosnia—anything. The ball was rolling, and there was no stopping it now. He could tell from the look on Carlucci's face.

"McFosters," said Carlucci. "He's gone. Had it. Finished - kaput - disappeared off the face of the earth."

"As planned?" asked Minton.

"Exactly as planned."

There would be no trace of him. There was no record of him arriving in Washington. Not a living soul saw him. Nothing.

***

In his Downing Street office, alone except for the Cabinet Secretary, Prime Minister Tony Weaver was getting a similar briefing.

Verbally, and in hushed tones, of course. Nothing was to be put in writing anywhere about any of this, by anyone, ever. No paper, no leaks.

"McFosters checked in at Belfast airport, all right," reported Sir Robin Algar. "No doubt about that. The media were there to see him off."

But he seemed not to have arrived.

"According to Washington," continued Sir Robin, "no one has seen him at the other end."

"Exactly as planned?" asked the PM.

"Precisely so."

"And no one in Washington saw McFosters at all?"

"No one living." Sir Robin allowed himself the suggestion of a grin. "Certainly not the gentleman sent to meet him in the arrivals hall, outside customs. He is still there. And McFosters' bag is still going round on the carousel in the baggage hall. An extraordinary thing altogether!"

"Well I'll be damned!" exclaimed Weaver. "You know, I really did wonder if the Americans had the guts to go ahead with all of this. But the game's on now, all right. Well I'll be damned!"

"Shall I ask Jane to come in?" asked Algar.

"Yes, do. And tell her to bring the whisky!"

***

McFosters was the first.

Chapter Two
IN THE BEGINNING

It's odd how things happen sometimes. Tony Weaver was in reflective mood as he sat in his office at No.10, not quite believing what was happening or how it had all started. Almost by accident, really. It's not so unusual for small, simple and often quite insignificant things to happen by chance. They do, all the time. More often than not, people don't even notice. Little coincidences, of no importance or relevance to anything much at all, are part of life. But this was different. All this was pure chance, too, really. A casual remark. Almost an aside. But it had set in train a cycle of events that was changing the course of history and the destiny of nations. And changing them fast in a world where already, after the war on terrorism had been declared, things would never be the same again anyway. The Prime Minister simply had to take time to reflect, just to keep up.

The day had started like most others, he recalled, except that there had been no emergency calls overnight, so he was rested and refreshed when he got to the office, just after eight. It had made a change to have breakfast with the family on a weekday, too—he had enjoyed that. Sir Robin Algar, the Cabinet Secretary, was already in, of course. So were half a dozen other key officials, getting papers ready for the planned events set out in his diary. No travelling today, not even across the road for PM's questions in the House. A few meetings with colleagues, going over the most important agenda items for tomorrow's Cabinet meeting, the usual mountain of paper work, and the regular call, now back on a more leisurely weekly basis after the frenzy of events a few months ago, to Bill Minton, the American President. Sir Robin would give him a written briefing for that, and they would go through it together later, with the Permanent Secretary from the Foreign Office. It was now, once again, a routine enough event for the Foreign Secretary not to be involved directly, although he would have read and agreed to brief and the lines to take.

As Tony Weaver reached his office, Jane Parsons, his senior personal secretary, handed him a sheaf of papers, and almost immediately followed him to his desk with his first cup of coffee of the day.

"Good morning, Prime Minister."

"'Morning, Jane. Anything special in this lot?" he asked, waving to the now full in-tray.

"No more special than usual, Prime Minister," she replied, collecting his over-night red boxes. "Sir Robin would like to see you when you're ready, and Andrew is waiting to go through the press cuttings with you."

"OK. Give Andrew a coffee, and tell Sir Robin to bring his in with him. I'll see him now."

He moved across to an armchair next to the coffee table in the bay window overlooking the rose garden, taking his cup with him, and heard the disappearing Jane say, as she did every morning at about this time, "The Prime Minister will see you now, Sir Robin." He brought his coffee with him, without being told. He always did.

A tall, slim and elegant man, in his mid-fifties, Sir Robin Algar was one of Tony Weaver's favourite people. A career civil servant with an excellent classics degree, he had risen rapidly to the very top, serving en route as a diplomat in Washington, and Permanent Secretary in both the Treasury and the Foreign Office, before heading up the civil service from his present post as Cabinet Secretary. Those who criticised him at all, usually did so through jealousy, but pointed to his sheltered life and lack of experience in the 'real' world outside the confines of Whitehall, either in industry, commerce or the military. Up to a point, they had a point, but ignored the very real demonstration of his versatility and razor-sharp intellect when he spent three years seconded to a lame duck industry, which he managed to turn to profitability. Others did remember, though, and it was said that he was frequently headhunted for much more lucrative positions outside the civil service. Such was his loyalty, though, that he had so far not been tempted. He undoubtedly enjoyed his work—his enthusiasm rubbed off on others—and was very much on top of the job. He appeared unflappable, knew everyone worth knowing, and seemed to know what was going on in every nook and cranny of Whitehall. What he didn't know, he very soon found out.

Tony Weaver motioned him to another armchair.

"Jane's got the red boxes, and I have signed everything except that letter to the CBI. You'll see that I've scribbled on it a bit. Let me know if you agree with what I've suggested."

"Yes, of course, Prime Minister. I may have trouble with Trade and Industry over that, as I know they were wedded to what they thought was a carefully crafted letter on a difficult subject, but if we can square away the Secretary of State, we should be alright."

"I'll speak to him myself if you have any trouble." Weaver didn't expect for a moment that Sir Robin would have the least bit of trouble.

"Thank you, Prime Minister."

"Now, what about today, Robin? For a change, it looks straightforward enough and pretty routine, judging by the diary at least."

"As you say, straightforward enough, I think, although fairly busy. So far as I can see, you have all the papers and briefings you need to see you through. Unusually, there are no lunches and no speeches today, although there is a draft of one for you to give in your constituency on Friday. That's been prepared by your people at party HQ, of course, although I have taken the liberty of having a quick look at it myself, and nothing in it seems to conflict with any stated government policy. Later on we have a slot in the diary to talk about tomorrow's Cabinet, and this afternoon you have your regular telephone conversation with the President of the United States. If I may, I'll sit in on that as usual. I shall be here or in the Cabinet Office most of today, although I do have a few meetings of my own to attend to as well as a couple with you, but I can be contacted if you need me for anything urgent while I'm out."

"That sounds fine - thank you, Robin. Anything special for the President this afternoon?"

"Nothing I'm aware of that isn't already covered in your briefing notes, unless there's something in the papers this morning. Shall I ask Andrew to join us now?"

Andrew Groves joined them, nursing what must by now be a cold mug of coffee. He had his own mug, which he reckoned held more than most cups, although it badly needed a good wash. Andrew and the mug were somehow right for one another. He was a bit on the scruffy side of smart. His suit could have done with a press, his hair was a bit ruffled and untidy, and his shoes - well, they used to be Hush Puppies, but most of the nap had long since worn off. He shuffled in briskly, a fist full of papers in the other hand and cuttings under one arm, a stooping figure, no doubt the result of long hours hunched over a typewriter trying to beat it to death with two fingers.

" 'Morning, Prime Minister." He slumped into a vacant armchair, and dumped an untidy pile of paper on the floor beside him. "Not much in the media this morning to worry about," he said, thrusting onto the two laps facing him a neatly produced and concise summary of the main items of interest over the last 24 hours from the TV, radio and papers. "I told them yesterday there was nothing important in your diary today—if you see what I mean—so they managed to get their main story from Brussels. Some clown apparently wants us all to grow straight cucumbers. Why do they do that?"

"Why don't you go and find out?" asked the Prime Minister, annoyed. "That sort of headline is most unhelpful, and even damaging to us at the moment, given the state of the debate in this country about our future in the EU. And it can't help other potential member nations, either. There ought to be the same sort of consultation and co-ordination between member states that we enjoy here between government departments, to make sure there are no surprises."

"Well, I certainly could shoot over for a day. I haven't met Pierre van-Leengoed officially since the G-8 meeting earlier this year, and we didn't have much chance for a bi-lateral chat then. Too much else going on, if you recall. But I've known him for a long time now, and we occasionally have a weekend together, as I'm sure you know, so it would be good to have an excuse to see him again. I might take James Wellington or one of his chaps from the Foreign Office, too, just to avoid upsetting anyone. I'm sure between us we could sort something out."

"By all means consult with James first," said the Prime Minister, "but I'd rather you went on your own, if you wouldn't mind. There's something else I'd like you to check out while you're there, if you would. Let me know when you have a date, and I'll brief you then, but make it soon if you can."

Andrew and Robin exchanged glances. What was all this about, then? No doubt they'd soon find out, so neither chose to ask.

They finished going through the day's news summary. Plenty of coverage about the latest twists and turns in the Middle East, including yet another suicide bomber who, for once, had managed to blow himself up without hurting anyone else. But that hadn't stopped the Israeli administration from using their helicopter gun-ships against yet another series of Palestinian targets, including a police station on the West Bank. The new outbreak of BSE in Devon, although very limited, continued to get plenty of coverage, especially from those who thought the government was directly responsible for it and could have prevented it. Not least, some European 'allies', who could see the chance of more exports for their own livestock, were busy jumping on the bandwagon again. There was quite good coverage of the latest government initiatives announced the previous day, especially the deliberate leak of a rumoured consultation document about the possibility of re-introducing tax relief on contributions by pensioners to private medical insurance. But there was virtually no mention of the anti-terrorist war, no doubt because the initial storm had passed, and there was not much sign of activity against new targets.

There was no need to change the briefing for the Washington call.

Another piece of paper was thrust forward.

"Today's announcements by other Ministers—nothing unexpected. Overseas Aid is top for questions in the House, but again no major initiatives are planned, and no embarrassing questions have been tabled. But I shall be there just in case. Someone's bound to ask if we're doing enough for Afghanistan or Pakistan—they always do."

Both men were always impressed by how on top of events he always seemed. There was no doubting that he was in charge of co-ordinating government communications, or that he was one of the hardest working people in Whitehall. Weaver had no idea what time he got to the office each morning, to get all this read and summarised and prepared for such an early briefing, but he knew he did it all himself. He almost felt guilty about it. Groves lived in Surrey and drove to work—liked to miss the rush hour and the congestion charge at both ends of the day, he always said. He certainly did in the evenings. He had seen him leave around eight on a good day, and he knew he often stayed on if there was an important debate in the House. Robin drove to work, too, but only from Battersea. All Weaver had to do was walk down stairs, and even that was an effort some mornings. He almost felt guilty about it.

"I've got a copy of the briefing for your call to the States," Groves continued, almost without pause for breath, "and I'll brief the media accordingly when I get the word from Sir Robin. I've already spoken to the President's press secretary and agreed the line we are planning to take, so there will be no crossed wires. There's nothing in the media there to worry about either, but if anything breaks during the day, I'll let you and Robin know."

He started to scoop up his papers, obviously keen to get on. "Anything else?" he asked.

"Robin?"

The Cabinet Secretary shook his head, still scanning the press summary.

"That's all, then, Andrew. Thanks very much," said Weaver.

"I'll be around if you want me." Andrew took a last swig from his mug and strode for the door.

There was nothing special about the rest of the day—it went as planned, for once.

Around teatime, Sir Robin appeared prior to the Washington call, with Sir Arthur Bailey, his opposite number from the Foreign Office.

"Nothing in your brief needs changing, Prime Minister," he said, "and there's nothing to add, either. I've been in touch with colleagues in the White House and at the Embassy, and they are all content."

Together, the three of them went carefully through the written briefing.

In the outer office, one of the technical specialists from the Briefing Room was checking over the equipment, testing the scrambler and opening the line in readiness. Even though there was nothing of great international import to discuss today, secure communications were essential for any bilateral conversation between heads of state.

The phone call was routine enough. Sir Arthur left, and Sir Robin stayed on in case something came up which wasn't in the briefing, as well as to listen on the extension and take notes. The door to the outer office was shut. A weekly sequence of events, when things were normal. Not that things ever were, really, but when none of the crisis around the world had a direct or major new impact on either country, then weekly was usually enough to keep the special relationship in the public consciousness. It had to be said, though, that until recently the special relationship hadn't been quite as special as it used to be. America had been following it's own interests rather too earnestly of late, almost regardless of the impact of their policies on the rest of the world, what with the Land Mines Treaty, the ABM Treaty and Star Wars, and the Kyoto agreement on global warming. In all these areas, American industrial interests had been put first, and international agreements second. The threat of recession and unemployment, no doubt, was a powerful influence, and to be understood after the horrific events surrounding the World Trade Centre. But the United Kingdom was now one of their closest allies again, and there was a distinct coolness in the relationship with Israel, who, Minton felt, could have done more and said less in the run up to the offensive both against bin Laden and his al Qa'Aeda group, and against Saddam Hussein.

But the special relationship, even before the joint action against Iraq, had kept the two leaders in touch, and allowed their officials to swap notes. So it was that afternoon, as always. Well before the hot line was opened, both leaders had been briefed by their senior officials and advisers, who had agreed the agenda between them much earlier still. They had also agreed the joint press statement that would be issued afterwards, providing their men stuck to the script.

They had.

Bill Minton and he had exchanged pleasantries, asked about the families, commented on the weather - all that. Minton, Weaver recalled, had even asked about the cricket, although that was a bit uncalled for, especially as we had just lost another test match. Besides, Minton knew as much about cricket as he did about baseball, and probably cared even less. But he supposed it was meant to be friendly, and that was what special relationships were all about. Certainly, he and Minton had personally always got on well enough when they had met, special relationship between the two countries or not, and their friendship allowed a certain level of informality not normal between heads of state. In fact, if there hadn't already been one, they could well have started the special relationship going.

Eventually they got down to the usual things. Famine in Africa, environmental issues like global warming (he knew this was sensitive, so stuck to his brief in as friendly a way as he could), easing the third world debt burden, and so on.

There was nothing new to say about the war against terrorism. The Taliban had gone, and with them Osama bin Laden, while Iraq was quietly getting back to normal, in spite of the insurgents. Others, like Iran and Libya, were being allowed to sweat it out for a bit, although attention was still focused on the Middle East, where both Israel and Lebanon were accusing each other of terrorism.

It must have been, he reflected, while they were chatting about that ever-continuing crisis. Yes, that's when it was. That's what really started the whole chain of events. No doubt about it.

"So you're sending the Secretary of State to the Middle East again next week?" he had asked.

"Certainly. It seems to me that some pressure is needed to get talks going again, so we all hope that a few days intensive shuttle diplomacy will concentrate their minds, and perhaps even lead others in the coalition to bring pressure to bear as well. Somehow, the vicious circle of violence and revenge has to be broken, although how anyone in the Middle East can control fanatical suicide bombers or kids throwing stones, escapes me. Frankly, I don't think they're capable of controlling anything, and it's my firm belief that we shall soon have to get the old allies of the coalition fired up again to do something about the extremists, on both sides."

"I agree, and you can certainly count on us to give you our whole-hearted support. Let us know if there is any specific area where we can help during this current effort. Are you offering any carrots or sticks this time, by the way?"

"Nothing special," replied the President, "usual stuff about the possible effect of continuing conflict on financial support, trade or arms sales, depending who we are talking to. But we are hoping to develop a bit more international support this time round. Certainly, Jordan seems to be ready to add weight to our efforts, and even Syria appears to be getting more and more exasperated and ready to help, since we pushed Israel off to an arm's length relationship after their behaviour during the run up to the Afghanistan raids."

"None of this usually makes much of an impact, though, does it?" asked Weaver. "Especially on the hard-liners on both sides."

"You're right," said Minton. "I guess one day we'll actually have to do something that hurts. The problem is, who to hurt first."

"And if you hurt them both at once, it has no effect at all."

"Right again—except that whatever we are likely to do in that part of the world hurts someone here back home, too. That's always a problem for us. Loss of exports, effect on the dollar—something difficult to handle, you bet, whatever option we discuss."

"And votes?"

"Yup. And votes. Especially the Jewish vote in this case if we're not careful, and there's lots of 'em," agreed Minton. "Trouble is, there is no half way house between the demands of either side. No compromise, no deal, nothing."

"The whole situation in the Middle East is very similar to Northern Ireland really, isn't it?" opined Weaver.

"Exactly similar," agreed the President. "One side insists on staying part of the UK, while the other demands to be made part of the Republic. There is just no middle ground. And much as we try to support all you are trying to do, we are very conscious that the efforts being made by NORAID are working against you. And, of course, we have a huge Irish-American vote here, much of which supports what they see as the Northern Irish struggle for freedom. So that in itself is a bit limiting on what we can do, and how far we can go. But you know all that—the art of the impossible! It's a pity we can't find a third party they'd both be happy with!"

There was a pause.

"Mr. President, perhaps we should talk more about that," said the Prime Minister quietly. "Between ourselves, soon."

Another pause. The informality had gone. Officials on both sides of the Atlantic fidgeted.

"Happy to, Prime Minister. It's time you came over again, and we could find a quiet weekend retreat somewhere if you wanted."

"Thank you for that," said Weaver. "I'll be in touch to arrange something shortly, if I may? Perhaps this weekend?"

The hot line went cold. So did the officials who were listening. This wasn't in the script.

Sir Robin looked at him quizzically as the call ended. Tony Weaver was suddenly at his crisp and efficient best.

"Cut outside Robin, and see if Jane or the chap from the Briefing Room heard anything. Make out you missed something, if you like. Hurry. And leave your clipboard here, please."

Sir Robin Algar looked almost offended as he put his notes into the outstretched hand and turned towards the door.

The technician was just leaving, and Jane was hunched over her computer, peering into the screen. She never usually listened in, and hadn't today. The other members of the outer office had been too busy to take much notice of anything except their own concerns. The Diary Secretary was busy, as always, trying to fit quarts into pint pots—there were always more calls for 'essential' meetings that there were hours in the day. Typists had been typing, clerks had been clerking, but the man from the Cabinet Office Briefing Room always listened, through a pair of earphones, although it was only to ensure top quality reception and that the scramblers at both ends were talking the same language. Nevertheless, he would have heard every word that passed between the two leaders. There had been no one else in the outer office during the brief discussion, and even if there had been, they would not have known what was going on. So Robin reported.

"I want to see that man's personal file as soon as possible," said the Prime Minister, "complete with security clearances, when he was last vetted and so on."

"Very good, Prime Minister. I'll get on to it right away."

"When you have, come back and I'll explain. Make the call from Jane's office, and tell her no one is to interrupt us."

Sir Robin Algar had worked with plenty of government ministers in his time, from both political parties, and had managed to get on with them all, even if he hadn't always agreed with what they were trying to do or how they were trying to do it. Some had been pretty sharp characters, while others had to be led by the hand to get anything done at all. But he had never before met anyone in politics quite like Tony Weaver. He had impressed while in opposition, even on the backbenches, but he had shone in the shadow cabinet and had mesmerised members of his own party and the electorate at large as opposition leader. The fact that he would one day be Prime Minister was a political inevitability. He didn't look anything special, it had to be said, but he had a razor-sharp brain behind his furrowed brow, and he knew how to use it. Every now and then, Robin thought he could see something of his military training coming through. Although it was a long time ago now, he took the Sword of Honour at Sandhurst, and was well on his way to the higher ranks of the Army when he decided that, as he put it, he would rather sort out political cock-ups from the front bench than from the front line. And that, in Sir Robin's view, was where he had particular strengths. He could cut through traditional thinking to introduce radical and innovative, but nonetheless practical policies, and lead from the front to get them into place. He was courageous enough to think the unthinkable and overcome prejudice, and seemed able to plan a sequence of events to achieve his desired outcome, rather like a game of three-dimensional chess. He had introduced, in his time, what anyone else would perceive as 'wild ideas'. And yet, quietly and mostly on his own, he had worked out the detail, assessed the risks, balanced them against the benefits, worked out who would support and who would oppose, and eventually demolished the opposition by his crystal clear logic to push through measures which no-one else had thought of or would have believed possible. Not all, Sir Robin admitted, had yet stood the full test of time, but not one so far had come unravelled or showed any signs of doing so. In all this, his first priority was one of benefit to his country. He had been known, in the past, to support opposition policies because he believed them to be in the nation's best interests, and was prepared to sweep aside petty party politics to achieve the best that was available. "Innovative thinking and beneficial policies are not the sole prerogative of government," he once declared. Sometimes, the strength of coalition was preferred to the weakness of opposition for its own sake.

In his rather privileged position, Sir Robin often got wind of the way the Prime Minister's mind was working before anything was said officially or privately. The odd question here, a reference there, a request for an old briefing paper, an informal chat with a colleague—little things often began to point to a neat piece of lateral thinking that was being carefully developed before being launched on an unsuspecting Cabinet. He worked so closely with Tony Weaver that they had come to respect one another's confidences and to understand how each worked. So much so that Sir Robin had more than once managed to get on the same wavelength, to the extent that he was prepared rather than surprised when the new policy was eventually given a discreet public airing. He was almost invariably the first to share in the Prime Minister's thinking. His view was valued, and his vast experience of how government worked—how to achieve the impossible—made him a perfect sounding board. Once the confidence had been shared, they had then worked quietly together to take the developing policy forward, he taking discrete soundings of the Whitehall machine while Tony Weaver used his political antennae to judge the mood in Parliament, until the point was reached that early, tentative draft papers could be put together. Here, Jane would be brought in to the act, or his own Isabelle. Both devoted personal assistants of the old school—utterly loyal, totally trustworthy, discrete and hard working.

Jack Bennett's file would be there within the hour.

"When it arrives," he told Jane, "let me know on the intercom, and I'll come out for it. Otherwise, no phone calls or visitors until further notice."

"No problem," she replied, "There is just one diary slot we should perhaps re-arrange, in case you're closeted for too long." She looked questioningly at the Cabinet Secretary.

Sir Robin shrugged. "Your guess is as good as mine," he said. "For once, I haven't the slightest idea what we shall be talking about, or for how long. Perhaps you'd tell John I'm still here, and get him to tell the Foreign Office that nothing special happened. Oh, and tell Andrew he can brief the media as planned."

It was not like him not to know what was going on—not even to be able to hazard an intelligent guess at what was happening. He was used to the cold incisiveness of the Prime Minister's policy development, and his courage in putting forward the un-thinkable, but it was always, in the past, in relation to domestic policies. This plainly was not. At least one foreign power was going to be involved in this one, and this made Sir Robin feel most uncomfortable. Even if the PM was only planning to take advantage of his personal relationship with Bill Minton to bounce a few ideas around, it probably wasn't a very good idea to air possible solutions to this country's problems abroad, before they had been aired at home.

What the devil is going on?

One way to find out. He went in, to find Weaver with his back to the door, gazing out of the window, lost in thought.

"That file you wanted will be here within the hour," said Sir Robin. "I've asked Jane to let me know when it arrives."

"Good. It's getting late—you'd better ask her to bring in the tray and some ice, too! We could be here some time yet. I hope you've nothing planned for this evening, Robin. Say if you have, and we can talk some other time."

Not bloody likely, Robin thought. His own SPS, John Williams, would know to warn his wife about dinner tonight, but it was only a family affair with his stepbrother and sister-in-law.

"Nothing planned," he said, turning in the doorway to Jane.

"I heard," she said. "I'll get the ice. Whisky?" she asked.

"Please."

He sat in his usual armchair at the coffee table. But this was far from usual. He had no papers, and he was not there to brief the Prime Minister. The Prime Minister was about to brief him.

"Sorry about this." The Prime Minister tapped Sir Robin's clipboard. "I didn't want any prying eyes finding out anything they didn't need to know. You know what Private Offices are like—the people there can read anything up side down at fifty yards! And we must have total and absolute secrecy."

"I quite understand," said Sir Robin, although he patently didn't.

"One thing I shall insist upon," continued the PM, "is that there shall be nothing, repeat nothing, in writing about this issue. No minutes of meetings, no agendas, no memos, no file notes, no papers, no discussion documents, no drafts, no invoices, no bills, nothing—absolutely nothing—on paper. If I proceed with what I am about to discuss with you—and a lot depends on your reaction to what I have to say—only those people who we can guarantee to be absolutely trustworthy will be involved, and their numbers will be kept to the very minimum necessary to achieve our objective. There must be no leaks, and nothing to leak which makes any sense—hence no papers. If we proceed…" Sir Robin noticed that already the PM was talking about 'we' and not 'I', "…if we proceed, there will obviously have to be a public record of everything that takes place, and I shall look to you eventually to produce that archive material."

"Understood," said Sir Robin, who still didn't, and was already beginning to feel even more uneasy. He noticed that both men had already finished their first glass of Scotch. There was a tension in the air, which Robin had never before noticed when in Tony Weaver's company.

"So I shall leave it to you to decide whether or not you keep these notes," the clipboard was still on the coffee table, "and if so, how you secure them so that no-one can possibly gain access to them apart from yourself.

"There's just one thing which we should perhaps do before we settle, and that, if you agree, is to start organising my trip to the States. Perhaps you would ask Jane to set the ball rolling making the necessary plans. It would be helpful if I could go this coming weekend, if that's convenient to you and the President.

I'd like you to come with me, if you can. Tell Jane and the Foreign Office and anyone else who needs to know that it's about the Middle East, and that it's a public demonstration of our support for everything America is trying to do out there. Get the Foreign Office to prepare a briefing on our position as a matter of urgency—what more we do to help, the usual thing. We need a smoke screen, and it won't be a complete waste of time, as officials can discuss it formally in Washington while you and I are with the President, and Andrew can brief from it. While you're setting that up, I'll pour another glass!"

Sir Robin slipped out, briefed Jane, and had a quick word with Arthur Bailey, who sounded quite surprised.

"I thought you said everything went according to the brief," he queried.

"So it did, but I think this is an afterthought on the PM's part, and he quite firmly believes it would be helpful to the Americans to have such a display of support at this time. I must say, I agree, and I'm sure you do, too."

Sir Arthur had little choice. "Yes, of course. I'll get things moving straight away, and let you know as soon as I can if Washington can accommodate us at such short notice."

Sir Robin knocked quietly and went back into Tony Weaver's office, to find that the PM had switched on the anti-bugging recorded tape of a party in full swing. No-one eavesdropping would be able to pick up a conversation between two people against that background, and although the office was swept by security at least once a week, Weaver was obviously leaving nothing to chance. When he had said 'no leaks', he had meant 'no leaks'.

The Cabinet Secretary took his seat opposite the Prime Minister, feeling distinctly apprehensive, and nodded.

"I hardly know where to begin," began Weaver.

Chapter Three
MEANWHILE, IN WASHINGTON

"What the hell's going on suddenly?" demanded Bill Minton as the phone call from London ended.

Bill Minton had been President of the United States for some three years now, and was acutely conscious of the fact that if he were to stand any chance of serving for a second term, he would very soon have to start making careful plans for his re-election. He had, at least, already made the decision to run for a second term, although the decision had almost been made for him. His party hierarchy wanted it, party activists and grass-root members across the States wanted it, and many foreign leaders had hinted that a second term would be in the national interest as well as in the overall interests of the international community, which above all needed stability at the moment. Not least, his wife, Millie, had urged him to stand again.

The Democratic Party was in something of a turmoil, and had no real prospect of winning, largely because they had no really credible candidate or policies that in any way appealed to the electorate. Minton, on the other hand, had introduced several popular domestic reforms to education and the health system not least, as well as tightening up on law enforcement. This was a direct follow-on from his predecessor's foreign policy initiatives to combat terrorism, which he had supported and was taking forward. Many of his domestic initiatives still had to be brought to fruition, and for the country to change leadership now would be to lose these reforms when there was nothing worthwhile on offer to replace them.

So it seemed to him, and his political advisors, that he had a good chance of being re-elected, and probably with a decent majority, in spite of the closeness of the last two presidential election results. One of the main reasons for this belief was that the man who appeared, at the moment, to be the front-runner for selection by the electoral colleges as the Democratic candidate was a very loose cannon. Indeed, it was being said that he was so far right wing that even the South African whites were afraid he might win.

But he recognised that nothing is ever certain in politics, and especially not in American politics. It was virtually impossible to take heed of all the lobby groups that existed, for a start, and it was certainly impossible to go anywhere near meeting all their often disparate and conflicting demands. Some were two-bit, wild-eyed organisations, with no real power base or support around the country, while others represented very much minority or specialised views. Generally speaking, these could all safely be ignored. But there were others, mainly ethnically based, which could certainly not be ignored, particularly with the world in its present state of flux.

Almost any candidate, of whatever party, could write off the majority of the small but not insignificant Muslim and Islamic vote for a start, after events in Afghanistan and Iraq and the ructions they had caused. The overall situation in the Middle East, and the growing anti-American feeling throughout the region, was also not a good sign. The only effective way to recapture that particular vote would be to virtually cut off any further help to, and support of Israel, but that was plainly impossible. The strength of the American Jewish vote was such that it simply couldn't be sacrificed or risked. Having said that, it was already a less certain commodity than it had been a few years back, due to the coolness which had developed, and largely remained, during the intensive round of diplomacy in the Middle East while trying to build the anti-Taliban coalition. But Minton certainly wasn't about to do anything himself which would further weaken his support from that section of the community, although, on the other hand, there seemed little he could do to strengthen it, either. Certainly the 'road map to peace' hadn't achieved much.

Somehow, in spite of America's own best efforts and the valiant support of their closest allies, it had proved largely impossible to convince the Muslim world that the fight against terrorism wasn't a fight against the whole Islamic community. Sure, there were countries in the region that were prepared to pay lip-service to being convinced, but they largely sat on the fence when it came to actually giving any practical support. What was desperately needed was to shift the fight against terrorism to a non-Arab terror organisation. But where?

The fact was that most of the violent militants were anti-American or anti-Jewish, and from the Arab world, with bases and support in such places as Iran, Syria and probably still Libya. Shifting the fight there would, and had, only make a bad situation worse.

But the hawks in his own administration were determined to see such groups as Hamas, and Hizbollah, backed by Iran and Syria, thwarted before they looked outside the Middle East, although Indonesia, with its own brand of Muslim fundamentalists, had been talked about. And up to a point it made sense while there was still such a built up of military forces in the area, but he had often been sorely tempted to suggest that they should shift their attention to, say, ETA and the Basque separatists, if only to prove the point about not being anti-Muslim. But for all their evil, they were not in the same category as al-Qa'Aeda, and not truly international terrorists, either, so he had held his council. Nevertheless, he remembered that the Spanish government had once, some time ago, asked the European Union to do something or other about them. He really should find out what, if anything, was done—they probably only froze their assets, or something, and it obviously hadn't made the slightest difference. Bombs still went off in Madrid and Bilbao, and judges and other senior figures were still shot from time to time. He knew that America had higher priorities at the moment, but the fact remained that if they could only do a little to help and make the maximum out of it in PR terms, it would not make much difference to the Hispanic votes at home one way or the other, but might just help to convince the Arab world that terrorists meant terrorists, and not exclusively Muslims.

Ireland was different, though, and quite unexpectedly and without warning, the brilliant young Prime Minister from across the Atlantic wanted to talk to him about it, and in a hurry, and privately.

"What the hell's going on, suddenly?" Minton asked his Cabinet Chief, as the phone call to London was ended. "What's he on about? We weren't expecting that, were we?"

"No, Mr. President, we were not. There's certainly no hint from the briefing of anything new coming up, and I can't begin to guess what he wants to talk about."

Colin Carlucci, as the President's Chief of Staff, was always present when Minton spoke to foreign leaders, and was responsible for making sure he was properly briefed beforehand. Minton was shaping up quite well—certainly they'd had worse Presidents—but he still needed leading by the hand every now and then, and he knew it. To his great credit, he never shied away from asking for help, advice or support when he thought it was going to be needed.

This call, though, was slated to be even more routine and low key than most of the weekly contacts with London. The Secretary of State's office had prepared the brief as usual, and gone through it with the President only last night, but there was no reason for him or anyone else to be present. They knew London was taking the same low-key approach, too. Of course, there was a section in the briefing book about Northern Ireland, but nothing had changed since last week, and it was not expected that it would be raised at all, least of all as an issue. Weaver had caught the President on the wrong foot, no mistake, so he had really had little chance but to react as he had done. Indeed, thinking about it, Minton had reacted exactly right, Carlucci concluded.

"Was the call taped?" asked the President.

"Always."

"Then see if you can get the Secretary of State in here to listen to the end of it—if not, the Deputy. Let's see what they make of it, and whether they have a clue what this is all about. Use my phone from here, if you like."

"If he's free," said Carlucci to his opposite number, "the President would like to see the Secretary of State in the Oval Office as soon as possible, please. Something came up during the call from London which we weren't expecting and which wasn't covered in the brief." A pause. "Good. Thanks.

"Mr. Bragan's on his way. I'll organise the tape in here, shall I?"

Miles Bragan was probably the safest pair of hands, as Secretary of State, in America's living memory. Both quick witted and sure footed, he had taken very little time to stamp his authority on the world stage, and earn the respect of his peers in most of the major powers. It wasn't just that he was a nice man and easy to get on with, but rather that he always took a measured view and made up his own mind even if that went against the party line. Neither hawk nor dove, he was a stabilising influence wherever he went, at home or abroad, and was a powerful negotiator.

Both sides in the Middle East were rather dreading his upcoming visit to them, truth be known. He had almost shamed them into the ceasefire they had reached some six months ago, and which, until recently, had more or less held fast. Certainly, plenty of talking had gone on during that time, and although nothing approaching real progress had been agreed, there had been encouraging signs that limited agreement would be possible given more time. But now time had run out once again, and escalating violence had started up all over again. Of course, each side blamed the other for starting it, for over-reacting, and for being responsible for the breakdown in talks. Although neither would admit it, both sides also felt rather ashamed at letting Bragan down, and knew that they were about to have their heads banged together again, in the nicest possible way. They also fully expected, and hoped, that he would be able to produce yet another face-saving formula which would allow a few more months of stumbling progress to be made.

" 'Morning, Miles," welcomed Minton.

"Good morning, Mr. President; Colin. What happened?" asked Bragan.

"Absolutely nothing, until right at the end," replied Minton.

Bragan sat across the oak desk from Minton, next to Carlucci who had the tape ready to play.

"I won't bore you with everything that passed between us," continued Minton, "it was just like the brief said it would be in terms of the subjects we discussed, and as relaxed and friendly as ever. As you suggested he would, Weaver offered every support for your trip to the Middle East, and offered specific help if we wanted it in any particular area. The conversation somehow almost drifted from there into making comparisons with Northern Ireland—play the tape, Colin, from where we were talking about votes, after I'd said how difficult it was to take any positive action because of reaction back here."

Carlucci set the tape recorder going, and Bragan leant forward.

"You're right," said Minton. "I guess one day we'll actually have to do something that hurts. The problem is, who to hurt first."

"And if you hurt them both at once, it has no effect at all."

"Right again - except that whatever we are likely to do in that part of the world hurts someone here back home, too. That's always a problem for us. Loss of exports, effect on the dollar - something difficult to handle, you bet, whatever option we discuss."

"And votes?"

"Yup. And votes. Especially the Jewish vote in this case if we're not careful, and there's lots of 'em," agreed Minton. "Trouble is, there is no half way house between the demands of either side. No compromise, no deal, nothing."

"The whole situation in the Middle East is very similar to Northern Ireland really, isn't it?"

"Exactly similar. One side insists on staying part of the UK, while the other demands to be made part of the Republic. There is just no middle ground. And much as we try to support all you are trying to do, we are very conscious that the efforts being made by NORAID are working

against you. And, of course, we have a huge Irish-American vote here, much of which supports what they see as the Northern Irish struggle for freedom. So that in itself is a bit limiting on what we can do, and how far we can go. But you know all that - the art of the impossible! It's a pity we can't find a third party they'd both be happy with!"

Bragan noticed the pause.

"Mr. President, perhaps we should talk more about that. Between ourselves, soon."

Another pause, Bragan noted, and the informality gone, too.

"Happy to, Prime Minister. It's time you came over again, and we could find a quiet weekend retreat somewhere if you wanted."

"Thank you for that. I'll be in touch to arrange something shortly, if I may? Perhaps this weekend?"

Carlucci switched off the tape.

"So what the hell's going on, suddenly?" asked the President, for the second time.

A puzzled Secretary of State shook his head slowly, frowning. "Three things, Mr. President. First of all, it seems to me that your conversation didn't drift into talking about Northern Ireland. I think you were deliberately led into the subject. Secondly, I have no idea why you were, or what the Prime Minister has in mind. My guess would be that his officials will be as puzzled as we are by what he's up to. You and I both know him well enough now to know that he's a very sharp cookie, and that he often plays his cards very close to his chest until he's good and ready to let an idea get an airing. I think that's where we're at now. Finally, Bill, I think you responded exactly right."

"Well, thanks for that, at least," responded the President. "But I'll be damned if I can understand why no-one here has a clue what's going on. I thought our links with the UK were so good that we shared almost everything, and what we weren't told we found out anyway."

"That's normally true, but sometimes even top officials in Downing Street and Whitehall are taken by surprise since Weaver took office, and as I've said, my guess would be that this is one of those times."

"Well, check it out if you will, Miles. I don't like being caught flat-footed like that."

"I'll get on to it right now," replied Bragan. "I'll see if the security people have got wind of anything on their net, too. But perhaps I could make a suggestion?"

"Go ahead, Miles, anything."

"It's pretty obvious that Weaver's in a hurry now, and that he wants to see you soon and privately. If my suspicions are right, and that this caught the other side flat-footed too, then I suggest we keep quiet ourselves until we know more. Casting the net too wide in an effort to find out what's going on is only going to get other people inquisitive, too, and that is probably just what Weaver doesn't want. Normally, I would get someone on the line to the British ambassador, and have a word myself with their Foreign Secretary, but this time, I recommend that we don't. Weaver will be on again himself soon, or Sir Robin Algar or someone like that, to fix the visit—we can do a little probing then, perhaps. But I think we should let them make the next move, as they made the first. It's their call, after all, and it wouldn't be helpful to make things difficult for them."

"I guess that makes a lot of sense, Miles, but I want to know what's going on."

The President's executive secretary stuck her head round the Oval Office door. "Sorry to interrupt, Mr President, but I've had an urgent call which I really should discuss straight away with Mr. Carlucci."

They all knew that Laura Billings wouldn't butt in if it wasn't urgent—she'd been around the White House for far too long.

"Would you mind, Mr. President?" asked Carlucci.

Minton waved his OK.

"Thanks, I'll get right back."

As the door closed behind them, Miles Bragan said, "I think we should brief the media later today as if nothing untoward has happened, and stick to the line agreed with London. I also think it would be sensible, for the time being at least, not to let this tape get into circulation. If you agree, I'll take it with me and keep it in my office safe until we can be sure there's nothing to prevent us putting it with other recent archive material. I'll also find out who else may have been listening in to your London call, and check them out for security. This may all be unnecessary, but I'm sure you would agree that it would be better to have Weaver thank us for doing this than for him to blame us for not."

"You're right, Miles. Until we know more, I suppose we should tread warily. From the way Tony Weaver spoke, we may not have long to wait, anyway. But let me know if your discrete enquiries turn up anything meanwhile."

One of the Oval Office catering staff knocked, and bustled in with a tray of coffee and cookies.

"We'll need an extra cup this morning, please Sam."

"Comin' right up, Mr. President, sir. Mah trolley's right here, outside." The cup appeared as if by magic, proudly borne by Sam. "They's yo' favourite this mornin', Mr. President sir," he said, pointing to the tray. "Chocolate chip cookies, as ever. I git inta trouble out there," he thumbed towards the outer office, "fer spoilin' you." His old black face was nearly all grin and white teeth.

"Just so long as you don't spoil me too often, Sam, or you'll have Mrs. Minton after you as well."

"Yessir, Mr. President, sir." Sam and the grin disappeared.

He passed Colin Carlucci in the doorway.

"Mr. President, things seem to be moving fast. Laura's had London on the phone, and your office has had a call too, Mr. Bragan. The Prime Minister would like to come over this weekend."

"Goddam it," exclaimed the Secretary of State, "they are moving fast, and we've missed the call and the chance to probe. What did they say, exactly?"

"They say that you agreed, Mr. President, to an early visit to Washington to discuss the Middle East situation, as a public demonstration of their support for your upcoming visit, Mr Bragan. They propose a small party, with maximum publicity, and are quite sure it will be helpful. Apparently, officials are already working on drafts." Carlucci sounded quite out of breath.

"Can we do this weekend?" asked Bragan. "What are the diaries like?"

"Laura's done a quick check, as you'd expect, and it seems we can do it with only a bit of juggling. And the Vice President is in town."

"Let's go for it, then. Anything said about a private meeting between me and Weaver?" asked Minton.

"Nothing, so far as I know," said Carlucci.

"That could just prove I'm right," said Bragan. "Their officials don't know about that side of it."

"So neither must ours," directed the President. "Colin, as my Chief of Staff you are to make sure that only those are told who positively must know. Is that understood?"

"Absolutely, Mr President. And if I speak to anyone on the other side, I'll make sure it's Sir Robin Algar and nobody else. He's bound to know—he knows everything."

"So how shall we engineer the private meeting?" asked Bragan.

"I'll talk to Millie right away," replied the President, "and we'll try to fix up a weekend at her brother's place off Long Island—you know it, you've both been there. It's quiet and its secure. If we can't get there, we'll have to think about Camp David, but that might be a bit too public. We'll do the Middle East business here in Washington, and then I suggest we leave you, Miles, with their Foreign Secretary—what's his name…"

"Robert Burgess," helped Bragan.

"…Yeah, you and Robert Burgess and your officials to deal with the statements and media briefings, while Tony Weaver and I cut across to New York for an extra day. Colin, you'd better come too, as I expect Sir Robin will stay behind as well, but if you agree, Miles, we'll keep it as small as that. Perhaps you could find out if a day is long enough, will you, Colin? I sure hope so. We'll play the Washington trip straight, but without saying we're going New York, by simply letting it be known that, as old friends, we're having a quiet day together for private talks and a bit of relaxation. No statements afterwards—nothing. It's private, OK?"

"Sounds good, Mr. President, and it certainly will be very helpful to me to have the public backing of the British Prime Minister and Foreign Secretary before I go whistle-stopping around the Middle East next week. We can make as much noise as we like about that side of their visit, subject to their agreement, but I suggest," said the Secretary of State, "that we keep very quiet, even within Washington, about the private visit, at least until we know what's afoot. If you agree, Bill, we must deal with as few people as possible, tell them as little as possible, and put nothing in writing yet. We can always sort out the paperwork later if we need to."

"Agreed," said the President. "OK with you, Colin? Can you keep things to yourself so far as possible?"

"Yes, of course, Mr. President. I'll obviously have to bring my private office in on the act, but I'll restrict that to Alex if I possibly can. He's totally trustworthy as an executive secretary, and has been around long enough to know the ropes on occasions like this."

"Thank God," said Bragan, "that we've all got such excellent outer offices. I fear we tend to take them too much for granted sometimes."

"OK then. Let's get started," said the President. "On your way out, would one of you ask Laura or one of her people to get Millie on the phone for me? And make sure you keep me in touch with developments."

As his two most trusted colleagues left, he turned to gaze out over the Rose Garden. After all that, he still didn't know what was going on. But then, neither did they, yet.

***

Miles Bragan and Colin Carlucci walked together down the White House corridor, and stopped outside the Secretary of State's office. Bragan, with his hand on the doorknob, turned before going inside.

"You know, Colin, I don't think the President has picked up half the clues from the Prime Minister's little chat."

"Neither do I," agreed Carlucci, "But then I'm not quite sure I've worked it all out yet. I need time to think."

"Don't we all," agreed Bragan. "But first we must act. We haven't got long to set all this up, and it's a diversion I hadn't bargained on before my trip to the Middle East. I suggest we swap notes again a bit later, before we talk further to the President. I'll let you know if I'm summoned, if you'll do the same."

"Sure." Carlucci walked on towards his own office.

Bragan took a deep breath as he watched Colin stride off, and turned to go into his own office, frowning.

The Secretary of State's office was always a hive of activity, and large. In terms of staff, his immediate support office was structured much the same as the President's, with a chief of staff and deputy chief, a secretary, an executive assistant, two special assistants, a scheduler, or diary secretary, a staff assistant and two personal assistants. All these people looked after Bragan's immediate day-to-day needs, including running his diary, fixing meetings in Washington and elsewhere, and arranging his travel around the world. In addition to this so-called private office, an executive secretariat liased with other departments and agencies within the White House, particularly in terms of preparing his briefing material and making the arrangements for his official trips at home and abroad, including staffing his mobile office which travelled with him and kept his itinerary on track. The secretariat also was responsible for his and the Department of State's Operations Centre, a 24-hour communications and crisis management organisation.

They were all busy, and about to get busier.

Greg Harvey, his chief of staff, was in the outer office and looked up as Bragan bustled in.

"Come in, will you, Greg?" Bragan asked. "What's been going on while I've been with the President?"

"Only that Prime Minister Weaver is coming over at the weekend for talks about the Middle East—but I guess you know that."

Harvey shut the door behind him.

"There's more to it than that, Greg," said Bragan, "but we aren't sure quite what. First things first," he reached into his pocket for the tape cassette. "I want this double sealed and put into my safe after I've initialled the seals. Access is denied to everyone except myself for the time being. It's the tape of this morning's bilateral with London. I want to know who else might have listened in to that conversation, by name and position, and I want to see their files, complete with security level."

He told Harvey briefly what was causing the fuss, and how it had all started.

"Until we know more," he concluded, "we have agreed that only those who must know are told about the private session in New York. Neither you nor I will be there—on present plans, just the President and Colin. We are assuming that officials in Whitehall don't know what's behind all this, and that only Sir Robin will be with Weaver, so we are playing it the same way until we are told otherwise by London. That's why we're securing the tape, and keeping quiet. There's to be nothing in writing, either—no memos, no leaks. OK?"

"Got it!"

"Did you take the London call while I was in with the President?" asked Bragan.

"Yes, I did. Robert Burgess was looking for you, but in the end I spoke to Sir Arthur Bailey. I said I would get you to speak to the Foreign Secretary later if you could reach him. Bailey was very apologetic about the short notice, but said that it seemed our two leaders had agreed to meet, so there wasn't much we could do about it, and was this weekend convenient? As if we really had a choice! There was absolutely no mention of anything except the Middle East, and no hint of either men wanting private time together, so I guess you're right, and they don't know."

"I think they soon will," said Bragan. "If the President can fix for them to stay at Millie's brother's place on Shelter Island, then he'll ring Weaver and invite him to spend the extra day there for a private visit and a bit of relaxation. We'll be left to handle the Middle East talks part of it if they haven't been concluded by then. Otherwise, the President and Prime Minister can take the press conference before they disappear. I'm sure the President and Colin will get what they can out of Weaver and Algar, but I'd give a million dollars to be a fly on the wall!"

"Well I'm sure we'll be fully debriefed late Sunday or early Monday," said Harvey, "and it will be interesting to see who else can be brought in on the act at that stage. I just hope we can delegate a bit if there's a lot of fall out—there's already the usual mild panic setting in before the start of our shuttle diplomacy in a few days."

"I know," said Bragan. "Interesting days ahead."

"God preserve us from interesting days!" quipped Harvey.

"Now," said the Secretary of State, "would you mind getting down to the Ops Centre, and as discreetly as possible, find out if there's anything new come in recently about Northern Ireland? Talk to whoever's in charge on duty right now—head man and no one else. I suspect there's nothing, but I need to know. And I'll try to get through to Burgess."

"I'll get right back to you as soon as I can," said Greg.

***

"Hi, Millie. It's Bill."

Every time, Millie wondered why he said that every time. It couldn't possibly be anyone else. It wasn't as if he just picked up the phone and dialled through himself. There was always a secretary who got the number for him, said hello nicely when she answered, told her who it was, and then put him through to her. So it was hardly a surprise when he said, "Hi, Millie. It's Bill."

"Hi, honey. Having a good day?"

He always wondered why she always said that.

"It looks like being an interesting one," he replied. "In fact, it already is. But I really called to see if you knew whether Chuck and Steph are using the beach house this weekend. If they're not, I would like to use it just for the day Saturday—got an unexpected head of state coming across who wants a day off!"

"So far as I know they're staying down town in their 57th Street apartment this weekend. Chuck said something about having a quiet weekend and taking in a theatre. I bet he'll try to get to the ball game, too. Shall I ask?"

"Yes please. Probably only be about four of us, plus the usual security people, and you, of course, if he brings his wife. You've met before, and I know you get on. But if Chuck isn't there and he can get the staff in for us, it would be much better than the Camp. We need to get away from prying eyes, I think, and Shelter Island is perfect for that. Do you want to try the other line while I hang on?"

He hung on, and was relieved to hear Millie get through quickly.

"Bill, honey, you're in luck, and he said you're more than welcome to use it. He didn't even ask who it was."

"Neither did you, and I wouldn't have told you if you had—not yet. Tonight, perhaps. But that's good news. Say thank you for me, Millie, and I'll get my people to make all the arrangements as usual. Bye now."

He hit the intercom button. "Laura, see if you can get Prime Minister Weaver on the phone for me please. Usual security, and ask Colin if he can get back while I talk."

***

Bragan had just finished speaking to Robert Burgess when his chief of staff walked in.

"Absolutely nothing new on Northern Ireland, either across the Atlantic or here," he announced. "There's apparently still no sign of the cash from the last two fundraising dinners, which Sinn Fein promised to give to the New York Appeal Fund, so I think we can kiss that goodbye—they've probably bought more Semtex with it by now. But I can't think the Prime Minister would want to talk about that specially. We've already had an exchange of views on the subject, and each understands where the other stands. It's still our call to do something, though, if ever we can work out what. But there's nothing on the intelligence network at all that we don't already know about. No Sigint or anything—not that we listen to everything, as you know. We usually get what we want just by asking, and what we don't ask about they usually tell us, anyway. I've checked with the Political Affairs Under Secretary too, and there's nothing on their net either."

"As I thought," said Bragan, "but thanks anyway. In that case, we'll just have to wait until we're told."

"What do you think it's all about?" asked Harvey.

"Greg, I wish I knew," replied the Secretary of State. "I have a hunch—no more than that—but I'm not even going to share that with you at this stage, if you don't mind. If I'm half right, though, that wily Prime Minister is cooking up a scheme for dealing with Northern Ireland once and for all. A third party both sides in Northern Ireland would be happy to deal with could be what he's looking for and what he wants to talk about. Whatever he has in mind, it looks like it is going to involve us in a big way. We shall see."

Carlucci knocked, and stuck his head round the door. "I've been summoned, again," he said. "The old man's getting back on the phone to London, and wants me there. I'll let you know what happens, although I expect you'll be summoned too, soon. Anything from your chair?"

"Nothing. And I mean nothing - ops. and int. haven't had a smell of anything new for weeks, so we're still groping for ideas, I'm afraid."

"I'll tell him. I haven't been able to talk to Sir Robin - he's with the Prime

Minister, and has been for ages. Since this morning's call, in fact. Something's up, no doubt."

"Maybe you'll get a clue in a minute, Colin," said Bragan hopefully.

"You'll be the first to know," said Carlucci, and disappeared towards the Oval Office.

Bragan's intercom went. It was the President.

"Can you spare a minute, Miles?" he asked. "I'm just getting back to Tony Weaver."

Chapter Four
THE SEED IS SOWN

"I hardly know where to begin," repeated Weaver, "because I hardly know where it all began."

Sir Robin Algar shuffled uncomfortably. He hoped this wouldn't take too long, or be a waste of time.

"But I'll tell you straight away what I aim to achieve," continued the Prime Minister, "and that is an end to all the nonsense surrounding Northern Ireland."

The Cabinet Secretary heaved an inward sigh. It *was* going to be a waste of time. *Yet another solution to 'the problems'*, he thought, as if he hadn't heard enough of them in the past. He had imagined that Weaver would be above thinking he could resolve that particular issue.

"I believe there really is a workable solution, given good will, total secrecy, and a good deal of support and loyalty from a very few people. Let's face it, the Irish, both north and south, have been a thorn in our side for far too long now, and people are totally fed up with the situation—not just people here, but the good people over there too, on both sides of the political divide. And the situation has been a monumental strain on the Treasury for years and years, as you know, not to mention the military."

The Prime Minister's face was grim but determined. He looked strained.

"I know exactly what you're thinking, Robin, and you may well end up being right," he said. "I may end up with egg on my face, like all the others before me who believed they had found the ultimate solution."

Sir Robin Algar nodded, and this time sighed audibly.

"I'm afraid I do think so, Prime Minister. Although of course you haven't yet spelt out any detail of your proposals, but I can see you believe America will have a major role to play—or rather, you hope they will."

"I believe they will. My proposals for Northern Ireland will benefit America and help to solve a few problems for the US administration as well, and my job will be to persuade them of that. If they are with us, and we get the planning right, then the whole thing should not take too long at all. First, though, I must persuade you that we may not, after all, be wasting our time."

He took a sip of his Scotch, frowning to assemble his thoughts into a logical order.

"Cast your mind back to our most recent visit to the Province. It was an unusual trip in many ways. For a start, it lacked some of the formality of earlier visits. We had a very useful informal lunch in the Officer's Mess at the Army Headquarters in Lisburn. It was then," continued the Prime Minister, "that I began to get a feeling of a possible way out of the mess which successive governments, our own included, have got us into over the years. In fact, two of the people we met there first put the thought in my mind. And they damn well wouldn't have done, but for that informal setting—not least because I would probably never otherwise have met them. They were both thinking along the same lines, it seemed, although in fact they had only met a few times before I butted in on their conversation. And they both believed, from their independent and totally different backgrounds, that a solution was possible and achievable, if radical."

"I certainly remember the lunch well," recalled Sir Robin. "Drinks in the crowded bar first, then a self-service buffet in the dining room across the hall. A mix of people, too. Junior military officers there as well as top brass, civil servants from both MOD and the Northern Ireland Office, and a couple of junior Ministers accompanying the Secretary of State."

"Exactly," said Tony Weaver. "Men and women there who one would never ordinarily meet on a visit like that, and because it was a small, rather cosy mess…"

"…Especially the bar," interrupted Robin.

"… Yes, especially because the bar was small and intimate, it was possible to get away from the people who usual surround me, and talk informally to some very interesting people with very interesting views—convictions even."

"Yes, I was able to do that, too," said Sir Robin. "And like you, I found it very welcome and refreshing to get away, as you put it, from 'the people who usually surround us'."

"I don't know whether you managed to speak to them yourself, but there were two individuals I remember in particular. And I will tell you now that I have spoken to them again since, privately."

***

It had been obvious since the troubles started that there was never going to be a political solution to Northern Ireland's problems. The balance had always been wrong. Since partition: that's where the cock-up had been made. Dividing Ireland at all had been a mistake in the first place, and then they got it all wrong as well. Asking for trouble, that was. And now they've got it, and can't sort it.

At least, they could; but probably not in a democracy. Churchill had said that democracy was the worse form of government - apart from all the others. And he was usually right about most things.

Bill Clayton wondered how he knew that. Not the sort of thing that usually stuck in his mind, that wasn't.

Major William Jefferson Clayton did not appear to be one of the brightest of Army officers by any means, but somehow or other they'd managed to find him the perfect job. His father, a retired general of some repute, claimed he had been put where he could do least harm. He was by no means convinced that Bill was upholding the family's military tradition, although he did grudgingly admit that not everyone could survive in the Intelligence Corp.

Bill wasn't actually surviving at all. He was doing very well indeed, thank you. Academically, he had always struggled. He gave up history at school because he couldn't remember the dates, and did woodwork instead. He could do that while thinking about something else.

Sandhurst had been a nightmare in the classroom, and a doddle everywhere else. Bill was as tough as old boots and very fit, without really trying to be. And in spite of appearances, he was by no means brain dead either. The fact was, he was good—very good—at anything that interested him. It was that sort of brain.

And what had always interested him was finding out what people were up to. What they were really thinking. What they were really planning to do, rather than what they said they were going to do. Call it inquisitive, if you like, or even down right nosy, but give him a pile of seemingly unrelated facts, and he could very soon sort the wheat from the chaff and work out what was going on.

He also had a gift for knowing what information he needed, and the skills to make sure he got it. Uncanny, really. He'd tasked any number of soldiers to seek apparently daft bits of intelligence, but they had eventually come to see how crucial they were to him. It was as if he was doing a giant jigsaw in his mind. He, and only he, knew what bits he'd got, how they would fit together, and what bits he needed to complete the picture. Indeed, only he knew what the picture was. Not the sort of thing they teach you at school. At least, not the schools he went to. It was a natural skill he had been able to fine-tune in the Army, to their great advantage. There simply weren't enough around like him.

The Army had not been slow to recognise his value in Northern Ireland. He was a widower, which gave him all the time in the world without any domestic pressures to divert his attention. He loved what he was doing and where he was doing it, and didn't want to be posted away from the Province. So, as long as it suited the Army and Bill Clayton, that was where he was going to stay. His Headquarters at Chicksands desperately wanted him there, to lecture. But he desperately didn't want to go there, of all places. So normal rules and regulations had been bent, and his Corps had to put up with the fact that one of their men was effectively missing—at least, for the time being. And higher ranking officers at the Army's Lisburn HQ in Northern Ireland also had to get used to the fact that he was special, and was likely to be called upon at any time to brief very senior people direct and at short notice. Where he was concerned, the chain of command virtually didn't exist. It wasn't always, either, that Bill chose to share all his intelligence with anyone else as a matter of routine— they'd had to get used to that, too. Altogether, an unusual situation for a relatively junior officer, but he was altogether a rather unusual man.

Those in the Security Services who knew him—and in the other two armed services—recognised his razor sharp mind, and weren't slow to take advantage of it when they could. Some—mostly in the RAF—maintained that the words 'Army' and 'Intelligence' were contradictory. They hadn't met Bill Clayton.

He knew exactly how to sort out the Irish problem.

And he thought it was just - *just* - possible to get away with it, even in a democracy.

But he wasn't about to tell anyone. They wouldn't listen, anyway. Far too busy trying to recoup all that had been lost during the cease-fire. Somehow, they hadn't realised that that was all it was—a bloody cease-fire, not a surrender.

So far as he knew, he and his team had been able to keep up to speed, more or less, with what had been going on. And plenty had, of course. That's what cease-fires are for.

New people recruited. New plans drawn up. New arms and explosives bought—and some delivered. New active service units formed and trained. Some of those had been deployed to the mainland, too, like the one that did

Docklands. They were new. And they were good.

But not as good as he was.

He knew who they were and where they were and all about them.

Not that he could do much about it. The normal system of justice simply wouldn't work, in spite of all the evidence they had. It was impossible to get any witnesses to come forward. Like many magistrates and members of the judiciary, they were scared stiff—and with every cause. So it was a waste of time trying to get these people into court. There were other ways of dealing with them though, and it could be done, but not in a democracy, where nobody listened to anything at all out of the ordinary. Which is why he wasn't about to tell anyone that he really thought they could put an end to all this nonsense, if they had the will and really put their minds to it.

But then he met junior Minister James Anchor, quite by chance. It was an informal occasion, he remembered, and they chatted quite amicably over their drink. They got on well, swapped ideas, and there it was. They had both, it seemed, been thinking along much the same lines. They agreed to meet again. The more they met, the more their ideas developed, the military mind playing off the political. It became almost a game for them. But they resolved never to mention it to anyone else, because they knew that no one else would take it seriously.

***

It was extraordinary what Northern Ireland did to politics. On the mainland, the parties were united, generally speaking, in their approach to the troubles. In fact, it was about the only subject where there was ever agreement.

But across the water, the parties never agreed about anything, and probably never would. They didn't even agree about uniting against what some—as if they were governed by some other body—called "the British Government." But then they had religion, which was a stronger influence than politics. Except that it never was able to influence events, or the people who had control of events. But it did influence politics and politicians. What church you went to, or what religion you belonged to, was more important than anything else. You didn't need to think about politics—not in the democratic sense. Your religion decided your politics, where you lived, where you went to school and everything.

Being a mainland politician, representing one of the major parties in your constituency, and representing your constituency in Parliament, was a relatively straightforward affair. True, there were often divided loyalties to be reconciled, between what the whips wanted you to do, and what your constituents thought you should do. Almost without exception or question, you obeyed the whip, especially if you were ambitious. Almost without exception, too, your constituency party understood that.

Life became more complicated when you were a Minister as well. There was now a third force seeking to influence what you did. In particular, you had far less time to bother with local constituency affairs. There were, after all, grave departmental matters of state to be attended to now. Generally speaking, your constituency party understood that, too. Of course, you still had to spend a bit of time with them—a weekly surgery, or something equally tiresome. After all, they voted you in, and could just as easily vote you out if you weren't careful.

But being a junior Minister in the Northern Ireland Office had to be about the most bloody awful job in the world. James Anchor thought so, anyway, and he hadn't been there long. Not that he was about to say anything, mind you. Some quite senior people had whinged about going, gone anyway, and then been finished so far as their career was concerned. James was having none of that, scared as he was, like the rest of them.

Fascinating but frustrating, that's what it was. There always seemed to him little chance of making any impact on anything much. It was like trying to square a circle with knobs on. It couldn't be done. Better men than him had tried and failed. No sooner did you seem to be doing something that pleased one bit of the equation, than other bits started to sound mightily displeased. And doing nothing didn't please anyone, either. It was because they said we'd done nothing for eighteen months that they set off the Docklands bomb.

Actually, things did start getting done pretty soon after that. Talks were set up that some people didn't attend, while others who hadn't been invited turned up and weren't allowed to attend. Elections were announced that nobody wanted. Dates were announced for more talks—that sort of thing. It wouldn't work, of course. None of it. It didn't stop the bombings, either. Nothing ever had.

But it did seem obvious to James that one thing might make an impact, and so far as he knew, it hadn't been tried before. Probably because it was so far right wing to be out of sight. The sort of thing that couldn't be done officially. But it could still be done, with care. Blind eyes had been turned before.

The trouble was, James had no idea where to start—not the slightest. It wasn't the sort of suggestion you made at a meeting, or even to close colleagues over a scotch. In fact it wasn't really the sort of idea you could ever mention, come to think of it. In spite of his excellent Cambridge degree, James had a reputation for being a bit of a scatterbrain, and a bit vague. Indeed he was, in a professorial sort of way, and he was sure that this would count against him if ever he should be brave enough to hint at his theory. But he had a sharp mind, was quick to reach the right conclusions, and had a sense of humour which helped him get by, often while others were catching up with his thought processes.

He remembered being told when he arrived that if he ever thought he had the solution to Northern Ireland's problems, he had either been there too long, or been wrongly briefed. But this was different, he was sure. This was his idea. And it seemed so blindingly obvious, that he was quite convinced that there must be others wandering about the Province with the same idea.

Like him, they were probably too frightened to mention it to anyone else. He certainly wasn't going to.

But then he met Major Bill Clayton, quite by chance. It was an informal occasion, he remembered, and they chatted quite amicably over their drink. They got on well, swapped ideas, and there it was. They had both, it seemed, been thinking along much the same lines. They agreed to meet again. The more they met, the more their ideas developed, the political mind playing off the military. It became almost a game for them. But they resolved never to mention it to anyone else, because they knew that no one else would take it seriously.

***

Then they both met Tony Weaver over a pint in the Officer's Mess at Lisburn.

James knew the PM quite well, as a matter of fact. Indeed, it was he who had suggested to James that it might be a very good career move if he went to Northern Ireland. He hadn't been in Parliament all that long, and for the Prime Minister himself to suggest an appointment as a junior Minister was something ambitious politicians couldn't refuse. Not that James liked it— Northern Ireland, that is. He would have preferred some rather quieter backwater, like Transport or Trade and Industry, to be honest. But this was not to be sniffed at, so he went.

He had been quietly chatting to Bill Clayton in a crowded corner of the bar. They'd met several times before, and had, in fact, become quite friendly. They were deep in quiet discussion when the Prime Minister hove into view, empty glass in hand.

"You chaps are looking a bit intense," said Weaver. "Might I enquire what about?"

James introduced him to Clayton. Bill saw the empty glass, and set off to refill it and his and James's. He'd been looking for an excuse.

"Interesting chap, that is, Prime Minister," said James. "I came across him some time ago. He's certainly got his head screwed on and seems to know everything there is to know about what's going on around here. Delightfully unstuffy for an Army officer, if you know what I mean."

"I've certainly met a few of the more pompous variety this morning," said Weaver. "What were you on about just now?"

"Oh! The usual thing," replied the junior Minister. "How to sort this mess out—you know!"

"Is that all!" laughed the PM. "You'd better let me in on the secret, if you really do think you're on to something."

"Well, it's odd actually that, although we're from quite different walks of life, so to speak, we do seem to have been thinking along much the same lines. Put my political assessment with his military judgement of what is possible, and we are beginning to arrive at something quite interesting, although probably totally impractical."

Bill Clayton came back with the drinks, hotly pursued by a rather flushed looking civil servant.

"Could you spare a moment, Prime Minister? I'd rather like…"

"Actually, not now if you don't mind," interrupted Weaver, "I'd rather like to finish this conversation before I start another one. If you don't mind."

An even more flushed civil servant backed off, hovering near enough to keep away others anxious 'to have a word', or 'catch the Prime Minister's ear', but without being near enough to actually overhear Weaver's conversation.

Weaver turned to Clayton, thanking him for his newly charged glass.

"The Minister was telling me that you have been reaching some exciting conclusions between you, Major. I'm interested," said Weaver. "Anything you can share with me?"

Clayton looked at Anchor, aghast, wondering what on earth he had said to excite the PM's interest.

"If you insist, Prime Minister, then of course I'd be happy to share my thinking with you," said Clayton. "But I must emphasise that they will be my own thoughts and not reflect any official thinking whatsoever."

"Understood," said Weaver.

"And they are," continued Clayton, "unrefined to say the least. Simply an expression if you like, of what could be done, given the political will, and providing total secrecy could be guaranteed. Much of what I have in mind might not be strictly legal or within the bounds of what's possible in a democracy."

"Much the same in my case," said James Anchor. "I hadn't meant to suggest, Prime Minister, that we had developed any profound thinking about the future of the Province—only that we had discussed some rather revolutionary ideas which, on the face of it, might just be capable of being put into effect. But Bill and I had agreed that it would be impossible to share our thoughts with anyone publicly, let alone consult with others. Now you want us to share them with you, of all people!"

"We'll both get the sack," grumbled Clayton.

The Prime Minister could see that he meant it.

"James, you know that I have always held you in the highest regard," confided the Prime Minister. "It's because I think you have a brilliant political career ahead of you that you're here in the first place, young as you are. So if you think that what you and Major Clayton have been discussing is worth discussing, then I think it's probably worth listening to."

"Thank you for that, Tony," said Anchor. "But the bar is no place to even outline our thinking. Is there anywhere else, Bill?"

"Certainly. Come into the Mess Secretary's office next door. If he's in I'll kick him out. We can shut the door, and we've got about five minutes before lunch, that's all."

"To solve the problems of centuries," mused Weaver, as they moved out of the bar into the small next-door office.

On their way, Bill grabbed a colleague by the arm.

"Charlie, stand outside this bloody door and don't let anyone come in—not even the General. Give us a knock when they go in for lunch. If anyone asks, tell them the PM and the Minister wanted a private word. No need to let on that I'm here, too, OK?"

A rather bemused subaltern, who was on his way to do something far more worthwhile, like catch another quick half before lunch, came smartly to attention and nodded. He wasn't quite sure what to do if challenged, as he didn't even have his hat on, never mind a gun.

But the moment the door shut, a slim young fellow in a dark suit joined him.

"I'll stand guard with you," he said, showing his Special Branch ID card.

"PM's personal protection," he said. "There are others outside, and I'm armed, which you probably aren't. So what shall we talk about"?

Charlie felt better, but he knew another beer was out of the question this side of lunch.

***

"And I thought you'd gone to powder your nose before lunch!" the Cabinet Secretary laughed. "Instead of that, you were discussing how to change the tide of history!"

"Don't joke about it, Robin. I really believed those two, between them and independently, were on to something. It's certainly a theory I intend to pursue and develop. Their thinking was very unrefined, and I suspect that they would never have taken it any further forward but for my intervention. They thought their original concepts were far too radical to be put in to effect, or to have the slightest chance of being taken seriously. But I have already taken their thinking a good deal further forward, and the more I do so the more I come to believe that there may just be the germ of a solution in what they have said. But we shall have to tread extremely warily. The political implications of getting it wrong are too ghastly to contemplate, both nationally and internationally. James Anchor's role in this may already be drawing to a close, but we shall need to rely quite heavily on Major Clayton's fund of knowledge if we agree to take this forward."

"So what on earth did they say to you?" Sir Robin Algar looked serious again.

It was obvious that the PM, with such a sharp brain, would not be taken in by some hare-brained scheme, and it was equally obvious that Weaver did not think that this was one.

"In a nutshell, a three-pronged assault. I hope you're ready for this."

"Try me," said Sir Robin, leaning forward.

Chapter Five
THE BRIEFING

"I'm sure I don't need to tell you, Robin, that there's only ever one way of solving any problem, and that is to remove the cause of it."

The Cabinet Secretary nodded.

"And the cause of the problem in Northern Ireland," continued the Prime Minister, "is that the Unionists want to stay part of the United Kingdom while the Republicans want unification, and the British out of Ireland altogether. On the face of it, two irreconcilable requirements, which mean, we have always assumed, that the cause of the problem cannot be removed. All that consecutive British governments have done is play for time. We have given too many concessions over the years, and sacrificed too many lives. Now, public opinion is swinging towards cutting loose from Northern Ireland, getting rid of the problem—the eternal thorn in our side—one way or the other, even if, some say, it means granting unification. The fact that civil war would inevitably follow does not seem to bother many people, say some of the pollsters. But it bothers me, and I believe there could be another possible way ahead, if we initiate three areas of action simultaneously. All three areas of activity would have to be very closely co-ordinated and effected over a very short period of time if they are to work at all, either on their own or together.

"First, there would have to be what I shall call a military offensive, where we clear out the terrorist leadership and hardliners, both unionist and republican, and those terrorists masquerading as politicians, while at the same time getting rid of their arms and weapons. In parallel, we launch a major financial effort to empty their coffers totally, so that they cannot re-arm. And thirdly, we negotiate a political solution acceptable to all the parties involved, including the British public. This, I believe, is where America has a major role to play, having agreed the overall strategy. Hence my need to see President Minton privately."

To the Prime Minister's obvious annoyance, the office intercom buzzed. Sir Robin Algar stood to deal with it. "Shall I?" he asked.

"If you would. But I thought Jane knew not to interrupt."

"It's probably the file you asked for—you remember? The technician from the COBR?"

The PM nodded.

"Yes, Jane?" Sir Robin bent over the machine on the desk.

"Sorry to interrupt," she said, "but you did ask to be told when Jack Bennett's file arrived. I've got it here now."

"I'll come and get it," said Algar.

On his return, the Cabinet Secretary asked, "Do you want to look at this now, Prime Minister, or later?"

"Later—when I've explained a few more details about this proposed strategy. You will see then why we need a careful look at that man's background. But you can tell Jane that she can go home when she's ready, once the night duty staff are all in—there's no need for her to hang around."

"Very good, Prime Minister."

With the door firmly shut behind him again, Sir Robin Algar returned to his chair with the folder. "You were going to tell me about the three-pronged approach you had in mind, Prime Minister, one of which–" he looked anxiously at the man seated opposite him, "–involved 'clearing out'—I think that was your expression—the terrorists. You hadn't in mind internment again, had you?"

"No, certainly not." Tony Weaver was emphatic. "That didn't work last time, and in fact proved to be quite counter-productive."

"Exactly," said Algar. "It proved a great challenge to the terrorist gangs, who simply filled the vacuum as we created it by recruiting more and more members. It was a politically difficult gambit, anyway, in terms of civil liberties, and our international allies were uneasy about the whole episode."

"They will be even more uneasy about this proposal, let me tell you, if ever they suspect that the 'clear out' is a direct result of any official HMG policies."

The PM frowned. "Which is why we have to be ultra careful about how we set this up, and who knows about it. As I said earlier, we must ensure the utmost secrecy about the whole affair, and only the minimum number of the most trustworthy people must know the whole plot. Let me say again what I said a short while ago. Nothing must ever be put in writing about any of this.

Which is why I still have your clipboard." He waved it in the air to add emphasis.

"Any briefings must be given verbally, and face to face whenever possible. We shall need a special and exclusive code for those occasions where something simply has to be put on paper."

The Prime Minister paused briefly for thought.

"There will be times during this when money has to change hands—expenses, fees, that sort of thing. It will have to be in cash—no cheques, nothing in writing. We'll need to work out how that is to be done, and sweep up the paper work afterwards.

"But I'm drifting into detailed tactics before I've outlined the major aspects of the strategy."

Weaver sipped his whisky.

"Let me brutally frank about this, Robin. When I say 'clearing out', I mean removing them permanently out of harm's way. In a word, execution—nothing less," pronounced the Prime Minister. "And without a formal trial. I don't plan legislation to re-introduce the death penalty, or anything like that."

"But my dear sir," exploded the Cabinet Secretary, "you cannot possibly be advocating such a course of action as official government policy. That would be simply outrageous!"

"Now you just listen to me, Robin," interrupted Weaver, leaning forward and jabbing the air with the clipboard. "This sort of thing has been done before, as you well know, and not just by those to whom democracy is a foreign word, but by British governments, by American administrations, and by others who have felt sufficiently compelled by the need to be able to justify the means. And it is still done from time to time. What I have in mind differs only in scale, and in the way it will be carried out."

"I shall need some convincing of this." Sir Robin Algar looked deeply worried. He was certainly not expecting such a Wild West approach from such a level headed and sophisticated politician.

"And I shall need to convince many others, too, as I in turn was convinced by James Anchor and Major Clayton. But don't you even begin to feel sorry for these people, Robin. They entered into their life of terrorism and violent crime quite willingly and fully knowing the risks, without a second thought for their victims or even their own families."

Weaver looked closely at Sir Robin Algar.

"But you are my litmus paper, as well as my most trusted colleague, inside or outside of politics. If you do not agree to the whole plan as I shall outline it to you this evening, then nothing further will happen, and I shall have no further convincing to do. You may think that places an unfair responsibility on your shoulders, Robin, but the ultimate responsibility for all this rests with me, and I simply cannot canvas these ideas too widely. Can you imagine putting this to a Cabinet Committee for recommendation?"

"Perhaps not!" agreed Algar, with a grin. "And I appreciate your trust and confidence."

"But you are right to show such concern," continued Weaver. "It's a concern I shared when I initially discussed the outline of this in the Officers' Mess in Belfast. And I can tell you that I am still concerned, but now rather more of the consequences of failure than the consequences of proceeding."

"You talked about justifying this. Take me through that," asked Sir Robin.

"The authorities here, and across the water, have enough evidence against most of the terrorist leadership, from both sides, to convince anyone of their involvement in murder, explosions, rioting and no end of other criminal activity. But they simply cannot get them into a court of law because of the power and the level of influence the terrorists gangs wield, together with the degree of intimidation they are able to exercise against any possible witnesses—not to mention a few leading lawyers, barristers and policemen, as well. So justice as we know it is not available to us to rid society of these scum. Justification for ridding society of them, on the other hand, we do have, in spades.

"Major Bill Clayton is a most interesting man," continued the Prime Minister. "And he is probably one of the most knowledgeable men in the Province—certainly about the main players in and supporters of the various terrorist groups. He knows who they are, where they are, what they have done in the past and, in many cases, what they plan to do in the future. He has been able to infiltrate every one of the terrorist organisations, and in one or two cases their political wings as well, either by getting members of his own team into them, or by turning existing members. The dangers which these people face and the risks they take simply do not bear thinking about."

"I well remember the case of Captain Robert Niarac some years ago," mused Algar.

"Exactly so," continued the PM. "His cover was blown, and he paid the ultimate penalty. It was a very public affair, too, but there have been others who have not been so exposed to the glare of publicity. Special Branch and MI5 know only some of Clayton's sources, he tells me. There are others known only to him. He does not necessarily share all his intelligence sources or information with others, either—even within his own service—for fear of betrayal."

"But he has entrusted some of this intelligence to you, has he?" asked Sir Robin.

"No, he hasn't. And neither will he. What he will do, though, and in one or two cases already has done at our subsequent private meetings at Chequers, is to present us with sufficient evidence to convince us of the guilt of known terrorists and others in the political wings of the terrorist organisations. Much of this would readily stand up in court if ever presented in evidence. Some of it, however, is more circumstantial in the absence of witness statements and so on. But I am convinced that he is well enough informed to be able to bring forward adequate evidence to prove, to any reasonable man, the guilt of most of the top people in all these organisations. In other words, he can provide the moral justification for the elimination of sufficient people to leave their organisations totally leaderless and impotent."

"How many are we talking about?" asked the Cabinet Secretary.

"I can't tell you that, because I haven't yet asked the question myself. All Clayton has said so far is 'enough'. There is an interesting twist to this, incidentally. Clayton is convinced that, on past experience, the terrorists organisations themselves will help us in this task of elimination, particularly of the lower level members, by mounting tit-for-tat operations of their own. A little black propaganda from the Psy. Ops. people will help to get that under way, he is convinced, and the police should be able to control it. You can imagine how important that will be in diverting attention and countering any allegations that might start flying around about the government having instituted a 'shoot to kill' policy."

"Neat," commented Sir Robin. "Very neat. But how will this part of the plan be executed, if I may use the word? And by whom?"

"I think the 'by whom' part is probably the easiest. We have plenty of Special Forces about who are highly trained and well able to put such a plan into effect. We shall—Clayton's suggestion this—take a leaf out of the IRA's book, play them at their own game, and operate with very small, self-contained units, who will be unknown to one another. Once their task is completed, they will return to their normal duties, or, if necessary, be given another, seemingly unrelated, task. They will have no clue that they are or have been a part of a much bigger operation, although some may later guess at it. But they will never be able to prove it. Nothing in writing, remember. And—again Clayton's idea—no bodies, if we can manage it. No bodies, no post-mortems. Either that, or natural causes where that can be arranged. People are either seen to have died naturally, or they disappear, or they are killed off by their opposite numbers as part of a tit-for-tat operation."

"And we only act against those where there is judged, in normal circumstances, to be sufficient evidence to have brought a conviction in court?" queried Sir Robin.

"Right," said the PM.

"So who takes the decision? Who decides that we are morally justified in taking the lives of these people?"

"You do," replied Tony Weaver.

The Cabinet Secretary blanched, and picked up his now empty whisky glass.

"Have another," said the PM, reaching for the decanter. "You look as if you need it."

"That was below the belt," complained Algar. "I certainly wasn't expecting that reply when I asked the question."

"Your responsibilities in this affair will be more than just allowing it to proceed if I convince you of its practicality," said the Prime Minister. "I will underwrite your recommendations if you wish. You will work with one other, a law officer of your choice, in whom you must have absolute trust. But there will be much to be done, and it must all be done by the minimum number of people, for the sake of security, if for no other reason."

"What else do you have in store for me?" queried Algar.

"To answer that, perhaps I should move on to brief you about another phase in this operation. To my mind, although perhaps not to yours, this is almost more tricky than the area I've already touched upon, not least because the risks of leaks are greater," responded the Prime Minister. "And you will have a pivotal role to play, certainly in the planning of it, because of your many contacts at high level. I'm talking now about money."

"Right," said Sir Robin. This was certainly an area where he would feel more at home—he hoped, anyway. "You talked earlier of a major effort to 'clear their coffers'. Tell me more."

"Well," said Tony Weaver, "it will be no good trying to get international agreement to freeze their assets, even if I thought for a minute that such agreement would be achievable, or bring the required results. For a start, it would be a very public step to take, which would in itself not make much sense as a stand-alone policy. So people would become suspicious and start to speculate about our real motives. No, our efforts here need to be clandestine, too, so as not to draw attention to our anti-terrorist campaign and also so as to be more effective than any international effort might be."

"So what have you in mind?" probed Sir Robin. "Off the top of my head, I can't envisage any scheme that would deprive all the terrorist organisations of their considerable funds. And surely, we would also need to ensure that their funds are not immediately replaced. How would that be done?"

"Preventing the funds from being replaced might not, in the end, be as difficult as it sounds," claimed the Prime Minister. "Much of their money has traditionally come from overseas supporters, like NORAID in America, from Libya and, to a certain extent, Iran and Iraq. The IRA has also been earning an income from training other terrorists, for instance in Colombia. But they have all increasingly been raising their own funds through their own activities."

"I've seen a few intelligence documents about this," said Sir Robin. "I wish now I'd read them more thoroughly before passing them in to you."

"We all have too much to read," said the PM. "but at present Northern Ireland's terrorist groups are raising some £20m a year through organised crime, and this is far more than they need for their day-to-day operations, particularly since bombings and other explicit acts of terrorism have decreased since the cease fires were declared. But they spend a lot supporting their own victims, prisoners' families, training and so on."

"What sort of crime raises that sort of money?" asked the Cabinet Secretary.

"Armed robbery, smuggling, counterfeiting, drug dealing, social security fraud, extortion, you name it. A major source of income," continued Weaver, "is fuel laundering, made possible by the large differences in fuel duty between Northern Ireland and the Irish Republic. Even the small terrorist organisations, like the Loyalist Volunteer Force, which has a tiny membership, raises some £2m a year, while the four main loyalist para-military groups raise about £4m a year between them."

"So they're all earning more than they need," said Algar.

"Considerably more," said the PM. "They have countless millions stashed away in accounts all round the world."

"I begin to see why stopping their fund-raising might be easier than tracing that lot," said Sir Robin.

Tony Weaver grinned.

"Bill Clayton already knows where most of the major accounts are," he said.

"Does he, by Jove?" exclaimed Algar.

"He does. And what you have to do is find a way of getting the money and closing the accounts!"

"Is that all!" said Sir Robin. "And even if it did prove possible to get at it in some way, what's to stop this annual flow of £20m, or more perhaps, replacing it almost at once?"

"Several things," said the Prime Minister. "First of all, the groups will be leaderless. There will be no-one left of any significance to go about the fund-raising business. The income from crime will dwindle, as the gangs get broken up, foreign support will also fall away very quickly, especially from the States, when word gets around that terrorism in Northern Ireland is collapsing, and finally, Robin, there will be nowhere for supporters to deposit any cash even if they wanted to, because you will have closed all the known accounts."

"I will?"

"I certainly hope so. It's crucial to the whole operation that their funds are denied them, otherwise, they will, in time, simply re-group and re-arm as they have in the past. And, incidentally, as they are now. Decommissioning has achieved nothing, in effect. The IRA in particular, and the smaller loyalist groups, are simply using their wealth to replace all the weapons which the decommissioning body thinks it has put beyond further use."

"I was going to ask you about that," said Algar. "You mentioned earlier that part of your grand plan was to get rid of their arms. If the decommissioning body can't do that, how can we?"

"Easily," replied the PM, confidently. "Probably one of the easiest parts of the whole thing—except, perhaps, for the brave souls who will actually have to do it."

Tony Weaver got up, stretched, and walked across his office to switch on the table lamp.

"Let me remind you what's been happening so far," he said, topping up their glasses from the decanter. "The IRA has by far the largest stock of arms, ammunition and explosives. Loyalist stockpiles are relatively insignificant, although the Republicans would like to see them decommissioned, in the same way that everyone else wants to see the IRA's put beyond use. So the gallant Australian general, who is now heading the international commission formed to get rid of these arms, concentrated his efforts on Republican weaponry, egged on by the Unionists, who made all kinds of threats against his failure. But the Republicans were never going to give up their main—if not only—source of power and influence. That would be too much like surrender. However, after considerable procrastination, some arms dumps were eventually 'decommissioned', to the General's satisfaction, and to the delight of the Unionists. Only a few small dumps, however, containing a relatively insignificant number of weapons, were actually sealed permanently, but their contents were almost immediately replaced from abroad—usually Libya.

"In all the other cases, the terrorists had been busy during their years of apparent inactivity, secretly tunnelling alternative entry points to all their major dumps, normally disused bunkers or nuclear shelters in the Republic. Once completed, these dumps had then been ceremoniously decommissioned, usually by the immediate sealing up of the entrance with tons of concrete after a final inspection by the General and his team. Within days, the weapons had been moved out via the new tunnels to freshly developed sites or other existing dumps."

"So the sum total of all those years of negotiation has been virtually nothing," said Sir Robin. "In spite of what the general public impression might be."

"Quite."

"Thus, the time has come for direct action?" asked Algar,

"Quite," repeated the PM.

"How, exactly?" asked Sir Robin Algar.

"Details yet to be worked out," replied the PM, "but our learned Major Clayton and others know the exact location of all the major dumps. Spy satellites are wonderful! As a matter of interest, the Dublin government knows where they are, too, but they're not about to do anything. So we shall."

"With their agreement?"

"Or without," replied the PM. "But I very much hope that when push comes to shove, they will be with us. I also very much hope that it's the Americans who will be doing the shoving."

"Ah!" exclaimed Sir Robin. "Now we come to the politics of it all, no doubt, and our mystery visit to the States this weekend. I can see that it might just be possible to get rid of arms, perhaps money, or even people, but how does one create a lasting political solution out of all that?"

"With great difficulty," sighed Weaver. "But this is where James Anchor has made a considerable contribution to the thinking behind this plan, and he has convinced me that there is a solution, in spite of the difficulties. However, it has to be agreed quickly, at the outset, and be ready to be put in place immediately the conditions are right, and terrorism is finally ridden from Northern Ireland. If we cannot get early agreement to that, then there is probably little point in launching the other aspects of this initiative."

"What does America know of this plot so far?"

"Absolutely nothing," said Tony Weaver, "because up till now, there's been absolutely nothing to know. But the chance came up this afternoon to get us invited to the States, and it was too good a chance to miss. From America's point of view, the timing couldn't be better for launching this initiative, as there's so much in it for them. With Presidential elections coming up soon, and Bill Minton wanting a second term, he can hardly refuse the bait. At least that's my hope."

"But we are taking this at a bit of a gallop, aren't we?" asked the ever-cautious Head of the Civil Service. "We're not leaving ourselves much time at all to think through the details or consult colleagues if the Americans are to be brought in on it this very weekend."

"My dear Robin, we are not going to consult," countered the Prime Minister. "If you agree with me that it's worth the huge political risk to tackle the troubles head on, now, then we'll do it. The details will look after themselves, and we shall be telling people what to do, not asking them."

Here was the sharp brain of Tony Weaver at its' crisp best, thought Sir Robin Algar. He guessed that the PM already had a pretty clear idea of the detail, and knew what needed to be done, by whom, and when.

"But why the sudden rush?" asked Sir Robin again.

"Why not?" countered Weaver. "The sooner we get this thing started, the sooner it will all be over. And I don't want the whole thing to take forever, either. It must be done at great speed, with every aspect closely coordinated, otherwise those who oppose us will have time to develop their own tactics, and thwart our plans. I do not intend that anyone shall have time to work out the end game, until I tell them, by when it will be too late."

Algar looked increasingly worried.

"Of course," continued the PM, "we shall need to brief a select few on the whole plan, but others need only know about that part which directly effects them or in which they must get directly involved. You, for instance, will need the help of one of our top criminal lawyers, and you will need to enlist the help of one of your financial friends from the City if we are to break the terrorists' banks. But your lawyer need not know about our planned bank raids, if I may call them that, any more than your financial advisor needs to know about plans for top terrorists to be taken out of circulation. And almost no-one needs to know about the political solution I have in mind, until I'm ready to make a statement to the House and put the whole thing into operation."

"You were going to move on to discuss the politics of it all," said Sir Robin, "but I take the point about people who 'need to know' and those who don't. I suppose you will want to be kept informed about who is taking the lead in various fields, who else is being asked for advice, and so on?"

"I absolutely insist on it," said Weaver emphatically. "And I shall want to know before they are contacted, formally or informally. We can discuss later the sort of people we shall need with us—the absolute minimum, you understand—but first of all let me try to brief you on what I have in mind as the political solution."

"Please," said Sir Robin, wondering if the brilliant man across the table from him really had hit on the kind of workable solution that had escaped so many others before him.

"Let me remind you where we are starting from," began Weaver. "Years of effort have shown that the gap between the two communities of Northern Ireland is simply unbridgeable, and it is so because we got partition all wrong all those years ago. There never was a balanced community in Northern Ireland, and since then no solution has been found which is acceptable to both. Neither, it has to be said, has a formula ever been found which might, in time, bring a solution. Peace talks don't bring peace, and therefore something like the Bosnia solution, for all its faults, is not available to us either. The Northern Ireland Assembly has done nothing but buy a little time, and power sharing will never work while each side has a huge arsenal with which to reinforce its demands at the slightest whim. So, without a solution to the problem in prospect, we must try a little lateral thinking, and see if we can't remove the problem itself."

"There are those, of course," interrupted the Sir Robin Algar, "who believe that there is a demographic solution on the horizon. Given that the Catholic population tends to be procreating faster than the Protestants, they will, in time, be in the majority."

"Yes, but that's no solution," countered the Prime Minister, "it simply reverses the problem, and puts the boot onto the other foot, so to speak. When Republicans are in a position to seek union with the south through the ballot box, it will be the unionists who use violence to resist. No, the only solution is to remove the problem."

"And how on earth do you begin to remove the political problem?" asked a puzzled Cabinet Secretary.

"This is James Anchor at his brilliant best," replied the Prime Minister, "I asked him exactly the same question, and the answer really is so blindingly obvious that I am surprised it has never been suggested before."

"It may be an obvious solution," said Sir Robin, "but is it a practical one?"

"I think it could be. We remove the problem by removing the United

Kingdom from the equation," said the Prime Minister, "and the Republic of Ireland."

Robin Algar looked aghast. This would never work, he was sure.

"How?" he asked, simply.

"By replacing both nations by a third, acceptable to both the feuding parties."

"You mean the United States of America?" Robin Algar was incredulous.

"That's exactly what I mean," said the Prime Minister. "Think about it. Present British rule is acceptable to one side, but not the other. Similarly, Irish rule would be equally acceptable to one side, but not the other. So no solution rests within the *status quo*, and no solution rests in giving way to the Republicans. That's the problem. So remove the problem, and a solution becomes possible, given a third party who just might be acceptable to both persuasions."

"But are you seriously suggesting that we somehow give Northern Ireland away to America?" Sir Robin Algar was now ever more convinced that he had been wasting an evening.

"More than that," replied Tony Weaver. "I'm suggesting that the Republic of Ireland also gives up its independence, and that the whole island of Ireland becomes America's fifty-first State."

Robin Algar slumped back in his chair, and took a rather large swig from his glass. He looked across at the man opposite him—a man who he had always held in the highest esteem, probably the sharpest brained and best Prime Minister he had ever served. He could see from the intense look on Weaver's face that he was serious about this whole business. He was even now looking to Sir Robin with an almost pleading expression on his face, willing his old friend and ally to agree, or at least give some sign that his idea might at least be worth discussing further. For his part, the Cabinet Secretary could see now why Weaver was so keen for the minimum number of people to be briefed on the whole scenario. This was instant political death if handled wrongly, or indeed, if made public at all until the time was right. 'Only people who were totally trustworthy', Weaver had said. Were there any trustworthy enough? Was he, even? Weaver obviously thought he was, so he supposed he ought to be flattered by that. And now that Weaver had dared to share his thinking with him, he had in turn handed Algar enormous power. He had handed the Cabinet Secretary his whole future as a politician.

Could this seemingly hare-brained idea possibly work? wondered Algar. Tony Weaver obviously thought so. Indeed, in a few days' time he was going to share his ideas with the American President, unless Algar could persuade him otherwise. What the hell was Minton going to think of it? Come to that, what would the people of Ireland, north and south, think of it? Sir Robin could not conceive of any way in which they could possibly be persuaded that such a wild idea by the British government was a good one—never. And what about the Irish—the Dail and the Taoiseach? And what about NATO? And Europe? Good God, the work involved if ever this goes ahead! But nobody must know, of course—only the most trustworthy. Who could you trust in Brussels?

And yet…and yet! It would certainly be a solution. People had talked often enough about towing Ireland into the Atlantic and cutting the rope, just to get rid of the problem—this was towing it right the way across!

Sir Robin Algar was suddenly conscious that the Prime Minister was still looking at him intently. How long had they sat in silence?

"I was thinking, Prime Minister," said Algar, breaking the silence, "that constitutional changes of this magnitude, and involving three sovereign states, are not easily or quickly achieved."

Tony Weaver noticed the formality of tone.

"Nothing worth doing, Robin, is ever easy," countered the PM. "Nevertheless, it can be done, and it could be done relatively quickly, if all three sovereign states put their mind to it. And you are right to highlight the enormity of the constitutional changes involved. But I believe that the transfer of sovereignty could be put in place while all the myriad of detail is worked through in slower time. And there is no end of them, as I'm sure you have been quickly working out. Things like human rights, nationality laws, currency, rationalisation of various treaties and international agreements entered into by one of the parties but not the others, the rule of law, representation of the people, defence and foreign policy—will that do to start with? They and the rest must all be tackled with speed and equanimity."

"How do you propose to convince the Americans of this?" asked Sir Robin.

"Ah, so you're not immediately trying to dissuade me from going, then?" responded the Prime Minister, evading the question.

"Not immediately."

"In that case, you will need to wait until we're over there to hear the detail of my arguments. They are powerful, though, and I would be prepared to bet that Minton will want to proceed. There are equally powerful arguments to be put to Dublin, and indeed to our own people—we all have something to gain by going ahead, and nothing but stalemate if we do nothing. It is an eternal conflict which promises only third world status for Northern Ireland, even if we can keep the province from civil war, and that will inevitably drag us down with it. The world mood now is to get rid of terrorism in all its forms, and that includes ridding Northern Ireland of it."

The two men sat discussing all the issues involved in this dramatic plan for several more hours, Sir Robin Algar engrossed by the audacity of the Prime Minister's thinking. And he had to admit to himself that Weaver was probably right to assume that President Bill Minton would see some benefit in getting involved. After all, the Americans had only recently set up their own Homeland Security Department, and although this was primarily designed to defend the country against WMDs, the so-called Weapons of Mass Destruction, it would also be capable of preventing and countering just the sort of terrorist attacks that the UK had been enduring since 'the troubles' started. Following September 11, the US had been sickened by worldwide terrorism as a whole in a new realisation of what it meant, and the Americans themselves had identified the IRA as being one of the more formidable players in international terror. In the past, politicians had been accused of putting votes from the Irish/American population before British lives, but IRA activities in Colombia, McFosters' visit to Cuba, and their links with Libya and Iraq has received sufficient publicity for the Americans to realise that their tacit support now had to stop. But the 'stopping' had been rather more token than effective. It was true that Sinn Fein's web site had been banned, but funds were still being raised for the oppressed Irish 'back home' in the belief that the cash was being used to relieve the hardship of British rule, rather than buying yet more weapons. The vote was still a powerful influence.

Weaver's theory was that the Irish/American vote could be retained, if not strengthened rather than weakened, through decisive action against terrorists on both sides of the divide. World opinion would also be heartened by seeing that America had at last acknowledged that there was more than one way of cracking a nut, and that defeating global terrorism did not just mean repeated Afghanistan campaigns or war against Iraq. It had been difficult enough to deal with the threat of Iraq's build up of WMDs and their means of delivery, but they were not the only terrorists in the world, and Weaver knew that Minton was looking for some way to prove to the Arab world that action against terrorism was not synonymous with action against the Muslim world. Well, this could be the proof he was looking for. It would also secure for him the Irish vote—he was returning their fatherland to them, after all—and with it a second term for himself and the Republicans.

The Prime Minister stretched. It had been a long evening, but he hoped, a valuable one. It had been essential to brief the Cabinet Secretary, and win him over as an ally, without whom none of this would be possible.

"Robin," he said, addressing Sir Robin Algar, "we've covered a lot of ground in the last few hours, and there are many more hours of discussion and debate yet to be had. But you may feel I've said enough already to outline to you the broad tenets of my proposal. I need your support in order to proceed, but I don't need your decision tonight—that would be unfair. But I shall need to know before the weekend, as we shall need to discuss the line we take with the President."

"We certainly shall," agreed Sir Robin Algar. "But I think—even dare to suggest—that if I can be persuaded, then between us we should be able to persuade him."

"We will need to be particularly clear, too, about ensuring that he understands about the need for absolute security, and only to confide in those that he—and we—can trust totally."

"Yes, without a doubt. We in particular will need to be convinced of the security of his people as well as our own."

"Well," said the PM, "if you really do now understand how absolutely essential it is to be totally strict about the 'need to know' policy, and to be equally convinced that those who do know can be trusted, then we need to make a decision about our friend here, Mr. Jack Bennett." Weaver held out the file. "I'd like you to look at this most carefully, and, knowing what Bennett will have heard, advise me whether or not Bennett can be trusted, or whether we need to take some further action."

Algar took the file. "What further action had you mind?" queried Sir Robin.

"If you judge that he can't be trusted, then we shall need to consider whether he should be removed, completely and permanently."

"But with that threat hanging over me, forever at the back of my mind as I read his file, you will forgive me if I say now that the temptation will be to declare him safe, just to save his life," said Sir Robin plaintively.

"That thought had occurred to me, Robin," said the Prime Minister. "But I think I know you better than that. Now, if there's nothing else, I suggest we adjourn. It has, after all, been a long day for both of us."

"Just one last question if I may," said Sir Robin, as both men stood.

"Of course." The PM hovered by the door

"I cannot see how the Irish will ever agree to any proposed solution from any UK government, let alone a strategy with such far reaching implications as this. Surely you must see that, Prime Minister?"

"Of course," said Weaver again, this time with the glimmer of a smile.

"But their agreement is essential to the whole thing—without it, no political solution along the lines you suggest can even be contemplated. Exactly how, in God's name, will you set about achieving that?"

"I shan't," replied the Prime Minister. "The Americans will do it. In our talks with them we must persuade them—insist, even—that it will be their initiative, not ours."

"Oh, and by the way," said Weaver, as Algar turned for the door. "You'd better take your clipboard."

Chapter Six
SPECIAL RELATIONS

Andrew Groves and Pierre van-Leengoed had greeted one another like long lost brothers when they met at Zaventum, Brussels' International airport.

It had been some twelve years since their first meeting, and they had immediately got on well together. In those days, van Leengoed had been working in the Dutch Government Transport Department, in charge of their railways directorate, while Groves had been Head of Information at the Department of Transport in London. Their paths had crossed at a United Nations meeting of Transport Ministers in Geneva, when they had both been part of their respective delegations. They had immediately struck up a rapport, which, over the years, had developed into a strong friendship. The Dutchman had moved into public relations work, still as a civil servant, which had meant that he and Groves had even more in common, and that their professional paths tended to cross even more than they used.

Now they were both top of their profession, although, if he was honest, Groves was rather envious of van Leengoeds' job as Director General, Press and Communication at the EU. He wouldn't have minded that himself. Not that he was grumbling about the job he had instead—far from it. But perhaps NATO would come up one day—that would be nice.

Groves and van-Lee, as he was known, both enjoyed the 18km rail trip from the airport to the centre of Brussels. They shared an interest in railways that had developed during their work in their respective transport ministries, and their interest in the subject had lingered on. They each pumped 3.40 Euros into the machine for their single ticket, and sat in animated conversation during the 20-minute journey, Groves clutching his overnight bag. They left Centraal station, and headed for the Grand Place, a short walk away. Over their first glass of draught Kronenbourg, sitting outside at their favourite bar opposite the Hotel de Ville, Groves changed the subject from personal affairs to the real purpose of his visit.

"There's something very odd going on in London," said Groves, "and I don't understand what it's all about. What's more, no-one seems about to tell me, either."

"That's unusual," said his friend, "You usually get to know just about everything that's worth knowing."

"Well, not this time," replied Andrew.

"I must say," said Pierre, "I did think it odd that you should be sent over here just because some fat-head - is that OK English?"

Groves nodded. Like most Dutchmen, Pierre spoke excellent English.

"Just because some fat-head mentioned the advantages of straight cucumbers! People here are always getting stupid quotes in the papers."

"That's not confined to Brussels, either," said Groves. "But we'll talk about bloody cucumbers tomorrow, if we must. That's only the excuse—the official reason—for me being here. The Prime Minister has asked me to make discreet enquiries about something else, quite different and unrelated, and that's why I want your special help."

"Sounds interesting." said van-Lee.

"It is, and it's the bit I don't understand," replied Groves. He took a long sip of his beer, looking around him to make sure they were not being overheard. "The PM specifically wants to know about the activities of Sinn Fein within the EU," he continued, leaning forward. "As you may remember, they are the political wing of the IRA, and they have an office here in Brussels. He's asked me to find out who they've been briefing recently, what sort of line they are taking, what press coverage they've had over here, that sort of thing. But I don't know why, which means I don't really know what I'm looking for."

"Well," said Pierre, philosophically, "it's not the first time, and it probably won't be the last, that Ministers have asked you and I to do something which sounds screwy."

"Quite," said Andrew. "I can understand people getting cross about idiots who bang on about straight cucumbers—we have enough problems in the UK at the moment trying to convince people that the EU is a good thing, and with the debate hotting up about the single currency, this sort of thing doesn't help."

"Of course not. I can see that."

"But the sudden interest in the Brussels office of Sinn Fein is beyond me," said Groves.

"Well," said van-Leengoed, "it shouldn't be too difficult to find out what they're up to. I'll get one of my guys on to it."

"No, please don't do that," said Groves. "I hate to ask you this, but could you possibly take it on yourself? The PM has asked for the utmost discretion, and for only you and I to know that he has shown this interest. That means we have to do the legwork ourselves somehow."

"Still no problem," grinned his colleague. "I had hoped we might be able to dash home to Bergen op Zoom this evening—I know Marie-Ann is dying to see you again—but we don't have much time as you are flying home tomorrow. So I suggest we stay at my flat tonight, instead."

"As it happens," said Groves, "I could be persuaded to stay on a bit! The PM is going to the States this evening, and is staying over for a quiet weekend with President Minton. They seem to get on almost as well as we do! But I shan't be going—the Foreign Office is taking the lead—so I don't have to report to Tony Weaver until Monday. And I did warn Joan that this might take longer than just one day, so she won't be too surprised if I ring to tell her I shan't be home until later on Saturday."

"Brilliant!" van-Leengoed was obviously delighted. "But I still think we should stay at the flat this evening, and head for Holland later tomorrow if we can. It's only an hour away in the car, I know, but the flat is so handy for the office, it will give us more time. I've fixed for you to see a close colleague of mine in DG VI tomorrow morning at about ten to talk cucumbers. As you can imagine, I have quite a lot to do with the Agricultural directorate and its people. But we can nip into my office at the Berlaymont Building later this evening so that I can raid the files, look at the briefing material on the EU computer network, check the press cuttings and so on, when there's no-one much about. There's one man I might have a quiet word with tomorrow—or even at home this evening. He works in DG I, the external relations directorate, and keeps his ear very close to the ground. He could be a useful source. He won't mind, he can be trusted and he will have a finger on the Irish pulse. I promise I will be tactful—he won't have a clue why I'm asking, and he's sensible enough not to enquire. And he certainly won't know you're over here. Now let's have another beer!"

Which is what they did.

"I'd heard," said van-Lee, "on the news at lunchtime, I think, that Weaver was going to America. Something about a public show of support over their new Middle East initiative."

"That's right," said Groves. "That's why the Foreign Office is taking the lead, and my number two is going as well just to look after the boss. But they are all coming back after the meeting and press briefing, except the PM and the Cabinet Secretary, who are staying on for a quiet private weekend with the President."

"That could be quite a good weekend you're missing, by the sound it. US Presidents don't usually go wanting for anything!"

"But I think there's more to it than that," said Groves. "It all seems to have been arranged in a great hurry, and as you know, these trips, especially those ending in a 'quiet weekend', are normally in the diary weeks in advance. I think the Middle East thing is just an excuse for going."

"Like your cucumbers!"

"Exactly! If the two leaders really wanted a quiet weekend on their own, fishing or something, why is Sir Robin Algar staying as well?"

"And if he is, why aren't you?"

"Something odd there somewhere, if you ask me," said Andrew Groves. "Unless I'm just getting unduly suspicious of politicians in my old age."

"Could be that!" agreed Pierre, jokingly.

"What about some dinner, then?" said Groves, tipping back his glass.

"Good idea. We'll eat first, and go to the office afterwards. Everyone will have gone home by then. Where shall we go?"

"Anywhere but your flat, if don't mind. With all due respect, Mr. Director General, I could do without your cooking tonight! I've had a bad day already!"

"Well, we could try 'The King of Spain' over there on the corner, or cut through to the Rue des Boucher, where there's more choice."

"Let's pretend we're tourists, and find somewhere in the Rue des Boucher. There are some quite cheap little places there, as I remember, and I insist on paying."

The taxi from their chosen restaurant took little time to get to the EU Headquarters building, which was, by then, almost deserted of the usual hoards of European civil servants. Groves sat himself at the conference table in van-Lee's office, and started to wade through the folders of press cuttings that Pierre had retrieved from registry. Van-Leengoed himself sat at his desk, frowning into the computer, and they worked in virtual silence for well over an hour.

"There's damn-all in these folders, Pierre," said Groves eventually. "It seems as if Sinn Fein hardly existed, never mind had an office here."

"It's funny you should say that, but I've found nothing of any significance either. Perhaps I should ring Fabienne Pithan in External Relations—see if he knows anything."

"Why not, if he can be trusted."

"I'll say I've had an enquiry from a foreign editor."

It wasn't a long conversation. The Sinn Fein officials in Brussels did very little to draw attention to themselves, and were rarely seen at any official functions, mainly because they weren't often invited. When they were, they went, but very few people went out of their way to be sociable to them. They occasionally called a press conference to brief about the latest atrocity by the British Army, but few journalists bothered to attend, and even fewer wrote anything. Fabienne really wasn't sure why they bothered with an office in Brussels at all, or what the occupants of it did all day.

"How very odd," said Groves. "There's really no evidence of them doing any active or serious lobbying at all."

"Interesting, too, that hardly anyone within the Commission takes much notice of them, either," added van-Leengoed. "No obvious power-base or field of influence at all."

"I wonder if this is what Tony Weaver expected," pondered Groves.

"And why he didn't just ask your ambassador?" asked van-Lee.

"Security, I guess," said Andrew. "I know the ambassador was told I was coming over, to try to persuade you to stop these unhelpful press stories, but as you know that was little more than an excuse for seeing you. He certainly wasn't asked about Sinn Fein activities over here, and so doesn't know that the Prime Minister is interested. Nobody does, apart from you and I."

"And even you don't know why he is."

Groves frowned. "It would help to know what we're looking for and why, wouldn't it?" He looked at his watch. "Can we spend another hour or so just double-checking? I don't propose to take any notes—I have to brief verbally, so I must make sure I have a clear idea about what I'm going to say."

They slept well at the flat, after a decent nightcap, and took a breakfast of coffee and croissants at a small restaurant near the Berlaymont building, which was full of Eurocrats doing the same thing.

"Can't get near this place at lunchtime," observed Pierre. "You wouldn't think we had a half-decent restaurant in the building—heavily subsidised, too."

"Just nice to get out, I suppose," said Andrew.

"Probably," agreed van-Lee. "Especially as many of them come from the member states, and can only get home at weekends. It saves them cooking in their pokey little apartments after work."

"I never really understood why you have an apartment here, living only an hour away," said Groves.

"Well, the office pays for it, it's very handy after official evening functions that I can't dodge, and Marie-Ann stays there sometimes too, when shopping, or when we go to a theatre."

"Very nice," said Groves. "I only live about an hour from Downing Street, too, but I have to battle through the traffic every night, or go by train, which would be even worse."

"You're only jealous! But if we grab lunch in the building today, I can try to get away early so we can have a bit of time at home."

"Don't worry about me," said Groves. "If I can have access to today's papers and a phone, I can check in to see what's going on at home while you do whatever you must, catch up on the news, and make a few notes about your attitude towards cucumbers, if I really feel I should! And I'll change my flight to one tomorrow afternoon, if that's all right with you and Marie-Ann?"

Andrew Groves, Pierre van-Leengoed and his colleague who acted as spokesman on agricultural affairs—a harassed, rather worried young German, who was aging before his time—duly met the chosen official in DG VI on the dot of ten. Groves let forth about cucumbers and the dangers of unguarded comments to the media, while DG VI and its spokesman claimed that it was all the fault of the anti-European media, mostly based in UK, who grabbed at any chance to knock the CAP in particular and the EU in general. Groves already knew of the delightful openness of the Berlaymont building, and the ease with which almost anyone could gain access to almost any official. It was an attribute of the Commission that he almost envied, except that it made controlling and keeping in touch with what officials said to the media virtually impossible. Coffee flowed, views were exchanged, and at the end of the meeting, both sides concluded that they had made their point. DG VI, however, were impressed and slightly alarmed that the UK Prime Minister had chosen to send his top man to deliver a bollocking personally, rather than have a minion ring them up, which is what usually happened.

In the end, it was about four o'clock when they eventually hit the A12 out of Brussels towards Antwerp and Bergen op Zoom, in Pierre's new Audi.

On Saturday morning, Marie-Ann was in the kitchen, bustling about preparing lunch, when she answered the phone.

"Andrew, it's for you," she said, bringing in the portable. "Says his name is Tony Weaver," she announced.

Pierre sat bolt upright, and Andrew grinned, taking the phone.

"Thanks," he said, "It's the Prime Minister!"

"And he just spoke to me," said Marie-Ann, in awe.

" 'Morning, Prime Minister," said Andrew, as Pierre and his wife beat a hasty retreat. "I hear from the news that you had a good meeting in the States."

"Very good indeed," replied Weaver, "and I'm glad it got positive coverage in Europe. I'll tell the President. He was well pleased to have our support for this new initiative, and, although I say it myself, I think it was because we were here that the Russian President managed to bring himself to have a long telephone conversation with the President last night to offer his support as well. Every little bit helps."

"That was reported here, too," replied Andrew. "I've been in touch with the office, by the way, and there's nothing for either of us to worry about, so I'm told."

"I am getting the same message," replied Weaver. "How have you been getting on?"

"Fine. A good meeting about cucumbers, and they're in no doubt about how unhelpful that sort of thing is. Of course, they blame the media, but they realise they shouldn't make unguarded comments in the first place. You'll have my report on Monday, unless you'd like it e-mailed now."

"No thanks, Andrew. I'm really rather more interested in the other matter. What did you find out?"

"As a matter of fact, Prime Minister, it's almost a nil return," replied Andrew, who had just worked out what time it was in Washington. He briefly, but guardedly, outlined what little he and Pierre had discovered.

"Excellent—that's good news, Andrew. Many thanks."

"Is that why you rang?" asked Andrew with his usual bluntness. "It must only be about six in the morning where you are, and you had to track me down, too."

"You're right on both counts," replied the PM. "It is early, but it's a glorious morning, and I'm told I'm being taken fishing later, so I thought I'd make contact before we both disappear for the weekend. See you Monday."

And with that, Weaver hung up. He guessed that Andrew would be bewildered by his call, but he really did need to know the outcome of the Brussels investigation before he continued his private discussions with Bill Minton. Perhaps he should have explained, too, that he was no longer in Washington, but on some out-of-the-way island in New York.

Events yesterday had gone well, he thought. All overseas visits seemed to start and finish with a press conference, and this had been no different. He had taken the lead outside Downing Street and at Heathrow, but on arrival at Dulles he had shared the platform with Foreign Secretary Robert Burgess. They had taken a few of the political correspondents with them, as they did when there was room and when they thought the extra briefings on the aircraft would pay off.

The series of meetings in the White House had been both amicable and useful. At his level, he had been able to impress upon the President and the Secretary of State the importance which the UK attached to this new round of diplomacy as part of the war against terrorism, while at parallel meetings between officials, drafting the final communiqué had proved relatively easy. The UK's offer of meetings at diplomatic level in the Middle East to further support the Secretary of State had been warmly welcomed.

Lunch, as always at the White House, had been jolly good, although not as lengthy as it often was, as officials seemed to be working faster than usual and finding fewer obstacles in the way of reaching a finally agreed statement. So lunch was soon followed by a final meeting of the two leaders and their immediate senior officials behind closed doors, after which the final plenary session was held, where the communiqué was agreed. They had tea while it was being turned into a press release, in itself a more positive and hard-hitting document than usual.

In the end, it was late afternoon before Weaver and Minton appeared on the White House lawn to brief the assembled media, which kept a respectful and safe distance away. They each made only the briefest of statements, and took no questions, as the main briefing was to be held inside by Robert Burgess and Miles Bragan. Plenty of time for questions there.

Eventually, they strode across the lawn, pausing now and then to wave at lurking TV and cameras, passed the immaculate Marines, and climbed into the waiting Presidential helicopter. As they turned at the top of the steps for a final gesture of solidarity and a cheery wave together, they could see their two wives, Millie and Susan, being escorted to a second helicopter, with Robin Algar and Colin Carlucci. Apart from security men, that was the size of the party heading off for a quiet and private day on a remote but lovely island off New York. But it was a day that was going to change the course of history.

"I hope you're gonna like this place," said Minton, as they took off. "It belongs to Millie's brother, Chuck, and I just love it. He uses it for weekends, but every now and then I can get there, and we're lucky he's staying at his apartment in New York this weekend. It's real quiet, well secluded and secure—our guys make sure of that when I'm there—and it's better than Camp David because it's out of the way, and not many people know I go there from time to time."

"Where exactly is it?" asked Weaver.

Minton groped for a map. "Let me show you," he said. "Now, see here's New York—Manhattan," he stabbed a finger, "and here's Brooklyn right at the bottom of Long Island. And here, sheltered between the north and south forks of eastern Long Island, is Shelter Island—that's where we're heading."

"It doesn't look very big," commented Weaver.

"It's about 8,000 acres, and most of that is nature reserve. It's quiet and peaceful, with natural harbours and a couple of marinas for those who like boating, good fishing, plenty of bird life, and good beaches. There's also a 35 mph speed limit!"

"Full of New York commuters, I suppose?" queried Weaver.

"Some. But it's a village sort of life, although with some superb ranch-style properties, and many people just use it, like Chuck, to get away from everything at weekends. But some people commute, by sea-plane, even!"

"Sounds too good to be true."

"I'm sure you'll just love Beach House—certainly Susan will. It's on a headland outside Dering Harbour Village. Eight bedrooms, all with en-suite, swimming pool, private beach and moorings, huge grounds, you name it."

"What does Chuck do for a living to afford all that? Presumably he owns the apartment in New York as well," queried Weaver.

"Something to do with insurance—Millie knows, but I'm never sure. He certainly earns plenty. In fact sometimes that worries me, Tony. There are too many people in the States earning too much, and too many not earning enough. We can redistribute some of it through the tax system, but too much social engineering could well kill off the wealth that keeps the country as a whole going. It's a difficult balance, as I'm sure you know. But we don't need to talk that kind of shop, unless you want to," said Minton.

"That's not quite what I wanted to talk to you about privately, Bill," replied Weaver.

"I guessed not. What I suggest is that we have a quiet evening—I'm sure you and Susan could do with a freshen-up and rest after all your travels today. Then we'll have a leisurely supper—I thought something light after the White House lunch—and a look round the house and grounds together, and you and I can get down to business tomorrow, if that's agreeable, with Robin and Colin. I take it that Robin knows what this is about, and that I can have Colin with me?"

"Yes, of course."

"I've arranged a fishing trip for the morning, in Chuck's launch. I know you enjoy that when you get a chance, and there's some excellent striped bass to be had with the right tackle. The girls can tour the island, or go shopping or whatever they want to do, but we'll be able to talk quite freely together with no one to overhear what we're saying. Two security guys will drive the launch for us, and help with the fishing tackle—the rest can tag along in another launch. It's all laid on."

"Thank you, Bill. That all sounds absolutely ideal," replied Tony Weaver. "But I think we may need quite a bit of time to ourselves, as there are a lot of issues surrounding the subject I want to discuss. So could I suggest that we might start this evening after supper, perhaps while walking in the grounds? Then we can sleep on things and resume tomorrow. I wouldn't want to totally ruin the fishing!"

"OK - that's no problem," replied Minton. "It won't be dark 'til gone ten tonight."

Soon, they were touching down in the extensive and immaculately kept grounds of Beach House. It was easy to see why Bill Minton so enjoyed his visits—there was an immediate air of peace and tranquillity about the place. As they approached over the creek, Weaver had noticed large flocks of seabirds take to the air from the sky-blue waters. He had a good view of the marina and yacht club, and of the North Ferry terminal, as they swept over the beach, avoiding the village, and turned to land on the striped lawn. Peaceful though it seemed, he had also noticed the security personnel around the house and in the grounds. The whitewashed house itself was huge, and reminded him at first of a Spanish hacienda. Certainly there was an Hispanic influence in its architecture, but it still had the style of a ranch from America's South and the typical American homestead—although on a grand scale.

They waited for their wives to join them, and headed for the house, being met on the way by a matronly housekeeper, who took the Weavers to their suite on the first floor. They had arranged to meet for a drink on the patio by the swimming pool, overlooking the bay, at about seven—plenty of time to change and relax. Time too, for Tony to rehearse how he would approach the President with such a monumental proposal as he had in mind.

He went over his thoughts with Robin Algar, when they met as pre-arranged shortly after six. He and Robin sat in earnest consultation on the balcony of the PM's suite, while their wives chatted amicably in the sitting room. They all agreed that they had never seen such opulence and luxury—certainly not at Chequers!

Drinks on the patio in the warm evening sunshine were followed by a buffet supper of local prawns and fresh lobster, accompanied by a chilled sparkling wine from California. The whole party appeared totally relaxed—in fact, only the wives really were, and even they sensed that their men-folk were tense about their forthcoming discussions.

Eventually, Minton stood. "Come on, Tony, my friend, let me show you the grounds. I can't bear the suspense any longer of not knowing what you want to discuss so privately."

They set off down the steps, and headed across the lawn to the wooded area behind the house, Algar and Carlucci following, closely but out of earshot.

Colin Carlucci turned to Sir Robin. "It won't matter if we lose sight of them—I know my way around here. It's almost a nature trail, although I guess you and I will be too engrossed to take much notice of our surroundings."

"That's a pity, but I'm sure you're right," replied Robin. "My instructions are to brief you on exactly the same areas that they will be covering," he nodded ahead of them, "so that if they need to talk things over with us, either together or separately, we'll all know what we're talking about."

"That's good," replied Carlucci. "As you can imagine, we've been scouring the briefing books and Int. reports and everything, trying to work out what this is all about. We guess it's something to do with Northern Ireland, but that's as close as we've got," he confessed.

"In broad terms, you're right," said Algar. "But it also has a lot to do with the fight against terrorism, and international politics. We have proposals to put to you that have wide ranging ramifications for both our countries. The Prime Minister has suggested that we deal with the terrorism aspects this evening, and move on to the political implications of our ideas tomorrow, after you have at least had a chance to digest some of what we have in mind."

"Sounds like a pretty full agenda," said Carlucci.

"It is," said Algar. "There are two things to emphasise, though, before we begin. The first is that we naturally don't expect a considered reaction this weekend. The President will obviously need to consult with you, the Secretary of State, and others before any response will be possible. But the second point, which is absolutely crucial, is that your consultations be confined to the very minimum number of people necessary, and that they are absolutely, one hundred percent, trustworthy. I can't emphasise that strongly enough—you'll see why total and absolute secrecy is imperative as I outline our thinking."

"Understood," replied Carlucci. "I'm sure the President will be happy to proceed on that basis, and so am I."

"I must also ask you, as the President himself is being asked, not to take, or make in the future, any notes. There must be nothing in writing—no paper, no leaks. Neither the PM nor I have any notes to draw upon for our briefings this weekend. I just hope I remember everything!"

Sir Robin Algar took a deep breath. He knew he was embarking on one of the most important briefings of his career, but without the comfort of notes or slides or view foils or video clips or auto-cues—nothing but his own memory.

He started by outlining the background. The UK's support for America's fight against international terrorism had been unswerving, but that fight was increasingly being perceived as a war again the Muslim world. There was an urgent need to show that this was not the case, and the British government wanted to suggest that America should now devote its attention to the terrorist gangs which operated in Northern Ireland. The United States had, after all, once identified the IRA as being one of the more formidable players in international terror, so here was a chance to do something about it.

"We have worked out a strategy for defeating terrorism in the Province, for bringing peace to the area, and for instituting a lasting political solution," pronounced Algar. "But we can't do it without the total support of the United States. We are here this weekend to ask for that support, and to try to convince you that America has as much to gain from successfully prosecuting this policy as anyone else."

"By God, that sounds ambitious," exclaimed Carlucci. "And you are really convinced that all this is possible, after all these years of the troubles?" asked Carlucci.

"Certainly," replied Algar. "I have to admit that at first I couldn't believe that it would work. Nothing ever has in the past, as you hinted. But this is largely Weaver's own plan, and I think that if he is politically brave enough to attempt it, then I can be brave enough to support it. And I do now believe it can be made to work, given speed and absolute security."

"Tell me about the politics of it," said Colin. "We've always been briefed that the gulf between the two sides is un-bridgeable."

"Politics tomorrow," replied Algar. "Let's deal with beating the terrorists first, and get your views on that, because, again, we can't achieve this on our own."

Ahead of them, they could see the President and the Prime Minister, both ambling towards the belt of trees, heads bowed, the President with his hands in the pockets of his jeans, the Prime Minister with his hands firmly clasped behind his back. Armed security men were comfortingly evident, but unobtrusive.

"Why don't we sit here," said Carlucci, as they approached a bench, overlooking Dering Harbour and the yacht club. "I can't walk and think at the same time."

"OK. Now let me briefly outline the problem as we see it, and how the PM believes we can overcome it," continued Robin Algar. "It's quite simple, really, if audacious. You know, I'm sure, Colin, that the Unionists want to remain part of the UK, while the Republicans want to join the south and get Britain out of Ireland altogether. That's the real and basic problem—all the others flow from it. As Weaver sees it, the first thing we must do is create peace in the province, and that means an end to talking. That is simply achieving nothing. But if we were to remove the terrorists, their funds and their weapons, then a political solution becomes possible."

"And how do you remove the terrorists?" asked Colin Carlucci. "You can't declare war on them, as we did in Afghanistan, and I seem to remember that internment was tried before and didn't work."

"Exactly," replied the Algar. "That didn't work last time and it won't work now. By 'remove', the Prime Minister has in mind permanent removal, and he doesn't mean new legislation to re-introduce the death penalty, either."

Carlucci frowned. "If you mean what I think you mean, he surely can't be serious, can he?"

Sir Robin Algar recognised exactly his own incredulity when Weaver had first suggested this to him.

"Deadly serious, if I may say so. There is enough evidence to send all these people to death row if it was just possible to get witnesses into court. But the level of intimidation and the power exercised by these evil men is such that the normal course of justice is denied us. The Prime Minister believes that, done carefully, we would be totally justified in removing them from civilised society. He believes, and I agree, that there is no need, either, to feel in any way sorry for any of them. They are terrorists, murderers, and operate huge organised crime syndicates without a moments thought for their victims, or even their own families. Weaver is quite convinced that we shall have right on our side in this crusade, and that in the end the majority of people in Northern Ireland and elsewhere will be heartily thankful when they come to realise that these thugs have disappeared from the scene and are no longer a threat to civilised life."

"And you want us to help?" asked a stunned Chief of Staff.

"We shall certainly be asking for your total and unswerving support, as you have had ours so far. This is seen as just another step in the battle to rid the world of terrorism—but this time they are not Muslims. And I dare say that there will be a time when we shall need your practical assistance as well."

"Convince me, then. What's the plan?" asked Carlucci.

"Nothing in detail yet, obviously, but we see three stages to the whole operation designed to bring peace to Northern Ireland, and something assembling normality for the people of the Province."

"Keep going."

At least Carlucci was still listening, thought Algar. He wondered how Weaver was getting on with Minton.

"The Prime Minister sees getting rid of the terrorist leadership and hard men on both sides of the divide as the first stage. Up to a point, we may just be helped by their own enemies on the opposing side of the political divide, through tit-for-tat retaliatory actions, if they can be made to believe that the opposition is carrying out the offensive. They won't need much convincing of that. But we shall need to take great care how we go about it, too. Deaths must either look as if they have come about naturally, or there must be no bodies, and hence no postmortems. We simply must avoid accusations of a 'shoot to kill' policy by the security forces."

"This looks a terribly risky policy to me," said Carlucci. "The political risks simply don't bear thinking about."

"That was my point exactly. Hence the need for absolute and total secrecy, and only telling those who are guaranteed to be trustworthy—like you."

"Gee, thanks. I'm not sure whether I'm pleased to be hearing all this or not." said Colin. "But you mentioned three stages—what are the others?"

He's still with me, thought Robin. *But for how long, that's the question.*

"We must then get rid of the huge stockpiles of arms and ammunition which are still held by both Unionists and Republicans," he continued. "We know where most of the dumps are, and the decommissioning process simply hasn't worked. Nothing worthwhile has been achieved, and even when some small quantities have been given up, it has only been a hollow gesture on the part of the terrorists, as they have immediately gone to their suppliers, and replaced their stocks. We simply can't wait any longer for this process to work. There's only one way to put their arms and ammunition beyond further use, and that is to decommission it all ourselves."

"I seem to remember from our intelligence reports that most of the arms dumps are in the south, across the border," said Carlucci. "How do you plan to square all this with Dublin?"

"You're right," said the Cabinet Secretary. "The people in Dublin know where most of the dumps are, too, but, apart from monitoring them, have so far chosen not to do anything about them. The idea is that we will deal with them, with or without their agreement, but hopefully with it."

"This brings us to the politics of it all," said the Chief of Staff.

"Tomorrow!" said Robin Algar.

"OK. So what's the third stage then?"

"So the third stage," replied Algar, "must be to empty their bank accounts and neutralise their paymasters so that they have no cash with which to re-arm when we deal with their stockpiles."

Carlucci stood and stretched. "Let's walk on a bit. It's beginning to get dark. We can cut off the corner, and catch up with our two bosses."

They ambled off through the trees, into the gathering dusk.

"Tell me how you think you are going to deal with their funds?" demanded Colin.

"That's going to be a job for me, apparently, since I have contacts in the City of London and in banking who I can trust, and who could be useful. We know where most of the accounts are, and I shall have to find a way of getting at them, clearing them of funds, and closing them down. Trying to get the international community to agree action to freeze their assets would take forever, and then largely be ineffective. It's also too public, and could draw attention to what we are trying to do elsewhere. But I shall need help from this side of the Atlantic, especially where NORAID is concerned. We know the IRA and Sinn Fein have several accounts here."

"Yea, we know that, too," said Carlucci. "The problem is the Irish/American vote. That's why we haven't been able, or perhaps I mean willing, to do more to help you in the past. We rely too heavily on it. But given the will, and the political direction, we could help, for sure. It's certainly true that 'corporate America'—the business community, which tends to give financial support to the Irish Republican cause—has become very disenchanted in recent years with the antics of people like McFosters. His visit to Cuba did him and his cause no good at all. He forgets that the States is largely anti-Castro, and that there's a trade embargo in force between the two countries. And the IRA has even been training Colombian terrorists, so it seems, and that went down like a lead balloon here, too. Of course, it depends on the President, not least of all, and his perception of the political damage this could all do to the party. But I suppose that's politics and tomorrow, again!"

"Correct, Colin!"

They were nearly back at the house now, and could see the two world leaders ahead of them, heads still bowed in earnest conversation. *At least they are still talking*, thought Robin, *as we are.*

"There's one thing that won't have escaped you, Colin, and that is that we must synchronise the anti-terrorism work very closely with all that needs to be done on the political front, and complete both with the utmost speed. Getting terrorism out of Northern Ireland must be done covertly and swiftly, whereas the political process which will follow, rather than parallel, must be completed with the utmost openness and public participation."

"And shall we be involved in that, too?" asked Colin.

"Very much so, as you will see tomorrow."

The four men met up again on the lawn.

"Well, Mr. President?" queried his Chief of Staff.

"Well, indeed!" responded Bill Minton. "If you've heard half of what I've heard, you will be as breathless as I am. But I congratulate you, Tony, on some very creative and positive thinking. I'm almost sure that, provided we can so plan things that no finger of suspicion points at either of our two administrations, your plan to eradicate terrorism from Northern Ireland could just work."

"I agree," said Carlucci, "but Mr. Secretary Bragan will need to be consulted and convinced, as will several others. I just hope we know enough people in the right places who we can trust enough to get in on it."

"We shall have that problem, too," said the Prime Minister. "Paramount in all this will be total and absolute secrecy in all areas of the anti-terrorist action, as well as in the planning of the political effort which will be needed to complete the exercise. Then, total openness is called for, as democracy swings into action. I have to say, Bill, that I am very grateful indeed to you and your staff for immediately realising that there was this need for total secrecy. Without my asking, you actually did exactly what we did—no public record of the phone call, nothing on paper, nobody briefed. Except that you have indicated to Miles Bragan that something is afoot and let him hear our taped conversation, and I haven't yet told the Foreign Secretary. I'll do that when I know whether or not you're with us."

"Colin," said the President, "you and I will need to talk about this later, although I guess you're not looking for a commitment this weekend, are you, Tony?"

"No, of course not."

"Then let's have a quiet glass of something, and talk further as a foursome. But I do confess to being very puzzled indeed about the political solution you must have in mind," said Minton.

"Me too," said Carlucci. "Totally at a loss."

"I really do think, Bill, that we all have enough to think about tonight, and that we should leave discussion of the political processes until the morning," insisted the Prime Minister.

"I suppose you're right, Tony," conceded the President. "But there is such a gulf between the two sides in their political aspirations that I simply cannot see how they can ever both be satisfied with any sort of compromise."

Tony Weaver sat back, sipped his cognac, and looked across at the Cabinet Secretary.

"Shall I give them a clue, Robin?"

"Entirely up to you, Prime Minister. This is your show."

"Very well then." He turned to Bill Minton, grinning. "Just a clue, then, until the morning. The great problem with Northern Ireland politics is that the Unionists want to remain part of the UK, while the Republicans want nothing to do with the UK. There is only one solution to any problem, and that is to remove its cause. In the case of Northern Ireland, the cause is the UK."

There was silence.

"If you are seriously suggesting that you remove the UK from everything to do with Northern Ireland, and leave them to sort themselves out, which is what I assume, then you will have an even bigger mess, surely, and a complete political vacuum," claimed the President. "That sort of action would surely lead to even more violence on the streets, rather than less, and something approaching civil war. I have to tell you, Tony, that I most certainly would not be able to support such a policy, or recommend to others that it should be supported. The situation in Northern Ireland is not one where you can just walk away and leave that sort of vacuum."

"But I have a proposal which would fill that vacuum," responded Tony Weaver. "A formula for political action, which, hopefully and with your support, would be acceptable to both sides."

"What sort of formula?" demanded the President. "Come on, Tony! It's getting on for tomorrow already!"

"I know that," replied Weaver, "and I'm already beginning to feel the effects of jet lag—it already is tomorrow in London! But my plan is to brief you both fully in the morning, and as we shall all be together, I assume on Chuck's launch, I can brief you and Colin at the same time. Robin, you might actually be able to catch some fish while I do that!"

"Not likely," said Robin. "I want to be there to hear the reaction."

"Oh, all right," said Minton, "But you did say you would give us a clue, Tony.

If not, Colin and I will be up all night trying to guess at it."

"OK then. Just a clue, and then I'm turning in. It's been a long day," said Weaver, standing. "It's a formula drawn from your own history, Bill. I call it the Hawaii Formula. Goodnight, and thanks for an excellent day. See you at breakfast."

Chapter Seven
THE HAWAII FORMULA

Prime Minister Tony Weaver and Cabinet Secretary Sir Robin Algar made their way indoors towards their first floor suites.

"I can almost hear them scratching their heads," said Weaver. "They may just guess at the common link between Hawaii and Northern Ireland, but somehow I doubt they will guess what I am going to propose. I think we shall certainly have their undivided attention tomorrow."

"I think we had it today, too," replied Algar. "And I also think that we will end up getting their support for the covert part of this operation, if only because they can't think that they will have much of a role to play in helping us get rid of the terrorist gangs over there."

"They may change their minds when they hear what we have to say tomorrow, though," said the Prime Minister, "especially when they learn that we want them to take the lead in all this."

"That's certainly a risk," agreed Sir Robin. "But then this whole venture is a risk—even telling them about it in the first place runs the risk of an enormously embarrassing leak."

"Well, we shall see," said Weaver. "In a way, the fishing trip will be an unwanted distraction, although from a security point of view, it probably couldn't be better in terms of not being overheard. But there's a lot of ground to cover in just a morning. What time are we due to leave?"

"I think the plan is for us to have a barbeque lunch—probably fish, if we catch any—and then a final round of informal talks, so we have rather more time than just a morning. We're due out on the early evening flight from JFK," replied Algar. "I'll go up to the office the check up on things before I turn in, but I'm afraid there will be some red boxes put on the inbound flight for you to deal with on the way back. With any luck, we shall be back in Downing Street soon after eight o'clock Sunday morning."

"That sounds OK," sighed the PM. "But we shall need some time on the aircraft to agree how well we think we've got on, and what we need to do next. Perhaps more important," he reflected, "who we need to tell next. Don't spend too long in the office—we need all the sleep we can get."

They parted on the landing, outside the Prime Minister's suite, as Sir Robin went up one further flight of stairs to the temporary offices that had been established - one for the President and one for the UK Prime Minister. Both had secure communications links, via satellite, and a handful of staff, sufficient to cope with any emergency while the two leaders were away from their own permanent offices.

All seemed to be at peace with the world—or at least, there was nothing going on at the moment that couldn't wait until the PM's return, which was good. There would be nothing in the red boxes that was of particular moment, all pretty routine Cabinet papers to read and letters to sign. One of the Garden Room girls had come over with the party, and so would be on the Jumbo going back tomorrow if Weaver needed to do any dictation. Flights had been confirmed, and the PM's car would be ready and waiting for him on arrival at Heathrow, as would the Cabinet Secretary's. The President's office next door had been in touch to fix the helicopters to Kennedy airport tomorrow, so just about everything that needed to be done seemed to have been done.

A thankful Robin Algar bade the duty clerk 'goodnight', and returned to his suite on the floor below. He needed a rest, and it would be a happy break to find out what his wife, Betty, had been up to in Washington while they were at this morning's meetings about the Middle East. Was it only this morning? God, it had been a longer day that he had thought. And tomorrow was going to be even more trying, he imagined.

But when he eventually got to bed, having admired the results of a shopping trip with the President's rather extravagant wife, Millie, he found he couldn't sleep. There was too much to think about, churning over in his mind all that had happened during their walk through the grounds this afternoon, and too much more to rehearse for tomorrow's fishing trip.

Tony Weaver was having the same trouble in the suite next door. Which was why, as dawn was breaking, he decided to find out what Andrew Groves had discovered in Brussels. The European angle of this scheme had always worried him more than a little, and although he suspected that Sinn Fein might be more supportive of the whole plan than the Unionists, they had the potential to stir up trouble through their office in Belgium.

He dressed quickly and quietly, and walked up to the third floor office. They patched him through to the duty officer in Downing Street, who in turn was able to give him Groves' phone number in Holland. He decided to use the phone in his suite, rather than alert those in the office—security wouldn't be a problem with his call if he was careful, and he know Groves to be a cautious man of few words.

Andrew had sounded almost as surprised as the lady who answered the phone, and immediately realised that his end of the phone line was insecure, even if what he thought to be the Washington end wasn't. At the end of their brief but reassuring conversation, Weaver had hung up without telling Groves where he was. He felt a bit mean about that, but didn't mind—the fewer people who knew the better.

Breakfast was lavish. There was everything available they could wish for—fresh fruit, scrambled egg, grilled bacon, hash browns, waffles—everything. While Susan tucked in from the groaning sideboard, Weaver himself asked for two hard-boiled eggs. They arrived in solid silver eggcups, already shelled. Weaver noticed that every place setting had its own solid silver condiment set, that there were fresh flowers on the table, and at least two people were serving in the dining room.

"Chuck knows how to look after himself," remarked Bill Minton when he joined them. "Good job he's paying for all this and not the taxpayers."

"I must remember to drop him a note of thanks," said Weaver.

"He'd like that, I'm sure," said Minton. "How did you sleep?"

"Not a lot, to be honest, but we were very comfortable. I was up early."

"Me too," said Minton. "Colin and I stayed talking for some time after you'd retired, and put together a few theories of our own about what you want to talk about later this morning."

"Robin and I guessed you would," replied the Prime Minister. "There would have been something wrong if you hadn't." Weaver grinned. "We shall be interested to see if you guessed right."

"We'll get going as soon as we're ready—the suspense is killing us," said Minton. "But I'll tell you now, Tony, that Colin and I are sure we can get the necessary support to help you with your plan to rid Northern Ireland of terrorism. Obviously, we shall need to talk to Miles Bragan and perhaps a few others, but we don't see any great problem."

By then Colin Carlucci and Robin Algar had joined them.

"That's very encouraging news, Mr. President," said the Prime Minister.

"I hope at the end of today you will be able to support the whole of my plan."

"I've arranged for one of the best fishermen on Shelter Island to take us out this morning," continued Minton. "Guy called Captain John Hill, ex-Coast Guards, totally reliable, and still with a security clearance because of his reservist commitment. I saw him arrive in his launch just as I came down."

They were soon ready to bid farewell to their wives, and head across the manicured lower lawn towards the jetty at the northern end of the small private beach.

"This certainly is a beautiful spot," commented Algar. "And look at the size of Chuck's launch!"

The two Marine Corps security men were already on board, chatting quietly together, as Captain Hill walked up the jetty to greet them. He was soft spoken man, with a tanned, lined face under his peaked cap.

"Mr. President, gentlemen," he greeted them, half saluting. "Everything's ready when you are, sir."

"Right, then, let's get this show moving," said the President. "As you know, we must be back here about noon, so we don't have long to catch lunch."

"Long enough," replied John Hill, with a warm smile. "I gather you will be doing rather more talking than fishing, but I'll quickly show you the ropes as we head out towards Montauk Point. Should be plenty of bass out there. Some Spanish mackerel and a few Skipjack tuna, too, I shouldn't wonder, but we'll use light tackle and go for the striped bass. You can see from the masses of birds out there that there's plenty of shrimp and sand eel about, so the fish won't be too far away from a good meal."

As they pulled out into open water, they could see two small Zodiacs ahead of them, no doubt the rest of their security team.

"Let's go below to the cabin and start our discussions, before we get to the fishing grounds," suggested the President.

As they settled in, one of the Marines poured steaming fresh coffee for each of them, left a plate of cookies on the table, and went on deck, firmly closing the door behind him.

"Please tell Captain Hill that we'll join him when we're ready," said Minton to the retreating figure. "You carry on fishing if you want, but we are not to be disturbed."

The President turned to Prime Minister Weaver. "We're all ears, Tony."

Weaver had decided to take the bull by the horns, and not waste time on too much background. He took a deep breath.

"With your help, Mr President, I believe we can bring peace to the Province, as we discussed yesterday. But peace without stability will not last, so we need to install political institutions that both sides of the divide can accept and work in as well as work with. I no longer believe that Britain can play a part in that process." Weaver could see he had already captured the attention of both men. "The fact is that the British government is one of the main causes of the problem in Northern Ireland. As you know, the Republicans want nothing further to do with the UK, and are determined to achieve union with the south. The Unionists on the other hand want nothing to do with the Republic of Ireland, and are determined to stay a part of the UK. I have to say that my own soundings suggest that the Republic is none to keen on union with the north, although it naturally has to go through the motions of supporting the Republican cause, rather than the Unionists'. But the gap between the two sides is unbridgeable, so the other part of the problem is thus the Republic itself. If we can remove the problem, that is both the UK and the Republic from the Northern Ireland scene, then a solution becomes possible."

Carlucci, frowning, was deeply mystified, and looked questioningly at Algar. The President shook his head.

"I simply can't see how that can be done without creating a total vacuum, and inviting civil war," said Minton.

"Exactly what I said initially," said Sir Robin Algar. "But I now think there is a way forward after all."

"My theory," continued Weaver, "is simply to replace both nations by a third, which would be acceptable to both sides of the conflict in the north. And I believe that nation could be the United States of America."

There was a stunned silence, broken only by the steady throb of the powerful twin outboard motors of the launch.

"How the hell!" exclaimed the President, eventually.

"More to the point," said Carlucci, "Why the hell?"

"Let's deal with 'why' first," said Weaver "and look at the advantages which I believe could flow to America. First of all, some 50 million Americans claim Irish ancestry, and form the third largest ethnic group in the US. You're one of them, Bill. A majority of them support the republican cause in Northern Ireland, and would be unlikely to insist that the province remains part of the UK. You would be returning their fatherland to them if sovereignty of Ireland could pass across, and your party would secure the Irish American vote - well, just about forever. You would then also be freer to deal with Muslim fundamentalist terrorism and the problems of the Middle East, because loss of their votes would make little difference to your power base. Secondly, you would have a much firmer foothold in Europe, with all that means for trade and influence, the NATO alliance and so on. I believe that Ireland's membership of the EU could be retained, with careful negotiation, even if it became your 51st State. In UK terms, the Irish State would become a sort of American Hong Kong. From the Irish perspective, they gain peace and prosperity as part of a far more wealthy and powerful nation than the UK, they gain unity under a third party friendly nation, with a special relationship already in place. As for the UK itself, we save our exchequer a small fortune which the conflict, peacekeeping efforts, direct rule and everything else is presently costing us, and yet none of these costs would pass on to the US. Furthermore, we would rid ourselves of a huge problem which successive governments have failed to resolve and which is seemingly insoluble, while at the same time building even closer ties with the US without jeopardising our existing ties with Europe."

Minton and Carlucci were now sitting forward, leaning on the table, cold coffee in front of them. Weaver certainly had their undivided attention, Algar noted, without so far any sign of outright rejection. He had to hand it to the Prime Minister—he certainly knew how to judge his audience and how to present his case. He had seen it so many times in Cabinet and in the House. And now on a motor launch, somewhere off New York.

"Very neat," said Minton at last. "Very neat indeed."

"A fifty-first state, for God's sake!" exclaimed his Chief of Staff.

"Frankly," said the President, "I can't see how it would be done, even if my colleagues and I were to agree that it was a good idea."

"The same way as Hawaii transferred to the United States in 1959," replied Weaver.

"But if I remember my history right," said Carlucci, "the Hawaiians wanted to become a state. The Irish don't."

"Not yet," responded Algar, "but we think they might when it's put to them and the advantages are fully understood. Certainly we believe the Catholic north will be supportive, and that the Republic itself could be persuaded to enjoy the benefits of both membership of the EU and a direct relationship with your economy in return for giving up, in name anyway, its present sovereignty. The Unionists in the North will be more difficult to persuade, but we can offer them inducements, we think, which might help them to vote 'yes' in any referendum."

"Why do you think the south will be prepared to give up being a sovereign state?" asked the President.

"Mainly for economic reasons," replied Weaver. "They have enjoyed unprecedented economic growth and prosperity since joining the European Union, but the so-called 'Celtic Tiger' economy is now beginning to look a bit tired. They won't be slow to see the benefits of boosting their economy while remaining in Europe, or of peace across the Province."

"What about Europe—how will they react?"

"One thing I can tell you is that Sinn Fein won't be stirring them up. Although they have an office in Brussels, it seems to be virtually ineffective. But I believe the EU will also see the benefits to trade of closer ties with the US. Huge new markets will open up for its member nations, especially the more recently joined and poorer member countries," said Weaver.

"There are so many questions," said President Minton. "We can't deal with them all here, and we shouldn't try. Let's concentrate on the major principles involved, and leave the details till later. For a start, I shall need to brush up on my American history, to remind myself how Hawaii did actually accede to the United States."

"The whole process took years," replied Algar, "so we shall need to speed things up considerably if we take that route. But the basic constitutional mechanics of the transfer seem to me to be almost tailor-made for the transfer of sovereignty of both Northern Ireland to the US from the UK, and for the transfer of sovereignty from the Republic."

"If I remember my recent history," said Carlucci, "Hawaii twice applied for annexation to the United States, and was twice refused before establishing itself as a republic. It was only after the war, and what happened at Pearl Harbour, that things really started to move, and even then the Senate rejected the first bill which the House of Representatives passed."

"That's right," said Minton. "But we need to act faster than that this time—forget annexation and establishing a republic as the first steps. We will need to move straight to legislation to admit Ireland as the 51st state, if we're going to do anything at all."

"In the Hawaii case, that part of it all eventually happened quite fast, including approval by Hawaii's voters," said Carlucci. "So let's hope we can do it fast again, if it comes to it."

"I agree," said Weaver. "The faster we can move on all aspects of this, the less chance there will be for opposition to get itself organised well enough to throw spanners in the works."

"There seem to me to be any number of hurdles to be crossed first, and the plan could fall at any one of them," commented Minton. "For a start, just think how many people and institutions need to give the scheme their blessing before it can go ahead, including both houses of Congress."

"I don't underestimate the scale of the task ahead of us," said Weaver, "but with terrorism beaten and a peaceful background, our job will be made ten times easier."

"It seems to me," said Minton, "that the key to all this will be coordination."

"And speed," said Carlucci.

"And secrecy," added Weaver, "until we are ready to launch the idea on an unsuspecting world, by which time all the plans must be in place for constitutional talks, referenda, elections and the rest of it. The planning of all that will have to be carried out by the minimum number of the most highly trustworthy officials while we deal with the terrorists, so that the political solution can be put in place immediately there is seen, by all the parties concerned, to be a chance of lasting peace."

Carlucci sat back. "Personally," he said, "I can see many good reasons for taking this seriously and discussing it in detail further. But I cannot see how anyone in Ireland, north or south, will possibly take such a proposal seriously. It will simply be seen as a cop-out by the British government, and yet another UK plan to be kicked into touch by one side or the other."

"I agree," said Weaver. "That thought had occurred to us, too. This may be asking a lot, but if we are to proceed with this, then the idea must be proposed by the United States for it to stand any chance of being accepted, either in Ireland or by the international community at large."

"That sounds a bit devious to me," commented the President. "Is this the UK copping-out already?"

"No, of course not, Bill. Colin is absolutely right. If the UK were to put forward such a plan it would get nowhere. We might as well suggest transferring sovereignty to, say India or Spain. It would be laughed out of court. But if the proposal came from this side of the Atlantic as a final solution to the problems which have beset Ireland for so long, then it might have a chance, and you would, in my view, gain great credit for putting forward such a statesmanlike proposal."

"And gain even greater international credit if it could be made to work," interjected Sir Robin Algar.

"I have to say, too," continued the Prime Minister, "that I believe it to be absolutely crucial that the proposal is brokered by you in the south. I can hardly go to the Taoiseach to suggest that he hands over sovereignty of his country to you, whereas you could go to him to suggest that a unified Ireland and a lasting settlement would be possible under your auspices and with your patronage."

"You're asking an awful lot, not just of the United States," commented the President, "but of the people and institutions of Europe, the people of Ireland, and your own electorate in Great Britain."

"An awful lot is always demanded of politics and politicians, if ever we are to achieve anything worthwhile," retorted Weaver. "Diplomacy will certainly be working overtime in Europe and the South, but as to our own electorate—well, I believe the people of Great Britain have had more than enough of Northern Ireland and its problems. Certainly, recent opinion polls have shown even more strongly than before that most people would be glad just to get out of the Province and leave them to get on with it."

"Which is not a solution at all," commented Carlucci.

"Of course not," agreed Algar. "Even with the terrorist gangs more or less disbanded and their weapons denied them, it would lead to civil war and a bloodbath, which the Republic in the south would, and could, do little to prevent."

"I'm not suggesting that my proposed solution is the only one, Bill," said Weaver. "Leaving them to get on with it certainly isn't an alternative, but if anything better and easier occurs to either of you, then I'd be happy to discuss it."

"Nothing ever has," said Minton. "And I have to say that there is a certain neatness about your proposals, breathtaking and audacious though they are at first sight. What do you think, Colin?"

"Convincing the people of Northern Ireland seems to me to be the most difficult part of the whole plan, and that's really down to you, Prime Minister, even if the idea does appear to come from this side of the Atlantic. But if we can crack that, then I can see that this really might be a runner," opined Carlucci.

"I am inclined to agree," said a thoughtful President. "It has potential merit for all sides, apart perhaps from the Unionist's point of view. You said you might be able to offer them inducements, Tony. What had you in mind?"

"I haven't properly thought it through yet," replied Weaver, "but I'm sure we can think of some constitutional device which could sway them from their bigoted leadership. Something like seats in the UK Parliament for a limited number of years, as well as in Congress, joint citizenship, that sort of thing."

"The democratic processes will certainly need some careful thought, but I like that idea," said Minton.

"I'm pleased to hear you say 'will' rather than 'would', Bill," said the Prime

Minister. "Was that a slip of the tongue, or are you already starting to think that we may be on to something after all?"

The President chuckled. "I'm thinking positive!" he said. "But I do at least have some powers of my own as President. For instance, I can negotiate executive agreements with leaders of other nations, and negotiate and ratify treaties with the consent of two-thirds of the Senate."

"I'm thinking positive, too," said the Chief of Staff. "And the more I think, the more I can see that this is a really clever idea, if I may say so, and certainly one worthy of further thought and careful consideration and development. Do you agree, Mr. President?"

"Personally, I do," replied Minton. He turned to Weaver. "Of course, I can't speak for my Cabinet colleagues, or the Senate or House of Representatives, and we certainly need to do more work before this is ever put to all of them—or those on your side of the Atlantic, Tony. How do we take this forward, if we should decide to do so?"

"I think, as a first step, we both need to get agreement in principle to taking this forward from a minimum of our closest and most trustworthy colleagues and advisors. That will allow us to start proper planning. The anti-terrorist and financial aspects we can take care of quite easily, I think, but the political elements of all this will take a considerable amount of detailed planning. I suggest we will need to establish a small joint committee of constitutional lawyers and others to advise us on the steps we need to take, and the order in which they need to be taken."

"Sounds a sensible way forward," commented Minton.

"They can start work while we are still ridding ourselves of the terrorists gangs, their money and their arms," continued Weaver. "That way, we shall be ready for the second phase of this exercise as soon as it becomes apparent that a lasting peace is about to break out in Northern Ireland."

"Presumably you would hope by then to have, shall we say, taken care of most of those likely to be violently opposed to the proposed political settlement."

"Quite so, Bill," agreed Weaver.

"How would you structure this constitutional committee, then?" asked Minton.

"Since your country would effectively and publicly be taking the lead, should you agree, then I think it only right that you should provide the chairman," replied Weaver. "Not only right, if I may say so, but natural, if you are to propose a solution along the lines of the Hawaii formula. For a start, a state constitution will need to be drafted, and proposals drawn up about the structure of the state legislature. Then it will need to consider how the two present halves of the proposed new state are to be represented in that legislature, and in your own Congress. It will probably also be sensible to consider a degree of representation continuing in our own UK Parliament for a time, and this will need to be specified. Finally, it will be necessary to set up the machinery through which all this is agreed - either through referenda, national and local elections, free votes in Parliament and so on. The committee will have an enormous amount of ground to cover in a very short timescale."

"We'll need the best brains in the business, that's for sure," responded the President. "Any ideas, Tony?"

"Again, we need to give that more thought. But there is one man I would like to be part of our team," replied the Prime Minister, "and that's James Anchor, one of my Ministers in the Northern Ireland Office. Some of this was his idea in the first place. He won a first in American Political History at Cambridge, and he suggested that the Hawaii solution could apply here. He has a first rate mind, and is totally reliable. We may need a couple of others—perhaps you will have some ideas, Robin—but we do need to keep the committee as small as possible, and fill it not just with our top brains, but also with people who can work fast. And we shall need to include a representative nominated by the Taoiseach, at some stage, when you have broached the subject with him."

"I agree with all that," said Minton. "But we need to do first things first. If I tell you now, Tony, that I am prepared to consult further among a limited number of my top people"—the President looked across at Carlucci, who nodded—"then that allows you to do the same when you get back."

"Mr. President," said Weaver formally, "I am delighted and relieved to hear you say that. I confess that we hadn't dared to hope that we would be able to get this far so quickly during our informal discussions, and I really appreciate your speedy reaction and ready support."

"Forget it, Tony," responded Minton. "It will get more difficult as we get into more formal discussions, but brilliant thinking like yours deserves a positive response, at least initially. Let's see how far we can run with this."

"The question of security becomes even more important if we are to move forward," said Weaver. "We really must make sure that we put nothing in writing unless we really have no option. No paper, no leaks, or at least a far reduced risk of leaks."

"I agree with that, too, Tony," said Minton. "Of course, our small constitutional committee will eventually need to put their plans on paper, or record them in some way."

"Perhaps," suggested Robin Algar, "we should devise a special one-off code for this operation, available to only the minimum number of those involved, and as complex as it can be devised."

"That's a good idea, too," said Carlucci. "I'm sure our people could work together to put together something that's virtually un-crackable, especially if it will only be used by a limited number of people for a limited time."

"It would certainly be very useful for communicating between us as this progresses," said Minton. "We certainly can't do all the talking on our own, Tony, over the phone."

"We shall need to look at the security of that, too," said the Cabinet Secretary. "Perhaps a special hot line, with a video link. I'll get the Briefing Room team to look at that immediately when we get back."

"I suppose that's right," said the Chief of Staff. "Once you've left this evening, we shan't be able to have quiet and private chats like this again, so we need to talk through issues like that right now."

"There's one other thing, too," said the President. "We need to be quite clear in our minds and agree between us a timetable for consulting with the Taoiseach. I suppose I shall have to raise it with him first, perhaps informally at such a weekend as this, but then it will be useful—probably essential, come to think of it—to have you alongside for joint talks."

"Absolutely," agreed the Prime Minister. "Michael O'Leary's early agreement is essential, not least so that his people can play a part in the deliberations of the constitutional committee at a later stage."

Bill Minton looked at his watch. "My brain's going round in circles!" he said. "We have time for further discussions after lunch, so let's see if we can catch anything worth cooking."

As they stood and stretched, they realised that the launch had been at anchor for some time. John Hill came to the cabin door as they emerged.

"There's more coffee if anyone wants it," he said, "and the sport is looking good. I've already been broken by a small Skipjack tuna which was too lively for the light tackle I was using, and one of our Marine colleagues has taken a good bass of just over ten pounds."

"That sounds good," said Minton. "Come on, Tony, you're supposed to be good at this."

"Not this," replied Weaver. "A three pound brown trout on a dry fly I can sometimes manage, but not this big stuff."

"Show our guests what to do, then, John," demanded the President. "They will soon be casting to catch bigger fish than these."

Tony Weaver looked about him, and drew heavily on the fresh sea air. He hadn't realised how stuffy the cabin had become. At least the atmosphere between the four men had not been, and he was astonished at how much progress had been made and how easy it had seemed after all to put his proposals forward. So far, anyway. He was feeling tired, and needed to relax. Normally, fly-fishing was the only thing he had found that was a complete diversion from the day-to-day stresses of office. It was not possible to concentrate on fishing and anything else at the same time.

The launch had now weighed anchor, and was heading back towards Shelter Island and Dering Harbour. He had needed little tutelage to familiarise himself with the salt-water tackle, and had cast out over the stern. He sat admiring the scenic beauty of Montauk's cliff lined rocky coastline as the launch drifted past. There were white sailed yachts skittering across the ruffled waters on the brisk breeze nearer the shore, while, on the other side of the launch, further out, a small float plane left a creamy wake as it took off from the watery runway, marked out with orange buoys. There were sea birds everywhere, including many he had never seen before. Some looked like a variety of plover, and he wondered if one might even have been an osprey. Bill had told him that there were bird sanctuaries along the island's shoreline, which was home to many protected species.

The sun was warm, and he felt the tension ebbing away when, suddenly, he was awakened by a savage strike as a large fish took his lure. He could tell it was large by the way it was bending the rod, and by the way it fought to free itself. John Hill was already at his side, giving quiet instructions on how to handle the rod and the fish. The others looked on. Afterwards he reflected that this was just like any other aspect of his life. Patient diplomacy, sometimes leading to a false sense of security, and a rude awakening as the pace suddenly quickened. Then, there was Robin Algar at his side, quietly guiding and encouraging, while others looked on. In the end, he landed a beautiful striped bass of about twelve pounds, on his eight pound breaking strain line. Would he and Robin land an even bigger fish, he wondered? As Bill Minton had hinted only a short while ago, they would soon be casting for the catch of a lifetime.

As they crossed the lawn of Beach House towards the pool, they could see that the barbeque was already lit, waiting for their trophies to be cleaned and gutted and cooked. Lunch was good, no doubt about it, and their freshly caught fish, lightly grilled, simply melted in the mouth. They lingered over the meal, behaving more like human beings again, enjoying the company of their wives and hearing about their morning's walk along one of the island's many nature trails. This was certainly a delightful place, so peaceful and yet so near to such a turbulent and noisy city.

They were all reluctant to return to the work of the morning, but Weaver knew that their American friends had questions to ask and more points to discuss while they could do so freely and openly in one another's company. It would be more difficult to take this forward when back in their offices. They would have to be more circumspect about what they said, and how they said it, and who might overhear them.

Robin and Colin paid a brief visit to their temporary offices upstairs. Robin Algar passed on the Prime Minister's request for James Anchor and Bill Clayton to be in Downing Street for a lunchtime briefing on Sunday. The two Heads of State moved away from the poolside to a small summerhouse on the other side of the lawn, where, eventually, their right-hand men joined them. The solemn mood of the morning seemed to have gone. Whether it was the fishing, or the lunch, or the Californian wine didn't matter. The fact was that the four men felt more at ease with each other and with the subject under discussion. There was almost an air of excitement about their final informal talks. The President and his Chief of Staff were talking enthusiastically, rather than quizzically, about the prospects for developing Weavers' plan, while the Prime Minister and his Cabinet Secretary were more relaxed and encouraged by the apparent keenness of their friends and allies. Weaver was sure that, if this enthusiasm lasted, Minton would be able to carry his colleagues when it came to briefing them to gain their support.

It was agreed that, as a first step, the President would brief Secretary of State Miles Bragan, and that Weaver would talk to both the Foreign Secretary, Robert Burgess, and to James Anchor. At the same time, steps would be taken to develop a special code, which the two sides could use when communications between them might otherwise be difficult or compromised. If the early discussions went well on both sides, then the two leaders would take the next step, which would be to discuss tactics for ridding the Province of terrorists and their arms with their Intelligence and Security chiefs. Weaver would take the lead here, and on the financial side of the operation, too. It was hoped to reach this point within a week. The operation to deal with the terrorist gangs would be launched as soon as possible and completed with all speed, while the constitutional change committee was formed and started deliberating on the steps needed to bring about a permanent political solution. In spite of their newfound euphoria, the four men were crisp and businesslike in their discussions. The more they talked, the more they agreed on what needed to be done. If only all international negotiations were as amicable and free flowing, the world might be a better place.

Their discussions broke up when the two Presidential helicopters clattered into view.

"I hope our ladies have packed," said Weaver. "Just look at the time."

"They have!" observed Carlucci, as staff emerged from the house carrying the luggage towards the landing pad, followed by the men's wives.

"Bill," said Tony Weaver, "I can't thank you enough for looking after us so royally, and for listening to our ideas with such patience this weekend."

"It's been great to see you again socially, Tony," replied the President, "and you, too of course, Robin. We've covered a lot of ground and mapped out what could be a turning point in one of the most difficult parts of the world, and in the fight against terrorism. I'll certainly do my best to convince colleagues here that this should be taken seriously, and taken forward with all speed."

"I appreciate that, Mr. President. But don't let us forget that these have been very much personal and informal talks. There is more to do before we can open any more formal negotiations, but I share your hope that we can at least reach that stage, and very soon."

The President and the Prime Minister shook hands warmly, and soon Weaver and his Cabinet Secretary friend and colleague were on their way to JFK, and home.

The President and his Chief of Staff watched as the departing helicopter turned south.

"That Prime Minister's a pretty sharp cookie, isn't he?" said Bill Minton. "Pity there aren't a few more brains like his around—the world might be a better place."

"But where do we start, Mr. President? Where the hell do we start?"

"We start," replied Bill Minton, "by getting back to Washington, and getting out the history books. I need to know more about how to take on board a 51st state, if that's what we're gonna do. And more than anything, we need to talk to Miles Bragan. Make sure he's in the Oval Office when we get there. Let's get going, and see what we can do for that Mr. Weaver—and for ourselves."

Chapter Eight
SPREADING THE NET

There was the usual gang of newsmen, mostly photographers and TV cameramen, on the White House lawn when Minton and Carlucci got back. Minton always suspected that they hung around for the same reason they attended air shows—in case there was an accident. But the helicopter landed safely, and the President and his Chief of Staff hurried towards the building's entrance, with a cheery wave, and yes, thank you, we had a good day and enjoyed the fishing.

As they reached the President's office, Laura Billings greeted them.

"Yes, thank you. We had a good day, and enjoyed the fishing. Is the Secretary of State around?"

"He's in his office, waiting for you. I gather you passed word that you wanted to see him as soon as you got back."

"Quite right, Laura, but there really was no need for you to come in as well. It is Sunday after all."

"It's no problem," replied his executive secretary. "I'll get Mr. Bragan for you if you're ready."

"I'm here already," said Bragan, striding into the office. "I heard the chopper."

"And before you ask," said Minton, "we had a good day and enjoyed the fishing! Come in, and we'll tell you all about it."

"Not all about the fishing, I hope. OK if Greg joins us?" asked Bragan, as his chief of staff arrived.

"Sure. Come in. We'll have some coffee, please, Laura," said Minton, turning to shut the door.

"So what happened?" asked Greg.

"One of the Marines landed a skipjack, and the Prime Minister a lovely bass, which we had for lunch," grinned Colin Carlucci.

"And the United States," added the President, sinking into his swivel chair behind the historic 'Resolute' desk, "caught its 51st State."

"You obviously had more than striped bass for lunch," said the Secretary of State. "Will you two please stop arsing around and tell us what Prime Minister Weaver wanted to talk about in such a god-damned hurry."

The President stopped grinning.

"I've told you already," he said. "I knew you wouldn't believe it—I hardly believe it myself—but we have been offered a 51st state. Weaver has a plan to rid Northern Ireland of terrorism, and believes that unification with the south would then be possible, under our governance rather than the UK's."

"I'll be damned!" exclaimed Bragan. "Was he really serious?"

"Not 'was', 'is'. Very serious indeed," replied the President.

Sam knocked, and came in with the coffee and his usual grin.

"You're here, too!"

"Yessir, Mr. President, sir! We all thought someth'n was up when we got your message, an' I just knew you all would be needin' coffee, so here I am."

"Sam, I think we all need something stronger to go with this, too," said Carlucci. "Any bourbon about?"

"Sure thing, Mr. Carlucci, sir. I guess Miss Laura will have some tucked away someplace. I'll git her to bring it in."

When they were settled and the door firmly shut again, Bragan turned to the President.

"Perhaps you'd better start at the beginning, Bill," he said. "If Weaver has some plan to shuffle off his problems on us, then I want to know what we get out of it, too."

"There's plenty in it for us, Miles," replied Minton. "If I hadn't thought that, I wouldn't have bothered you this evening. I know what your schedule looks like, but I think we need to start moving, and move fast."

"Incidentally," broke in Carlucci, "we were right to be so security conscious about this, and not to start putting memos about. We still need to keep all this off paper, and away from others, at least until we four have talked more and decided what, if anything, to do. Do you agree, Mr. President?"

"Absolutely," replied Minton. "There must be no record of this meeting, and you must keep the tape of that phone call secure, too, Miles. Weaver and Algar did all their briefing without any notes whatsoever—and briefed exceptionally well, too, as you might expect. I hope I can recall everything they said—if I skip anything, Colin, fill the gap, please."

Carlucci nodded.

"I'll start where Weaver started, with the anti-terrorist part of the operation, then move on to the politics of it all."

President Bill Minton outlined as best he could the scenario that had been sketched out by Prime Minister Weaver, while his Chief of Staff, Colin Carlucci, filled in the detail when prompted.

"We covered the fight against terrorism during the afternoon yesterday—was it really only yesterday?—and slept on that before moving on to the political dimension today," concluded Minton.

"Not that anyone, on either side, slept much," said Carlucci. "There was too much to think about, not helped by the Prime Minister's tantalising clue of what was in his mind, when he dubbed the political solution 'the Hawaii formula'. We simply couldn't work out the connection."

"Off hand, neither can I, except that Hawaii was the last state to join the Union," said Bragan.

"And that's exactly the link," said Minton, "but of course at the time we had no idea what was coming later."

"There seems to me," continued Minton, "to be considerable benefit in the US getting to grips with the IRA and other terror gangs in Northern Ireland. You know, Miles, that for a long time now I've wanted to get our war against international terrorism away from the Islamic world. I had thought that Spain might welcome our involvement with their fight against ETA and the Basque separatists, but they are by no means 'international'. And we could hardly suggest interfering in the UK's internal affairs, in spite of all the Irish/American support for what they see as an Irish liberation movement. But now we are actually being asked to help out, and at a time when the IRA really has started to get too big for its boots, what with their involvement in Columbia and McFosters' trip to Cuba and all."

"And it doesn't seem," interjected Carlucci, "that we shall actually be asked to do much of the dirty work, either. The UK seems happy to tackle that head on, with only limited practical help."

"A change of direction now sure would be useful for us," agreed Bragan. "It would help to make life a bit easier for me in trying to broker a deal in the Middle East."

"Life gets even easier," said Minton. "Just wait till you hear about the political proposals."

"Shoot!" said Bragan. "Just what is all this about a 51st State?"

"It means exactly that, if everything works out as Weaver suggests and predicts," said Minton. "His theory is that because the UK is a major part of the problem, it can't also be part of the solution. Nothing they've ever tried before has worked, and now everyone has had enough. Action, and no more talking, seems to be the theme, with a third party, which both sides can trust and work with, stepping in as the catalyst for peace and political stability. That's us."

The President lent forward.

"First of all," he said, indicating the first finger of his left hand, "we get rid of the terrorist gangs in the north. That includes their arms, their top people, and their money."

"Is that all?" said Bragan.

"Listen. This gets better," continued the President, pointing to his second raised finger. "While that is being done, we convince the Republic that they should give up their sovereignty in the interests of a lasting peace, increased prosperity, a unified Ireland, and life under the Stars and Stripes. Third, we form a special, joint committee of our top constitutional brains to work out the political timetable—a draft state constitution, legislative structure, level of representation in Congress—all that, and a timetable for consultations, referenda, elections, and so on. Weaver thinks this could all be based on the sort of procedure used to gain statehood for Hawaii in 1959, but much, much quicker."

"So the UK shuffles off one of it's longest standing and most intractable problems on us, does it?" asked Greg Harvey. "Just like that? Does Mr. Weaver think we're mad, as he obviously is?"

"He's not as mad as he might sound," responded Carlucci. "If he can, as he claims he can, bring a semblance of peace to Northern Ireland, then there's all to play for. But peace without a lasting political solution is useless, and there's no way the UK can engineer that. They never have been able to, and they never will. It simply has to be a third party."

"So I ask again," quizzed Bragan, "what's in it for us?"

"How about this for a ball game, then?" countered the President. "We gain a 51st state, on the very edge of Europe, which is already a member of the EU. Weaver reckons that membership will stand, not least because of the huge economic and trade advantages which will flow to Europe and it's newer, poorer member states. If it's good for them, it's good for us, too. We establish a firmer foothold and greater political influence in Europe and NATO, apart from the economic benefits. And here's the crunch. We return their homeland to some fifty million Irish/Americans, Miles, and the third largest ethnic community in the States. I'm one of them. Just think what that does for votes."

"I think I'm beginning to see things your way, Bill," said Bragan.

"They would vote for us forever!" exclaimed Minton. "And that means that we can take a little less notice of the Jewish votes and the Muslim votes."

"And I can really get stuck in to the Middle East," said the Secretary of State.

"Exactly," said the President. "Exactly so."

There was a pause.

"How very neat," said Bragan eventually, with a grin. "How very, very neat."

"And how very, very risky," said Carlucci.

"Surely to God the Irish will never take any notice of such a British proposal as this, will they?" asked Harvey. "They're not that stupid!"

"If we take this forward," said the President, "it won't be a British proposal. It will be ours, for that very reason."

"Ouch!" exclaimed Bragan.

"Think about it, Miles," said Minton. "Only we could convince the South to give up their sovereignty, and it will probably cost us to do it, too. But they will have a price—you and I both know that there's a pretty high degree of corruption at every level of society in the Republic, although it's not as obvious to outsiders as it is in many other countries. But public undertakings of massive inward investment and so on will do the trick, I'm sure. The Brits have the big problem, and that's convincing the Unionists in the North. But Weaver reckons even that can be achieved, if we play the constitutional cards right—things like dual citizenship, representation in both the UK Parliament and in Congress, that sort of thing."

"It all begins to look feasible, suddenly, and not so mad after all," said Bragan. "The more I think about it, the more I see that there is, after all, plenty in it for the States, and plenty in it for the UK as well."

"Certainly, they get rid of a problem that's been round their necks for centuries," said Carlucci, "and Weaver reckons that none of the costs relating to direct rule, the security situation and so on will fall on us. Without terrorism, the costs to the British exchequer, and therefore to us, will disappear."

"Furthermore," concluded Minton, "this country will gain enormously increased power and influence because of our diplomacy in proposing and concluding a resolution to such an age-old international problem."

"It's a daring and audacious plan," said Bragan, "and I raise my hat to Prime

Minister Weaver for having the balls to think it through and put it to us as he has. And it could just work, to the advantage of both our countries."

"And to Ireland," said Harvey, "if they can be persuaded."

"So far, Mr. President, I'm inclined to say that we should run with this one, and I sense that you are of the same mind," said Bragan. "But I'd like to hear more about how they propose to defeat the terror gangs in the north, and what our role is likely to be in that."

"Colin, you start, while I organise more coffee," said the President. "And help yourselves to another shot of bourbon, if you like. This could be a long night."

It was.

***

Major Bill Clayton has been enjoying a quiet Saturday afternoon, in much the same way that he enjoyed any lengthy period away from the office. Since he was widowed a few years back, he had determined never to get morose, and always to keep himself occupied. It didn't do to dwell too much on the past, and as he had no children of his own, he busied himself looking after other people's, in a remote sort of way. He had always wanted kids, but what with his turbulent military life, and his wife dying so tragically so soon after they had married, it was not to be.

So there he was, trying to get an old clockwork steam engine to work again. The main spring had gone, but he thought he either had a spare somewhere, or, if not, could shorten the broken one a bit to make it fit again. It might not run for so long between winds with a shortened spring, but what small boy who'd never had a train set before was going to notice that? Winding it would be another problem. There wasn't a key, but he'd face up to that when he had to. Probably a spare somewhere. He remembered that his uncle had sent him a couple of spares a short time ago. If not, he'd just have to make one. He'd done that before, many times.

Bill Clayton enjoyed working with his hands. It gave his brain a rest, although it also gave him a bit of thinking time when he needed it. The Army let him use a spare garage round the back of the Officer's Mess, and this was now his workshop—his toy hospital. Every year, he managed somehow to collect and repair enough toys to fill a five ton truck, which, at Christmas, did the rounds of orphanages and the children's wards of local hospitals. Not that he went with it. Catch him dressing up as Santa Claus? No thanks! But the

Army got lots of good publicity out of it—hearts and minds stuff—which is why they didn't charge him for using the garage.

And he enjoyed the solitude. Only now and then did someone bang on the garage door, usually clutching a cardboard box full of broken bits and pieces, and other things which just needed a touch of paint, and even more that were beyond his skills to repair, and which got carefully taken apart for use as spares. He enjoyed rummaging around to see what challenges the box contained for him. He could even manage soft toys, although he had to get help for that. But there was a pleasant old biddy who worked behind the bar who was quite handy with a needle, and she could usually manage to get the odd ear back onto a rabbit, or an arm on to a teddy bear. She was quite good, too, at making a dress for a naked doll when the need arose, thank goodness. He could never do that, and it would be a waste to throw the thing away. But he preferred boys' toys, if he was honest.

So there he was, gently taking this old Hornby tin-plate engine to pieces, listening to quite a good rugby match on the radio, when there was a thump on the door. *More work*, he thought. He was right, too, but it wasn't the sort of work he was expecting, or particularly wanted. It was the Duty Officer.

"Sorry to bother you, sir, but you're wanted on the phone right away. Someone from London. They're hanging on."

Clayton swore quietly under his breath, got the grease off his hands with an even oilier rag, and followed the Duty Officer into the Mess.

He took the call still wiping his hands down the seat of his trousers. He was supposed to be better dressed than this in the Mess, he thought, hoping he wouldn't be noticed.

It was the Prime Minister's Office. The Prime Minister was on his way back from Washington, said the duty chap in London, and would like to see Major Clayton, please, in Downing Street around mid-day tomorrow, if that was possible. And, by the way, did he happen to know where Mr Anchor was? The Prime Minister rather wanted to see him as well, at the same time, but the said duty officer hadn't yet managed to track him down. The people at Stormont were being particularly slow this afternoon, it seemed, and really ought to be able to contact Ministers straight away if they're wanted, don't you think?

"Leave it to me," said Clayton. "I think I can find him. We'll be there tomorrow."

The Downing Street chap thanked him awfully. Clayton hung up, and said, "Bugger!"

He went back to his room, and picked up the phone. He got hold of James Anchor first try.

"Your people at the Castle have been trying to find you," he said. "And Downing Street thinks it's a disgrace that they can't get hold of Ministers when they're wanted."

"Well, I'm not duty Minister this weekend, but I did tell them where I was going," replied Anchor. "At least I think I did. I certainly told someone. What do they want, anyway, and how do you know?"

"It's my job to know—that's what I'm paid for. Anyway, our presence has been requested again," replied Clayton. "Weaver passed a message when he left the States. He wants to see us at mid-day tomorrow. Shall I fix it?"

"Would you mind?" asked Anchor. "You know the calibre of people we get on duty over the weekend—we'd probably end up in Berlin or somewhere."

"Leave it to me," said Clayton, for the second time that afternoon. "Nine o'clock plane out, and last plane back be all right?"

"Sounds fine if you can fix it," said a grateful junior Minister. "Do you suppose we'll get lunch?"

"Not on the nine o'clock plane out of Aldergrove, you won't."

"No, no—I meant in Downing Street. It was pretty good at Chequers, I remember."

"Different place altogether," replied Clayton. "The Navy used to do the catering at Chequers. Downing Street is contractors."

"Sounds like a sandwich in the 'Red Lion' again then, if all else fails."

"What about buying me lunch instead in that posh restaurant of yours in the House of Commons?"

"Not open on Sundays. What will you tell the General?"

"With any luck at all, I shan't have to tell him anything," said Clayton. "He's in Wales for a break this weekend, and the Colonel's away shooting poor bloody pheasants. God willing and a fair breeze, I should be out and back again before they notice."

"Your lucky day," responded Anchor.

"Not from here, it isn't. But I can't keep dodging off to see the PM without someone finding out soon. I'll have to warn Weaver that I must tell the boss what's going on."

"Tricky. Are you on a secure line, by the way?"

"I doubt it," replied Clayton. "And I know you're not, because I know where you are."

"I won't ask how! See you tomorrow, then," said Anchor.

Clayton tidied up, and walked across to the headquarters to see the duty corporal in the Transport Office.

"'Evening, Major. How can I help?" he said, standing up.

"I need two seats on the 0900 out of Aldergrove to Heathrow," replied Clayton.

"What day, sir?"

"Tomorrow. And back tomorrow, too, on the last flight out."

"It's a bit short notice," said Corporal Harrington, sitting down again. "There's plenty of room on Monday's—I checked it out earlier this morning for someone else."

"Tomorrow," demanded Clayton. "Please."

"You and who else, then, sir?"

"Mr. James Anchor, Minister of State, Northern Ireland Office," replied Bill Clayton.

"At least I can off-charge his seat," said the relieved Corporal. "I suppose there's no chance of getting a reason for your trip this time, is there, sir?"

"Not a hope," replied the Major.

"The auditors are beginning to get quite stroppy, you know."

"Tell you what, then," suggested Clayton. "Put it down as 'liaison'."

"But that's what you always say," complained the Corporal.

"That's because that's what it always is," explained Clayton. "Liaison. In London. We've been summoned," said Clayton, trying to be helpful.

"Ah," said the Corporal. "Then if I can say by whom, that'll keep them quiet."

"Well, you can't," retorted Clayton. "Liaison in London will have to do—again."

The duty Corporal sighed. He knew full well that Clayton took priority over just about everyone, and he knew why. But he did wish it wasn't always him on duty when the Major strolled in.

"If the auditors give you a hard time, refer them to me, OK?" offered a helpful Clayton.

"Thank you, sir. Tickets at the BA check-in tomorrow, then, by 0730. If there's any problem, I'll let you know."

"Thanks, Corporal. I look forward to not hearing from you!"

***

The resident Heathrow press corps was in attendance, as expected, when Weaver and Algar, a respectful distance behind him, emerged from the VIP suite in terminal four. Weaver waved cheerily, and in answer to their questions, said airily that, yes thank you, after their Middle East talks, he'd had a relaxing day with his friend the President, and enjoyed some fishing.

The Prime Minister headed straight for Downing Street, while Sir Robin Algar, as they had agreed on the aircraft, set off for home. It had been decided that the Cabinet Secretary did not need to be there when Weaver had his discussions with Anchor and Clayton later, since the ground that was to be covered during that meeting had been thoroughly discussed during the flight. Since Algar had not been at the earlier meetings of the trio—indeed, he didn't even know about them—there seemed no real point in him being present at this one either. It was, after all, only to brief the two men from Northern Ireland on what had happened this weekend, and to get them geared up for the next stage of the operation. And Algar had some planning of his own to do, too, before getting to the office the next day. All this new activity had to be fitted in to an already horrendously busy schedule, and done so discretely.

In the flat, Weaver slumped into his favourite armchair.

"You look exhausted, my dear," said his wife, Susan. "And I was so hoping you would enjoy your day with Bill. You get on so well together, and it was a lovely spot he took us to."

"It was nice," replied Weaver, "but I had a lot on my mind I wanted to talk about with Bill and Colin Carlucci, so I couldn't really relax."

"Such a pity. Us girls really got on well and had a wonderful day together. And the shops are so inexpensive, compared with London prices. But you did go fishing, and I know how much you enjoy that."

"And I caught a fish," replied Tony Weaver. "That was fun, while it lasted, although I think I may have landed an even bigger trophy at the same time."

Susan looked puzzled, but knew better than to ask.

"I have a theory about Northern Ireland, which I wanted to share with Bill. I think he might support it—I hope so. I should know in a day or so."

"Well, you can put your feet up for a bit now, I hope," said Susan.

"Not for long, I'm afraid," replied the Prime Minister. "I've asked James Anchor and Major Clayton to come over for a quick briefing at around lunchtime, so I'll have to go down to the office for that. That reminds me—I'd better get some sandwiches organised."

"While you're doing that," said his wife as he reached for the phone, "I'll put the kettle on."

It was a quarter to twelve when Anchor and Clayton arrived in Downing Street, and they were immediately ushered into the waiting room across the corridor from the PM's office. Moments later, Tony Weaver stuck his head round the door.

"Come on in, gentlemen," he greeted them. "Good of you to come over at short notice."

"Not at all," replied Anchor. "You're the one who's had the journey. You must be tired after your flight from Washington."

"New York," corrected Clayton.

The Prime Minister looked at him quizzically.

"And I hope you enjoyed the fishing," Clayton added.

"How do you know that?" he demanded.

"It's his job to know things, Tony," replied Anchor with a smile. "It's what he gets paid for."

"Ah, yes. Of course. And that's why you're here, Major."

The Prime Minister motioned towards the armchairs, and the three of them sat round the coffee table.

"There'll be sandwiches and a glass of wine soon, if you'd like that, but let me first quickly tell you about my conversations with the President yesterday. As you know," he looked towards Clayton, "I had the Cabinet Secretary with me, and Mr. Minton was accompanied by his Chief of Staff, Colin Carlucci. I broadly outlined the scenario that we three have sketched out at our earlier meetings, and I think I can say that, after their initial and natural shock and disbelief at the audacity of our proposals, they ended up appearing broadly supportive of what we have in mind. Naturally, too, they need to discuss all this with a few carefully selected colleagues, as I shall need to share it with some of my own soon. But I hope and expect that I shall have a positive response within the next few days. So we must be prepared to start work immediately when that happens."

"You assume, do you," asked Anchor, "that your Cabinet colleagues will go along with the idea?"

"I don't assume, James, but I shall persuade them. Tomorrow, I plan to brief Sir Percy Lewis, the Attorney General, Roy Salisbury and Peter Coombs, the Secretaries of State for Northern Ireland and Defence, Robert Burgess, the Foreign Secretary and Alison Judd, the Home Secretary. I shall then hold a second briefing with the Chief of Defence Staff, the Commissioner of the Metropolitan Police, and the Chief Constable of the Northern Ireland Police Service. Can either of you think of anyone else?"

Neither could, off hand.

"I shall brief the whole Cabinet about the political proposals only when it becomes clear that the first phase of this operation is succeeding, and that terrorism in Northern Ireland is becoming a thing of the past. Without that, the political solution won't work, so they won't need to know about it. Bill Minton and I have agreed to co-ordinate dates on this, because we shall then need to go wider as well—to the UN, NATO, the European Council, and so on."

"What about the Irish Republic?" asked Bill Clayton.

"The President has undertaken to brief the Taoiseach, Michael O'Leary, fairly soon after he has convinced his colleagues to take part in this plan. Hopefully he will be meeting a select few of them tomorrow as a first step, as I am."

"That should be fun," said Clayton. "I only ask because at some stage, I shall need to liase with the Guarda special branch, as well as the Yard's."

"And with all these people being told, I begin to worry about security," said Anchor.

"I agree," said the Prime Minister. "As always, there will be nothing about this scheme in writing—absolutely nothing. I propose to tell the people I brief tomorrow that they must not pass on a full briefing to anyone else, either. If they think someone needs to know the whole picture, they tell me, and I will brief them if I so decide. Otherwise, they confine themselves to briefing senior individuals about the range of specific tasks which they alone will have to carry out or take responsibility for."

The two men were listening intently, and nodded.

"For example," continued the Prime Minister. "The Chief of the Defence Staff will have to brief some of his single service chiefs about their individual role, and particularly about the role of the Special Forces, and the unit commanders will then need to be tasked to carry out a specific aspect of the operation. But none will have the whole picture, or even know that there are other units playing a similar role. Once a group of men has carried out a specific task, it will be disbanded, and although individuals may be tasked with other aspects of the operation later, no-one will be able to link the two as part of a larger operation."

"That's exactly the way the IRA operates," commented Clayton. "Small units, unknown to one another, individually tasked, none knowing what the others are up to, or even who they are."

"And I see no reason why we should not play them at their own game," said Weaver.

"Neither do I," agreed Clayton, whose idea it had been in the first place, anyway.

"Finally," said the Prime Minister, "I shall make it abundantly clear to colleagues before I start tomorrow that they are about to be briefed about a highly dangerous and sensitive operation with world-wide implications, with no guarantee of success, and that the time has come to put their jobs, and possibly their lives, on the line. Any who are not prepared to take that risk will be invited to leave at that point. Otherwise, their loyalty and commitment to the operation will thereafter be assumed to be total. Then, to emphasise the need for absolute secrecy, I shall let them know that some of what we have in mind could be interpreted as state terrorism, with all that implies for war crimes and so on. They will then be given a last chance to withdraw."

The Prime Minister looked closely at both men.

"I am only telling you this because, for both of you, that point has already been passed. You are part of it, and there is no going back for either of you."

They nodded.

"Whatever the Americans decide, this is a secret which all those of us who know the full plan will take with them to the grave."

"And especially us," said a solemn James Anchor. "We thought of it."

"I obviously need to say no more," said Weaver.

"I begin to think that I need to say something though, Prime Minister," said Clayton. "Any time at all my boss and the General are going to wonder what I'm up to. I can't keep dodging off to see you without, one day, having to tell them where I'm going, and then I shall have to tell them why."

"When I see CDS tomorrow, I will tell him of your role in this so far, and the role I want you to play in the future. I guess you'll soon hear from the General after that, but only tell him about your role—no one else's, and not the whole picture. If you have any real problems, let me know direct," said the Prime Minister.

With a quiet knock, Jane Parsons stuck her head round the door.

"Jane! What are you doing here? It's Sunday."

"Doesn't matter," replied his secretary. "They told me you'd fixed a meeting this afternoon, so I thought I'd put in an appearance. Your sandwiches have arrived—shall I have them brought in?"

"Yes please. We could all do with a break."

"I've had Sir Robin on the phone, too, Prime Minister," said Jane. "I'm arranging the two meetings you wanted for tomorrow. Will an hour be long enough for each of them?"

"I'll make sure it is, Jane, thank you."

"I'm afraid the rest of tomorrow's diary begins to look very pear-shaped, but I'll do my best to fit everything in."

"It might be an idea, Jane, to leave at least an hour a day free for the next month or so, if you can manage that," said the Prime Minister. "I've a feeling I shall need to arrange a few more things at short notice in the weeks to come, and that would make life a bit easier for you."

"I'll see what I can do, Prime Minister," promised his secretary. "By the way, I take it you want Sir Robin at the two meetings tomorrow?"

"Certainly."

"I'd better get on to his SPS then, to make sure he knows what's going on, although I'm sure Sir Robin will have phoned John himself."

Once food and a glass of wine had been served, they had the office to themselves again.

"We'll work through, if you don't mind," said the Prime Minister. "If all goes well, we shall be in a position to start things going later next week or the week after that, and I want to make sure that both of you are ready for it."

"There's certainly a lot to do," agreed Clayton. "Anything specific you want me to tackle, or just general preparedness?"

"Bill, I want you to concentrate on two areas specifically. You will need to be ready to brief, when asked, on where the top people are in all the major organisations, and how they can best be got at. As we discussed before, you will also need to be able to provide as much evidence as you can about their involvement in terrorism or criminal acts relating to terrorism. The decision about their fate will rest on that evidence, but it's not a decision you will have to take. Details of the arms dumps are important, too, although I guess that is more general knowledge. But someone will be asking you for their weak points, and how best they can be targeted. Finally, I shall want you to prepare a list of all the major terrorist bank accounts, with as much detail as possible—where they are, account numbers, who is authorised to draw on them, how much is in them and so on. Somehow, you will have to get all that to Sir Robin Algar."

"I thought he'd be wanting that," said Major Bill Clayton, reaching into the inside pocket of his jacket. "Would you be so good to pass this on to him when you next meet?" he asked the Prime Minister. "It's in writing, I'm afraid, but on note paper bought at the local newsagent, and the envelope is a used one, sent to an uncle of mine in Sussex sometime ago."

"I'm impressed," said Weaver, "but not entirely surprised. Is everything here?"

"There are a few details missing about a couple of accounts in the States, but I've got people working on that, so I should be able to fill in the gaps soon. As for the rest, I'm ready to brief almost at once, but I must warn you, Prime Minister, that there is one IRA arms dump that is going to be very difficult to deal with. It's buried in a hillside across the border in the Republic. It used to be a Remote Centre of Government during the Cold War; it's very deep and almost nuclear proof. So far as I can gather, the decommissioning body doesn't even know of this one. It's their biggest dump by far, stuffed full of Semtex and countless weapons of all kinds, and is regularly inspected by their Quartermaster, Seamus O'Hara, and two or three of his top men. If we can find a way of blowing it with them inside, that would be an added bonus."

"Any ideas?"

"Oh, yes. But we could discuss that later, perhaps, when we know who's on our side."

"Understood," said Weaver. "And thank you for this." He waived the rather tatty envelope in salute. "It probably goes without saying that from now on you should only brief up the chain of command, and not downwards."

The Prime Minister turned to James Anchor.

"That goes for you too, James. And if either of you comes across any dissention or disagreement or difficulty, tell me and I'll sort it—don't you try to do so, and don't ask anyone else higher up the chain, either."

The two men nodded agreement.

"Now, James," continued the Prime Minister. "I want you to get your brain into gear, and to forget Northern Ireland for a few weeks."

"How can I possibly forget Northern Ireland for a few weeks?" queried James Anchor. "This whole show is about Northern Ireland, and even if it wasn't, I have Ministerial responsibilities there."

"It's your Ministerial duties I want you to forget," responded Tony Weaver. "I need you over in the States, as a member of the Constitutional Committee which I hope Bill Minton will form soon. With your degree in American political history and your well-developed thinking about the transfer of sovereignty using what you called, and what I have now called 'the Hawaii formula', I can think of no one better suited to representing our interests there. I have in mind that the Attorney General should join you on the committee, unless you can think of a better constitutional lawyer to represent the UK?"

"Not off hand, although it's a pity Erskine May isn't still alive, don't you think? The only other possibility might be the Lord Chief Justice, but obviously the more you have, the more debate there will be and the harder it will become to get decisions taken. As a matter of interest, how shall I engineer my absence from the office?"

"You need a holiday—probably three weeks or so, to recover from a mild but worrying attack of angina," suggested the Prime Minister.

"I do?" asked Anchor with a grin.

"I suggest something like that," responded the Prime Minister. "Start displaying the symptoms now, and you'll be ready to disappear on indefinite leave when the time is right—probably about three weeks, with luck. I'll brief Roy Salisbury tomorrow."

"And I'll arrange a doctor's certificate, if you need one," said Clayton helpfully.

"If you're not careful, you'll arrange for me to have the real thing, the way you're going," responded Anchor. "But I'll give some serious thought to the constitutional aspects of all this, Prime Minister, so I'm well prepared when summoned."

"Excellent. Although the States will be taking the lead officially, we need to be sure that our own interests are fully covered, and that we can't be faulted in the way we consult the people of this country and let them have their say. In particular, we must be sure that the people of Northern Ireland are properly represented when the change of sovereignty is finally made, if it is, and especially the Unionists. You may like to consider things like dual nationality, and parliamentary representation in both countries for a period of time. Things like that."

"It might be worth considering," suggested Anchor, "whether the Foreign Office should be part of this committee as well. They're bound to ask."

"That had occurred to me, James," replied the Prime Minister. "And there would certainly be merit in that, not least because of our existing treaty obligations in Europe and elsewhere. But I'll make a final decision when I see how the President plans to be represented."

A weary-looking Tony Weaver finished his glass of wine, and pushed aside a plate of half eaten sandwiches.

"If you've no other points, gentlemen, I think we should call it a day. I shall be setting up a special hot line for this operation, with new one-off ciphers and that sort of thing. Don't hesitate to use it to contact me direct if the need arises."

"Does the operation have a code name?" asked Major Clayton.

"It does not," replied to Prime Minister, "and I think if we can manage without one, we should. Code names get written down and leaked."

"Then let's do without," agreed Clayton.

The two men left No.10, and headed off towards Whitehall.

"He doesn't waste much time, does he?" commented Bill Clayton.

"I hope he realises what he's doing," replied James Anchor. "I feel quite responsible."

"So you should, as it was your idea in the first place."

"And yours," responded Anchor.

"I could murder a beer," said Clayton.

"Looks like the 'Red Lion', then," said Anchor. "There's plenty of time before we need to get to the airport."

"How are you feeling, by the way?" asked Clayton.

"Awful," replied Anchor.

"That's good! Where will you go for your holiday, then?"

"Hawaii would be nice," he said.

Chapter Nine
IGNITION

Sir Robin Algar was in the office even earlier than usual.

He had made as many discreet phone calls from home as he dared the previous day, but now he needed the security of the Whitehall machine around him before he could take things much further. There were several things he needed to do urgently, and he knew that much of his time that day would be taken up with the two special meetings the Prime Minister had called. He would be at both, although he wouldn't be taking the minutes as he usually did at such gatherings. There wouldn't be any minutes.

The Cabinet Secretary had to make sure, too, that no one else took any notes, and that would be tricky. He knew that he would have to personally 'disarm' each member of the two meetings as they arrived, and relieve them of their briefcases, notebooks and any portable dictating machines they may have. They wouldn't like that, but it had to be done to ensure the utmost security. It had gone through his mind that he should also ask them to leave their pens and pencils in the outer office, but he had concluded that there was little point in rubbing salt in their wounded pride by going quite that far. After all, they would have nothing to write on, as they would be sitting at an empty table. He certainly wasn't going to let the private office staff put out paper as they usually did.

He imagined Colin Carlucci would soon be going through the same sort of procedures in the President's office. Algar knew there was nothing either of them could actually do until each side was certain that the other was totally committed to the plan and all its ramifications. But he felt certain that they would get the green light in a day or so, and wanted to be ready to put things in motion as soon as he could. He knew that Secretary of State Miles Bragan would be leaving for the Middle East later that day, and just hoped that the President would be able brief him before he went, if he hadn't already. If not, it would be the end of the week before they had any news of the American attitude, as Bragan was planning to be away for at least two days.

In the meantime, he saw no reason why the new hot-line video conferencing link should not be set up between the two leaders. They had been pondering such an idea for some time, so now let's do it. At the same time, the new cipher was probably worth starting work on, as he couldn't imagine things like that were devised at all quickly.

It was also in his mind that, even if they found no support from America for the whole plan, which would mean that every aspect of it would be abandoned, it would still be worthwhile emptying the terrorist's coffers. At least that would put a severe brake on their activities for the foreseeable future, although he really didn't know where to begin. The Prime Minister had, almost casually, given him responsibility for that aspect of the operation, and in a way it made sense, as he did have some quite good contacts in the financial world. But he had to admit that he had no real idea about where to start tracking down the accounts they used, never mind—what had the PM said?—'emptying them'. Algar remembered that Weaver had also said that his Army contact in Northern Ireland—Clayton, wasn't it?—knew where most of the money was, but the Cabinet Secretary found it difficult to believe that an Army Major could know anything of the sort, even if he was part of the intelligence network. But it might be useful to meet this man at sometime, not least because Weaver thought so highly of him. He knew that Clayton had been over for another briefing only yesterday, with James Anchor, and he wondered how that had gone.

There seemed to be so much to do, apart from the normal routine of Cabinet Office life, that he hardly knew where to begin. Not that there ever was anything normal or routine about life where Tony Weaver was concerned. But now the workload had been piled even higher.

Soon, there would be the normal early morning 'prayers', with Andrew Groves in attendance. He would have seen from the diary that there were two extra meetings today, and would obviously wonder what they were all about. Algar had no doubt that he would be kept in the dark by Weaver, although eventually Groves would have to be brought in to the picture. Groves, and his colleagues around Whitehall, would have a pivotal role to play in moulding public opinion, and especially the Ulster Unionists, in favour of the political solution once the operation started. But not yet. Other things had to fall in place first, and as long as there wasn't a leak of any sort, Andrew Groves had no need for the time being to know what was being planned.

The first man he needed to speak to was Paul Bridges, the retired Air Commodore who ran the Cabinet Office Briefing Rooms. He dialled the number himself, as neither John Williams nor Isabelle Paton had yet arrived in his outer office. As luck would have it, Bridges himself answered the phone.

" 'Morning, Paul, Robin Algar here."

"Good morning, Robin. You're early for a Monday."

"I have a feeling," replied Algar, "that it's going to be one of those days. But I need to talk to you. Can you spare a few minutes?"

"Yes, of course. I'll come up straight away."

When Bridges arrived, he shut the door firmly behind him, and sat in front of Algar's desk.

"How can I help?" he asked.

"We need another secure hot line to Washington," said Algar, without beating about the bush. "And I wondered how quickly one could be set up, and whether it was possible to have a video conference facility with it. But it must be really secure—latest scramblers, everything."

"Shouldn't be any great problem," replied Paul Bridges. "But could I ask what's suddenly brought this on? Is anything wrong with the present link?"

"No, there's nothing wrong with it at all, and we shall keep it in use for routine and regular contacts between the Prime Minister and the President," replied the Cabinet Secretary. "But we've been thinking for some time that a second direct link between them would be very useful, particularly with a video link, but with access available only to the two men. As you know, the present hot line has links to the Foreign Office and God knows where in the States. But both men agreed over the weekend that future discussions between them on a particular topic needed to be much more secure than at present and with a much more restricted access. I can't tell you now why the need has suddenly become urgent. Very strictly 'need to know' at the moment, I'm afraid."

"Understood," replied the Air Commodore, who had one of the highest security clearances possible. "It so happens that we have already set up a few video conferencing links to the States recently, including one to the Secretary of State's ops room, so it will be no real problem to set up another, providing we can find the satellite space. If we can't, we'll have to give up one of our existing links."

"That's very encouraging," said Algar. "I must emphasise, though, the need for the highest possible security."

"You shall have it," replied Bridges. "The difficult bit is scrambling the video, although that's becoming easier with agile digital data links."

Sir Robin Algar looked puzzled.

"The picture needs to be coded too," explained Bridges," because some hackers can lip read if they should intercept it."

"Ah," said Algar, as the penny dropped.

"I do suggest, though," continued Paul Bridges, "that even if the link is to be discreet between the two Heads of State, this end of it should be in one of the emergency rooms downstairs, rather than in the PM's office. I'm quite sure the American end won't be in the Oval Office, either. Too easily bugged and too many people in and out all the time."

"Sounds very sensible," replied Algar. "I'm sure the PM will agree to that. How long will it take to set up?"

"Allowing time for a few test transmissions, I would say by the end of this week, if all goes well. I'll get my people on to it right away."

"That's excellent, Paul. Thank you."

"If this is all so hush-hush, will the White House know what I'm talking about when I get on to them?" he asked.

"Talk to my opposite number. Colin Carlucci is the President's Chief of Staff, and may well already be making similar moves. He'll certainly know what it's all about," replied Algar.

Air Commodore Bridges stood to leave.

"Could I ask your advice about one other related matter, while you're here?" asked the Cabinet Secretary.

Bridges sat down again. "Of course."

"You will have gathered from what I've already said that the two leaders are embarking on something of quite unusual sensitivity. So sensitive, indeed, that I can't even tell you about it yet, although I'm sure I shall be able to soon."

Bridges nodded. "I'm not in the least offended," he said, with a smile.

"At the moment, nothing at all has been put in writing or committed to paper by either side as an additional precaution against leaks, and only the minimum possible number of individuals are in the loop," continued Sir Robin. "But the time will come, and soon, when communication between the two sides will have to be on paper rather than verbally. For that, I think, we shall need a special code or cipher. How do we go about setting that up? Any ideas where I might start?"

"You just have started," replied Bridges. "There are several wizards with codes, especially in MI5, and I know quite a few of them. Our own codes and ciphers are always being changed, of course, both the diplomatic and defence ones, so there are plenty of experts about. Will this one just be for use between the two Heads of State, or will lower mortals also need access?"

"Wider access than just the two of them, including perhaps Northern Ireland, but still very restricted indeed," replied Algar. "But I don't want it universally available—just for those involved on this particular project.

"I'll dig up someone for you, and bring him along to see you, if that's all right," offered Bridges. "You can then brief him yourself as much as you can, and leave it to him to deliver."

"Sounds good," replied Sir Robin.

"I'll be in touch later today, hopefully. If that's all, I'll toddle along," said Bridges, standing again.

"Thanks for your help." said Algar.

John Williams, Algar's SPS, put his head round the door as the Air Commodore left.

"Thought I heard voices, but didn't like to interrupt," he said. "Is everything all right?" he asked. "You're in early."

"There are two extra meetings this morning, John, so I thought I would try to get a few things done before 'prayers'."

"You should have said, and I would have come in early too," responded Williams. "How was the trip to Washington?"

"Very satisfactory, but a lot of extra work is flowing from it, I fear, and not all to do with the Middle East, either," replied Sir Robin. "But I can't tell you much about it, I'm afraid—something the two Heads of State are cooking up between them at the moment. I'll brief you as soon as I can, but in the meantime, say nothing to anyone, please."

"Very good," replied Williams, thinking that he really had nothing to say to anyone even if he wanted to.

"The Air Commodore will be in touch with you soon to arrange another meeting. Make sure you fit him in as a priority when he rings. We're setting up another hot line to the White House. And when you've settled, could you try to get Alistair Vaughan on the phone? He's Head of Security at the Bank of England. I'd like a quick word with him before 'prayers', if that's possible, and then probably a meeting with him soon. With any luck, he'll offer me lunch somewhere!"

***

They agreed that Simpsons, in the Strand, was about half way between them, so that's where they arranged to meet the next day.

The morning meeting went off smoothly enough. As expected, Andrew Groves' curiosity about the extra two meetings scheduled for afterwards went unsatisfied, and he was asked not to probe any further. Having dealt with the weekend's media, he contented himself with a dissertation about straight cucumbers, and left.

The first of the special meetings, with the carefully selected Cabinet Ministers, went rather better than either Sir Robin or Tony Weaver had expected. They immediately got whiff that something was in the wind when they arrived and were ushered into the Cabinet room having had their brief cases confiscated. They all signed up readily to the Prime Minister's demand for total loyalty, dedication and secrecy, even though they had no idea what they were agreeing to. But they knew it was either a case of that, or find something else to do while on the backbenches. And they had worked with Weaver long enough to know that he was unlikely to ask them for any greater sacrifice than he was himself prepared to make. Until, that is, he started to brief them about the first phase of his plan for Northern Ireland. Then the discussion became quite lively, especially when they were told that, if phase one was successful, there would be a second, even more dramatic proposal to put to them, but that they were not going to be told about that until later. Sir Robin Algar was able to report that he had already set in train plans for a special video link hot line and a one-off cipher for use during the operation, and that he was meeting a top official from the Bank of England tomorrow. Even the Prime Minister looked impressed, and eventually all those present undertook to support the project, on the understanding that it would not go ahead without the unqualified support and help of the United States.

As they left, the Prime Minister motioned to Algar to stay behind.

"Well," said Weaver, "so far so good. We eventually got the support we needed, but I would hardly say they were enthusiastic about the project."

"Understandable, I suppose. Its going to make life difficult for all of them, especially as they are not yet authorised to consult within their own Departments, and they can see the risks which will accompany failure."

"At least we all sink together, so I suppose they took comfort from that," said the Prime Minister. "I'm glad you've already made a start—that helped to get them on side, I'm sure."

"I'm not at all certain where to start with my colleague at the Bank of England though," said Algar, "but I couldn't think of anyone else to give me a lead."

"Perhaps this will help," said the Prime Minister, handing over the package from Bill Clayton.

"And who, may I ask," queried Algar, looking at the grubby envelope, "is Edward Benbow from Fittleworth in Sussex?"

"Major Bill Clayton's uncle, as it happens," replied Weaver. "But the envelope isn't important. Look inside."

"Good grief!" exclaimed Algar, as he skimmed the list of terrorist bank accounts. "If this is only half accurate, it's going to save an enormous amount of time and effort."

"Most of what Clayton does is on the ball, so I hope that is, too. He handed it to me yesterday, when I was briefing him and James Anchor about our visit."

"I suppose, even if nothing else happens, cutting off the terrorists' supply of cash would do no harm," said the Cabinet Secretary.

"Exactly," agreed the Prime Minister. "As you've already made a start, keep going!"

By then, the Police Chiefs and CDS had arrived for the second crucial meeting to be held that day. General Sir Giles Guthrie, the Services chief, had thought to bring his ADC with him, an elegant-looking captain from the Grenadier Guards, whose mission was to take the notes. In the end, he stayed in the outer office with the briefcases. Apart from that, the meeting was a good one—indeed, those present even showed some enthusiasm for the task in hand. Getting rid of the terrorists was going to save them all a good deal of manpower and effort.

There was token resistance from the NIPS Chief Constable. "It's our job to uphold the law, of course," he said, "and I would find it difficult to live with some of what you propose, Prime Minister. Murder is murder, after all."

"It's also your job to prevent crime," responded Weaver. "Regard this as an exercise in long term crime prevention."

The two policemen looked at one another, nodded agreement, and grinned. From then on, the operation had their complete support.

"I am sure all of us totally accept the need for secrecy if this plan is to succeed," said Sir Giles, "and I applaud what you are already doing, Prime Minister, to set up discrete secure systems. But I wonder if I could ask a question, without in the least wishing to appear impertinent?"

"Go ahead," said the Prime Minister, wondering what was coming. Guthrie was nobody's fool.

"I know you have weekly audiences with the Sovereign," said the General, "and I suppose at some time you will have to brief on this subject. But, ahem, we all know that the King is something of an, um, er, how shall I put this—eccentric? Writes letters to all sorts of people with all sorts of sometimes, ahem, odd views. Could be a risk here, if you don't mind my saying so."

"The thought had already occurred to me, General," responded Tony Weaver. "I plan to brief the King only about the political scenario, and even then not until the establishment of peace in the Province, if that is achieved. I shall brief you, gentlemen, my Cabinet colleagues, and Parliament all at about the same time. He will not be told about our role in ridding the Province of the terrorists, only that they seem, in some way, to have ceased operating and left the country."

"Excellent," said the General, and went to gather up his papers—except that there weren't any. "I can assure you of my total support."

"Good," said Weaver. "When I know that we have the support of our American allies, I will let you know. Until then, no one else is to be briefed by any of you. If I had wanted any of your subordinates briefed, they would have been here today, and I would have done it myself."

They shook hands and left, collecting brief cases, notebooks and ADCs on the way. The Prime Minister and Cabinet Secretary made their way to the PM's office, and sank into armchairs.

"We've made good progress, Robin," said Weaver. "Let's hope they can all be trusted to keep their mouths shut until I tell them otherwise."

"I'm sure the military will be no problem," responded Algar, "and I think you put enough of the fear of God into your Cabinet colleagues to ensure that they toe the line, too."

"Do you realise that we now have all the initial support we need, on this side of the Atlantic? I wonder how things are going in the White House."

"I wonder."

"I'm very tempted to get on the blower to find out," said the Prime Minister. "but I shan't. It would be better for them to ring me, but I hope they're not too long about it. The suspense is killing!"

***

In Northern Ireland, James Anchor was also going through the motions of dying. He had not been having a bad day, really, all things considered. Plenty of paperwork, of course, and the odd meeting with officials seeking his views about this and that, but nothing really taxing for a man of his capabilities. He had lunch at his desk, because there was no official luncheon for him to attend that day, and he preferred his own company anyway. If he hadn't been divorced, he might have been able to slip away home for lunch, like most people who lived within range, but there was nothing in his flat, comfortable though it was, to attract him there for lunch on his own. So he stayed where he was, making the best of a sandwich from the canteen that his secretary had fetched for him, and read the *Times*.

Later that afternoon, he had to chair a rather irksome meeting with a dozen or so officials, all of whom had a view and wanted to make sure that everyone else knew what it was. Housing policy was not his favourite subject, but the people before him were being paid to take an interest and to 'do something' about it. So he listened patiently, rather wishing he'd had a better lunch. Sandwiches two days running were probably not a good idea. Which was really why he had already taken two glasses of water, and had surreptitiously rubbed his chest a couple of times. Eventually, he excused himself from the meeting, his right hand firmly clasped to his left rib cage.

He returned a few minutes later, full of apologies. Yes, of course he was all right, really—kind of you to ask. Touch of indigestion, he was sure: nothing more than that. Too many sandwiches for lunch, probably. He took another glass of water, and sat under the worried gaze of officials, still clutching his chest.

***

On the other side of Belfast, Major Bill Clayton called in one of his staff.

"Off hand," he asked, "how many weapons have we captured that have been used in terrorist killings?"

"Off hand," replied his second-in-command, Captain Brian Foley, "I've no idea. But I could find out."

"Please," said Clayton. "And find out where they are and whether I can borrow them."

"Now what are you up to, sir?" quizzed Foley. "Or are you not going to say."

"Right as usual," agreed the Major. "But I shall want a couple from each side, Republican and Unionist, and the more they've been used the better."

Captain Foley left, shaking his head. It was so often impossible to work out what the boss was up to, but in the end, there was always a good reason for his often bizarre demands.

"And while you're at it," Clayton called after him, "get some captured ammo to go with them."

Foley thought there might be a clue in there somewhere.

"And get the Chief Clerk in here!" Clayton shouted after the retreating figure. So loudly, in fact, that the Chief Clerk heard him from two offices away, and scurried in without further bidding.

"Ah! Sergeant Wilson—just the chap I wanted. You must be psychic!"

Sergeant Catherine Wilson was just about getting used to everyone being a 'chap' so far as Clayton was concerned.

"I've got a little job for you, Sergeant."

"Yes, sir?"

"I want you to dig out all those dossiers we've built up about the villains of this parish—you know, the ones which try to list all the evidence against them—and trot across to the NI Police HQ at Knock with them," said Clayton. "Go through them with one of your chums in special branch or the anti-terrorist squad, or both, and make sure they're all as complete as we can make them. Then I want a duplicate of each folder. They must be classified at least Secret, so I'll sign the authorisation when you're ready, and then sign for possession of the duplicates. I shall be taking them to London later, but nobody needs to know that. Any questions?"

"Only the usual one, sir," replied Sergeant Wilson, "but I expect I'd get the usual answer, so I shan't bother asking."

"Good man," said Clayton. "On the button as always! Off you go."

He watched her disappearing figure. As sergeants go, she wasn't a bad looking one, even in uniform, and he had once seen her out of uniform, jogging. Even better. She was damned good at her job, too.

***

By close of play on Monday, there had still been no contact between Washington and London. Surely they would hear something on Tuesday? The five-hour time difference really was a nuisance. It would be the afternoon before they heard anything, whatever day the news came through. But it was obvious to both the Prime Minister and his Cabinet Secretary that Tuesday was going to be yet another long, and anxious, day. A day when they could do nothing but wait patiently for America to catch up with them, and pass on their decision—go or no-go. But there was plenty of routine government business to keep both men busy while they waited. And at least, so far as they could see from Andrew Groves' morning briefing, there had been no whiff of a leak about their grand strategy. In fact, there was almost encouraging news, in that the President of Sinn Fein, Martin McFosters, had announced that he was to pay yet another visit to America the following week. This could just present a golden opportunity to take some action in pursuit of their long-term objectives.

Sir Robin Algar was able to punctuate an otherwise terrible day, during which some unpleasant decisions had been taken, with a pleasant lunch with his old colleague Alistair Vaughan. They sat quietly at one of the small alcove tables upstairs at Simpsons, and chatted amicably until they had tipped the carver who had served them from the trolley, and were tucking in to their rib of beef.

Vaughan's role at the Bank of England was to oversee and protect all the Bank's operations, from the physical security of cash and bullion to the security of its many complex and highly sensitive computer systems. But to protect them, he had also to know how they could be compromised, and this was where Algar needed to probe. Normally foolproof and impenetrable procedures would have to be thwarted if he was ever going to be able to siphon off the vast reserves of cash built up by all the terrorist organisations operating in Northern Ireland.

Understandably, Vaughan initially refused any help whatsoever, although he had been impressed by his quick look at the contents of Clayton's envelope.

"What you propose is quite illegal, as I'm sure you know," he said. "If I should help you to breach the accounts you say you have details of, then you or your staff would be able to use that information to breach almost any account you wanted, or pass the information to an accomplice who could do the same."

"That isn't actually what I'm seeking from you," corrected Algar. "I don't need your direct help or involvement, now or at any time. What I need to know is whether what I have in mind is possible, given all the countermeasures which I'm sure you have in place to prevent such a thing, and secondly whether you know of any genius anywhere who might be able to achieve such a thing. At worse, you might have to turn a blind eye in an effort to assist the government in achieving what I'm sure even you would agree is a worthwhile objective—denying terrorists the wherewithal to carry out their murderous activities."

"Well," replied Vaughan, helping himself to another glass of excellent claret, "I suppose that is a bit different. But I can tell you that I wouldn't be prepared to go even that far unless the Prime Minister personally discusses this with the Governor, and I get the green light from him. It's my career we're talking about here as well, you know."

"Of course, I quite understand that, and what you ask can easily be arranged. Do I take it, from what you've said, that there is someone, somewhere, who could help us achieve this?"

"Well," replied Vaughan cagily, "I think there could be, but whether you'd want him to act as your agent is another matter. And getting through all the accounts on your list would take some time, especially those in the States and Switzerland."

"Are we talking about days, weeks or months?" asked Sir Robin.

"Certainly a week or so, working full time," replied Alistair.

"We could live with that," responded Sir Robin. "But any longer would allow the opposition to gather their wits about them and start moving cash around, which would then make the task even more difficult."

Vaughan nodded.

"Who is this man, by the way?"

"He used to work for the bank, in our computer organisation. Only young, but a real wizard and an expert programmer," replied Vaughan.

"So why do you have doubts about us wanting to use him?" asked Algar.

"Because he's already in gaol. Serving eight years for fraud, doing exactly what you propose—lining his pockets by hacking into our own computer systems and transferring cash from other people's accounts into his own."

Sir Robin Algar grinned. "I'll let you know. Can I offer you a glass of port?"

The two men arranged to meet again in a day or so.

***

Two things that happened later that afternoon caused a flurry of excitement. First of all, Sir Robin Algar had a meeting in his office with Air Commodore Paul Bridges and a cipher expert, and, much later, Tony Weaver had word that the President would want to talk to him on the hot line tomorrow afternoon, at about nine o'clock Washington time.

Isabelle brought in Paul Bridges, and introduced a tall, rather bent man, with a shock of grey, unruly hair.

"This is Mr. Ernie Stevens, from GCHQ," said Isabelle.

The two men shook hands. Stevens somehow looked like a scientist, rather than a civil servant, although he was that, too, of course. He wore a check jacket with leather patches at the elbows, and a shirt that was obviously not used to having a tie tied at the neck. Although he had no papers with him, Stevens had a pair of half glasses perched on the end of his nose.

The three sat at the coffee table, as Isabelle brought in a tray.

"I thought it might be a good idea, Robin," said Bridges, "to bring you up to speed first with a slice of modern technology that you probably won't often come across in your job. Otherwise, you won't have a clue what Ernie's talking about. As you know, experts tend to forget that not everyone shares their knowledge, and Mr. Stevens is one of our top cryptanalysts."

"Thoughtful of you," replied the Cabinet Secretary. "And although I am, I suppose, responsible for all of them as Head of the Civil Service, I never seem to have the time to meet as many of the scientific members of it as I should. So it's particularly nice to meet you today, Mr. Stevens. Are you based in Cheltenham?"

"No," he replied. "One of the outstations—Eastcote, in fact. It's easier to get to other places from there, including Heathrow. I travel quite a bit."

"I see," smiled Algar, looking towards Paul Bridges.

"Well," began Bridges, "there's so much going on these days in this field that I hope you will find a quick 'tour de force' useful, because one of the most important and rapidly developing aspects of modern conflict is information warfare. In that respect, you are absolutely right to demand the highest possible level of security for whatever operation it is you are now planning, because modern computers and the people who use them can pose an huge threat, as well as being an enormously powerful tool in the right hands. For some time now, the Americans have been conducting special training in the use and protection of computer network operations, and we have sent people to some of those courses."

"I've been on one myself," said Stevens, "and since then I have been developing our own training programme for the military and others in crucial civil and commercial organisations. You will see the importance of this cyber warfare training and increased awareness when I tell you that the annual level of reported hacking attempts on the US Defence Department computer networks more than doubled last year, to over fifty thousand."

"Most of the attempts were unsuccessful, and probably carried out by youngsters, but some were undoubtedly hostile," continued the Head of COBR, "so protection of our information systems is vital."

"Once someone gets into a network, he can do untold damage," Stevens went on, "A determined hacker can take control of your system by secretly installing his own operating programme into it—what we call a Trojan Horse—and there are hundreds of these systems available on the internet if you know where to look for them. Once in, the attacker can steal passwords and gain full access to all the file systems."

"I had no idea," frowned Algar.

"It gets worse," said Bridges. "Hackers can devise automated tools which will extract encrypted passwords, they can alter the security and system logs to hide their presence, so ensuring that they can always gain access, or they can simply deny access to legitimate users by flooding the system with so much traffic that it can't handle it all."

"There are countermeasures, of course," said Stevens, "and we are constantly devising new methods of encryption and layered defences to combat increasingly sophisticated threats. But unless we can protect our information systems and control cyber-space, future conventional warfare becomes almost impossible."

"It certainly seems now," continued the Air Commodore, "that the days of massive armies facing massive armies are fast coming to an end. In future, victory will go to the force which has best harnessed the information revolution, and gained control of cyberspace."

"Has fiction really turned into fact so swiftly?" queried Sir Robin.

"Let me give you an example from the first Gulf War," said Ernie Stevens, adjusting his glasses. "My own organisation mounted a joint operation with the American National Security Agency, and inserted a virus into Saddam Hussein's command and control system, which caused widespread disruption. His military commanders were forced to keep in touch over far less secure networks, which our intelligence agencies were able to bug. So we knew what they were doing, and gained a huge tactical advantage."

"Well I'll be damned," said an amazed Cabinet Secretary.

"So the old days of Type X codes and first echelon ciphers are over forever," continued Ernie Stevens. "We're into an age of two level super enciphered codes, now. Put simply, this means that the message is coded into five-figure groups, taken from a code book, and that is then enciphered by adding random numbers from a one-time pad. The recipient does the same thing in reverse, and the pads and books are frequently destroyed and replaced."

"I'm very glad that was the simple explanation," said Sir Robin.

"The point is," said Ernie Stevens, "that all this can be done by computer these days. We don't actually use books and pads now, although we still call them that because computer cryptology uses much the same principles. The drawback is that instead of needing to operate a physical security system to protect the code books and so on, we now need to control cyberspace to prevent the computers and their contents being compromised. And there is one further major development that we have been working on, with the Americans at the Los Alamos National Laboratory in New Mexico, and that is quantum cryptography, using satellites for transmission over long distances.

"Basically, we transmit a digital key for deciphering coded information. Those keys are long random strings of numbers, which again receiver and sender must possess, but they are not anymore sent electronically. As we've said, electronic signals can be intercepted and decoded. So we are exploiting the unusual properties of quantum mechanics, and encoding the keys as minute particles of laser light, which we send along optical fibres, or through the air via satellites.

"So," concluded Stevens, adjusting his spectacles again, "this all means that we can offer you an almost impenetrable code, specific for your operation. But I need to know more about the operation before I can start work on it."

"I see," said Algar, for the second time that afternoon, although he really didn't see at all. "What more do you need to know?"

"I need to know the operation's code word, for a start," replied Stevens.

"It doesn't have one," replied Sir Robin.

"Then you'll have to give it one," demanded the man from GCHQ. "Otherwise, how will the people at our communications centres recognise your traffic when you start sending messages?"

"I see what you mean. I'll let you know, through the Air Commodore, if that's all right?"

"That'll do," came the reply. "I assume that all your traffic will be Top Secret, which means we only need one cipher. But how far afield will the traffic be sent?"

"Your assumption is correct, but why do you need to know where we shall be sending messages? I'm not sure I know myself."

"Then you need to give it some thought," said Ernie Stevens. "Remember what I said—both senders and recipients need access to the same codes and ciphers, and I don't want to disseminate them worldwide if that's not necessary, for obvious security reasons."

"I see," replied the Cabinet Secretary, who meant it this time. "Obviously, we need to keep the list of destinations as short as possible, so off hand I'd say the White House and the Pentagon in the States, one or two people in the Irish Republic's government, our own Foreign and Home Offices, and MOD as well as Downing Street. If there are any more after I've spoken to the Prime Minister, I'll let you know."

"Thanks. The fewer the better, really. Consider too, if you would, whether the normal means of sending secure communications might serve your purpose some of the time, rather than always use the special system, if that would restrict its use."

"I'll certainly do that, Mr. Stevens, and thanks for your time and patience," said Sir Robin Algar, drawing the meeting to a close. "Could you spare another minute please, Air Commodore, before you leave?"

Stevens shook hands, and left, adjusting his glasses.

"I take it," said Sir Robin when he had closed the door, "that Ernie Stevens is a mathematician by specialisation."

"Yes he is," replied the Air Commodore. "But he also has a PhD in particle physics, and speaks six languages, although he would be the first to tell you only four fluently. You can image how valuable he is to us, although there are plenty more around like him in that field of work."

"I was fascinated by what you had to say about cyber warfare. Much of that was new to me," confessed the Cabinet Secretary.

"Well it's a new field, and so far has been subject to very little public debate," said the Air Commodore. "But it means that the most powerful nations are the most vulnerable, of course, which is why America is so keen to get ahead of the game. Viruses and computer programmes have already been developed that can turn off a nation's electricity, steal its foreign currency, open the sluice gates of dams and so on, all from thousands of miles away."

"Foreign currency, eh?" said Algar. "That's interesting, because I had lunch only today with Alistair Vaughan from the Bank of England. He's Head of Security there. I wonder if he's heard about that?"

"I know Alistair," replied Bridges, "and I can tell you he probably knows more about it than anyone in the country."

"Fancy you knowing him," commented Algar.

"It's a fairly close community I work in. I first met him when he was a Commander at Scotland Yard in charge of the serious fraud squad among other things, and I was Provost Marshal. We still keep in touch."

"Really?" said the Cabinet Secretary.

"In fact, I knew you had lunched together today, and I know what you talked about. He rang me to see if I was in the picture, but of course I didn't have a clue. It sounds an interesting and useful idea you put to him, though. I'm sure he'll help, if he can, that is, without stepping too far outside the law. And of course if I can help in any way, you only have to ask."

"Well, since you now know about it," said Algar, "what do you think about using this convicted felon to tackle the job we have in mind?"

"I don't really see any alternative," replied Bridges. "Someone like Ernie Stevens would easily be able to do it for you, but that would be a bit too close to home for comfort, if it went wrong."

"I must talk to the Prime Minister before reaching a decision, but that's a useful view to have with me."

Sir Robin Algar felt decidedly uncomfortable. Too many people knew too many other people, and already word was getting about.

"You look worried, Robin," said the Air Commodore. "You mustn't be. The people you are talking to are totally trustworthy, you know, and won't gossip to anyone who is likely to be a security risk."

"But Alistair rang you on an open line, and that's a security risk," complained the Cabinet Secretary.

"As a matter of fact, he used a perfectly secure line," responded Bridges. "There was no risk."

"Well, that's a relief anyway. I suppose you know Major Bill Clayton, too?" probed Sir Robin.

Air Commodore Paul Bridges grinned, and stood to leave. "Everyone in this business knows Bill Clayton."

* * *

The following morning, Sir Robin Algar anxiously awaited Andrew Groves' briefing about the media. But there was still no hint that anything had leaked, and certainly the Downing Street Press office had not received any media questions at all out of the ordinary. Although relieved, he was still anxious.

The Cabinet Secretary stayed behind after 'prayers' for a final word with the PM, during which he quickly briefed him about the events of the previous day.

"At the end of it all," Sir Robin concluded, "there are three things outstanding, Prime Minister, where I'd like your view. First of all, we need, I think, a code word for this operation, for the reasons I've described, and secondly, I need to know whether you're happy to use the man suggested by my contact at the Bank of England to tackle the financial side of this plan. According to Bridges, we could do it ourselves, but he doesn't recommend it in case things go wrong—which they could, of course."

"There's probably no real alternative," replied the Prime Minister. "At least this chap has proved to the satisfaction of an Old Bailey jury that he can do what we want done!"

The two men laughed.

"It's not funny, really," continued Tony Weaver, " and we shall have to be very sure about security while this man's working, and especially when he's finished. He'll obviously have to go straight back inside afterwards, to minimise the risk of him talking."

"We may even have to take better care of him than that," said a grim faced Algar. "But we'll cross that bridge later, when we see what this man can deliver."

"In the meantime, I'll phone the Governor, and ask him to authorise Vaughan to co-operate with us," said Weaver. "As to a code word, I had decided not to give one to this operation, in case it leaked, but I suppose we do, after all, need one as your man from GCHQ suggested. What shall we call it?"

"Op. Hawaii would be neat," suggested Algar, "but I'll need to make sure it's not already in use. I'm sure Paul Bridges will be able to find out for us. And that brings me to my final point, Prime Minister. The Air Commodore now knows that we want an additional secure hot line to Washington, he also knows we need a special code and cipher system for a Top Secret operation, and he knows I have met with the Head of Security at the Bank of England, and why I did so—Vaughan is an old friend of his, and a retired commander from Scotland Yard by the way. I'm quite sure he must have linked these events together, and I would now like your permission to brief him about the whole project."

"He has a very high security clearance, doesn't he?" asked the PM.

"Just about the highest you can get, and it's regularly reviewed. He's not only totally trustworthy, he is going to be a key player in this whole business, and is already more involved than most people."

"Right. Let's do that then. Go for the code name we agreed, and brief Bridges, but only on the first stage."

"I'll get on with that, after we've heard from the White House. Oh, and by the way, Bridges knows Clayton, too! It seems everyone knows Bill Clayton, except me. I really must meet this man, and soon."

"I'm sure he'll be over again in the next day or so if all goes well, so I'll make sure you meet," agreed Weaver. "But we still need word from the White House before we can really get things moving. What time are we expecting Bill Minton's call?"

"About half past two. I'll come to your office half an hour or so before that, as usual, shall I?" asked Sir Robin.

"Yes please, but nobody else needs to be here, or even know about the call if we can avoid it getting around."

Sir Robin Algar was already in the outer office when the Prime Minister got back from his official lunch in the City, just after two. A man from the Cabinet Office Briefing Room was already there, preparing to open up the line and check the scramblers, as usual.

"Prime Minister, could I introduce you to Grant Piper, from COBR," said Jane Parsons. "He's taken over from Jack Bennett, who always used to open up the line for us."

"Jack on leave, then?" asked the PM as they shook hands.

"Haven't you heard?" asked Jane. "I'm so sorry, Prime Minister, I thought you had been told already, but poor Jack was knocked down by a car and killed on Monday evening, on his way home."

"How awful," said the Prime Minister. "I am sorry to hear that."

"And the bastard didn't stop, either," said Grant.

"That's terrible!" said Weaver.

"The funeral is on Friday afternoon," said Jane, "and one or two of us thought we might go, if that's all right with you, Prime Minister."

"Yes, of course," said Weaver. "And if there's a collection for flowers, then I'd like to put a tenner in, if that's appropriate. How about you, Robin?" he turned to the Cabinet Secretary.

"I've already, um, contributed, Prime Minister."

Weaver immediately understood.

"There won't be many at the funeral," said Piper. "He didn't have much of a family—wasn't married, or anything—but his father's coming over from Ireland. Tipperary, I think."

It was 2.30 precisely when Minton was put through to Weaver.

"Just a quick call," said Minton, "but I thought you'd like to know that we have what they call at Cape Canaveral, 'ignition'. And I must say a good deal of enthusiasm, eventually, among the colleagues I've spoken to."

"That's very encouraging news, Bill. Thank you for your efforts."

"Not at all, Tony. We all appreciate here that you've got the sticky end of the stick, at least initially, and wish you good luck as well as sending you our support."

"In that case," responded Weaver, "as I think you also say at Cape Canaveral, let's go for lift-off."

"Let's do that, and let's talk again soon when we have the new links in place. Thank you for starting that ball rolling, by the way," said the President, as the call ended.

"That's it, then," said the Prime Minister to Sir Robin Algar grimly. "Let's get started. Although, it seems you already have," he added.

Chapter Ten
LIFT OFF

Even by Downing Street standards, the hours that followed the call from America were frantic.

The Prime Minister and his Cabinet Secretary had immediately decided that they should pass on the news to all those who had attended Monday's special meetings, but at the same time had concluded that the circle needed to be drawn even wider than that.

"It's no use Cabinet Ministers knowing the score," said Sir Robin Algar, "if their outer offices don't also know what's going on. That's where things are going to be made to happen."

"You're right," agreed Tony Weaver. "And it's no use the Chief of Defence Staff knowing if nobody else does in the military—he's not going to mount all these little operations on his own."

"I have to say that I think we can leave it to those in uniform to decide who else they need to brief to get the job done, but I worry about the politicians and civil servants, if I may say so," declared Algar. "There is a natural tendency to gossip in the corridors, which we shall have to kerb."

"At the moment, it's the military and the police who are going to be busy, so perhaps the problem isn't so bad as we fear," said the PM.

"On the other hand," countered Sir Robin, "MI5 must be briefed, and they report to the Home Office, as does Scotland Yard and therefore the anti-terrorist squad and special branch. MI6 is a Foreign Office responsibility, and since the CIA lifted its ban on assassinations following 9/11, the people at Vauxhall Cross have developed a highly secret military wing that they can task directly, mainly staffed by members of the SAS and other special forces. That's MOD again. The Northern Ireland Office will have a responsibility for the NI Police Service who must get involved because of it's own anti-terrorist branch and special branch, and the Prison Service, another Home Office responsibility, will have to agree to us using the man who is doing time for fraud. I'm very much afraid, Prime Minister, that we can't sideline Ministers and their officials as much as we would like."

Tony Weaver sighed, and stared thoughtfully out of the window, across the rose garden.

"I will pass the word to my Cabinet colleagues," he said eventually. "I will remind them of the huge political risks we are about to take, and, with that in mind, leave it to them to tell those officials who really have to know, taking guidance from their Permanent Secretaries as to trustworthiness, security clearances, and so on. I'm quite sure all the Permanent Secretaries will immediately contact you, Robin, so you can also take the opportunity to emphasise the sensitivity of it all."

Algar nodded.

"I will also," continued the Prime Minister, "contact the CDS and police chiefs, as they attended the meeting here, and give them the same instructions about who they brief. Only those who need to know in order to get the job done must be told—none other. But I will also personally brief the heads of MI5 and MI6 to ensure they not only work closely together, but also with the police and military. I think you could deal direct with the Prison Service when you need to, perhaps after you've put Paul Bridges in the picture and spoken again with your man at the Bank of England."

"I can't think of anyone else we ourselves need to tell," agreed Algar. "I'm quite sure things will start to happen fairly quickly on the military side, especially when your man Clayton gets the all clear from his general."

"We can get hold of all these people on a secure line, too, I think," said Weaver. "But I might just have Andrew Groves in and tell him what's going on. What do you think? He can at least be on the lookout for leaks, and take extra care to monitor the media for news of relevant activity across the water."

"Yes, that would be sensible," agreed Sir Robin. "Perhaps I could sit in on that. After prayers tomorrow?"

"Agreed," said the Prime Minister. "I think you and I should each brief our private offices now, and then get cracking on the phone before people start drifting home. In fact, our people could pass word to those at the bottom of the list not to go home until we've been on to them."

***

It was two hours later that Colonel Philip Dangerfield, Head of Intelligence at Headquarters Northern Ireland, stuck his head round the door of Bill Clayton's office.

"The GOC wants to see us both—now!" he said. "Any clue what this might be about?"

"Yes," said Clayton, as he followed Dangerfield towards the stairs.

Dangerfield paused, expecting more, but then took the stairs two at a time, remembering who he was with. He'd have to wait for an explanation from the General rather than from Clayton. He didn't have to wait long.

The General had received a secure phone call direct from the Chief of the General Staff, an almost unique event in itself. He, in turn, had received orders from the Chief of Defence Staff, who had himself been briefed personally by the Prime Minister. The General passed on to the two men what he had been told about the objects of the exercise, and how they were to be achieved. The upshot of it all was that Major Bill Clayton was to be given almost *carte blanche* to do as he thought best, and the maximum possible cooperation to help him do it. And as that order effectively came from the Prime Minister, that's all there was to it.

"We have at least," said the General, " been told what this is all about, and what it is that the government hopes to achieve. Sounds bloody dodgy to me, I must say, although I'm quite sure it can be done, given that the political will is there. There is apparently a second phase to this operation, involving a proposed political solution, and I may, repeat 'may', be briefed about that later. I suppose that depends on whether or not the politicians think they can do that part on their own, or whether they think they will need our help for that too. But I suspect we shall be left to get on with the shitty end of the plan, and they will bask in the political glory of it all when we've succeeded. But that's just me being jaundiced again, I suppose."

The General was well known for his jaundiced view of politicians, so neither man responded.

"Is there anything more you can tell me about this, Major?" asked the GOC.

"No, sir, not really," he replied. "Minister James Anchor will, I believe, be involved in the detail of the political planning after our part of the operation, providing we are successful. I was asked to get involved because it was believed that I had the kind of detailed information that was needed for a large part of the first phase."

"I gather you've already had meetings with the Prime Minister?" said the General rather peevishly.

"Yes sir. A couple," replied Clayton.

"I had no idea," said Dangerfield to the General, in an effort to protect his own back.

"I was told not to say that I'd been summoned to the presence," explained Clayton helpfully. "I couldn't at that stage have given a reason, so it was best that I kept quiet."

"Quite right, really," agreed the General. "By the way, the people at Hereford have already been briefed, and at my request, they are detaching an SAS lieutenant to work with you as their liaison officer, Bill. He should be with you tomorrow."

"That's good news, and very helpful, sir. Thank you." *Not such a bad general after all*, thought Bill Clayton.

"Oh, and one other thing," said the General. "I'm to tell you that, from now on, we are all only to brief upwards. See me first if you ever feel the need to do otherwise."

As the two men took their leave, Col. Dangerfield turned to the General.

"Does this have a code word, by the way?" he asked.

"Not only that," replied the General, "but extra special secure communications are being set up for its exclusive use. And I must emphasise again the need for the utmost security. There'll be all hell to pay if the wheel comes off this one. It's 'Op. Honolulu,' by the way, but God knows why."

Clayton knew, but, as always, wasn't about to say.

There was a note on his desk when he returned to his office, from Captain Foley, who had already gone to the Mess for supper. The note outlined the history of the four handguns he had 'borrowed' from the Police, and which were now secured in the armoury with captured ammunition as requested. The armoury was under strict orders not to release the weapons to anyone except Foley or Clayton, which was good thinking and typical Brian Foley, thought Clayton.

Having read the note, Bill Clayton strolled to the Registry, where he knew Catherine Wilson was still working.

"Shove this in the safe for me please, Sergeant?" asked Clayton. "How are you getting on with those dossiers, by the way?"

"Not bad, sir," she replied. "I spent most of today at Police Headquarters, and there's a bit more work to do on some of them tomorrow. But the copies should all be ready for you by lunchtime."

"Excellent," said Clayton. "In that case I think I'll take them to London on the twelve o'clock shuttle. I'll stroll across to the transport office on my way to the Mess."

The hapless Corporal Harrington was on duty again.

***

It was quite late when Paul Bridges responded to the phone call from Isabelle Paton, and made his way yet again to the Permanent Secretary's office. By then, almost everyone who needed to know about the plan did know, and Robin Algar guessed that a lot of other people would be working late that evening as a result.

"Come in, Paul," said Algar, waving towards an armchair. "Make yourself comfortable—join me in a glass of something?"

"Wouldn't mind a scotch if you're having one," replied Bridges.

"I think we've earned it today," said Algar. "Thanks, by the way, for your quick response about the code word for this little saga. Have you passed it to Ernie Stevens?"

"Yes, I have," replied Bridges. "Sorry we couldn't use 'Hawaii', but that's already a contingency plan for something else."

"It was only a thought," replied Sir Robin. "I'd better tell you what 'Op. Honolulu' is all about."

The Cabinet Secretary succinctly outlined the first phase of the proposed plan, which now had the wholehearted support of the United States.

"The Americans will probably not have a great involvement in the beginning," said Algar, "but if we succeed, then there will be a second, even more daring effort to bring about a permanent political solution to an Ireland without terrorism. And the States will be involved heavily in that. But if we don't succeed in bringing peace to the province, then all bets are off, and a great many political careers will be at an end, I suspect."

"I can see why they are involved," said Bridges. "And they must have some role to play, even if only in bringing an end to the financial support given by NORAID, surely."

"Yes, of course. It will be no use our friend Alistair Vaughan helping us to empty their coffers if the Irish Americans are still busy filling them, especially as they only support one side of the political divide. But they made a start some time ago, by banning their web site, and Sinn Fein's."

"Now I know a bit more about the plan, I'll have another word with Alistair tomorrow. He really must be persuaded to be more cooperative," said Bridges.

"The Prime Minister is speaking to the Governor as well, so I think he'll get the message all right. He was just a bit afraid of acting against his own future best interests, I think."

"You were certainly wise to set up the dedicated secure communications links," commented Bridges. "It doesn't bear thinking about if there was to be a serious leak."

"Secrecy is the essence of success here," agreed Algar. "I think the financial part will be OK—it's small and self contained. And I think, too, that the combined military/police operation directed against individuals will be carried out by very small units, none of which will have the slightest idea of the broader picture. Only a few at the top who are directing things will have that. The noisy public part of it will be dealing with their arms and ammunition dumps, and I'm not quite sure how the military will handle that."

"Certainly not quietly!" agreed Paul Bridges. "I suspect they will delay that part of the exercise a bit until some of the major players are out of the way, so they can't kick up too much of a fuss. It will also take quite a while to plan that aspect too, I should think, not least because public safety will be a factor. The last thing you want is too much collateral damage."

"I'm not at all sure," said Algar, "that in some ways it might not be a good idea to actually claim credit for dealing with the decommissioning of arms in this way, after all the talking has achieved nothing. A few brownie points for the government taking a strong stand, and all that."

"Just so long as you don't arouse suspicion that the government has been involved in other aspects as well," warned Bridges. "This whole thing will need the most careful handling publicly."

"Absolutely," agreed Algar. "The Prime Minister and I will be taking Andrew Groves into our confidence tomorrow, for that very reason. As a matter of interest, Paul, when might the video conferencing be available? I can see we shall need to be using that rather sooner than I had expected."

"We've earmarked the old press briefing room for it—in the good old days, it was used for the daily briefing of lobby correspondence, until one of the PM's predecessors stopped it. It's next to COBR 'A' downstairs, as you remember, so handy for everything else, and we've started installation already. A large, flat, plasma screen will make them feel as if they're almost in the same room. It should all be ready, subject to test transmissions going well, by the weekend."

"That's good," responded Algar. "I can imagine it is going to be very well used in the days and weeks ahead."

***

Like most other people involved in 'Honolulu', Major Bill Clayton was in the office early the next morning, but not early enough to beat Captain Brian Foley or his chief clerk, Sergeant Catherine Wilson.

"'Morning, chaps," said Clayton, always cheery when he'd had kippers for breakfast. "Not having breakfast this morning, Brian?" he enquired. "The kippers are particularly good."

"I'll get a bacon roll later," replied Foley. "Suddenly, there seemed to be a lot to do this morning, what with you going off to London again later."

"Well, you should have stayed later last night, shouldn't he, Sergeant?" joked Clayton. "In the end, I couldn't get on the scheduled flight, but the RAF has a Hercules going back to Brize Norton before lunch, and they've been persuaded to go via Northolt and drop me off. Isn't that good of them?"

"Only if they land first!" replied Foley.

"Very funny! But I'll certainly be going down the ramp at the back," said Clayton. "They're stopping at the end of the runway, and going straight off again once I've left them. I'm being met by a staff car. With any luck, it will take me straight to Downing Street. Much better than Heathrow, especially as I shall have the dossiers with me. They will be ready, won't they?"

Sergeant Wilson was at the photocopier as he asked. "Nearly there, sir," she replied.

"By the way," said Clayton, "Our clever GOC has arranged for an SAS chap to be detached to us to act as our liaison officer."

"He's already here," replied Foley. "In your office, re-arranging the furniture."

"What!" exclaimed Clayton.

"Said it was all hush-hush, and he had to work closely with you, or something, so we've squeezed an extra desk in there for him," explained Foley. "Needed somewhere to put his radio, he said."

"Got lovely blue eyes," mumbled Sergeant Wilson.

"Jesus!" Clayton stomped off to what used to be his office.

A tall, slim man in a dark blue wooly-pully, turned to greet him. "Sorry about your office," he said, holding out his hand. "Nick Marsden, at your service."

He had dark wavy hair, and a good sun tan—blue eyes, too, noted Clayton, shaking hands.

"I was expecting a lieutenant from the SAS," said Clayton.

"Sorry again," said Marsden, "but you've got a Lieutenant Commander from the Special Boat Squadron. Same thing, really. I was on detachment to Hereford, and they sent me from there to act as your fixer."

"The General was nearly right then, I suppose. You certainly didn't waste much time getting here," Clayton complimented him. "How did you manage that?"

"They let me bring my own chopper," explained Marsden. "Thought it could come in handy while this little show is on, and the lovely RAF gave me a quiet corner of Aldergrove to park it when I arrived late last night."

"How did you get here from Aldergrove, then?"

"Bit tricky at two o'clock this morning, but I eventually found a taxi," replied the SBS officer.

"You were very lucky indeed," said Clayton. "Not just to find one, but to get here alive."

"Oh, it didn't have a driver," explained Marsden. "Once I'd got the door open, I hot wired it and drove myself. Unfortunately, the thing caught fire and burnt out shortly after I left it at the bottom of the hill. That's quite a climb, you know, with this bloody radio on your back, I don't mind telling you."

Captain Foley was hovering outside the door. Clayton turned to him. "Let me know what the police are saying about that taxi, will you. I want to know if there are any witnesses."

"There aren't," said Marsden. "I hung around for a bit to see, and not soul stirred. It was torched, not blown up, so it was all very quiet."

Clayton looked hard at Marsden. He was a professional, all right. No doubt about that. Suddenly, all this began to look as if it could be quite good fun, in a sick sort of way.

"What's with the wireless, then," he said, nodding towards the extra desk crammed into the corner. "We've got quite a good communications centre here, you know."

"I'm sure you have," replied Commander Marsden. "No offence, or anything, but I can chat direct to all my chums on this without bothering anyone else. Totally secure, too."

Clayton hit the buzzer on his desk. Sergeant Wilson answered.

"Be a good chap," said Clayton, "and get some coffee organised. Those kippers have given me a thirst. Then ask Captain Foley to double up on his order for bacon rolls—Commander Marsden looks as if he could murder one." Marsden nodded appreciatively. "And then," concluded Clayton, "get on to the Officer's Mess, give them my compliments, and get a decent room organised smartly for the commander. He hasn't slept for a couple of days."

"Now," he turned to Marsden, "tell me what you know, and why you think you're here."

"I gather," replied Nick Marsden, "that there are certain parts of the landscape over here which are surplus to future requirements, and that they either need to be moved on, or to be removed. I'm told you have the details. My job is to arrange the removal for you. The SAS Commander over here has been told that any tasking from me takes priority over anything else he thinks is important, and he is also getting a few reinforcements in the next day or so. Your General again, I shouldn't wonder. The plot seems to be to use very small, self contained units, each unknown to the other, and for them to move on once their mission is achieved."

"Is your area of operations restricted to Northern Ireland?" asked Clayton.

"Not at all—anywhere you like, world wide."

"That could be very useful," said Clayton. "But what about the States?" he asked, remembering McFosters planned visit there.

"Even there," replied Marsden, "although it depends what it is you want doing. I spent some time working with MI6, so I know my way around the American Special Forces, but there could be times when it would be best to go in at the top, and work down, if you see what I mean."

"You mean a direct request from the PM to the President, for example."

"Exactly so. Things could move faster that way."

"What about this, for instance?" asked Clayton. Over coffee, they discussed the McFosters visit, and soon agreed what to do.

"I'm in Downing Street this afternoon, so I'll set that ball rolling if I can. I suggest you get your head down for a few hours while I'm away, and we can meet again over a beer in the Mess this evening."

"Sounds good," replied Marsden. "I need to twiddle knobs on my crystal set for a bit first, though."

"I'll tell my people to get whatever you want—if you can't find it for yourself, of course," said Clayton, looking around at his once tidy office.

***

Sir Robin Algar was just leaving for lunch when Major Clayton arrived, with his brief case padlocked to his wrist.

"At last we meet," said Algar. "I've heard a lot about you," he said, shaking hands.

"Sorry to barge in like this, unannounced," said Clayton, "but you will be needing these dossiers I've put together for you, and I thought the sooner you had them the better. They combine all the evidence we have about certain people over the water, and their alleged criminal activity."

"I've already got an envelope full of material from you," said Algar, "but this all looks much more official."

"It is," acknowledged Clayton. "It's a combination of facts from all our sources—the sort of paper work the Crown Prosecution Service would need before reaching a decision. I gather you need it for much the same purpose."

The Cabinet Secretary paled slightly. "I'm afraid I do," he agreed.

"I shall need to know your verdict," said Clayton. "It might be easier if I assume you are content for us to proceed unless I hear to the contrary."

"The evidence is that good, is it?" asked Sir Robin.

"We think so, in almost every case."

"Let's do it that way, then," agreed Algar. "How soon do you need to know?"

"How long will it take you to get through them all, do you think? There's three-dozen or so in there. The sooner we set the deadline, the sooner we can get started."

The Cabinet Secretary thought for a moment, and looked at the diary on his desk. "The trouble is, I can't take any of this home," he said, almost to himself. "Let's agree that if you haven't heard about any of them by Monday, then I am content. By then, the new secure communications should be in place, too."

"Good," agreed Bill Clayton. "That gives me time for some planning as well. There's one dossier in that lot, though, where I think the Americans could do a better job than us, but they will need to act on Friday. If you agree, could you persuade the PM to have a word with President Minton, to see if he can set it up for us?"

For the next ten minutes, they discussed Martin McFosters.

Sir Robin Algar suddenly looked at his watch. "Look here," he said, "I'm going to be late for lunch. Is there anything else?"

"I need your signature for the dossiers," said Clayton. "They're classified." He handed over an official receipt from his jacket pocket, and pointed to where the signature was required. "And this," he added, fishing for a scrap of paper in another pocket. "It's McFosters' flight number," he said, handing it over.

"You think of everything," said Algar, signing. "How about joining me for lunch? I'm meeting a friend of yours, Alistair Vaughan."

"I know you are. He told me when I spoke to him this morning. It would be nice to see him again, so thank you, if you're sure I shan't be in the way, I'd very much like to join you."

Sir Robin Algar grinned. "Come on then. The car's waiting at the Whitehall entrance."

He paused, to hand over the files to John Williams.

"For the safe, please, John. I shall want this lot again later. Get on the phone and tell Mr. Vaughan we shall be a bit late, and that Major Clayton is joining us."

"He guessed I would be," said Clayton as they set off down the corridor.

"Did he, now!" exclaimed Algar. "And I suppose you know where we're going, too."

"Rules," replied Clayton. "It's your turn and you like steak and kidney pud!"

The two men laughed as they stepped out into Whitehall. *This was going to be better than a pint in the Red Lion across the road*, thought Clayton.

"As a matter of interest, Major, why did you ring him?" said Sir Robin as they settled into the car.

"Only to try to put a bit of steel in his spine," replied Clayton. "I gather he wasn't entirely co-operative on your first meeting."

"Oh dear," said Algar. "What you say is certainly true, but poor Alistair will also have been encouraged to help this morning by Paul Bridges, who you also know I think, and by the Governor of the Bank of England himself, following a call to him by the Prime Minister. He may just not be in a very good mood when we meet after all that."

Bill Clayton grinned. "The steak and kidney will cheer him up," he said. "Although personally I shall have something lighter, I think, since I had kippers for breakfast. And please call me Bill, if you like."

"Thanks, Bill. Do you think Alistair and his convict friend are going to be able to pull this off, as a matter of interest?" asked Sir Robin.

"Oh, I'm quite sure they will." Bill Clayton lowered his voice and turned towards the Cabinet Secretary. "As a matter of fact," he confided, "I managed myself, only last weekend, to spirit away a few dollars belonging to the IRA from the Manhattan State Bank in New York. In fact, I closed the account. I'm told that caused quite a fuss, as I'd hoped it would. I knew they had quite a big bill to pay, and in the end, they had to scratch around to find the money from other accounts."

The Cabinet Secretary could hardly believe what he was hearing.

"I'm still not quite sure how I managed it, even now," continued the Major, "but the point is that if I can do it, fiddling around on my computer in the office, then I'm sure the Bank of England can. I was going to tell Alistair, and ask him what I ought to do with the money. I opened a special account for it, to avoid any confusion. But perhaps you might have an idea. It's been on my conscience, a bit."

During lunch, at their quiet corner table at the rear of the restaurant, the three men discussed the next moves in the bid to rid the terrorist organisations of the money they needed to operate.

"I've never understood why they need so much," said Vaughan.

"Weapons are expensive," replied Clayton, "and apart from that, they have quite large full-time organisations, with staff who need paying a wage, and they make handsome regular donations to their so-called 'war widows', and to the families of their members in prison. All in all, there's quite a bit of cash flowing through their accounts, especially the bigger organisations, and shutting off the flow will cause quite a bit of grief."

"What about the timing of all this?" asked Sir Robin.

"In my view," replied Bill Clayton, "we need to wait until a few of the major players are out of the way before we start shutting them down. Lower ranking members will make less noise and be able to do less to about it. I would prefer to start with the IRA and other Republican organisations, and then move on to the UDA. You'll see that the lists in my envelope are numbered - that's the order I think we should deal with them, if that's possible. It would be really neat, though, if your man could get everything prepared, and then shut down several accounts all at once. But however we do it, it's essential at the same time for the Americans to shut off the flow from their end."

"That's all in hand," said Algar. "We only have to say the word. And what about shutting everything down with a bang, rather than a gentle haemorrhaging, Alistair? Can that be done, do you think?"

"I'm sure we shall be able to close a few accounts on the same day, but not all of them at once. The whole exercise will take a couple of weeks, I should think, depending on how well our friend gets on cracking the various bank ciphers."

"There is one particularly important piece of timing, which will take a good deal of coordination," said Bill Clayton, leaning forward. "There's a large and important shipment of arms due in a couple of weeks from Libya. The usual practice is for members of the IRA to oversee the loading of the consignment, and then deposit a post-dated cheque, cashable when the arms are safely delivered. The money will need to be in the bank when the cheque is drawn up, but not when it's deposited. It must bounce. By then, we shall need to have taken care of their biggest arms dump, so that the need for the shipment is even more urgent. And we may need help from the Americans to do that," he continued, turning to the Cabinet Secretary. "But again, timing will be crucial, because, every four weeks, fairly regularly, the IRA Quartermaster himself, and two of his top people, visit the dump to inspect it. If we could blow it with them inside, it would look like an own goal, and I plan to make as much of this operation as possible look like that."

"That would be very neat indeed if we can pull that off," agreed Algar.

"There is one problem, though," said Clayton.

"Only one?" asked an incredulous Alistair Vaughan.

"Well, it's not really a problem, I suppose," said Clayton thoughtfully. He turned to Sir Robin Algar again. "It's just that the dump's south of the border, in Tipperary. Used to be an old regional seat of government during the Cold War, so you can imagine the size of it, and how well reinforced it is. We could take it out without Dublin knowing in advance, but I just thought it might be better if they knew the plot first."

"You're right to raise it," said Algar. "This is one for the politicians, I think. My guess would be that, whether or not we tell them, depends on how well the talks have gone between the two presidents. I'll need to discuss it with the PM."

"I'll let you know about the timing of that when we've done some planning, but we shan't be able to hang about waiting for politicians to reach agreement. We either tell the South or we get on with it—we don't ask," said Bill Clayton firmly. "But it all has to start with your con doing his stuff more or less to order," said Clayton, turning to Vaughan. "Just how good is he, Alistair?"

"It was quite amazing what he managed to do before, without our help, so if we give him access to our top facilities, he should have no real problems," replied Vaughan. "But he'll need watching like a hawk from the minute he starts."

***

When he got back to the office it was quite late, and Bill Clayton was surprised to find Nick Marsden still there.

"I thought you'd be quaffing ale in the Mess by now, or sleeping it off, or something. What's keeping you here at this late hour?" enquired Bill.

"As a matter of fact," replied Nick, "I've had an awful afternoon, thanks. How was yours?"

"Nothing special," replied Bill. "Lunch at Rules with the Cabinet Secretary after our meeting, a quick chat with the Head of Security at the Bank of England, a word over the phone with the Prime Minister, and a terrible journey back to Heathrow in a chauffeur-driven government limo. To crown it all, the only seat left on the flight back to Belfast was in business class."

"Sounds a hard life over here," responded Commander Marsden. "I think I'll go back to Hereford."

"Don't you dare—things are starting to happen, and will really take off on Monday, with luck," said Clayton. "Perhaps even Friday. And you and I have got a lot to do before then."

He briefly told Marsden about the arrangement he had come to with Sir Robin Algar, how Vaughan had finally agreed to help with the financial operation, not least because of Clayton's own spectacular coup in raiding a bank himself, and told him that the Prime Minister had agreed to talk to the President about the McFosters trip.

"That's why I had such a lousy afternoon," said Marsden. "I'd only just got my head down, when some erk bustled into my room to say that the Prime Minister wanted a word on the blower. Being unused to your way of life here, I naturally thought the man was nuts. It took him several minutes to convince me that he wasn't, and when I eventually got to the phone, the PM's winger didn't want me after all, but your good self. Weaver then realised that when he spoke to you on the phone earlier, you were in London at the time, and it then took further minutes to convince him that I was your right-hand man. In the end, the message was that the President was sure they could help, and watch this space. He said you'd know what that meant. When I said, 'Oh, you mean McFosters', he rang off."

"Typical," said Clayton.

"Him or me?" asked Marsden. "Why don't we go and have that beer? I suppose you had a good lunch, and don't want supper, but I'm starving."

"Ever been to Rules, in Maiden Lane?" asked Clayton, by way of reply.

"Don't tell me you had steak and kidney after your kippers? How could you?"

"I'm still hungry, even now," said Clayton. "It must be the travelling. But if you can keep awake, we ought to spend a few minutes here first, while it's quiet. There's quite a lot to tell you."

"I can't wait," replied Marsden. "And I'll show you how the radio works, and brief you a bit on our capabilities. We should soon be ready for lift off, with luck. I'm quite looking forward to working with you, Major."

"I'll drink to that," said Clayton, "but a bit later."

"In that case, I'll wait, and try to keep awake," promised Nick Marsden.

"Tomorrow, " said Clayton, "I must introduce you to the chaps in special branch. You'll be working closely with them, and the anti-terrorist squad. First, though, let's go through these."

He went to the safe for the originals of the dossiers he had taken to London earlier.

"These are the villains we have to deal with," he explained, "subject to London's approval, which is why I took a set of these over there today. We shall have a decision by Monday, when we can get started. But there are extra dockets in all of them which London didn't need—like this one, for instance."

Bill Clayton pulled out some pages from one of the files.

"For some time now, we've been monitoring every move of all this lot," he explained, waving at the pile of files. "We know everything there is to know that's worth knowing."

"Such as?" asked Marsden.

"Such as what time they get up in the morning, what time the postman calls, how much milk they have left, where they shop, what they eat, their favourite pubs and restaurants—everything, but especially their routines."

"I'm impressed," said Nick Marsden.

"It's useful for two reasons," continued the Major. "First of all, if they deviate from the normal, it alerts us to the fact that something is up, but secondly, if we want to, shall I say, upset their happy lives in some way, then we have a range of options available to us which we can tap into without them becoming suspicious."

"Like delivering the mail one day, instead of the postman doing it."

"Exactly. We even know where and when some of them plan to have their holidays. In fact in one particular case that poses a problem, because he will be going to Greece for two weeks just when we want him to be around in Belfast."

"We shall have to get at him in Greece, then," responded Commander Marsden. "Shouldn't be a problem."

"That would be handy," said Clayton. "It's why I asked if you could arrange operations abroad. I'm not keen to have too many bodies lying around, if we can avoid it. Bodies mean postmortems, and they can be embarrassing. I think, too, we might be able to arrange one or two tit-for-tat shootings if we can set the cat amongst the pigeons with a bit of Psy. Ops work."

Clayton returned the files to the safe, gave Marsden the combination number, and told him about the terrorist weapons in the armoury.

"Browse through those files when you like," he said. "But I want to discuss how we get at their arms dumps, if you don't mind."

"This is getting interesting," said Marsden. "Much better than training at Hereford. How many dumps are there that we need to tackle?"

"Taking both sides together, there are four small ones, but none the less important in spite of their size. But they will have to be raided and the contents removed, because they are in more or less built up areas and we must avoid collateral damage if at all possible. They will be a job for your chaps, I think, but again, if we are careful, we can make it look like the work of the other side. There is a good deal of weaponry hidden away in houses and flats and drinking clubs, and we can get the police to take care of that I think."

Major Bill Clayton paused. "There's one, though," he continued, "which I admit is really causing me sleepless nights." He pulled out a map.

"Down here, in the south." He pointed to an area of Tipperary, near Cashel. "Near an IRA training area," he continued. "It's huge. Got everything in it you can imagine, from hand-held ground-to-air missiles to several tons of Semtex. It belongs to the Provisionals, and the Decommissioning Body has never got near it—doesn't even know it exists."

Clayton looked at Marsden, stood up and stretched.

"I think the Irish government knows it's there, not least because it's in what used to be their major RSG during the Cold War. Bloody miles deep and covered in more bloody miles of steel reinforced concrete."

Marsden frowned. "Not the sort of place you can wander into and empty with a removal van, I agree," he said. "Why haven't the Irish done anything about it, do you suppose?"

"The need for a quiet life, probably."

"Blowing it up would soon take care of their quiet life for them, wouldn't it?" commented Nick Marsden. "And it must have weak points, like doors and ventilation shafts."

"It does," agreed Clayton, "we've got some good satellite photos of it. But the weak points aren't weak enough for anything I can lay my hands on."

"If we can do it, will the bods in the south be very upset, do you think?"

"They might just be asked if they mind," replied Clayton, who told Marsden about his conversation with Sir Robin Algar earlier, including the regular inspections made by the IRA's Quartermaster and his top aides, and the shipment due from Libya.

"If that ever gets ashore," said Clayton, "and I hope we can prevent that, but if it ever does, it will go into that bunker."

"If it's still there," commented Bill Marsden. "Any ideas?"

"I think we shall have to ask the Americans to help with this one," replied Bill. "I can't think of any other way."

"I was thinking the same," replied Nick. "They've got some pretty smart new 'bunker-busters', which they used in the Gulf. If we could persuade them to let us have the use of one, that would do the trick nicely. Multiple warheads would drill a hole straight through that lot before the sharp end went off."

"Air launched?" queried Clayton.

"Not all of them," said Marsden. "There are some new submarine launched cruise missiles fitted with those warheads. Much quieter and less obtrusive than noisy aircraft."

"Range?"

"Two thousand miles, probably. Well out of sight."

"Would they do it, do you think?" asked Clayton.

"If they're really in on this Op. they will. We would probably have to get up close ourselves to light it with a laser as back up to their global positioning system, and to tell them when the target is occupied. A job for me, I think—what a splendid challenge!"

"Do you mean personally?" asked Clayton.

"Why not?" replied Marsden. "I haven't been to a good firework display for simply ages. Now, what about that beer?"

Chapter Eleven
A PROCESS OF ELIMINATION

Jim Farlow lived in Highgate, with his elderly mother. Or at least, he used to, until he moved into temporary accommodation on the south coast. His mother wasn't at all pleased when he left, for a number of reasons. For one thing, it was handy having Jim around the house. Since Mr. Farlow died, Jim had been the main breadwinner, and had kept the old Victorian semi at the top of the hill near the shops in pretty good order.

Not that Jim was much of a DIY expert or a handyman. He was much more interested in his books, and spent most of his time in his room upstairs playing with his computer. Or whatever he did with it. Mrs. F. was never sure. But he was a good boy, really, and obviously had a good job at the Bank of England, too, until he moved, judging by the size of the allowance he used to give over every week. Even now, he still managed to make regular payments into her bank, although Mrs. Farlow wasn't at all sure where they came from. She had thought it best just to be on the safe side when Jim moved out to go back to her old job as a dinner lady at Highgate Secondary School. Just in case. It didn't pay much, but at least it was regular, and provided her with a bit of company, too.

As for Jim, well, he was making the best of things. Living in Sussex was certainly better than Wandsworth, where he had lodged when he first left Highgate, but he still missed his old home and his Mum. Although he was now turned twenty-eight, he had never married, nor even really felt the urge to do so, preferring his own company to other people's, generally speaking. Even though he'd left home, his Mum was still as good as gold, really, and paid him regular visits. He always sent the fare money, of course. And because Ford was an open prison, she was allowed to bring him homemade cakes and buns and things, when she remembered. And he was allowed his magazines, to keep himself up-to-date, and soon would even be allowed out to the shops, under escort. But not yet. He still had four of his eight years to do, although he hoped the Parole Board would let him home a bit early, especially as they'd got the money back after he'd told them where it all was. Or nearly all of it, anyway. There were still a couple of accounts left with considerable sums in them which they didn't know about, which would keep him comfortable in his retirement, and give him a very handy cushion when he came out if he couldn't get another job. He knew this was a risk, but it didn't matter. Because they had no real idea how much he'd managed to salt away before they caught up with him, they thought he'd owned up to all of it. They must have been daft.

He was reading the latest issue of *PC World* when one of the warders appeared at the door of his room.

"You're wanted," he said. "You've got visitors."

Jim looked puzzled. "Not Thursday, is it?" he asked. "My Mum's not due down again 'til next week, anyway."

"This isn't your Mum, and it ain't Thursday, either," replied the warder. "Don't sit there arguing, get a bloody move on. These blokes have come down from London specially to see you, and I expect they've got better things to do, if they're honest."

They left the room—he refused to call it a 'cell'—and Jim automatically turned left down the corridor towards the visitors' centre.

"This way," said the warder, turning right.

"Visitors' room's this way, isn't it?" said Jim, pointing.

"These are no ordinary visitors," said the warder. "They're in the room next to the Governor's office, and that's this way."

Jim was even more puzzled—even a bit alarmed—as he retraced his steps, and followed the warder. He wondered, as he had a hundred times, why they were known as 'screws'.

Eventually, they entered the administrative wing, a part of the open prison Jim had not previously visited. In the office next to the Governor's was a tall, slim man in a suit and a smart tie, with a military looking moustache, and another, rather more scruffy civil servant looking bloke.

'Moustache' seemed vaguely familiar, somehow.

"I've got a job for you, Farlow," he said.

"And who might you be, to offer me a job?" asked Jim.

"And I thought you had a good memory," said Alistair Vaughan, introducing himself.

"Ah!" said Jim. "Yes, I remember you now. You gave evidence against me at my trial. After what you said about me at the Old Bailey, what makes you think I'm going to do anything to help you after all this time? I thought I'd seen the last of you."

"Well, you haven't," said Vaughan. "And don't blame me for the fact that you're in here, either. You were the one hacking into computers, you were the one moving money about illegally, and you were the one who talked about it. That's why we started recording what you were doing."

"O.K., I know," said Jim. "But why should I suddenly help you now? What's in it for me if I did?"

"Freedom, that's what," replied Vaughan. "By the way, this is Philip Walton from the Home Office - Prison Service, actually." Vaughan nodded towards the other man. "Show Farlow your I.D., then he'll know we're here officially," ordered Vaughan.

"So now what do you want?" asked Jim for the second time.

"I want you to do legally what you were doing illegally four years ago," replied Vaughan.

"You're joking!"

"I'm serious."

"And why should I? What's all this about?"

"We know from bitter experience the sort of brain you've got, Farlow, and how easy you seem to find it to hack into systems with the very highest security," replied Vaughan. "We want you to do it again, this time with our support and help. This time you'll be with us, not against us. The only difference is that you won't be lining your own pockets, but emptying other people's."

"Just as a matter of interest, who would I be working for exactly?" asked Jim Farlow.

"The British government, essentially," replied Vaughan.

"Which is why I'm here," chipped in Walton, suddenly seizing his chance to impress. "I represent HM Government," he explained proudly. "Not that I know anything about what's going on," he added, unnecessarily, "but I am in a position to guarantee concessions in return for your full co-operation."

"What sort of concessions?" asked Farlow.

"Play your cards right and do as you're told, and you could be out of here in weeks rather than years," said Vaughan.

"Tell me more," demanded Jim Farlow.

"You'll get a full briefing when you've agreed to co-operate, and not before," said Vaughan. "What we want you to do should take about three weeks—bit more, bit less, who knows. You'll be working in the Bank of England, like you did once before, and as soon as you've successfully completed the job, and we've sorted out your paper work, you can go home, a free man."

"With a free pardon?" asked Jim.

"Like hell," replied Alistair Vaughan.

"What do I get paid?"

"Bugger all," replied Vaughan. "Judging by the size of the allowance you give your mother every month, you've already got more than enough stashed away somewhere without us adding to it."

Jim almost blushed. They weren't so daft after all. He wondered just how much they knew, but he was impressed that they'd found out about the allowance he was paying.

"When do I start?" asked Jim.

"If that means you've agreed to co-operate, now," said Vaughan. "Pack your bags, Farlow, and look sharp about it. We've got better things to do than hang around for you all day."

"I don't need to pack, if I'm coming back here tonight," said Farlow.

"You're not ever coming back here," said Vaughan. "From now on and until you've finished your little task, your home is Pentonville. Then you can go back to Highgate."

"But Pentonville is terrible," wailed Farlow. "I've heard about it from people here. Three to a cell, sometimes. I don't want that."

"You won't be getting it," Walton said. "You'll have a cell all to yourself."

"Solitary, you'll be in," added Vaughan. "Just in case you feel like talking about your day at the office, like you did once before."

"I'm not going," said Farlow.

"You're going," said Vaughan, "Whether you co-operate or not. It's up to you how long you stay there—four weeks or four years."

"That's not fair," wailed Farlow. "I want a Royal Pardon."

"Glad to see you haven't lost your sense of humour," said Vaughan. "Now stuff your kit in a black sack, and let's get going."

Farlow's second nasty shock of the day was that he didn't travel to London in the car with his two visitors, but in a prison van, straight to Pentonville. He had a miserable night, too.

***

During the past couple of days, Clayton and Marsden had held a series of meetings with Special Branch at the NIPS HQ at Knock, and with colleagues in the SAS detachment based at Bessbrook Mill. Marsden's Lynx helicopter had already proved its value, and he had proved himself a very able pilot as well, quickly getting to know the geography of the Province. The people they met had already received a limited briefing, and everywhere they went, they found the new secure communications links already in place. London had worked fast. The two officers had been able to agree who was going to do what and when, and in what order actions were going to be taken.

Back at headquarters, they made their way to Clayton's office to take stock.

"Anything happening?" asked Bill Clayton, sticking his head round the door of the Registry.

"Not that you'd notice," replied Captain Brian Foley. "You two really seem to be stirring things up."

"That's what we're paid to do," replied Nick Marsden.

"A colleague of yours has turned up, Commander," said Foley. "Wilson's taken him down to the Sergeant's Mess for a meal, but he's got himself a billet at Aldergrove. Chief Petty Officer Sid Rudkin."

"Sid's a good egg," announced Marsden. "He'll look after the chopper and anything else we want. If you see him before we do, Brian, you might tell him it's on the playing field and that he can take it back to Aldergrove anytime he likes. I'll get in touch with him later."

"Aye, aye sir," said Foley, cheekily. "And there was a message from Downing Street on the new hot line, to say that McFosters has gone."

"Gone?" they chorused.

"Gone," repeated Captain Foley. "Apparently left Belfast for Washington, and never arrived."

"Ah!" said Clayton, nodding. "Anything else?"

"Your Minister friend, James Anchor, rang. Sergeant Wilson spoke to him, but he's apparently off to the States soon for a long spell of leave. Not been well recently, so it seems."

The new secure phone rang.

"It's Downing Street again, wanting you Major," said Foley.

"I'll take it in my office."

The two men hurried off.

It was Sir Robin Algar. "Things have started to happen, so I thought I should keep you up to date," he told Clayton.

"I've heard about McFosters," Bill Clayton responded.

"The Americans did a good job there," said Algar, "although I'm not quite sure how they pulled it off. We've got our man working on your list of accounts—started this morning. When he's not at the Bank, he's in solitary in Pentonville, and when he is in the Bank, he's got two armed guards with him, everything he does—every keystroke on the computer—is recorded, and every move he makes is monitored. He's not allowed to talk to anyone, so we're pretty sure nothing will leak."

"Poor sod!" said Clayton.

"He wants a Royal Pardon, too!" said Robin Algar. "He's been told we'll take good care of him when he's finished."

"I know what you mean," said Clayton.

"Finally, two things on the political front. President Minton is having talks with the Taoiseach, Michael O'Leary, at Camp David in a few days, and the PM is going to be there as well. The Constitutional Committee is being set up and will be convening in a week or so probably. Your man James Anchor is on it."

"Where will they meet?"

"Oddly enough, in Honolulu," replied Algar. "The Americans are confining them to their huge air base at Hickham, and they will be kept more or less isolated from the outside world until they've finished, or until the three governments have gone public."

"Nice touch, that," said Clayton.

"But everything now hangs on the meeting at Camp David, so far as the politics of it all is concerned," continued Sir Robin. "I'll let you know how that goes when I hear."

"More importantly," said Clayton, "I simply must know how your man gets on at the Bank. Will you be able to let me know, or shall I liase with Alistair?"

"Alistair will know before I do," replied Algar.

"I'll keep in touch with him direct, then," said Bill Clayton. "Things are moving here, too. We are about ready to start serious business now we know McFosters has gone, and there will be a series of raids as well in the next day or so on arms caches, mostly in private homes. Cdr. Marsden has been in touch with the Americans about the big dump down south, and we can be ready to take that out by the time of Seamus O'Hara's next visit, which will probably be early next week. The US Navy has offered one of their latest submarine launched cruise missiles, subject to Pentagon approval, and I'll let you know if there's any help we need in getting that. I'll need a chap down there to work the laser range finder, so I need to know whether the Irish authorities have been told to expect the big bang, or whether we shall be acting totally covertly."

"Leave that to me," said Sir Robin Algar.

Things were certainly moving fast now, and the whole military side of the operation already seemed almost unstoppable.

Major Bill Clayton rang Alistair Vaughan at the Bank of England.

***

Suddenly, the news media was taking an interest in Northern Ireland again. *The New York Times* had sent a man across specially, the first time they'd had a correspondent based in Belfast for almost three years.

The disappearance of Martin McFosters had stirred the imagination, and had stirred the real IRA into accusing the Unionists of having abducted him, although they had not been able to suggest why they should have done so. In Northern Ireland, details like that rarely mattered. The police had also been active, and were showing off the results of several successful raids on illegally held arms. Several IRA and Sinn Fein members had been arrested at the same time. The police had said they had been "acting on information received," and the nationalist population naturally believed that it was Unionists within the NI Police Service who were to blame.

Within days, two prominent Unionists were assassinated on the same night, one a leading politician, the other the Commander of the Belfast 'Brigade' of the Ulster Defence Force. Forensic tests showed that, in at least one case, the gun had been used before in other loyalist murders, presumably by the IRA. Almost immediately, the police were able to put on show more weapons, this time seized from two of the unionist paramilitary organisations. By now, they had taken quite a haul of guns and ammunition out of circulation, to the delight of the local population and Westminster. The Chairman of the Decommissioning Body was forced to admit that the police had suddenly been able to put more terrorist weapons beyond further use, in a matter of days, than they had been able to in years.

Ballistic tests soon proved that the Commanders of the Londonderry and Belfast Brigades of the IRA had both been killed by weapons previously used by members of the UVF some years before. The murderers who had used them then had recently been released early from prison under the amnesty.

By now, tensions were running high, and the Army had twice been called in to support the police in containing angry confrontations along the sectarian divide. The police, with Army support, had mounted successful raids on two major arms dumps, one Nationalist and the other Unionist. There were more sectarian murders, with high-ranking casualties on both sides, although neither side really understood what was going on. Both suddenly realised that they were being quietly and efficiently disarmed, and that their leadership was being whittled away. Certainly, it was the police, with Army help, who were somehow finding arms dumps, even quite small ones, and stripping them bare. But neither side nor the public believed the police could be responsible for the seemingly systematic assassination of the top terrorists—that had to be tit-for-tat, like the bad old days.

If anything, the IRA leadership, or what there was left of it, was less worried than the Unionist para-militaries. For a start, they had much more of everything, and had a new, very large consignment of weaponry on the way. They had, also, to avoid further arrests as much as anything, organised the collection of as much as they could of the arms and ammunition being held in private houses and drinking clubs. They were understandably furious when the removal van was stopped on the border, the driver and his mate arrested, and the whole lot, carefully hidden though it was in crates, wardrobes, mattresses, fridges and other items of household furniture, taken away before it got anywhere near Cashel.

***

By now, Major Bill Clayton and his team, ably supported by Lieutenant Commander Nick Marsden and his SAS colleagues scattered around the Province, were working flat out. They had beds in the office, and most meals, if you could call them that, were delivered from the canteen and eaten in snatches, having mostly gone cold. They had spent considerable time and effort in planning, and now needed every bit of energy to keep track of events as they unfolded. It would be only too easy now for someone to slip through the net.

"Those weapons you borrowed from the police are proving valuable, aren't they?" commented Marsden.

"I knew they would," replied Clayton. "That's why I wanted them."

"Talking of weapons, the new IRA arms consignment left Libya on schedule," reported Marsden, "and I've arranged for it to be met in international waters in two days' time."

"Good," said Clayton. "And what about the UVF Quartermaster, Connor Keenan and his wife? They are supposed to be leaving for their holiday in Greece tonight, and there's no way now we can stop them."

"All sorted," smiled Marsden. "There happens to be a County Class Frigate on a courtesy visit in Piraeus, and she also happens to have a small SBS unit on board for training. I've organised quite a good little exercise for them. Keenan will disappear. How's your chum getting on at the Bank?"

"Last I heard making good progress, and almost ready to close a few accounts for us. The US Federal Reserve is ready to move when we say the word, so we should be able to shut down a large part of the IRA operation fairly soon. We'll try our luck on a couple of small ones first, though, just to make sure this guy's really on the ball and knows what he's doing."

"I wish I knew how he's doing it," said Marsden. "With my mortgage, I could do with that sort of knowledge."

"You've got to be a real wizard to crack bank security encryption codes, and that's after you've hacked into their computers without leaving any trace of who you are or where you are. The 4758 crypto-processor the banks use was thought to be impregnable until he came along, and they weren't amused when he got into it. The military uses it too, as it happens. The damn thing took ten years to develop, too."

"Perhaps I'll offer your man a job after you've finished with him. By the way, since you've insisted that I don't go down to the fireworks in Cashel, I've decided to send 'The Cat' instead."

Clayton suddenly looked concerned.

"Is that wise?" he asked.

"Perfectly safe, so don't worry. Done plenty of Close Target Reconnaissance work before, and only used two of the legendry nine lives. Both those went in Iraq."

"I know The Cat is legendry within the SAS, after what happened in Iraq. Escaping captivity with those injuries, and then making it back to our own lines took more guts than most people could have mustered, and I also know that it was rare—almost unique—for the Regiment to keep someone on its books who is no longer fit for combat. But I'm still not sure this is a wise decision."

"Look," said Marsden, "combat training within the Regiment is one thing, but now it's high time The Cat got away from behind a desk and did something practical again. It doesn't do SAS people much good, shoving paper around, and a CTR will make a break. I can tell you, if you don't already know, that in spite of all the injuries inflicted during capture, The Cat is perfectly fit enough for a job like this, and well able to spend a few days in a ditch without being discovered, if that's what's necessary. I'll do the briefing myself, if you'd prefer."

"Thanks," said Bill Clayton. "I'd rather you did. But I still don't like the idea."

"Good. That's agreed then."

***

Father Sean Doyle was sitting quietly in his lodgings, working on the sermon for next Sunday. His housekeeper had only just cleared the tea things, when the phone rang. It was Andy Murphy.

"Is that you, Father?" enquired Andy.

"It is indeed, Andy," replied Fr Doyle. "How can I be helping you this fine afternoon?"

"You will have heard about Martin, Father?" asked Murphy. McFosters was one of Doyle's more important and influential parishioners. And he'd disappeared.

"Indeed I have," replied Doyle. "Is there any news of the man?"

"None at all, Father. It's all very strange."

"Let's pray he'll turn up unharmed," replied Fr. Doyle. "I'm sure the good Lord will look after the man."

"The reason I'm ringing," went on Murphy, "is to tell you that someone seems to be looking after our funds, Father. Looking after them rather too well, if you ask me."

Doyle sat forward. "What is it you're saying, Andy?" he asked.

"I'm saying that someone seems to have their hand in our till, Father," replied Murphy, "And what with you being our Treasurer and all, I thought I'd see what you knew about it."

"This is all news to me, Andy. Tell me what you've heard."

Andy Murphy was McFosters' chief of staff. What he didn't know about what was going on within Sinn Fein and the IRA wasn't usually worth knowing. Except that they left Fr. Doyle to run the organisations' finances, and had done so for years. Having a well-loved and trusted parish priest as IRA Treasurer had always seemed a brilliant idea. Nobody would ever suspect Sean Doyle of any involvement whatsoever.

"Before he went to the airport," reported Murphy, "Martin told me that there had been some problem with the Manhattan State Bank account, and he asked me to do a bit of probing while he was away."

"I wonder why he didn't ask me," pondered Doyle. "I'll check on it right away."

"There's nothing to check on," said Murphy. "As far as I can discover, the account has been closed and the money has gone. Every last penny of it."

"But that's not possible. Surely to God Martin didn't empty it himself before he disappeared?"

"It would explain his disappearance, I suppose, but could he have done it without you knowing, Father?"

"Well, yes, I suppose he could. He had access to the account, as I do."

"So you could have done it yourself?"

Doyle laughed.

"I know this is a serious problem, Andy my boy, but what would a man of the cloth like me be doing with a million quid or so? Now be reasonable. There has to be a better explanation. Martin wouldn't do a thing like that, either, any more than you or I. Leave me to have a word with the Bank, and I'll let you know what I can discover. And you be sure to let me know if you ever hear a word about dear brother Martin."

Father Sean Doyle was both puzzled and worried at the end of his conversation with Murphy. He wondered what to do for the best. Contacting Bill Clayton now would not be a good idea, he was sure of that.

***

Connor Keenan and his wife had a love of the Greek islands. They had been before, mostly to the larger and more popular ones, but this time they had gone to great lengths to find a smaller, quieter place. They had decided on Angistri, a tiny island not that far from Aegina, sparsely inhabited, but with a couple of good beaches and apparently comfortable apartments. None of the big tour operators had even heard of it, so they booked their own flight, and dealt direct with the English-speaking Greek owners of the apartment, who had arranged for them to be met on the quayside in Piraeus and ferried to the island.

Sure enough, they soon spotted a well-tanned young man wandering about with their name on a piece of cardboard held above his head. He spoke good English—indeed they discovered that he was English, but had lived in and around the Greek islands for years. He escorted them to a very sleek, fast-looking launch tied up some way from the main ferry terminal, took their bags, and helped them aboard.

"This thing's quite fast," he said, "so we shan't be long getting to Angistri. Once we're in clear water out of the harbour, we can get a move on a bit."

He was obviously an expert seaman, and knew his way round the busy harbour like the back of his hand. Soon, they were in open water, and he opened up the throttles of the twin outboard motors, until the bows lifted high out of the water.

"Now," he said, "come below, and start your holiday in style."

He led them into the tiny cabin, sat them down, and opened a bottle of ice-cool champagne.

"Make yourselves at home," he invited them. "I won't join you, if you don't mind—driving, and all that," he joked. "But you've got half an hour or so to see that off before we get to Angistri. I'll let you know when we are within sight of the island."

With that, he went back up into the cockpit. That was the last they saw of him. They were looking forward, and didn't see him as he slid expertly backwards over the side, or see him being equally expertly picked up by a fast moving Zodiac inflatable, which cut a huge semi-circle of white water through the blue sea as it headed back towards *HMS Cornwall*, anchored off Piraeus. The launch sped on, straight as a dye, out to the open sea. Nobody actually saw the explosion, although plenty heard it. When the first small boat arrived at the scene, there was nothing left of the launch or its passengers, except a few pieces of floating timber, and a huge pall of smoke.

***

Sergeant Catherine Wilson was looking tired, thought Major Clayton. Not surprising, really, bearing in mind the hours they were all working. But somehow, she looked, well, more than tired. Almost as if she had been crying, although, of course, he knew sergeants didn't do that.

Nevertheless, he called her into his office when Marsden and Foley were both out.

"Shut the door," he said, "and take the weight off your feet." He motioned her towards a chair. She frowned. "You look more than usually tired," he said, "and I just wanted to make sure everything was all right." Even he thought that he sounded rather more than usually formal, and a bit stuffy.

He coughed, awkwardly, and tried again. "Probably none of my business, but if anything's wrong and I can help, you only have to say." He hoped that explained everything.

"I'm quite all right, really," she said. "Kind of you to ask though, sir."

"There's no need to call me 'sir' at the moment. This is informal—private, if you like." He felt awkward again. "It's just that I didn't think you looked quite yourself. A bit upset about something, perhaps."

"I'm quite all right, really," she said again.

"Well, I just wanted you to know," he blustered on, "that in spite of everything that's going on, I can quite easily arrange for you to have a spot of leave, if that helps. If your mother's ill, or something."

"That's kind of you," said Wilson, "but I don't need any leave. I'll be all right in a day or so."

"Ah!" said Bill Clayton, "so there is something bothering you then." He tried not to sound triumphant. "You're not ill or anything, I hope."

"No, no. I'm really quite all right," she replied. "It's just, well, I may as well tell you. You'll probably find out anyway. It's just, well, your friend James Anchor."

"Ah!" said Bill Clayton again. "You've been seeing him a bit lately, he tells me."

"Just a few times."

"So what's happened?"

"Well, I thought we were getting along quite well, and he's a nice man. I quite liked him." Her eyes went a bit misty, and Bill could tell she was fighting back tears.

"Go on."

"So I was a bit surprised—upset, I suppose—when he suddenly announced that he wouldn't be seeing me again."

"Ah!" said Bill for the third time.

"He said he was going away for a few weeks."

"Not been well lately, I heard," said Bill. For all his strengths, he was not a good liar. "Sick leave, isn't it?"

"Maybe it is; maybe it isn't," replied Catherine Wilson. "The fact is he said there was someone else he'd been seeing as well. That's what upset me a bit." Misty eyes again.

"You didn't know," said Bill. A statement, rather than a question.

"Did you know?" she asked.

"Well, actually, yes, I did. Not that he told me, or anything, you understand, and I haven't been prying. It's just that it's my job to know what's going on, that's all. A woman in the Cabinet Office, I think."

"Oh," she said quietly. "Now I feel a bit of a fool as well."

"Not at all; not at all," he protested. "Fact is, I rather wanted to tell you, but, well, I somehow couldn't bring myself to, if you must know. I had a feeling it would make you unhappy, and I didn't want to be responsible for doing that."

"And he's not really ill either, is he?" she said. Again, rather more of a statement than a question.

"Well, actually no, he isn't," said Bill. "And he's not going away on sick leave, either."

"Off somewhere with his girlfriend, I suppose," she said.

"Oh, no. Not that, either. In fact, she won't be seeing anything of him for weeks—perhaps months—and won't even know where he is. He's been acting at being ill, and sick leave is his cover," explained Clayton.

"Cover for what, may I ask."

"You may ask," replied Bill. "And this time I'll tell you. There's a political dimension to our Operation Honolulu, which is brought into play if we are successful."

"Which we are being," she said.

"Very much so. And James Anchor has a major role to play in planning the political scenario."

"So where's he going?" Wilson asked.

"By a stroke of rare American genius, to Honolulu itself," he explained. "He and many others will be more or less quarantined on the huge USAF air base at Hickham until their planning is complete. Could be weeks, or even months."

"Thank you for telling me," responded Catherine Wilson. "I almost feel better already."

"Nice chap though he is," said Bill Clayton, feeling a bit red round the gills, "I'm personally rather glad you won't be seeing him again, if I may say so."

Before she could ask 'why', they heard a door slam down the corridor.

"Twinkle-toes is back," joked Clayton, relieved.

Catherine Wilson grinned.

"But we do need to talk again soon," continued Clayton. "After this show is all over, I think we should both move out of Northern Ireland. I'm sure we'll have had enough of it, by then—I know I shall—and it may not be altogether safe to hang around for too long. You're about due a posting, anyway, and I certainly am. Personally, I wouldn't mind the Joint Services Signals Unit in Cyprus. The Middle East being what it is these days, it's a very interesting place to be. And not a bad part of the world. Ayios Nikolaos is in the Troodos Mountains—good skiing, and good beaches not far away. Mercury Barracks themselves aren't bad, either. Why don't you think about somewhere like that? We're a good team, and I could probably fix it if you felt like joining me out there."

"It would certainly be nice to get into some good weather for a change," said Wilson.

"Well, give it some thought," said Clayton. "Brian Foley already knows he's off to Bosnia next, so I don't need to worry about his future. Just ours."

Wilson grinned again, and gave him an old fashioned look. Clayton realised what he had said, just as Marsden burst in.

"Not interrupting anything, I hope," he said. "I've been tearing around all over the shop while you two have been sitting here relaxing!"

"As a matter of fact, we have been discussing matters of state, and what happens when all this is over," explained Clayton. "Postings, and things. But we've just about finished now, thanks!"

"Good," said Marsden. "You should get out of the office more, both of you!" he joked.

"Is that all, sir?" Wilson asked Clayton.

"It'll do for now," replied Clayton. "The Commander is obviously busting to tell me about his day, so I'll talk to you again tomorrow."

"Very good, sir." Wilson turned, and left the room.

"Good looking girl, for a sergeant," said Marsden.

***

Alistair Vaughan rang.

"Our man Farlow," he announced, "is making good progress, thanks to your list, and he's ready to shut down three or four accounts."

"Which ones?" asked Bill Clayton.

"Numbers one, three and four on your list. He's sitting here waiting for the OK."

Bill thought for a moment.

"What about number two on the list?"

"Says he should be able to get into that tomorrow. After that, he thinks the rest will be relatively easy."

"Do it then," ordered Clayton. "And number two on the list as soon as he's ready." He hung up.

Marsden looked across.

"Money is about to move," Bill told him. "So I need to get in touch with

Father Sean Doyle in the Falls Road."

"What the devil for?" asked Nick Marsden.

"He's one of mine, that's why," replied Clayton. "Ex-Army Padré. Been IRA Treasurer for four years now."

"I'll be damned!" exclaimed Marsden.

"That's how I got my list of accounts," explained Clayton. "He could have given me a lot more too, and sent several of his parishioners to jail for life, except that he's as straight as a dye so far as the church is concerned. He's made it a point of principle never to pass on anything he's heard in the confessional."

"Pity about that, but good for him in a way," said Marsden. "But he could be at risk now anyway, if he has access to cash which is fast disappearing."

"Exactly."

Major Bill Clayton grabbed the phone, and spoke urgently to the Head of Special Branch.

***

The Cat sat in the ditch.

For two days and two nights. But this would be the last. Then a hot shower and a cold beer. Seamus O'Hara and his two assistant Quartermasters were on their way, the US nuclear submarine *September Eleven*, with her armoury of cruise missiles, was in position, and The Cat had a clear view of the target, within laser range. Whether it was safe to be that close, only time would tell. There wasn't a lot of shelter to be had under a hedge, and there were a hundred tons or so of Semtex due to be blown up at any time at all, as well as all the rest of the stuff in the arms dump. A flack jacket would have to do. It's all there was.

The talks at Camp David had, so it was reported, been long and difficult, but eventually successful. The Taoiseach was on side, persuaded eventually by the progress that had already been made in dealing with the terrorists in the North, and by the promise of future economic development and stability which being linked to the American economy, as well as to Europe, were bound to bring to a unified Ireland.

Or something like that. From The Cat's point of view, the important thing was that the Irish government had agreed to this little operation, and arranged for their version of Special Branch, dressed up as workmen, to close the only public road within miles. But they didn't know about The Cat, or how the dump was going to be hit. At least this time, recovery would be easy, too. No long, hard slog across the desert. The rendezvous was only about four miles away, and then a Navy Lynx helicopter ride back to base. The Cat had even been told the name of the pilot—Chief Petty Officer Sid Rudkin.

It was late afternoon when the three men eventually appeared. The guard on the gate let them in after a bit of a chat, and they parked their Range Rover a short distance further on, near the entrance. As soon as they were inside, The Cat broke radio silence.

"The targets have merged," was the agreed signal. There was no acknowledgement.

"Missile launched," came the message moments later from the submerged submarine.

The Cat illuminated the target with the laser guidance system, and passed the message, "target lit."

The cruise missile was the very latest GBU-28 'bunker buster', fitted with the BLU-113 warhead, and a GPS guidance system that was quite capable of hitting the dump on its own. The laser was added insurance. There would only be one chance, and this was it.

The Cat heard the message, direct from the US submarine, "Time to target, one minute forty seconds." The Cat crouched as flat as humanly possible while keeping the target illuminated and rock steady within the laser sights.

"Sixty seconds."

"Thirty seconds."

There were two simultaneous explosions, The Cat recalled afterwards. One, as the missile blew a hole on impact through the six feet of steel-reinforced concrete, and another, a mille-second later, as the warhead burst through the breach and exploded deep within the dump, ripping it apart. What followed defied description, with missiles, shells and bullets ricocheting across the countryside, and debris showering down on the motionless figure of The Cat as the munitions in the dump continued to detonate for several minutes after impact.

The IRA concluded, as it had been hoped they would, that Seamus or one of his colleagues must have had a fag going.

Stupid bastard. Couldn't have been anything else but an own goal, could it?

***

That same night, far out at sea off the west coast of Cornwall, the 2,000-ton, ocean going, Liberian registered, rusting tramp ship *Hercules* was boarded. There was a mixed crew on board of Libyans, Irishmen and Chinese. They took the word of the boarding party that they were UK Customs and Excise, searching for drugs. If that was all, they wouldn't find any. The manifest said they were carrying only timber and molasses. If they were honest, it wasn't much of a search, either, and the boarding party left within half an hour or so, apparently content.

As the men sped off in their launch back towards the Coastguard cutter, a dim silhouette on the horizon, the Irishmen treated themselves to a large glass of Bushmills whiskey each.

"That was close," said one. "Thank the sweet Jesus it was only drugs they were after."

"And obviously not a tip-off either, else they'd have torn the ship apart," said another.

"Then we'd all have been sunk!" joked a third.

They were still laughing and drinking Bushmills half an hour later, when the sabotaged vessel was ripped from stem to stern by the explosive charges the SBS team had left behind during their 'search'. They watched through night-vision binoculars with professional satisfaction, and passed a "mission accomplished" message to Lieutenant Commander Nick Marsden, listening out on his 'crystal set' in Bill Clayton's office.

***

Quite how the media got hold of the document, nobody quite knew. It was a hand-written list of the names and positions of all the top terrorists on both sides of the conflict in Northern Ireland, and quite a few politicians as well who were known to have close links with the terrorist organisations on one side or the other.

Many of the names, like McFosters, and Keenan, and O'Hara, had been roughly crossed off in pencil.

But copies of it appeared, as if by magic, simultaneously in Washington, New York, London, Belfast, Dublin and Brussels. Nobody worked out where it had come from, because nobody recognised the handwriting of Sergeant Catherine Wilson. The press went wild, and so did many of those not yet crossed out on the list when it was published. They scattered to the four corners, like chaff in the wind, just as Bill Clayton had hoped.

At a stroke, Ireland was virtually free of terrorists. The punishment shootings and the beatings stopped, and the extortion rackets dried up, and no one went round any more collecting protection money. Quite suddenly, life was taking on an air of normality not familiar to many of the population.

Most of the surviving names on the list were small fry, fleeing for their life, and of no great interest to Clayton and his team. The hard men of the leadership had gone, or else their whereabouts was known. Those who mattered, who still might pose a threat, could be picked off at leisure. Their movements could be monitored. Half a dozen of them had gone to London, and they worried Bill Clayton. He was sure they had gone to join forces with an existing small 'sleeper' unit of the real IRA, somewhere in the capital. For some reason, though, the Yard's special branch and anti-terrorist squad hadn't been able to track them down.

So it was no real surprise, although a considerable embarrassment, when, at two in the morning a few days later, four shadowy figures appeared in the pedestrian precinct at Trafalgar Square. There were not a lot of people about to see them, as they jogged towards the foot of Nelson's Column. Since the precinct had been created, most passengers for the night buses boarded them in The Strand, outside the Armed Services Careers Office as it happened, rather than on the Square itself, outside the National Gallery, which is where the buses used to stop.

The men made their way to the back of the Lions at each corner of the Column, and sat to get their breath, admiring the view. As if in unison, they rose to their feet, and trotted off to the far corners of the Square. Only the most observant would have noticed that their backpacks had been left behind. The four simultaneous explosions put hundreds of sleeping pigeons to flight. The bronze lions fragmented, just as the Empire had done, only much more swiftly. Nelson's Column, its lower section blown away, settled gently on its foundations before the top 160 feet toppled towards Whitehall in a final, defiant gesture towards the British government.

The shattered effigy of Nelson came to rest with his blind eye turned towards the Old Admiralty, a habit he had developed during his distinguished career.

***

Lieutenant Commander Nick Marsden and Major Bill Clayton were having a quick conference in Claytons' office, to assess progress so far and plan future actions.

Captain Brian Foley stuck his head round the door. "Sorry to interrupt, "he said. "News, just in."

"I thought you'd gone to Bosnia," joked Marsden.

"Not yet," replied Foley. "You're not getting rid of me that soon."

"So what's the news?" asked Clayton.

"It's Andy Murphy, McFosters' chief of staff," replied the Captain.

"What about him?" asked the Major.

"Well, I suppose we shouldn't laugh," replied Foley, "but they seem to have found his body in a spare drawer in the mortuary at the Royal Victoria Hospital!"

"What an extraordinary thing," said Marsden, with a grin. "Who on earth could have put him in there, I wonder?"

Foley and Clayton looked at him. They would miss him when he went back to Hereford.

***

It took Jim Farlow just over three weeks to complete his task, working long hours, seven days a week. It suited his new employers, and it certainly suited him, as it kept him out of Pentonville, where he was far from comfortable.

On his last day, there was inevitably a mountain of paperwork to be done, forms to sign and so on, to secure his early release, but eventually they gave him twenty quid, and led him out of the prison and into freedom. Both Alistair Vaughan and Philip Walton were there to see him go.

Jim took a deep breath of fresh air, as if it was somehow different from that inside.

"Where will you go now?" asked Walton.

"Home, I suppose," replied Farlow, as if he hadn't really thought about it. "I'd better ring my Mum from somewhere, I suppose."

"What I suggest," said Vaughan helpfully, "is that you stroll up the road to the tube station—it's only about five minutes from here. You can get the Piccadilly Line to Kings Cross, and change there to the Northern Line for Highgate. Hundreds of phone boxes at Kings Cross, too."

"I think I'll do that," said Farlow, and set off with his black sack over his shoulder, in something of a daze. He couldn't believe he was free at last to do what he liked again, to go where he liked, when he liked.

He didn't see Vaughan nod towards the two men across the street, or notice them follow him.

He went down the lift at Caledonian Road station, and turned left on to the westbound platform. The indicator said, - "1 Heathrow 3 mins." There was neat little icon of an aeroplane next to 'Heathrow'. Not long to wait. He ambled down the platform towards the back of the train. It was rush hour and already quite crowded, but he remembered that the train would be less full at the back. He looked at the adverts across the track, something he hadn't seen for four years. Insurance companies, new films, French wine, Eurostar, and airlines offering cheap fares. Jim thought he would take advantage of those, as soon as he was settled back home. He felt the breeze on his face as the train approached, and saw its lights reflect off the silver ribbons of rail before he saw the train itself speeding round the gentle curve into the station.

As the train screamed to an emergency stop, the two men slid away unnoticed onto the other platform and an eastbound train.

A lot of people were going to miss their planes that evening. And Jim would never take one anywhere, cheap or not.

***

They were in the Prime Minister's office. Tony Weaver himself, Sir Robin Algar, Andrew Groves and Major Bill Clayton.

It was evident now that both the Nationalist and the Unionist terror groups had decided that they were the victims of treachery from within their own ranks, reported Bill Clayton. There was a lot they couldn't explain, but they had initially concluded that, on the one hand, McFosters had disappeared and made off with the IRA's funds, while Keenan had done the same with the Unionist bankroll. But then, as more and more funds disappeared and more and more accounts were emptied and closed, including some holding quite small amounts, this theory became less and less tenable. There seemed no way to stem the flow, and what leadership there was left had eventually panicked.

"I am most grateful to you, Mr. Groves, for all you did to help my little list get into the hands of the media round the world," said Clayton. "It had an electrifying and immediate effect, and more or less completed the job of closing down terrorist activity in the Province."

"I agree," said the Prime Minister. "Throughout this whole affair, Andrew's handling of the media, and his ability to co-ordinate with colleagues, has been exemplary, and played a major role in the success of Operation Honolulu. Or at least the first stage of it. There is now a great deal to be done on the political front in the months and years ahead."

The talks at Camp David had been by no means easy, reported Weaver, but at least the Taoiseach was now totally committed to the unification of Ireland under the American flag, and all sides had begun working together within the constitutional committee to make that happen smoothly and fairly, and the team at Hickham USAF base were reported to be making encouraging progress.

"Things have gone so well, in fact, that the two presidents and I have agreed to make a co-ordinated public statement next week about what has so far happened to return the Province to something like normality, and what we plan for the future. Of course it will need careful drafting, and you will all be consulted," promised the Prime Minister. "But we need to keep the initiative, we think, and put our case on the public record in our terms, rather than having to respond to leaks and speculation later. There's a good deal of good news to put across, and we need to do that to get public opinion on our side."

Groves and Algar nodded, sagely.

"But it hasn't all been good news, I'm afraid," said Clayton. "I suppose in an operation like this there were bound to be failures and casualties."

"You mean the Trafalgar Square bomb?" asked Groves.

"No, not just that," responded Clayton. "The IRA treasurer was found floating face down in Strangford Loch at the end of last week, for example."

"So why was that bad news?" asked Robin Algar. "He was obviously the prime suspect, after McFosters, as the one getting his hands in the till, and an obvious target."

"Precisely," responded Clayton. "But he was one of my best men."

They looked shocked.

"An ex-Army Padré, and Parish priest in the Falls Road area. I couldn't pull him out in time to save him," said a grim-faced Clayton.

"I agree," said the Cabinet Secretary. "That is bad news. I'm sorry. He was obviously a very brave man."

"And Edward Benbow has been shot and killed," continued Clayton.

"And who might he be?" asked Tony Weaver.

"My uncle," replied Clayton. "Lived in Fittleworth, in Sussex, and was shot by two men on a motorcycle as he walked across the bridge over the River Rother, on his way home."

"This is obviously sad from your point of view, but is it in any way significant?" asked the Prime Minister.

"I believe it is—very," replied Clayton. "That list of bank accounts I gave you, Prime Minister, which you later passed on to Sir Robin, was in an old envelope addressed to my uncle. Where is it now?"

The Prime Minister looked across to Sir Robin Algar. The Cabinet Secretary looked ashen faced.

"I handed it, still containing the list, to Alistair Vaughan," he said.

Chapter Twelve
ONLY THE MOST TRUSTWORTHY

Major William Jefferson Clayton was a mild mannered man. He rarely lost his temper, and was rarely cross. But when he was cross, people knew about it.

He stormed into his office on his return from Downing Street, without pausing to say 'afternoon, chaps' as he normally did, spun his peaked cap towards the hat-stand as he always did, and missed, which he never did. To crown it all, he slammed his office door behind him. Well, that door hadn't been shut for … well, weeks if not months.

Captain Brian Foley and Sergeant Catherine Wilson, who had stood up when he crossed the outer office, sat down again.

They looked and each other in disbelief.

"Is he cross, or something?" asked Foley.

"Not exactly his usual bright self, is he?" responded the chief clerk.

They looked towards the closed door.

"Do you think we should do something?" asked Foley.

"I'll put the kettle on," replied Wilson, helpfully. "And you can take the tea in when it's brewed."

"No thanks. That's a woman's job."

"I hope you're not going to pull rank, sir, at a time like this."

"Oh, no! Of course not," replied Foley. "It's just that a woman's touch is probably what's called for 'at a time like this' in my view. So you can take the tea in to him."

"You *are* pulling rank," said Wilson.

"I'll have a cup, too, while you're about it," said Foley, as if to end the discussion.

"Do you think the visitors' china is called for 'at a time like this'?" asked Catherine Wilson. "Or would his old mug make him feel more at home?"

"I shouldn't think he'd even notice, or care."

"Mug, then."

"On the other hand," said Foley, "it might be a good idea to leave him alone for a bit, y'know. Shutting the door like that might be a sign."

They looked towards the door again. Foley edged towards it, and cocked an ear.

"Not a sound," he said. "He's not on the phone or anything."

"At least he's not throwing things about."

"Perhaps we should wait a bit, to see what happens," decided Foley.

"And what if nothing does?" asked Wilson.

"Then you can take the tea in," said Foley.

They agreed to wait, and didn't have to wait long.

"I'm going to the toy hospital," announced Clayton as he emerged, grabbing his hat from the hook where Foley had put it.

"But it's only Thursday," ventured Sergeant Wilson, immediately wishing she hadn't.

"If the phone rings, I'm out," said Clayton, and went out.

Foley and Wilson looked at one another again, still in disbelief. Nothing like this had ever happened before.

"I'll make the tea anyway," said Wilson. "In case he comes back soon. I can't believe this will last."

"And what if it does, and he doesn't?" asked the Captain.

"Then I'll have to go and get him," said the Sergeant. "A woman's touch is probably what's called for at a time like this."

***

Bill Clayton wanted time to think, and he always did that best on his own, in the garage full of old toys.

He was worried.

There were things going on which he hadn't expected and didn't understand. Not usual, that. He usually knew what was happening and why, and he wasn't often taken by surprise by the turn of events, either. But he was now. Could he be losing his touch? Surely not. But he needed to understand what was going on, or he couldn't decide what to do about it. He needed to think. He needed to get the facts sorted into some sort of order, if there was one.

It was possible that it all started with his poor, dear wife. Only been married a few months, they had, and almost immediately went to Northern Ireland for Bill to take up his present posting. She wasn't used to the military life, or to the security situation in the Province, and hadn't got used to the idea that Bill was in a high-risk job. She'd been shopping in Lisburn, as if she was at home in her cosy Hampshire home of Farnham. Protestant Lisburn in County Down was usual pretty safe, but you still needed to be careful and be aware. Dorothy obviously wasn't. It must have been while she was in the supermarket that someone had planted the bomb, under their car parked at the back. At least she didn't suffer. Killed instantly, thank God. They never did discover who did it, but Bill had always secretly and guiltily believed that he was the real target. They had recognised the car. On the other hand, it could just have been a warning for him to back off. In the end, it had had just the opposite effect.

But now his uncle. First his wife, and now his uncle. Were the two events related, or was it just a coincidence after all this time? A settling of old scores, perhaps, and not connected to the current operation at all. Not many people even knew he had an uncle. There certainly weren't many outside his small family circle. The Prime Minister, the Cabinet Secretary, Alistair Vaughan—that was about it, really. It must be a coincidence. None of them ever met his wife, or knew anything about him when he was posted to Northern Ireland. Come to think of it, though, he did know Alistair before his posting to Belfast, but he was a Commander at Scotland Yard even then. Surely he could be trusted. What had the Prime Minister said? "Only people who were totally trustworthy must be told." But that had included Vaughan. He had been brought into the loop by the Cabinet Secretary, no less. Could the Cabinet Secretary himself be trusted? It was he, of course, who had given Vaughan his uncle's old envelope, with the list of bank accounts in it. Had Vaughan then passed it on to someone else?

Who else knew? Closer to home, both Captain Foley and Sergeant Wilson could have seen the envelope and noted the name and address. And what about the mysterious Commander Marsden, who had suddenly appeared on the scene out of nowhere? He had been a pillar of strength through this operation, like the rest of the team. Surely he was absolutely trustworthy. But would any of them who had seen the envelope have known that Edward Benbow was his uncle? Had he mentioned it? He didn't remember. If someone was trying to get at him through his family, perhaps he should warn his father to take more care? Would he be next?

Then there was the death of Sean Doyle. He felt bad about that—really bad. If he'd been quicker off the mark, Sean might still be alive today. He just hoped he hadn't suffered too much at the hands of his IRA masters and captors. He was pretty sure he wouldn't have talked, whatever they did. He was thoroughly trained by the Army to be able to resist that sort of thing, but you never could be sure. Everyone had a limit to what they could take. But Bill Clayton had a nagging un-ease about the whole thing. Something wasn't right, somehow. The more he thought about it, the odder he thought the whole thing was. It just wasn't like the IRA to dump people into Strangford Loch, or anywhere else come to that, when they had finished with them. Their methods of disposal were usually much more thorough than that. There was usually no trace left at all—no bodies for the mortuary, no clues, no forensic evidence, nothing. No bodies, no postmortems—exactly the policy that had been adopted during Op. Honolulu. And yet there was poor old Sean, floating face down in the loch. He must find out what the result was of the postmortem. Find out how much the ex-Army padré might have suffered and how much he might have been tempted, after all, to talk, to put an end to it all.

He ought to get back to the office, really. There were things he had to do; people he had to talk to.

And yet, suddenly, Bill Clayton didn't know whom he could trust anymore, or who he dared talk to about all this.

There was a soft knock on the partially open door, and Sergeant Wilson peered in. It was her turn to ask the question now.

"Are you all right, sir? I've brought a hot cup of tea, if you'd like it."

"That's kind of you, thanks. And I'm fine. Just worried about a couple of things that I wanted to try to get my mind round. A cuppa will help no end. Come in and shut the door," he said.

"Is that wise?" she asked. "Shutting the door, I mean. People might talk."

"Frankly, I don't care," replied Clayton. "But I suppose you could do without gossip."

She went over with the tea, and shut the door behind her.

"I was just thinking," said Clayton, "that I should get back to the office, if only to apologise to you and Captain Foley. I'm sorry if I acted a bit cross, but I was."

"We did wonder."

"I hope I wasn't too rude. I would hate to think that I'd upset you in any way." Clayton realised that he wasn't very good at this sort of thing. "I hope you'll forgive me, Catherine."

He hadn't called her that before.

"Don't be silly, sir. No offence was taken at all, although we were surprised that you were so upset. We haven't seen you in a mood like that before."

"Was it that bad?" Bill Clayton was becoming even more embarrassed.

"It was funny, really. You shut the office door, which you haven't done for simply ages, and your hat missed the peg. We knew something must be wrong." Catherine Wilson grinned.

"To be honest, I suddenly felt I wasn't in control of events any more. Things have happened which I don't understand and wasn't expecting, and which I can't yet explain."

"I'll help if I can," said Wilson, "and I know Captain Foley will as well if you want us to. But what exactly is the problem?"

"The problem is that I'm no longer sure who I can trust and who I can't." said Clayton. "And I desperately need to talk this through with someone, just to get my thoughts in order, but the fact is there could just be a traitor at work within the small team involved in Op. Honolulu. I'm not saying there is, but there could be, and until I know for sure, one way or the other, I can no longer be sure who to confide in."

"This sounds quite appalling," said a shocked Wilson. "There must be someone in authority you can talk to."

"I don't yet need anyone in authority, as you put it, although eventually I shall. At the moment, I can only think of the Prime Minister as being beyond suspicion, but I shall need to know more before I go to him. No. At the moment, I just need someone intelligent who can listen, and help me sort out the facts."

"How about Commander Marsden?" queried the Sergeant.

"I can't even be sure of him, at the moment," replied Clayton. "Until I know more, I can't be sure of anyone."

"Not even me?" asked Wilson.

He looked at her, and his anguished expression softened. "Since you ask," he said, "and since there's no-one else about, I can tell you that I would trust you with my life—with anything and everything."

"Well, thank you," she said, simply. "So why don't you?"

He looked at her again, and sipped the now-cold mug of tea. He sighed.

"We'd better get back before Brian Foley comes to find out what's going on. Not that anything is, but I'm sure part of your task was to humour me back into the office."

"You're quite right, actually." Wilson grinned.

Clayton stood and stretched. "Let's go, then. But it would be nice to talk things through with you later, if you're not doing anything."

"Nothing," she replied. "Shall we meet up in the office after dinner?"

"If you're really doing nothing, why don't we meet before dinner?" suggested Clayton. "I know a quiet restaurant where we could grab a quick meal, and talk at the same time. We're unlikely to be seen by anyone from here, either."

"That would be really nice, if you're sure that's OK. I mean, I know we're not supposed to socialise, being different ranks and all that."

"What the hell! I'm happy to risk it if you are," said Clayton. "It would be a great pleasure to take you out, if I may. And I'd really like to talk to you, about all sorts of things; not just this."

"I'd really like that, too," she said. "I'm no traitor, either!"

"That's about the only thing I'm really sure of at the moment," said Clayton with a grin.

He suddenly felt a good deal better, and much happier. On the way back to the office, they arranged where and when to meet. Foley looked up as they got there.

"See?" he said to Sergeant Wilson, "I told you a woman's touch was what was needed at a time like this!"

"The mug of hot tea helped a bit, too," said Clayton. "Sorry I was a bit abrupt earlier on. I suppose I ought to see what's in the 'in' tray."

"Not a lot, actually, sir," said Wilson, the Sergeant Chief Clerk again. "A few memos, a couple of e-mails for you to look at and delete, and a letter marked 'personal'. Not handwriting I recognise, I'm afraid."

"That shouldn't take long then," said Bill Clayton, as he went into his office, leaving the door open this time. "Where's Commander Marsden, by the way?"

"Said something about exercising his horse, which I take it means that he's using the helicopter for something or other," replied Captain Foley.

"Nice to have my office to myself again."

Clayton settled as best he could, but he was still anxious about the recent turn of events. More than that, perhaps, he was excited about the prospect of a quiet evening out with Catherine Wilson. He was looking forward to that.

He was brought back to earth with a jolt when he opened the letter addressed to him personally.

It was from Father Sean Doyle.

It was short and cryptic, obviously hastily written a very short time before his death.

Clayton read it over and over again.

My dear Bill, it read. *I'm sure you know me well enough to recognise what is in my character and what isn't, in spite of what may be suggested. And I'm sure I know you well enough to be confident that you will spot a red herring when you see one. May the Good Lord bless you. Regards, Sean.*

The envelope contained a second scribbled note, almost more alarming than the first. But it would explain a few things, if it was accurate. He read that over and over again, too, even though it was only a few words. After a few moments' thought, he pushed the note into his pocket. He would keep that to himself for the time being, until he was sure whom he could share it with. But he at least now had something to go on, and a possible, if tenuous, link between all this and his uncle. He needed to know more, but would need time to work out how best to check this out.

Clayton stood slowly, patted his pocket, and went to the door.

"Come in, you two," he said.

Now what? they thought.

"Sit down, and listen to this. The letter I had is from Father Sean Doyle."

They both knew Doyle's background, and that he was—or had been—one of their best men. Clayton read the letter to them, twice.

"What on earth is that about?" asked Foley.

"There always seemed to me to be something odd about Sean's death," said Clayton. "It's one of the things I was trying to puzzle out earlier this afternoon. The odd thing about it in particular is that the IRA don't usually leave people who they have assassinated lying about, which is what we had assumed had happened to poor Sean. We assumed that they had decided it was he who was creaming off their funds, and that after they had tried to get him to talk, had killed him to put a stop to it or as punishment. This letter suggests that Sean somehow knew what was going to happen to him."

"It could also suggest," offered Sergeant Wilson, "that he committed suicide before they got to him. We need to know how he died."

"Then let's find out, quickly," said Clayton, reaching for the phone. "We need the results of the post mortem, and fast."

They sat there while he spoke to his contact at the Queen Victoria Hospital, where the postmortem had been carried out. He almost looked relieved at the end of the conversation, but immediately dialled again to speak to the Detective

Chief Superintendent in charge of the enquiry into Doyle's death.

At the end of it, he sat back and looked at them both.

"Well, I'll be damned," he said. "For the last few years, Sean has been risking his neck on our behalf, and so far as we know, he was never suspected as being anything other than a parish priest. Thanks to his exceptional bravery and total loyalty, he won't be now, either."

"Why, what happened?" asked Sergeant Wilson.

"You were right—it was suicide. There wasn't a mark on his body, so no torture, thank God. He was found full of barbiturates, which he took before swimming out to the middle of the Loch. That was obviously a deliberate attempt to avoid the attentions of the IRA, and the risk of being forced to give away his real role in life. But he didn't stop there. The police have found child pornography in his rooms and a computer full of downloaded material, mostly of recent origin. The police believe he was a paedophile, who was about to be uncovered. They are already appealing for possible victims to come forward."

"That letter makes absolute sense now," said Foley.

"That's one hell of a red herring he's laid, too," said Wilson. "Blackening his own character in such a vile way just to protect us and our Op. Honolulu."

"You'd better dig out his file for me, if you would," said Clayton. "I shall need to square this away with his poor parents, if they are still alive."

***

Catherine Wilson couldn't remember when she'd last felt like this.

It was a long time since someone she really wanted to be with had asked her out. And she really wanted to be with Bill Clayton.

His friend, James Anchor, had been nice, but somehow she never really felt comfortable with people who had been divorced. You only ever heard one side of the story, and there was always another. Anyway, they only went out a couple of times before he decided that whoever-it-was in the Cabinet Office was a better bet. But she had learnt a thing or two about Bill Clayton during idle chats over dinner, and the more she heard, the more she liked. She had always thought he was a nice man, anyway, but had never given a second thought to the possibility that they could, one day, become friends rather than just office colleagues. The Army didn't like officers mixing with NCOs, so that was the end of it, so far as she was concerned. But he was obviously not the least concerned about that, which made this evening's dinner an even more exciting prospect. And if he didn't care about gossip, why should she? He had far more to lose than she did. If the worse came to the worse, she could always leave the Army. The thought had crossed her mind more than once, anyway, especially since her time in Iraq. That had been a brutal experience, and she often wondered if she'd ever really get over it. The physical hurt had passed and the wounds had more or less healed, but she didn't think the mental anguish would ever leave her, unless and until she left the Army. She liked the military life for the company it gave her and the active life—that's why she had joined—but now it always reminded her of a quite horrid episode in her life which she would rather forget.

She looked at her scarred body as she dressed after her shower, and winced at the memory. She wondered if he'd mind, although she was jumping the gun a bit, and grinned. Wishful thinking! She still had a good figure, but the scars were not a pretty sight, and she would understand any man being put off by them.

It would probably never come to that, though. Certainly not tonight. Bill wasn't the sort of man to rush things, she thought.

She was intrigued to know what it was he so urgently needed to share with her—or anyone—about recent events. Although they still had a few odd ends to tie up, their part of the operation was more or less over, she had thought, while the emphasis swung towards the politics of it all. She knew that James Anchor was now in Hawaii as part of the planning for that phase, but frankly, politics didn't interest her too much.

Bill Clayton did, though, and she hoped there would be time for her to learn more about the man—and for him to learn more about her.

She didn't know the restaurant he had suggested, but she would find it all right. They had agreed to go independently—he in his old car, and she on her motorbike—and to meet there. He would book a table, although it was quiet he said, and probably wouldn't be crowded. Seemed a shame they would have to say goodnight in the car park, but it was probably for the best. What sort of parting would it be, she wondered? The excitement and anticipation was killing her! She shoved her long hair into a bun, struggled into her tight leathers, and grabbed her helmet. She would soon know.

Bill Clayton had left the Mess earlier than he really needed, although he knew his old VW would not be as quick as Catherine's Honda. But he couldn't hang around any longer. The suspense was killing him. He really wanted to get to know this girl, and the opportunity to do so had come about quite unexpectedly. He still couldn't believe that he had been brave enough to suggest meeting out, rather than in that bloody office, or that she had agreed so readily. That had to be a good sign.

He got there first, as he had planned. He was shown to the table, and would have ordered a drink, except that he suddenly realised he didn't know what she liked. He really didn't know anything much about Catherine, except what was on her file. And that didn't include her favourite tipple.

He didn't have to wait long for Catherine. Her face flushed from the wind, she handed the waiter her helmet, shook her long hair into place, and unzipped her leather jacket as she crossed the small restaurant towards him.

"Hope I'm not late," she greeted him.

"Bang on time," replied Bill. "I was a touch early—must have had the wind behind me for a change!"

He helped her into her seat at the table, as the waiter took her coat and hovered.

"I couldn't order a drink," said Bill, "because I haven't the slightest idea what you like. In fact I know very little about you at all, but hopefully that will all change this evening. How about some champagne, as this is our first evening out together?"

"That would be lovely, "she replied. "But we mustn't forget that we are both driving."

"Bring a bottle," he told the waiter. "I'm sure we could manage that between us. We shan't be hitting the road again for a long time yet, I hope."

They studied the menu and ordered their meal, although neither of them had much of an appetite, for some reason.

"Now!" said Bill. "Tell me all about yourself!"

"Certainly not," Catherine replied. "I want to hear all about you first! But you wanted to talk shop—that's really why we're here."

"No it isn't," he replied "We're here because I wanted to take you out and get to know you a lot better. But I do also need to unburden myself a bit at some time this evening."

"Work first," said Catherine. "Let's get that over, then we talk about more pleasant things."

"If you insist. But I hardly know where to start."

"The beginning is always a good place," said Catherine, philosophically.

So Bill Clayton started at the beginning. He told her about the death of his wife, which might or might not have been the beginning, and his fears that he was the real target. Then there was his uncle, and the old envelope of his.

"I remember seeing it," said Catherine. "It was in the safe for a bit."

"And the list of accounts inside was largely provided by Sean Doyle, as you know." said Bill. "So there's a sort of link between Edward Benbow and Sean Doyle, but is it a strong enough link to explain Uncle's murder?"

"Who else knew about the envelope and its contents?"

"The Prime Minister, the Cabinet Secretary, and Alistair Vaughan."

"The Bank of England man?"

"Right. Sir Robin Algar gave him the envelope and contents together. Vaughan was responsible for action to close the accounts."

"Using the convicted computer expert to do it."

"Right again, Catherine."

"Would he have seen the envelope as well, do you think?"

"Possible, I suppose. But one of the things I haven't yet been able to work out is why anyone would want to kill Edward Benbow."

The smoked salmon arrived.

When the waiter had gone, Catherine said, "Tell me about your uncle." If nothing else, it might give her a few clues about Bill's family background, and she really wanted to know more about him.

"An interesting and complex man, my Uncle Edward," said Bill Clayton. "My father was in the Army—retired as a general some years ago. His sister married Edward Benbow, who was also in the Army, although not the sort of Army my father had much time for. Benbow was in the Royal Artillery, rather than a teeth-arm infantry battalion. So far as my father was concerned, people in anything other than that were a different and inferior breed from those in the front line battalions. Which is why I'm a bit of a disappointment to him!

"But Uncle Edward did well. He retired as a major, and went into the MOD—the final blow to my father—and while there, got a degree in nuclear physics, and then transferred to the Foreign Office, or MI5 or something like that, as an arms inspector. Much respected in that role he was, too. Spent a lot of time in Iraq before he retired altogether. Since then, though, he has been called up on some sort of contract to help out in Libya since Gaddafi declared his Weapons of Mass Destruction, and he's been there quite often in the... "

Bill Clayton stopped in mid sentence, and stared at Catherine.

"Bill, whatever is it?" she said, alarmed.

"I wonder," he said quietly, "I just wonder if perhaps Libya isn't the link we're looking for."

"Libya?" she queried.

"Yes, Libya. Libya could just be the key to all this." He fumbled in the pocket of his best jacket. "I didn't show you this, but I will now. It's a handwritten, or scribbled, note from Sean Doyle. It was in with his letter, but didn't mean much to me at the time."

He handed it across the table, just as their main course arrived. Catherine kept it hidden until the waiter had gone, and then read,

"Your man Vaughan a fund-raiser – links to Libyan arms dealers."

"Good God," she exclaimed. "If that's true…"

The rest went unsaid. They were both deep in thought.

"Why Vaughan?" asked Clayton, thinking aloud. "What's his particular interest in all this?"

"If that note from Doyle is accurate, then I suppose it's always possible that Benbow discovered that Vaughan was involved in IRA arms running," said Catherine.

"Or that Vaughan was afraid he would."

"Suddenly, we need to know a great deal more about Alistair Vaughan, don't we?"

"We certainly do," agreed Clayton. "And I would also like to know about the weapon that killed my uncle. I wonder how good the Sussex Police forensic people are? I think I might pay them a call to find out."

He looked across at Catherine. "Fancy a dirty weekend in Brighton?" he asked with a grin.

For the rest of the meal, they forgot the shop, and delved into each other's personal background. They discovered they had quite a lot of interests in common, although a love of motorbikes was not one of them. The more Bill heard, the more attracted he was to the girl across the table. And the more she learned about Bill Clayton, the more inclined she was to think that a weekend in Brighton, or anywhere else, would be worth having.

Eventually and inevitably, the conversation drifted back to the problems surrounding Op. Honolulu, and they discussed how they might set about finding out more about Vaughan.

"I've met the man quite recently, of course," said Bill. "Had lunch with him and the Cabinet Secretary at a very posh restaurant in London. We mainly discussed how to get hold of the IRA cash, but I seem to remember that I also mentioned the arms dump in the south, and how difficult I thought it was going to be to get at it. I also mentioned the shipment of arms they were expecting from Libya. Good grief, if he is on their side and not ours, I just about gave the game away about everything we knew."

"You weren't to know," said Catherine.

"Of course not," agreed Bill. "But if that note from Doyle is only half accurate, we've been extremely lucky to get away with it so far."

"I'm sure the man could have done more to stop us," said Catherine.

Bill looked at her. "He should have killed me and not my uncle for one thing," he said.

"Bill, please don't say that," she implored. "You must take special care from now on, until we know the truth. Promise me you will."

"Agreed," said Bill Clayton. "I'll start by keeping off the back of that motorbike of yours!" He was flattered that she seemed to care.

"Talking of my bike," she said, looking round, "we should make a move. They must be waiting to close. We are the last here."

He looked at his watch. "You're right. I suppose we should, but I was just beginning to enjoy getting to know you better. Can we do this again?"

"Yes, please."

He helped her into her coat, and they made their way across the car park towards her Honda.

"Don't you go mad on that thing, now," instructed Bill sternly. "And don't expect me to catch up. My machine's not up to it."

"It's been a lovely evening—thank you."

"On the contrary—thank you for coming, and thank you for helping me get some thoughts into order. We've given ourselves more work to do, I'm afraid, but we'll keep this between ourselves for the time being if you don't mind."

She leant forward and kissed him gently on the cheek.

"See you in the morning," she said, and swung a shapely leg over the bike.

Bill stood there as she sped off, watching her disappear from view before going across to his old VW. He was careful to check it over thoroughly before he got in, started the engine, and followed Catherine at a more sedate pace.

***

Next morning, Bill Clayton was in the office early. He hadn't slept a lot, if he was honest. Sergeant Wilson was already there. He flipped his hat across the room for it to land, as usual, on the hat-stand.

"'Morning, sir," said Wilson. "I see you're more like your old self this morning."

"'Morning, Sergeant," he responded. "You're in early—anything wrong?"

"Not really. I just couldn't sleep, for some reason."

"Neither could I, and probably for the same reason."

"Commander Marsden left a message on the answer phone. He'll be in about mid-morning, but is on his mobile if you want him. Otherwise, nothing much has happened since you left last night."

"Nothing much has happened?" he grinned, "You're joking! But we'd better work out what to do about Vaughan, so come in."

"There's coffee on if you want some."

"Please. Bring yours with you, too."

She sat across the desk from him, and there was the briefest of pauses as they both remembered how different it was last night. Clayton broke the silence.

"We agreed that we'd try to sort out the Vaughan puzzle on our own for the time being, until we are sure who else could be trusted with the information we've got. Our major need is for more information about the man, but there's no one I dare ask at the moment. It's his lifestyle as much as anything else we need to look into, and his background, to see if we can find any kind of motive for his wanting to help the IRA. In any other circumstances, that would mean mail intercepts, phone taps, a look at his bank balance, investments, and so on. But none of that is available to us at present, because there's no one we trust enough to ask for it to be laid on."

"So we do it without asking," said Catherine Wilson.

"Easier said than done. We need help, not least because we can't both go swanning off at the same time. Someone's got to be here."

"What we really need is to get into his flat, or wherever he lives," said Wilson.

"So far as I know, he has a flat near Canary Warf—Limehouse, I think—which he uses during the week, and a house in the Home Counties somewhere. His wife rarely uses the London flat, as she can drive to town when she needs to."

"Perfect," said the Sergeant. "We'll set a honey trap for him. I can do that."

"I'll not agree to that for one minute," said Bill Clayton.

"Don't start being protective already," said Wilson. "I can take care of myself."

"I know you can, but I still don't like the idea one bit."

"I certainly wouldn't let it get out of hand, so stop worrying," said Catherine Wilson. "I can't think of a better way of getting into his flat, unless you want to go along with a battering ram or something. This way it's legal, and I only need to be there long enough to set up a few bugs, find his bank statements and so on. It shouldn't take more than a couple of visits, and if I can get my hands on his keys, I can let myself in for the second one, and he won't even be there."

Bill Clayton sighed. "I suppose I've no choice, really, but I don't like it.

Unless something better occurs to me, we'll do it your way, but not quite yet. I need to do some more research first, and then I'll try to fix for the three of us to meet."

"What sort of research?" asked Wilson.

"The note from Doyle said Vaughan was a fund raiser. I would like to know how. Did he have his hand in the Bank of England till in some way, like Jim Farlow?"

"Good point," said Wilson.

"And I want to find out if all the IRA money was actually transferred to the special HMG account from the banks Farlow raided, or whether some of it was creamed off by Vaughan before it got there."

"Only Vaughan will know that, surely, and you can't ask him."

"No, but I could ask the PM to find out from the Treasury. We know roughly what was in most of the accounts, so we should be able to check."

Captain Brian Foley appeared. "You're in early—anything happening?" he asked.

"Not really," replied Clayton. "Just thinking of a few loose ends that we should tie up. There's one I'd like you to tackle, if you would."

"Of course."

"You know the list of bank accounts which we got from Sean Doyle was in an old envelope addressed to my uncle, Edward Benbow, who was shot and killed a week or so ago. Could you get on to the Sussex police, and see how their murder enquiry is going? I'm interested to know if they've turned up any clues yet—motive, suspects, that sort of thing."

"I'll get on to it this morning," said Foley. "Anything else?"

"Not really, although I think I feel another meeting with the Prime Minister coming on soon. And other coffee please, Sergeant Wilson."

Chapter Thirteen
THE PRIME MINISTER'S STATEMENT

The Prime Minister rose to a packed House of Commons. Rumours that he was to make a momentous statement about the future of Northern Ireland had been circulating for some days, and it was known that he had been having a series of briefing meetings that very morning with senior colleagues and leaders of the opposition parties. At the same moment, the Leader of the House of Lords stood ("in another place") to repeat the statement to an equally full House, while in Dublin the Irish Taoiseach, Michael O'Leary, was also on his feet to make a similar announcement. In a carefully planned and co-ordinated lifting of the veil of secrecy, President Bill Minton gave a nation-wide address on radio and television from his White House office.

Hansard carried a verbatim report of the proceedings the next day.

HOUSE OF COMMONS OFFICIAL REPORT
PARLIAMENTARY DEBATES
(HANSARD)

**Prime Minister's statement
Northern Ireland: amendments to the constitution**

The Prime Minister (Mr. Tony Weaver): With permission, Mr. Speaker, I should like to make a statement about proposed constitutional changes to Northern Ireland and its structure of government that are of the utmost importance to the future of the Province and its people, as well as having a significance far beyond the United Kingdom itself. *[hon. Members: Oh!]*

I have taken the opportunity this afternoon to fully brief the leaders of the opposition and the main political parties in Northern Ireland, and copies of my statement, which is also being given in another place by the Leader of that House, will, of course, be placed in the library immediately I have finished, and made widely available to hon. Members, to the media and to members of the public. Mr. Speaker, I am sure you understand that my hope is that I shall be able to complete my statement this afternoon without interruption. *[hon. Members: Here, here]*

Mr. Speaker, it will not have escaped the attention of Members of this House, or members of the public, that there have recently been considerable changes to the way in which the people of Northern Ireland have been able to conduct their lives. I dare say that, to many, life has taken on an air of normality, which, in the past, they had not dared to hope for.

I shall briefly rehearse the reasons for this, which I hope will put to rest much of the wilder speculation to which we have been treated recently in some sections of the media. The fact is, however, that there are many aspects of the changes which have occurred in the Province which I am unable to explain, any more than the media has sensibly been able to, but there are other areas where the government has been able to help the process, and I propose to give details of those in this statement.

Let me first of all address the security situation in Northern Ireland. For reasons which I do not fully understand, and for which I have seen no satisfactory explanation put forward, it would seem that the vast majority of terrorists, from both sides of the sectarian divide, have left the Province. This appears, on the face of it at least, to be the result of a quite vicious feud that was sparked by the disappearance of the President of Sinn Fein, Mr. Martin McFosters. The bloodshed that followed was without precedence, even by Northern Ireland standards, and yet it was quite specifically targeted at the leadership of the terrorist groups. Thankfully, the population of the Province was largely unaffected by this sectarian violence, which was as short-lived as it was unexpected and unexplained. I can, however, repeat the assurance which has been given many times before in recent months, and that is that the Army and the Northern Ireland Police Service have not been engaging in some form of state terrorism.

Mr. Speaker, the Northern Ireland Police Service has, indeed, deployed considerable additional resources in an effort to track down the perpetrators of some of these violent crimes. An early result of this vendetta, however, was that most of the remaining members of the terrorist groups fled the Province, no doubt in fear of their lives, and no doubt also, spurred on by the list which appeared, giving the names and positions of major players in the terrorist gangs which have for so long plagued the people of Northern Ireland, and indicating those who had already either been murdered or had disappeared. Once again, the Northern Ireland Police Service continues its attempts to trace the origins of that document, although forensic tests so far have failed to produce any worthwhile leads. *[Interruption]*

No, I shall not give way to the hon. gentleman - there will be ample opportunity for questions when I have concluded my statement. A second, and far more welcome result of this internecine warfare has been the almost total cessation of the many and profitable protection rackets and extortion scams which the terrorists were operating, and an end to punishment shootings and beatings. As hon. Members will know, the lack of terrorist leadership and the almost total cessation of sectarian violence has allowed the Police Service, aided by the Army and acting on information received, to confiscate considerable quantities of illegally held arms and ammunition, both from private houses and drinking clubs, and from arms dumps. Some of these dumps were previously unknown to the Decommissioning Body, who were also unaware of the seemingly huge arms dump that blew up near Cashel, in County Tipperary.

I mentioned earlier, Mr. Speaker, that there were areas where the Government has been able to aid the process of bringing peace to the Province in ways which have not previously been possible. I can now tell the House that, with the fullest possible help and co-operation of President Minton and the American administration, and with the active participation of the Taoiseach and the Government

of the Irish Republic, we have effectively closed down the operation of Northern Ireland's terrorist groups. Not only has the leadership of these organisations been either disposed of in some way or dispersed, and not only have we effectively been able to disarm them in a way which would not otherwise have been possible, we have also jointly been able to close their access to all their sources of funding. In America, for example, NORAID has been wound up and, with effect from tonight, will be declared an illegal organisation, as will any other body or individual on either side of the Atlantic found providing funds to terrorist organisations. Furthermore, action taken by the three Governments has closed all known bank accounts in Northern Ireland and elsewhere, and emptied them of their funds.
[Interruption]

Well, I don't propose to give way, but I can tell the House that freezing accounts was not considered to be a sufficient solution, and that the money has therefore been transferred to HM Treasury - several millions of pounds. I don't propose to quote exact figures. I pay tribute here to the role played by the Bank of England and the US Federal Reserve in achieving this remarkable result. This has been a significant step forward in the action by this country and our allies in defeating the world-wide menace of terrorism, and helps to prove, I sincerely hope, that our actions are not simply directed towards Islam.

Mr. Speaker, I come now to the political future of Northern Ireland, and the constitutional changes that I mentioned a moment ago. Let me start by saying that the discussions which have led to the proposals being formulated, which I am about to outline to the House, have taken place in an atmosphere of total co-operation between the three Governments, and that we are all in complete agreement about the proposed future of the Province. Details are therefore being laid before those Governments today, in a coordinated public briefing operation of which my statement is a part.

Let me remind the House, although it is probably not in the least necessary for me to do so, that for decades, if not centuries, the two opposing parties in Northern Ireland have had aspirations which have proved impossible to reconcile. On the one hand, the Unionists have demanded that they should remain part of the United Kingdom, while on the other, the Nationalists have demanded quite the opposite for a united Ireland. As President Minton quite rightly pointed out in a speech to Congress last year, the common factor, which has prevented reconciliation between the two ideals, has been the United Kingdom itself. In recent discussions with myself and with the Taoiseach, Mr Michael O'Leary, President Minton has proposed that this barrier to future progress should be removed. In the situation that the cessation of terrorism has created, positive initiatives on the political front are now possible.

Mr. Speaker, we have jointly taken a bold step forward, and are prepared to work together to cement the peace which is now being enjoyed in Ireland into a lasting and stable political future during which the vibrant economies of all sides can flourish side by side. The President has proposed, and this Government and the Government of the Irish Republic have agreed in principal and subject to certain safeguards that I shall outline, that sovereignty of both the Republic and the Province of Northern Ireland should pass to the United States of America. *[Interruption]*

Mr. Speaker (Sir William Wakeham): Order, order. I must ask hon. and right hon. Gentlemen on both sides of the House to regain their seats and allow the Prime Minister to complete this important statement without interruption. Order! Members have already been told that there will be ample opportunity for debate later.

Mr. Tony Weaver: Mr. Speaker, I can quite understand my hon. Friends wishing to put their points now, but this is an issue which will be debated to the fullest possible extent in the weeks and months ahead, and time has been allocated this afternoon for questions after my statement. I would only say by way of a diversion now, and for the benefit of those members who have not yet had an opportunity to study the text of my statement, that those of my hon. and learned Friends who have been able to do so, and with whom I have had the briefest of discussions before coming to this Chamber, have given a generous and welcome degree of support to the measures which I have outlined to them. For this I am most grateful, and it gives me hope that other hon. Members will share their support when they, too, are fully aware of what is proposed. *[Interruption]* I'm sorry, but I shall not give way to my hon. Friend. My statement is nearly finished, and time presses on.

Mr. Speaker, the proposal to transfer sovereignty of both Northern Ireland and the Republic of Ireland to the jurisdiction of the United States, will of course, create a united Ireland. This will no doubt be welcomed by those Nationalists in the Province, who have long aspired to such an outcome, but may, at first sight, be thought to be abhorrent to the Unionists. However, the proposal will contain sufficient safeguards to fully protect the interests of both sides. For instance, there will be a provision for continuing representation in this House, and for the maintenance of British citizenship where this is wanted.

Let me tell the House that a joint, international, Constitutional Committee has been meeting at a secret location for some months now to draw up detailed proposals which will enshrine and safeguard the interests of all parties to this agreement. In mapping the way forward, they have drawn heavily on the precedence set when Hawaii joined the United States of America in 1959 as its 50th State. The Constitutional Committee has now drafted a State constitution for the united Ireland, and this will be put to this House in a few days time when a White Paper is published containing the full set of proposals which surround this venture. These proposals will similarly be put to the Senate and to the Dail. Any amendments agreed in any one of these places will be put to the other two, and when agreed by all parties, enshrined in a revised Constitution. It is not only the elected representatives who will be consulted, however, and I shall be bringing forward a Bill very soon which will make provision for referenda to be held both in the Province and on the mainland. As to the representation of the people, hon. Members will know that the United States Congress, through which all legislative powers are granted, consists of two houses, the Senate and the House of Representatives. Each State sends two members to the Senate, while the numbers of representatives in the House are elected on the basis of their population. It is envisaged that Ireland will have two Senators and four members of the House of Representatives, two of whom will be empowered to sit in this Chamber and take part in debates on any issue that relates to or might impact upon the State of Ireland. This facility will, it is proposed, remain in force for ten years after sovereignty passes across.

Finally, Mr. Speaker, the House will wish to know that initial consultations with the European Union, the United Nations and the North Atlantic Treaty Organisation have brought forward a welcome, positive response. The fact is that the people of Northern Ireland have become wearied by long periods of conflict, by a peace process that failed to bring peace, and by various attempts at self-rule that have failed to find a satisfactory political solution to the conflicting views found within the Province. I sincerely believe that the proposals soon to be put before this House will bring a lasting solution under the good offices of the United States, which has itself had a long and happy association with Ireland, north and south, from where some 50 million of the American population can trace their ancestry. I also believe that the 'do nothing' option no longer exists.

Mr. William Holden (Hampstead): I thank the Rt. hon. Gentleman for his statement, and for his usual courtesy in making it available beforehand to members of this House. I thank him also for the detailed personal briefing he was able to give some of us on the Opposition benches before coming to the Chamber. Both these moves have been invaluable in helping us to understand the proposal that he has outlined this afternoon, and which, as he said, will have far reaching consequences for this country and others if adopted. The government will know that, traditionally, there has been a high level of support for all policies relating to Northern Ireland on all sides of this House, and having now had a chance to hear what the Prime Minister has had to say, I believe that this support can be expected to continue. *[hon. Members: Here, here]*

It is quite plain that there is an enormous amount of work to be done before the proposed transfer of sovereignty can be effected, and in the coming weeks and months it is evident that Parliament and its various committees and institutions will be heavily involved in ensuring that the best interests of the people of this country are safeguarded. Our overall interests must be to ensure that terrorism never again returns to the Province, and that the peace and normality which is currently being enjoyed by the people of Northern Ireland is maintained and enhanced.

There are obviously also complex international negotiations to be completed, and I wonder if the Prime Minister is able to say anything more about them at this stage? For example, the Republic of Ireland is already a full and independent member of the European Union. Will the transfer of sovereignty of both the Republic and Northern Ireland to the United States bring automatic membership of the EU to the Province, or will the Republic be required to leave the Union?

Mr. Weaver: I thank the hon. Gentleman for his unqualified support. There are indeed many issues that require considerable further study and debate, and a considerable amount of diplomatic activity will inevitably be required. As to the specific point which has been raised, current thinking is that the new State of Ireland would become an automatic member of the EU, and that, for a specified period of time, probably ten years, both the US dollar and the Euro would be regarded as legal tender, with the Pound Sterling being phased out of circulation as the Dollar is phased in.

Mrs. Shirley Donovan (Antrim North): I, too, thank my right hon. Friend for his openness and frankness in coming to the House today. I share the views expressed by the hon. Member for Hampstead (Mr. Holden) in that I believe the proposals put forward will go a long way towards stabilising the situation in the troubled Province of Northern Ireland and provide solid foundations for the future. I salute the initiative taken by the President of the United States in suggesting such a long term solution to an apparently unsolvable problem, and I share his view that the people of America will be able to warmly welcome the kith and kin who live in what will become the 51st State. I look forward with great enthusiasm to taking part in the debates that will inevitably follow, and in being a part of the difficult and complex pattern of decision-making that must be completed before a transition can take place

I speak, as the House will know, for that part of the Ulster population that has been so staunchly in favour of remaining part of the United Kingdom. From what little I have heard and read today, however, I take great strength from the fact that those of us who wish it may maintain our British nationality for the foreseeable future. I am also pleased to note that, through virtually automatic membership of the EU, we shall have the right of free movement to and from its member nations, including Great Britain. It seems to me, Mr. Speaker, that the measures outlined this afternoon will give the people of Northern Ireland, from whatever part of the community, the best of all worlds. The Prime Minister mentioned, almost in passing, that he believed that future economic benefits would also flow from the transfer of sovereignty. Has my right hon. Friend any further information he can give the House on that important aspect of these proposals?

Mr. Weaver: I am most grateful for the hon. Lady's enthusiastic support for the proposals that I have outlined this afternoon. As I am sure she has understood, however, they are only outline proposals, and a considerable amount of work and effort remains to be done before the dream of a peaceful and settled Northern Ireland becomes a permanent reality. In respect to her particular point about future economic development, it is, of course, far too soon to be able to speak in specific terms, especially in an area where contracts must necessarily be negotiated.

However, I would make two points, Mr. Speaker. First of all, I believe that any part of the United States is almost certain to benefit from the overall prosperity of that great trading nation, and that, in the particular case of Northern Ireland, there will be an inevitable increase in tourism, with the impact that has on jobs and income, flowing almost from the start. Secondly, I know that the President has in mind encouraging - I put it no stronger than that - the letting of new contracts with Bombardier Aerospace for quantities of their 'Starstreak' ground-to-air missile for the US Army. As hon. Members may recall, this is a multi-warhead missile, produced exclusively by Shorts of Belfast. Furthermore, I understand that there are also likely to be new orders placed for Bombardier's Regional Jets, for use by US Coastguards, and that in turn will also bring additional work and job security to Shorts. I have no doubt that more trade development will follow.

Mr. Jonathon Bradshaw (South-West Cornwall): I congratulate the Prime Minister on this bold and imaginative move, but dare to suggest that it is the American people, rather than the people of Northern Ireland or the UK who will be the net beneficiaries. Would the right hon. Gentlemen agree with me that, in gaining what some would see as its fatherland as well as a 51st state on the very edge of Europe - indeed, an integral part of the European Union, - the United States benefits from a huge trading opportunity and vastly increases its sphere of influence over world affairs? Would he not also agree that this move is likely to be hugely popular with the 50 million Irish-Americans in the States, to the extent that the Republicans will probably enjoy the votes of that section of the community for many years to come?

The Prime Minister: What the hon. Member says is probably true in detail, although I do not believe that the United States has more to gain than the people of the United Kingdom as a whole. For one thing, the people of Northern Ireland will have in place a third party as their sovereign power which should be acceptable to both parts of the community, whereas at present the UK is unacceptable to one part, while union with the south would be unacceptable to the other. This solution will, I anticipate, prove to be acceptable to both sides across the whole of Ireland, north and south. Economic benefits are bound to flow, not least because of the special relationship which already exists, and without which this proposal would never have been possible.

It should be born in mind, Mr. Speaker, that the United States has always played a pivotal role in the peace process, acting as an honest broker across the sectarian divide, so it is no stranger to the recent history of the Province. Finally, this country will save many millions of pounds of public expenditure every year, not just because many of the present costs will transfer to the United States, but because we shall no longer need, for example, to maintain an Army there. We shall, of course, also lose tax revenue, but I estimate the net benefit to the Exchequer to be in the order of some £100 million each year.

Mr. Patrick McNeil (East Belfast): Will the Prime Minister please tell the House what will happen to the British Army based in the Province, and to the Northern Ireland Police Service? I notice he is already counting the savings to be made, so may I assume that, at last, the people of Northern Ireland are to be rid of them?

The Prime Minister: The proposals that will be put before this House include provision for the Northern Ireland Police Service to be disbanded upon the transfer of sovereignty, and for it to immediately reform as a US Federal Police Force. As the hon. Member may recall, all American Federal policemen are fully armed. *[laughter]* The British Army will similarly be withdrawn to barracks on the mainland, and will be replaced by an equal number of US Marines and Coastguards. It is also proposed that the Irish

Republican armed forces and the Guardai would likewise transfer to US Command. The hon. Member for East Belfast and his cohorts cannot, I am pleased to say, look forward to a period without law enforcement. *[laughter]*

Mr. Bernard Mercer (Edgbaston): On a more serious note, would the Prime Minister agree that the defeat of terrorism in Northern Ireland, by whatever means that has been achieved, has a significance for world peace and stability far beyond the narrow borders of that Province? Is it not a fact that the United States and its coalition partners have become obsessed in the past with the thought that terrorism only exists in the Muslim world, and that this has actually done more harm than good to recent efforts to achieve a peace settlement in the Middle East? Can the Prime Minister say whether the United States has any plans to help Spain tackle the problems of ETA and the Basque Separatists?

Mr. Speaker: Order. I am sorry to stop the hon. Gentleman, but his questions do not relate directly to the statement.

The Prime Minister: With respect, Mr. Speaker, I believe the hon. Member for Edgbaston (Mr. Mercer) does make a valid point, in that the defeat of terrorism has been perceived by many, especially in the Middle East, as a war against the Muslim community. Of course, this is not the case, and we and our allies have made it quite clear on more occasions than I care to remember that terrorism and those who support terrorism will be pursued wherever they are and whoever they are. Actions which we have been able to take in Northern Ireland to bring peace to the Province after decades of unrest there and on the mainland will, I hope, do much to reinforce that point, and to reassure those involved in the Middle East peace process that Islam is not the only target.

Mr. Iain McFadean (Glasgow Central): Would the Prime Minister agree that, when the constitutional position of Ireland has been changed as outlined in his statement, the point made earlier by my hon. Friend the Member for South-West Cornwall (Mr. Bradshaw) becomes very relevant, in that with the huge Irish-American vote almost guaranteed, the President, Mr. Minton, will be able to take a much tougher stance with Israel, as his Jewish lobby will no longer hold such power over him or be able to exert such a great influence over what he does?

Mr. Speaker: Order. I really must insist that hon. Members do not widen this debate beyond the subject of the Prime Minister's statement.

Mr. Ronald Briggs (Liverpool, Walton): The Prime Minister has displayed an endearing belief that Irish terrorism really is a thing of the past. How can he be so sure? What about the most recent attack in London, which destroyed one of the Capital's best known landmarks?

The Prime Minister: I firmly believe that terrorism in Northern Ireland is at an end, Mr. Speaker. We have seen no evidence of it for some considerable time now, and all our information is that the terrorist organisations are now without arms, without a leadership, without the large reserves of cash they once enjoyed which would enable them to re-arm, and indeed, in many cases they are also without members who are any more prepared to continue their sectarian violence. As I have said, there have been no explosions or bombings or shootings in public, and no punishment shootings or knee-cappings or beatings in private. Earlier victims of protection rackets are now free from the demands once made upon them, and the public at large is now coming to realise that it can lead a near normal life that has been unknown to them for many years. As to the bombs that destroyed Nelson's Column, my information is that this was a small IRA cell which has been based in North-West London for some time, but which has eluded the best efforts of Scotland Yard's Anti-terrorist Squad. I am pleased to be able to announce to the House, however, that, following a series of Police raids in North London early this morning, six men and two women are now being held at Paddington Green Police Station, and are being questioned about the bombing.

Mr. Ronnie Hancock (Blyth Valley): Mr. Speaker, that is indeed welcome news, and it is to be hoped that the perpetrators of that rather stupid and petulant bombing of one of London's most popular tourist attractions can at last be brought to justice. It was obvious to many of us that it was a last desperate act by a dying organisation, and we are fortunate that it did not result in any deaths or serious injuries to any members of the public. May I ask the Prime Minister if any decision has yet been taken about replacing the monument?

The Prime Minister: No decision has yet been taken, Mr. Speaker, although I am hoping that we shall soon be able to announce that this famous column will be replaced, using money taken from the accounts of the IRA and other terrorist organisations. *(hon. Members: Here, here)* At the moment, however, we await detailed proposals, and, I have to tell the House, a legal opinion about the rights and wrongs of using confiscated funds. As I am sure my hon. Friend the member for Blyth Valley is aware, it has also been suggested that, as a gesture to our European friends and allies, and in particular the French, we should no longer perpetuate the memory of Admiral Lord Nelson.

Mr. Edward Little (Dover Harbour): Many members on both sides of this House could suggest a more fitting gesture to offer to the French.

Mr. Speaker: Order, order.

Chapter Fourteen
THE ENVELOPE

After lunch, Major Bill Clayton wandered across from the mess to the Transport Office.

Corporal Harrington was having a quiet day, and had been looking forward to getting stuck in to his new paperback. He had to admit that, so far, the book itself was not living up to its cover, and that's what had persuaded him to buy it. So far—page 53 he was on—there had been no reference whatsoever to a tall, willowy blonde with big boobs and not much on. And Major Clayton, nice bloke though he was, nearly always spelt trouble.

"Why is it," asked Bill Clayton, "that it's always you on duty when I come across?"

"I often ask myself the same question, sir," replied Harrington.

"Anyone would think that you ran this place on your own."

"It sometimes feels like it, sir," replied Harrington. "How can I help?"

"Well," said Clayton, "for once there's no panic."

"That's a relief."

"I would like you to book me two seats on the first flight out on Thursday, please." said Clayton. "The day after tomorrow," he added, just to be sure Harrington knew what day of the week it was. Clayton had spotted the cover on Harrington's book.

"Who for, sir?" asked the Corporal.

"Me, and Sergeant Wilson," replied Clayton. "And before you ask, I've got a meeting with the Prime Minister in Downing Street, and Sergeant Wilson has a meeting at Scotland Yard. Try to book us back on the last flight, if you would—neither of us knows how long we shall be."

"Should be no problem, sir," said Harrington. "I'll get the tickets to your office in the morning."

"Thanks." Clayton turned to leave. "Oh, and, er, enjoy the book."

Harrington blushed.

"Early start on Thursday, I'm afraid, Sergeant," Clayton said when he got back to his own office. "I've asked for seats on the first flight out, and the last one back. Tickets delivered here tomorrow. We'll use my car to get to Aldergrove—save bothering the Transport office again. I give them enough trouble."

The Prime Minister's statement a few days earlier had really caused a stir, as everyone knew it would. So far, though, it had been difficult to accurately gauge reaction around the world to what he and the President had announced, but the early signs were reasonably encouraging. Certainly, there was unqualified relief that terrorism in Northern Ireland seemed to be at an end at last, although there was still the odd incident now and then, as there had been in Iraq. The Protestant population was more fidgety about the plan than anyone else, as expected, but even there, it seemed that the option of keeping a British passport or taking out dual nationality, coupled with the continuing representation at Westminster had been enough. There had also been a quiet 'spin' campaign going on for some time, to make sure they knew the alternatives—civil war or union with the South. The message that Britain had had enough had got through, and if continuing union with Britain was no longer an option, then the comfortable umbrella of the United States was better than the rest. There seemed to have been enough concessions to the Unionists for them to be reasonably content, at least for the time being. No doubt both sides of the divide would be seeking even more during the run up to the referenda and elections, when the people of Northern Ireland, and in the South, would finally express their views. And that process was due to start very soon, before too much opposition was allowed to build up on either side of the Atlantic.

Nick Marsden was in Bill's office, as he still liked to call it, when Clayton returned.

"I had been thinking, you know, that it was time for me to sling my hook, as they say, and get back to Hereford," he announced, "but suddenly, after Monday's political hoo-hah, we seem to be getting busy again. So if it's OK with you, I'll hang around a bit longer."

"I could still do with your back-up, if you don't mind. I shall be away from the office for bit in the next week or so I think."

"Agreed, then," said the Commander.

"As a matter of interest," asked Bill Clayton, "why are we suddenly busy again?"

"The PM's statement has brought all sorts of people out of the woodwork. You can hear the din of the whistle-blowers from here. We've had several very useful tip-offs from anonymous individuals who want to clean their slate and their consciences while there's time. There are a couple of quite important people we need to pick up—they were on our initial list—and there are a few small arms caches to deal with, 'as a result of information received', to use the jargon."

"That's good news," said Bill. "Tell me about the weaponry."

"Nothing really big," replied Marsden, "although one, a UVF haul, is well worth getting rid of. And lots more illegally held weapons are being turned in by their owners, too, according to our police chums at Knock. The police can actually deal with most of this, but I'll get a team together to deal with the ammo when we find it."

"Excellent. But I'm sorry we're getting busy again right now, as I'll miss a bit of the action when I go to London on Thursday," said Clayton.

"With the lovely Sergeant Wilson, I see!" Marsden pulled his leg.

"That's right. She's using a contact of hers to gain unofficial access to some records at Scotland Yard that I wanted to go through, and I'm meeting the Prime Minister again in the afternoon. There's no end to the fun, is there!"

"Brian Foley will be here, though, so we'll manage without you for a day," replied Nick Marsden. "What are the records Wilson is searching through, as a matter of interest?"

"If I can, I'll tell you when we get back, if they prove to be at all relevant. But they may not—we'll see."

***

It had been the fag end of last week when Catherine Wilson, wearing an even bigger grin that usual, had knocked on Bill Clayton's door.

"You'll never guess what I've done," she said.

"Surprise me," said Clayton.

"By devious means, which we won't go into if you don't mind, I've been given access to Alistair Vaughan's personal files at the Yard."

"You're joking!" exclaimed Clayton. "How the hell did you manage that, you clever girl?"

She raised a finger to her lips.

"Not a word," she said, "but I have managed to persuade an old chum of mine—ex Military Police—to let me have a quiet and unofficial look, if he can get hold of them from the vaults where the archives are stored. Thursday, unless I hear to the contrary before then."

"That's brilliant."

"I thought you'd be pleased," Catherine Wilson said. "It could provide us with just the information we've been looking for."

"Tell you what," said Bill Clayton. "I'll try to fix to see the PM on Thursday too—I need to see him again—and perhaps we can both meet Alistair Vaughan for lunch. How about that?"

"A great idea. If I don't get all we need from the files, I can chat him up over lunch, and if necessary, and if I'm asked, stay over."

"That's the bit I don't like," said Clayton.

"Don't fuss," she replied. "It may not come to that, but you know very well I can take care of myself if I have to."

Clayton nodded. "I still worry about you, Catherine."

"Nice of you, but please don't," she replied.

"I'll book us both back on the last flight, and hope you're there," he said. "Apart from anything else, it will give us a good chance to de-brief, over a drink."

"I can think of better places than that," she said with a laugh.

***

As it happened, Clayton couldn't get an appointment with the PM until late afternoon on Thursday, which didn't really matter as he might, by then, have learnt a bit more about Vaughan from Catherine's researches.

He had an uneasy feeling about that man, and his possible involvement with the opposition. It just didn't seem to ring true, somehow.

He had arranged to meet Catherine Wilson outside Scotland Yard at 12.30, from where they would get a cab to Covent Garden for their lunch with Vaughan at 'The Crusting Pipe' wine bar. He had given Wilson her return air ticket, 'in case she was delayed for some reason', as he put it; otherwise, they would meet at the check-in desk at Heathrow.

In the cab, Catherine Wilson was able to give Clayton a rather breathless debrief about her morning's work.

"Went right through his personal file," she reported, "and your friend looks as clean as a whistle to me. Not a hint of any trouble, no Irish connections, excellent annual reports, and a very high security clearance."

"Lifestyle?" queried Clayton.

"No evidence of anything excessive," she said. "Smallish house in a village called Lane End, near High Wycombe, and a smallish mortgage to go with it. Of course, he left the Yard a couple of years ago now, so I suppose things could have changed since then."

"Maybe we'll find out later," said Clayton, as the cab pulled up.

"Oooh! Shops!" said Catherine.

"Keep your mind on the job, if you don't mind, Sergeant," said Clayton.

Alistair Vaughan was already at the table when they arrived, and Catherine Wilson was introduced as Clayton's P.A.

"Very nice to meet you," said Vaughan, shaking hands.

"We can talk shop quite openly," said Clayton. "Catherine's got a high security clearance, and knows all about our recent endeavours."

"Good," said Vaughan. "We haven't met since my part in the venture was finished, but I was impressed how well that villain Farlow got on, and how quickly he got to grips with things."

"He seems to have done a good job for us," said Clayton, "although I haven't checked the figures to make sure he managed to transfer all there was. I hope to do that later," he added, watching Vaughan's face.

"I think you'll find not a penny piece missing," said Vaughan. "We watched him like a hawk all the time, and recorded his every move. Every stroke of the keyboard is on tape, by the way, if you should want it for your files."

"I'll take the tapes off your hands, if you like, although it might be best if we destroyed them eventually rather than risk them getting into the wrong hands."

"I agree," said Alistair. "There are no copies, of course."

"I could perhaps collect them from you this afternoon," said Catherine. "I shall have nothing better to do while the boss is in Downing Street, although a bit of West End shopping is always tempting."

"There's not much in the way of shops in the City," said Vaughan, "but Canary Wharf is worth a visit, if you have the time."

"I'd certainly love to have a look round Docklands," Wilson enthused. "I've never been, but I've heard so much about it. In fact I rarely get to London at all, and when I do, usual head for the West End or Knightsbridge."

"Don't all women?" asked Clayton.

They chatted on over a pleasant lunch and a bottle of Claret, but learnt nothing about Vaughan that they thought was in any way out of the ordinary—not a clue. The man was as open and frank as they could wish, and perfectly relaxed. He didn't mention Farlow's unfortunate accident on the tube after he left prison, although they all knew of Vaughan's part in arranging it.

Eventually, Clayton looked at his watch, and made to leave.

"Can't keep the PM waiting, but you two by all means linger over coffee or another glass. I'll settle up on the way out."

He and Vaughan shook hands, promising to keep in touch.

"See you at the airport, Catherine," he said as he left. "If you're going to be delayed, give me a bell on the mobile."

"I'll have to get back to the Bank soon, too," said Vaughan. "But if you've really nothing else to do, why don't I point you towards Canary Wharf, and perhaps meet you again later for a drink, when I can show you around?"

"That would be really nice, if you're sure it's not putting you out at all."

***

Bill Clayton saw the Prime Minister alone in his Downing Street office.

"It's very good of you to see me, Prime Minister, and I sincerely hope I'm not wasting your time, but something's come up in relation to Op. Honolulu that I thought you should know about. On the other hand," continued Bill thoughtfully, "it would be rather better in the end if I am eventually proved to be wasting your time."

"I told you at the beginning that if there were any problems you should discuss them with me direct. You'd better explain."

"Frankly," said Bill, "I am extremely worried that we may have a traitor in our midst. Someone we have trusted absolutely until now appears to have let us down, and not to have been on our side at all."

"Good grief!" exclaimed Tony Weaver. "If true, that is very serious indeed, and I see now what you meant about hoping that you are wasting my time. Are you suspicious of anyone in particular?"

"Yes, I am, although I should find it difficult to believe if it proved to be true." said Clayton. "My problem is, though, that until we can be certain of the man's identity, I no longer know whom I can trust. Which is why I asked to meet you on your own."

"I quite understand that," said Weaver. "Tell me what's happened to arouse your suspicions."

"It is all related to that wretched envelope of my uncle's, and his later murder. At the time, Edward Benbow was acting for your government, Prime Minister, as an arms inspector in Libya, following Gadaffi's admission that he had WMDs. Obviously, because of the envelope, his death is in someway related to Op. Honolulu, but for the life of me I have been unable to find the link or any explanation at all. But it all comes back to the envelope containing the list of terrorist bank accounts, which, you may remember, you passed on to Sir Robin Algar. He, in turn, gave it to Alistair Vaughan at the Bank of England. Alistair is an old and trusted colleague of mine, but I'm sad to say that he is my prime suspect."

"Why?" asked the Prime Minister, looking very worried.

Bill Clayton told Tony Weaver about the circumstances surrounding the death of Father Sean Doyle, the erstwhile priest of the Falls Road, but also one of Bill's top men, who had actually supplied most of the bank account details, gleaned through his other role as the IRA's Treasurer.

"You may remember me telling you that he was found dead in Strangford Loch."

The Prime Minister nodded.

"For a time, we imagined that he had suffered at the hands of the IRA, who probably assumed that he was responsible for the disappearance of their funds. But then this arrived in the post."

Bill took Doyle's letter from his pocket, and waited while the Prime Minister read it.

"Well," asked Weaver, "what do you make of it?"

"We now know," said Clayton, "that Doyle committed suicide, presumably because he feared torture or worse at the hand of his IRA colleagues. But he left a false trail, to ensure people didn't suspect any involvement with us. The public view of his suicide now is that he was a paedophile, about to be uncovered, although we know that he was no such thing. Now look at this, if you will."

Clayton produced the scribbled note that had been included with the letter.

The Prime Minister read it with growing concern. "Now I understand," he said, quietly. He sat, thoughtfully, for a few moments. "I find all this as difficult to believe as you do, but we really do need to take colleagues into our confidence if we are to get at the truth."

Clayton frowned.

"I shall take full responsibility for this, as I have for everything else which has happened in this area recently, but I want you to go over all this again, with Robin Algar, who I trust absolutely, and one other, who I believe you also know from the past—Air Commodore Paul Bridges. I'm told he has one of the highest security clearances available, and he also knows Vaughan well."

Clayton knew that Army Majors don't argue with Prime Ministers, so he had to agree. Eventually, in response to Tony Weaver's summons, both men joined them. Clayton briefed them, as he had the Prime Minister, and showed them the two notes from Doyle.

"I came direct to the Prime Minister with this," he concluded, "because frankly I didn't know whom I could trust anymore. I'm having Vaughan checked out, so there's no need for either of you to do anything on that front. So far, though, the whole thing remains a complete mystery, and Vaughan seems, at the moment, to be beyond reproach."

"Frankly, that doesn't surprise me, Bill," said Paul Bridges. "I've known him and worked with him on and off for years, but you were absolutely right not to dismiss this out of hand."

"And equally right to trust no-one until you had done some research," said Sir Robin Algar. "But like Paul, I would find this very hard to believe."

"I'm afraid I took the view that I shouldn't trust anyone who had seen that envelope, apart from my own team, of course, and you, Prime Minister," said Clayton.

"The fact remains, though, that the link with Libya could help to explain why Edward Benbow was murdered," said the Prime Minister.

"And at the moment," said Bill Clayton, "It's the only explanation available to us. There seems to be no other possible motive, except that Vaughan wanted to prevent Benbow from uncovering his arms dealing activities, and so arranged for him to be shot. It's quite possible that Vaughan could have been creaming off the IRA's funds as well as being a fund-raiser, and he could also have creamed the top off the accounts we've just closed. As an ex-Head of the Fraud Squad, he'd know all the dodges."

"A bent ex-copper," murmured Robin Algar.

"The problem is," said the Prime Minister, "that if we do confirm these suspicions, we can hardly have him arrested and charged. It would blow the whole of Op. Honolulu sky high."

"So what will you do next?" Paul Bridges asked Clayton.

"I'm waiting for the results of forensic tests on the bullets, recovered at the scene by Sussex Police, and Vaughan is under close personal surveillance. After that, God knows," said Clayton. "And I have to say that at the moment, Vaughan looks squeaky clean."

"That's a relief, but not all together surprising," said the Cabinet Secretary, "unless I totally misjudged the man."

"The whole thing makes no sense to me at all, to be honest," said Clayton. "Just cast your mind back to our lunch, Sir Robin. I mentioned, in front of Vaughan, plans to blow up the Arms dump south of the border, while the IRA

Quartermaster was inside. He appears to have done nothing to stop that, when he could have. And he appears to have done nothing to thwart our plans to empty the terrorist coffers—indeed, he suggested Jim Farlow as the man who could do it for us. It just doesn't make sense."

"I couldn't agree more," said the Prime Minister. "The whole thing is quite extraordinary."

"There was one thing I wanted to ask while I am here, Prime Minister," said Clayton. "Can you possible find out for me, very discretely, how much cash was actually moved from the various IRA accounts into the special Treasury account which was opened for it?"

"Why do you ask?" enquired Weaver,

"Well, Sean Doyle gave us a pretty good idea how much was in the accounts, and I would just like to be sure that none of it was creamed off during Vaughan's operation to close the accounts."

"That's a damned good idea, Bill," said Robin Algar. "If I may use a phone, Prime Minister, I can get a ball-park figure almost immediately."

"Go ahead," said the PM.

He did, and it was all there.

Another mark in Vaughan's favour, and a further deepening of the mystery surrounding his role in this affair.

Clayton wondered how Catherine was getting on.

***

Vaughan got away early from the Bank, and he and Catherine met again by the escalators at Canary Wharf station. He guided her to a nearby wine bar. He had remembered to bring the tapes, which she put in her briefcase. They were getting on well, but Catherine had still not discovered anything like an explanation for Sean Doyle's cryptic note. Eventually, and without a lot of persuasion, Catherine agreed that she could stay a bit longer to have dinner with him, and that she really didn't have to get back to Belfast tonight.

"Tomorrow morning really will do," she said. "So long as I let Bill Clayton know where I am, there won't be a problem, and I've got my return ticket, so I can easily re-book. This really is most kind of you, Alistair, but I haven't enjoyed a visit to London so much for a long time."

"Well, I'm really pleased," said Alistair. "It will be so nice to have your company this evening. I get a bit fed up on my own every night."

"Aren't you married, then?" asked Catherine, innocently.

"Oh, yes, but we have a flat near here where I stay during the week, and I get home at weekends, unless my wife is coming to town, as she is this weekend. She's coming down tomorrow afternoon and we're going to a concert on Saturday evening, so the flat is really very convenient for that sort of thing. Otherwise, we live in a small village in Buckinghamshire."

"How nice," said Catherine.

"The flat is certainly very convenient," said Vaughan, "specially when I have to work late. And it's not a bad flat, either. It's in one of the old warehouses they've converted, so it's very modern inside, and looks out over Limehouse Creek, which is pleasant."

"That must cost," said Catherine, probing.

Vaughan laughed.

"An arm and a leg!" he said. "The Bank pays for it, thank goodness. I could never afford it on my own, and would have to commute without it, which would be costly in time as well as money."

"I think I passed a few conversions like that on the little train you put me on," said Catherine Wilson. "They look very nice from the outside."

"They're very nice inside, too." He hesitated for a moment. "Look here," he said. "Please don't think I'm making advances or anything, but if you haven't anywhere to stay tonight, there's a spare room if you would like to use it. We always keep the bed made up in case, although hardly anyone ever stays. My son, sometimes, but that's about all."

"Well, I haven't booked anywhere," admitted Catherine, "And I was going to ask if you could recommend somewhere cheap. It's very generous of you, but I hardly like to put you to all that trouble, since we've only just met."

"It's really no trouble at all, honestly. I'll tell Gill to bring a spare set of sheets tomorrow, and the laundry can do yours—they collect on Monday. All part of the service provided for the flats."

"Well, if you're really sure," said Catherine, hesitantly.

"Absolutely," Alistair assured her. "So long as you think you can trust me!"

"I'll set Bill Clayton onto you if you make one false move!" responded Catherine. "Thank you again."

"Right, then. Let's think about where to have dinner."

"Before we do that," said Catherine, "I need to dive into Marks over there for a spare pair of tights, and things."

"Of course you do," said Vaughan. "I'm so sorry; I should have thought of that myself."

"Not at all," replied Catherine. "Look after my drink for me—I shan't be a minute."

Alistair Vaughan stood politely as she left, and watched her disappear towards the supermarket. *Bill Clayton was a lucky chap*, he thought. But then so was he, and he was looking forward to Gill coming down tomorrow. He got out his mobile phone to tell her about his unexpected visitor.

At the same time, when she was well inside the store and out of view, Catherine rang Bill Clayton.

"Where are you?" asked Bill.

"I'm in Marks and Sparks at Canary Wharf, getting a spare pair of tights and things like that." she replied. "I've accepted an invitation to stay the night in his spare room after we've had dinner. Where are you?"

"I'm at Heathrow already. I had a useful meeting, although we didn't get very far, but at least everyone now knows the plot. They're all as amazed as we are at the thought that Vaughan could be anything but straight."

"I think he is straight," said Catherine. "He's certainly not living a lavish lifestyle. He's already let me buy a round, and we've agreed to go Dutch over dinner, so your expense account is going to take a bit of a hammering, I'm afraid."

"We were able to check on the cash transfers, and everything that should have moved across seems to be there, so he hasn't been creaming any off," reported Clayton.

"If he did, he's not spending it," said Wilson. "I'd better a get a move on, or he'll get suspicious."

"Take care then," said Bill Clayton, "and ring the office tomorrow to tell them you've been delayed."

"Good idea," said the sergeant. "And don't worry about me. He's being a perfect gentleman, and is even ringing his wife to tell her I'm staying over at the flat tonight. She's coming down for the weekend tomorrow afternoon, so I'll be away well before then."

"See you tomorrow, then. Take care."

"G'night, Bill."

She hurried back to Alistair having completed her purchases, which were shoved into the briefcase.

"I've rung Gill," he announced, "and said you'd be away before she gets to the flat tomorrow lunchtime. I hope that's right."

"Oh absolutely!" she replied. "I'm an early riser, usually, so I'll get your breakfast if you like, before I go!"

"I wouldn't think of it," he said. "My breakfast is a cup of coffee when I get to the office, and I'm usually there about seven. So you sleep in, and then help yourself to whatever there is you want."

"A coffee will do me, too, but I'll wait until you've gone to give you a clear run at the bathroom. I'll leave the place as tidy as I can," she promised.

The rest of the evening passed pleasantly for both of them, but no amount of probing and no end of leading questions led Catherine to change her view of the man she was with. He was no bent ex-copper, she was sure, but she'd have a good look round the flat tomorrow before she left, just to be sure. But she had already made up her mind that she would not be bugging the place after all, unless Bill insisted.

Next morning, she waited for Alistair Vaughan to leave for the office before she stirred, although she had been awake for sometime. After she had showered and dressed, she made herself a coffee. Vaughan had thoughtfully put everything ready for her, and left a note telling her to help herself to anything she wanted, and he hoped she had slept well and been comfortable.

She used his phone to ring the office, and spoke to Captain Foley.

"Good morning, sir," she said. "I'm afraid I didn't finish my work at the Yard yesterday, so I've stayed over to finish it off this morning. I hope that's all right."

"OK by me," replied Foley. "I'll tell the Major when he comes in."

"Thanks," said Catherine. "If he should want me (*I wish*, she thought!) I shall have the mobile on. But I should be back this evening, and I'll ring again later to let you know."

She felt almost guilty as she pulled on her surgical rubber gloves, and started a systematic search of the flat.

Nothing.

She eventually left, and set out for the shops, where she managed to buy a pretty 'Thank You' card, and a large box of chocolates. She let herself back into the flat, wrote the card, and left it with her gift on the hall table.

She found their cottage in Lane End quite easily. The man on the Docklands Light Railway station had told her how to get to High Wycombe, and she got a cab from there to the end of the road where the Vaughans lived. It was about lunchtime when she arrived, so she guessed that Gill would already be one her way to Limehouse, if not already there. To make sure, she walked up to the front door, and rang the bell. Twice.

No answer.

She had no difficulty in getting in through the back door, which she closed quietly behind her. The keys were on the kitchen draining board, so she locked herself in, and pulled on her gloves again. As Alistair had said, it was a small house, and didn't take long to search. After about an hour, she had seen all she wanted to see, used his phone to call for a cab to meet her at the end of the road, and let herself out of the front door.

By the time she got to Heathrow, the late afternoon flight had checked in, so she got herself a seat on the last one of the day—24 hours after the one Bill had caught—and went for a meal. She was starving, and realised she hadn't eaten since dinner last night.

She phoned Bill Clayton on his mobile.

"I'm on the last flight," she said.

"Are you all right?" he asked.

"Hungry, that's all, but I'm just getting something to eat now."

"I'll meet you at Aldergrove." It wasn't a question.

"That would be nice," she said, "Otherwise I shan't see you until Monday."

"By the way, Alistair has been on the phone. He wanted to make sure you'd got back all right, and to thank you for the chocolates."

"I told you he was a gentlemen!" said Catherine. "By the way, I decided not to leave any bugs behind in the flat. I'm quite sure we'd have learnt nothing from them, and it saves having to go back for them."

"Not that it would have been any problem for you," said Bill. "Alistair's wife wanted to know how you got back into the flat with the chocolates. He said his PA couldn't have managed anything like that."

"What did you say?"

"I said you were in the Army and his PA wasn't!"

"I've been to their house as well," she announced, "And that wasn't difficult to get into either. Since I knew his wife would be out, it seemed too good a chance to miss."

"That's damned clever of you!" said Clayton. "I can't wait to hear about it. And I can't wait to see you again, either."

"A couple of hours, and I'll be there," she said, and hung up. She felt a quiver of excitement at what he'd said. She wanted to see him again, too. Thank God she didn't have to wait until the dreary office on Monday.

When they eventually met, she touched him lightly on the sleeve in greeting, but it was too public a place for anything more.

In the car, he said, "It's too late to go anywhere now, for a drink or a meal, but can we have dinner tomorrow?"

"Please let's," she said. They agreed on the now usual place—this would be their fourth visit—and the now normal travel arrangements.

"I'm really dying to know how you got on," he said, "although I take it you've found nothing in any way suspicious about Alistair."

"Absolutely nothing," she confirmed.

"But if you agree," he continued," I think we should wait for a proper debrief in the office on Monday. Commander Marsden doesn't even know about Doyle's first letter, never mind his scribbled afterthought, so I suggest we all have a brainstorming session and start from the beginning. Someone might just be able to suggest an explanation for all this."

"No shop until Monday then," she agreed "What shall we talk about instead?"

"Let's talk about us," said Bill Clayton.

Chapter Fifteen
DOUBLE BEDS AND DOUBLE AGENTS

Bill Clayton found it difficult to concentrate on Monday. Monday mornings weren't usually like this, but then neither had the weekend been quite like any other. He hadn't been to the toy hospital at all, but he had managed to spend more time with Catherine.

He could hardly believe the way his relationship with her had developed, or how quickly. For months on end, he had sat in his office, secretly admiring the girl who worked for him and who ran his registry. Admiring, and wanting to talk to her like a human being, rather than as a fellow member of the Army. But the fact that he was commissioned and she was not, was like an insurmountable wall between them—an artificial barrier put in their way by the Army. He had never dared hope that one day they might at least be able to see across that barrier, even if they could not break it down, and to regard one another as people with feelings rather than people with different ranks. But now the barrier was beginning to crumble, and they were at last able to start sharing their feelings towards one another. It had taken a huge effort on his part to first suggest that they should meet outside the cramped and stifling conditions of the office. It was gamble, which could have dramatically misfired, and yet, as if by some miracle, Catherine had agreed. Agreed so readily and without question that he believed she might, in some small way, feel the same about him.

Somehow, he managed to drag his mind back to the present.

Monday morning it was, and there was work to be done. He called his team together, into the now cramped office. They made themselves as comfortable as possible, clutching mugs of coffee that Sergeant Catherine Wilson had made.

"The first thing I need to tell you," said Bill, "is that this little team will soon start to wind up. Everyone, from the Prime Minister downwards, is full of praise for all the work we've done in helping to create the climate within which a political solution can be made to work at last. We all know what that solution is, but it would never have been possible if terrorism here had not been brought to an end. In the wider sense, we have contributed towards a major victory in the global war against terrorism."

They all nodded, sagely, inwardly pleased.

"There are still one or two loose ends to be tied up before our role in Op. Honolulu can be said to be finally finished, and in a minute, I want to discuss one of them which is proving particularly difficult.

"But we must now start concentrating on closing down this office completely."

They looked at him, puzzled.

"The Americans are coming," he said, "and soon. The FBI has already sent a couple of chaps to the Northern Ireland Police Service to start the process of turning it into a US Federal Police Force, and we must soon expect to get the CIA and the US Marine Corps breathing down out necks, because they will be taking over from us when the Army eventually withdraws to the mainland."

Nobody seemed to have thought of that.

Catherine sat in shocked disbelief. Surely the Army wasn't going to engineer their separation now, just at the very time they were beginning to get together? That would be just too cruel. That simply must not happen—it could not happen; she felt desperate, and suddenly brimming with unhappiness where only moments before she had been so elated.

"The first thing we need to do is have a very thorough search through all our files and records," Bill Clayton continued, "to weed out anything which we think Uncle Sam might not want to see, or might not need. We have to get everything into apple pie order for a hand-over, probably starting quite soon. Perhaps you could take the lead in that, Sergeant Wilson."

She nodded, as he paused.

"We are all going to be very busy, again."

"And we need to start thinking about a formal handover, Brian," he said to Captain Foley. "Would you have a word with the General's ADC to find out what they are doing, and how we can dovetail into it? And then start thinking about the format of a presentation of our own, going into a lot more detail, for the chaps who will actually be doing this job. All that will need careful drafting, visual aids prepared, and so on. The sooner we start, the better."

Clayton almost felt he was making work, just to take his mind off things. He turned to Nick Marsden.

"Nick, you've been a tower of strength during recent weeks, and we couldn't have done what we have without your support and professionalism."

"Great pleasure," he said, "Thoroughly enjoyed it, as a matter of fact. But I suppose this is leading up to telling me to push off, back where I came from."

"Almost," said Bill Clayton, with a grin, "although I wouldn't have put it quite like that! But you don't need to hang around to help us sort out years of old files."

"Not my favourite job, anyway," said Marsden. "I'm not good at paper."

"But I do want you to help us sort one final problem before you go." said Clayton. "It's been nagging me for a week or more, and I simply cannot think my way through to a solution. I'll start at the beginning, not just for your benefit, Nick, but also to help remind the rest of us of what we know so far."

He started with the death of his uncle, Edward Benbow, and told them something of his background and his most recent role in Libya. He went on to tell them about his uncle's old envelope, which had been used to house the list of terrorist bank accounts, and how the envelope had ended up in the hands of Alistair Vaughan.

"It has always seemed pretty obvious to me," he said, "that there has somehow got to be a link between that envelope and Benbow's death. Then our man Father Sean Doyle died. He had given us the list with most of the information we needed to close the terrorist bank accounts—the list which was put in the envelope. Doyle was an ex-Army Padré, working in the Falls Road as parish priest, and had for some time been the IRA's Treasurer. He was one of our best men out in the field, as you all know.

"In fact, it was his death which gave us our first clue as to a possible link between Edward Benbow and Op. Honolulu," continued Clayton.

He pulled Doyle's note from his tunic pocket.

"Nick," he said, "you haven't seen this before, but it was posted to me by Doyle shortly before he was fished out of Strangford Loch."

"My dear Bill," it read. *"I'm sure you know me well enough to recognise what is in my character and what isn't, in spite of what may be suggested. And I'm sure I know you well enough to be confident that you will spot a red herring when you see one. May the Good Lord bless you.*

Regards, Sean."

Marsden read the note with a puzzled look on his face. "Cryptic, to say the least," he commented. "What do you make of it?"

"It made no sense at all at first," replied Marsden. "We had all assumed that Sean was murdered by the IRA because they suspected him of creaming off their funds, but they're not in the habit of leaving their victims lying around. Then the post-mortem showed that he had committed suicide – he was full of barbiturates. We then assumed that he had taken his own life to avoid the attentions of a suspicious IRA, but the Police also discovered child pornography both in his flat and downloaded onto his computer, so they have assumed that he killed himself because he was about to be uncovered as a paedophile. We, on the other hand, and because of his note, thought it was all designed to divert attention from us, and to prevent the discovery of any possible link to us and our activities."

"Hence his reference to a red herring, and you knowing his character better than the evidence suggests," said Nick Marsden.

"Exactly," said Clayton. "But there was another, hastily scribbled, note in with his letter."

He showed it to Marsden.

"Pass it across to Brian—he hasn't seen it yet, either."

"Your man Vaughan a fund raiser – links to Libyan arms dealers."

"Vaughan, for God's sake," said Foley. "Why Vaughan?"

"That's what I had to find out, and fast. It seemed out of the question that Vaughan could be some kind of traitor, but if Vaughan thought that Benbow was about to uncover his links with Libyan arms dealers, then he could well have arranged for my uncle to be killed. And until I knew one way or the other, I could no longer trust anyone involved in our venture. There was no one, it seemed to me, that I could talk to about it, except the Prime Minister, and Sergeant Wilson."

"I was pretty safe," she said, "because I had only been on the fringes of this business, and because I'd never met Vaughan or Benbow."

"But you had seen the envelope," said Marsden.

"Quite so," continued Clayton "It was gamble, but it seems to have paid off. By pure good fortune, Sergeant Wilson had a contact at Scotland Yard. Somehow, she persuaded him to dig out Vaughan's old records from the vaults—you remember he was a commander there running the Fraud Squad before he went to the Bank of England. But we needed to know more about the man—his background, life-style, possible links to Ireland or Libya, that sort of thing. That's why we went to London on Thursday, Nick. You'd better take it up from there, Sergeant, since you did all the work."

"Very well, sir," said Catherine Wilson.

She glanced at her notes. This wasn't going to be easy. Normally she would have had no problem going over the events of last week, but suddenly things weren't normal any more. Not between her and Bill, anyway. She found it hard to concentrate, and even harder to believe that she and Bill were at last behaving towards one another like two human beings. Like two people who cared. She realised, too that Bill wasn't finding this easy either. The death of his wife had hurt him terribly, and she could tell that he had determined never to be hurt like that again. He had shut himself off from life, almost. Buried himself in his work, and when that wasn't enough to keep him away from mixing socially with people, had shut himself away in his toy hospital. She understood the reasons, but had nevertheless longed to be able to get close enough to him to help. Suddenly, as if by some miracle, the ice had cracked, and they had been out together. Not once or twice even, but four times. She began to think that he really might share her feelings, but knew how very careful she had to be not to send him back into his protective shell. If she showed her true feelings too soon, or too quickly, she would lose him. That's if the Army didn't wrench them apart again.

She struggled to bring her mind back to the office, and knew that Bill was having the same problems. They had to be so careful, both of them, not to betray their new fragile relationship to their colleagues. *Damn the Army*, she thought.

"The plan was," she said, "for me to go through the records at Scotland Yard in the morning, then meet Major Clayton so that we could both have lunch with Mr. Vaughan. It was my job to investigate the man as thoroughly as possible and as quickly as possible. If necessary, I was even authorised to set up a honey trap."

"Christ, Bill, that was risky," interrupted Marsden.

"I can look after myself quite well, thank you, sir," said Sergeant Wilson primly.

"Well, I know that, damn it. But it was still hellish risky," said Marsden.

"Anyway, in the end it wasn't necessary," continued Wilson. She glanced at her notes again.

"There was absolutely no hint, from his records at Scotland Yard, that Mr. Vaughan was anything other than what he seemed. Good security clearance, excellent annual reports, no hint of financial problems, only a small mortgage on a small house in Buckinghamshire, and no obvious Irish links—nothing. The man looked squeaky clean."

Bill Clayton took up the story.

"We probed as much as we decently could without raising his suspicions over lunch, but turned up absolutely nothing. Certainly not a lavish lifestyle—he let me pay! But I had half wondered, if Doyle's claim that he was a fund raiser for the IRA was true, whether he might have creamed off some of the terrorist funds from the accounts he was closing down for us. However, when I was with the Prime Minister later that afternoon, he was able to quickly check what had been put into the special Treasury account, and it was all there so far as we could tell."

"I stayed on after Major Clayton had left," continued Sergeant Wilson, "and Mr. Vaughan offered to show me around the Docklands area of London, and eventually to meet him again for dinner. He also offered to put me up in the spare room of the flat the Bank provided for him, and I accepted, as this would give me the perfect opportunity to scout round for bank statements and so on. I was also supposed to bug the flat, but eventually, because of a total lack of evidence of anything untoward, I took the decision not to. Throughout my time with him, he behaved impeccably, and even rang his wife to tell her I was staying in the flat overnight. She was due there the following afternoon, I discovered, so I took the opportunity to visit and search their house in Buckinghamshire after she had left for London."

"Bloody hell!" exclaimed Captain Foley.

"The point is, Brian," said Clayton, "That neither of us found anything in the least suspicious about the man. He is what he appears to be: as straight as a die and as clean as a whistle, if you'll excuse the mixed whatsits!"

"Which means," said Marsden, "that the dear departed Father Doyle had it all wrong."

"Which is exactly the point of this little brainstorming session. We still can't link Edward Benbow and his wretched envelope to Op. Honolulu, although the link has to be there somewhere."

"I agree," said Foley. "But I drew a blank as well, when I got on to the Sussex Police as you asked, sir. They have no clues at all about your uncle's murder, and no one locally has been able to suggest a motive. They've recovered the bullets from Mr. Benbow's body, and found the spent cartridges, but forensic tests have thrown up no links to any other crime."

"There are two things I'd like to know," said Commander Marsden. "I'd like to know more about that bloody envelope, but first of all I'd like to know if the gallant Sergeant can make some more of her excellent coffee!"

"Good idea," said Clayton. "Let's take a break for a few minutes and have a stretch. It's a bit cramped in here," he said, looking at Marsden's radio in the corner.

"I'll get rid of that in a day or so, and then you can have your office back," promised Marsden.

Armed with fresh coffee, Marsden repeated his question. "Bill, old chum, tell us more about this envelope. It's obviously central to the whole puzzle, because without it, no one would ever know that Benbow existed. By the same token, only those who have ever seen the envelope can be in the frame for his murder—hence you not trusting anyone. So! What's the history of the envelope? How did it get here in the first place, and how did it come to have that list put inside it?"

They all turned to Major Clayton, expectantly.

Bill Clayton realised that he hadn't traced events back that far himself. Perhaps he should have done. Where had it all begun?

"So far as I recall," he said, frowning, "Benbow had sent me a couple of keys for clockwork toys, wrapped up in that envelope. He'd picked them up in an antiques market place in Petworth, not far from where he lived. It was in my pocket when I met Doyle to collect the list from him."

"And where did that happen?" asked Marsden.

"In the Mess, here, would you believe," said Clayton. "It's coming back to me, now." He lent forward. "You know we have regular liaison meetings with all sorts of public bodies, including church leaders. We've never got round to having all denominations together," he continued, "but at the last one we had with members of the local Catholic church, Doyle was invited, as he always was to these events, as one of the most important parish priests in Belfast. I knew he was bringing the list with him, but it was hardly the sort of thing he could hand over openly in front of all his colleagues. The arrangement was for him to put the list into the envelope which I had given him, and for him to leave it in the loo, on top of the cistern, where I would collect it later."

"So Doyle actually saw the envelope," said Marsden, probing.

"Not only that," said Clayton, "he had it for long enough to note down Benbow's address."

"But why would he want to do that?" asked Foley. "He had no idea who Benbow was or what he did."

"Yes he did," replied Clayton. "I told him. Like everyone else who's seen that bloody envelope, he naturally asked who Benbow was. And I told him.

Everything, including his probing visits to Libya."

They all looked at Bill Clayton, as the significance of what he had said sunk in.

"What an absolute bloody fool I've been," said Clayton, "not to have remembered that before."

"But if the good reverend really was on our side, Nick, as you had every reason to believe, it wouldn't have mattered a jot," said Marsden.

"Are you suggesting he might not have been?" asked Foley.

"Only that it's a possibility we should perhaps look at," replied Marsden. "In the same way you thought the unthinkable about Vaughan. You now have to add Doyle to the list of people who knew about the envelope, and who you therefore can no longer trust. Except that he's dead, of course."

There was silence, while they all pondered this latest revelation.

"I need to get down to Sussex," said Bill Clayton eventually. "I want to talk to the local police, and in particular, I need to borrow the bullets and spent cartridges from them. I'll bet they haven't thought that they could have originated from here."

"Now that *would* be significant," said Marsden.

"What it is to have a fresh brain looking at things. Thanks, Nick."

"My pleasure," said Marsden.

"I'll go at the weekend," said Clayton. "In my own time and at my own expense, and not the firm's, I think. It's time I visited my aunt again, anyway. Brian, perhaps you would be good enough to get back to your contacts in Sussex, and ask them if I can pick up the spent ammo while I'm there, so that we can run our own forensic tests. I think Petworth is the nearest police station to Fittleworth, so it would be handy to collect them from there, if that can be arranged."

Catherine was having a bad day. Just to add to her growing misery, Bill now seemed to be planning a weekend away from her. She decided to go back to the office after supper, and bury herself in the job of sorting out their files and records, ready for a hand-over. It might just keep her mind off things, although in fact it didn't. The more she thought about the mornings' events, the more depressed she became.

The phone rang.

At half past eight in the evening?

"Sergeant Wilson," she said.

"Major Clayton!" came the response. "What on earth are you doing in the office at this hour, Catherine?"

"I thought I'd start going through the files," she said. "To try to get my mind off things."

"What things?"

"Well, the team breaking up for a start, you going away for the weekend to see your aunt, that sort of thing. I was feeling a bit depressed about things, to be honest."

"Well, don't," said Bill Clayton. "I've been looking everywhere for you, and never thought you'd be in the office, of all places."

"I just had to do something," said Catherine Wilson. "But now you've found where I am, what did you want?"

"I want to know if you're free to come with me to Sussex at the weekend, that's what."

"I thought you were going on your own," replied Catherine.

"I couldn't very well invite you to come with me in front of the rest of them, could I? But if you can't come, then I shan't go."

"Oh, Bill! Of course I'd love to go with you, if you're sure," she said.

"Brilliant," said Bill Clayton. "We'll go Saturday morning to miss the weekend exodus, otherwise we might be spotted. We can go from Belfast City airport straight to Gatwick, and pick up a car from there. We can put up in a pub for the night somewhere, if that's all right."

"Is this my dirty weekend in Brighton you promised?" she asked.

"Don't be cheeky!" replied Bill. "And no, it isn't! Most of Brighton's sordid, and in any case the Sussex police HQ is in Lewes, which is even worse."

"Suddenly, I'm feeling more cheerful," said Catherine.

"I should hope so," said Bill Clayton. "We can discuss the details over dinner one day this week, if you'd like."

"I'm definitely feeling better now!"

"How about Wednesday?"

"I'm not doing anything, and if I was I'd cancel it!" she said.

"We'll go somewhere new," said Clayton, "where we shan't be spotted. I'll let you know where, but I'm getting a bit fed up with this hole-in-the-corner business, aren't you?"

"It would be so much nicer if we could be open about things," she agreed.

"One day, my dear," said Clayton. "One day. By the way, you do realise that there's a downside to our trip, don't you?"

"What's that?"

"Meeting my aunt," replied Bill. "She's a nice enough old stick, really, and I'm sure you'll get on, but, well, it's family, if you know what I mean."

"I don't mind in the least," replied Catherine.

"And I really ought to drop in and see my father, while we're there. He lives in Worthing, not far away. Would that be all right, too?"

"Of course it will be all right. I'd really like to meet him."

"He'd like to meet you, too. I've told him about you. He's a bit of a fiery old sod—retired generals often are—but he's got a heart of gold beneath it all. I think you'll like him. But we'll go over the details at dinner on Wednesday. Now you pack up, and relax a bit."

"I will," replied Catherine. "I'm feeling better now I've talked to you."

***

They made their way separately to City airport on Saturday morning, in case someone saw them together. Frankly, Catherine no longer cared whether anyone saw them or not. Not after dinner on Wednesday. No peck on the cheek when they had parted then, but a proper, if hesitant, embrace.

They picked up their car from Gatwick, and headed for Petworth, to collect the spent ammunition.

"Do you know Sussex?" Bill asked her.

"Not at all," she replied. "Never been here in my life before."

"Well," said Bill, "you'll find it a bit different from the Fens of your childhood. There's not much flat in this county, apart from the water meadows and flood plains around the rivers that flow into the sea – rolling, wooded down land, narrow winding lanes, and picturesque villages mostly. I'll show you around properly one day, when we have more time," he promised.

"Meanwhile, I think we should go to Petworth first to collect the ammo, then that's the business side of our trip taken care of, more or less. You'll like Petworth. Plenty of old antique shops, and Petworth House is a stately home well worth a visit one day. After that, I thought we could head for Worthing to meet the old man, if that's all right with you, and then that's over, too."

"Whatever you like, Bill. I'm more than happy just being here."

"Dad's only got a small flat, so we shan't be able to stay there. It's on the front, overlooking the sea, and just right for him. Then, I thought we would head to Fittleworth this evening, and see my old aunt tomorrow. There's a lovely old Inn at Fittleworth—The Swan—where we can get a good dinner and spend the night, if they have rooms. I'll ring them from Worthing."

"All that sounds perfect. But how come you know Sussex so well?" she asked.

"Born and bred in the county," he replied. "This is home for me."

They found the police station in Petworth without too much trouble, and the Detective Inspector in charge of the case was expecting them. He handed over the ammunition in a sealed plastic bag, and confirmed that they still had no idea who had killed Edward Benbow, or why.

"Two shots fired at close range," said the Inspector. "There was a chap fishing just below the bridge who heard the shots, and saw two men on a motorbike speeding off towards Bognor. We assume they were the killers, but the man was too far away to be anything like a witness—no description of the men, or anything. It's all very odd," he continued. "Things like that just don't happen around here."

The couple managed to park in the town square, and had time for a quick look round, including the antiques market where Edward Benbow had picked up the clockwork keys. Bill managed to buy a map of Sussex in the newsagents, so that he could show Catherine where they were and where they were going.

"See?" he said. "Fittleworth is only a short way down the road from here, and we shall pass it on our way to Dad's place. But we won't stop; there'll be plenty of time for a look round tomorrow, but it is a lovely little place."

They got to Worthing quite quickly, and parked in the forecourt of the block of flats, to the west of the town centre, where the General lived.

"We used to live a bit further along the coast, that way," said Bill, pointing west. "Village called Ferring; I was born there."

Catherine wasn't sure she was altogether looking forward to meeting Bill's father. She didn't have a great deal of experience of generals, and certainly not socially. As it happened, she needn't have worried—they hit it off immediately.

"I've heard a lot about you, my gal," he said, "and I've been looking forward to meeting you. Bill's not usually wrong about people," he added. "Come on in, and make yourself at home."

He turned to Bill. His booming voice wouldn't let him whisper, but he did his best. "You were right, boy. Damned good looking."

Catherine was surprised and flattered that Bill had even mentioned her at all.

Bill asked if he could use the phone. "I thought we could put up at The Swan tonight, if they have rooms free," he said.

"Excellent place," enthused the General. "Stayed there m'self." He turned to Catherine. "Just sorry I can't put you up here," he said. "It would do me good to have you around the place. But you'll probably be more comfortable at The

Swan, and it's handy for visiting my sister, Edith, tomorrow. She's still a bit cut up about Edward, of course, but like me, can't wait to meet you."

Bill came back from using the phone in the hall.

"The don't have any single rooms tonight," he said, "but they've got a twin, with en suite and everything, so I said we'd have that, if it's OK with you, Catherine."

"Of course it's all right with Catherine," boomed the General on her behalf. "Something wrong with the gal if it's not!"

Catherine grinned. "Your father's quite right, of course," she said, "I shan't mind a bit."

"Told you so." The General beamed.

"I'll take a turn round the block while you're using the bathroom," announced Bill.

The General looked at Catherine, raised his eyes to heaven, and went in to the small kitchen to put the kettle on for tea.

"Any clues yet about Edward's murder?" he asked Bill later. "If you want my opinion," he continued without waiting for a reply, "you can blame the bloody Arabs for that. Been poking around in Libya, by all accounts, and no doubt he was on to their illegal arms trade."

"As a matter if fact," said Bill, "There could well be a connection."

He explained why they were there, and about the mystery surrounding his uncles' envelope. They chatted on for ages, and Catherine became more and more relaxed in the company of the two men.

Eventually, Bill looked at the old carriage clock on the mantelpiece.

"We really must get going, Dad," he said. "They will have closed the dining room at The Swan if we're not quick."

The General walked with them to the car park.

He put his arm round Catherine's shoulders. "I can't tell you how nice it's been to meet you," he said to her quietly. "Bill's a changed man since I last saw him—much more like his old self again. He's very fond of you, y'know."

They parted already the best of friends.

"I know we haven't got all that time, if we're going to eat this evening," he said, as they were on their way, " but we'll go into Fittleworth from a different direction so I can show you bridge over the river were my uncle was shot."

They drove along the coast, passed a sign to Ferring, and eventually went through Arundel, with its castle on the hill, and north up the A.29. They turned off up the road signposted to Fittleworth, and Bill pulled over as they approached the river. They leant over the little bridge.

"I wouldn't mind a quid for every time I've scrambled over that stile next to the bridge when I was a kid," he said. "I used to go fishing down there quite often with my father and Uncle Edward. And now he's dead. Murdered at the very spot where we used to have such fun."

Catherine put her arm through his. "Come on," she said. "Buy me dinner."

Neither of them noticed the two men on the motorbike.

They booked in at The Swan, but went straight into the dining room while the chef was still on duty. They lingered over an un-hurried meal, and it was quite late when they eventually gathered their bags and climbed the stairs to their room.

Bill opened the door, and groped for the light switch.

"Oh, look," said Catherine. "A four-poster! How romantic – I've never slept in one of those."

"Romantic perhaps," said Bill, "but the man said this was a twin room, not a double."

"It doesn't matter," said Catherine, softly.

"Well, it's too late too do anything about it now, anyway," said Bill, "I'll just have to sleep on the floor."

In an instant, Catherine decided to gamble everything. "You'll do no such thing," she said, moving closer to him. She started to undo his tie. "This could turn out to be the happiest day of my life."

There was barely a pause.

Bill put his arms round her, and pulled her close. "Mine, too," he whispered, "if you're sure."

Suddenly, the barrier that had kept them at arm's length from one another for so long was gone, and they were at last free to express their true feelings towards one another.

There was no doubt that they were both very much in love.

They nearly missed breakfast, and there were kippers on the menu.

***

It was the middle of the following week when Bill got the call he was expecting from the police forensic science laboratory.

"We've been able to trace the spent ammunition and cartridges you brought in," said his contact. "Interesting. The weapon has been used at least three times in the past. A couple of sectarian murders of Protestant hardliners some three years ago, then a kneecapping in the Falls Road, which we took to be a punishment shooting. But then nothing, until this."

"So it's an IRA weapon?" asked Bill.

"No doubt about it, but until now, it hasn't been used for about three years."

"Any sign of the weapon?"

"That's interesting, too," came the reply. "As it happens, we only picked it up within the last two weeks. We found it stuffed down the back of the sofa in Father Sean Doyle's flat."

Major Bill Clayton briefed his team on this astonishing news.

"You're not saying, are you," asked Brian Foley, "that Sean Doyle killed Edward Benbow?"

"No," replied Bill, "but it was his Smith and Wesson that was used, so he must have authorised it and provided the weapon."

"Why, on earth?" asked Catherine Wilson.

"Well, we can't ask him," said Bill, "but my guess is—and that's all this is—my guess is that he thought Benbow had been responsible in some way for blowing the *Hercules* out of the water, on her way from Libya with the IRA arms."

"The significance of all this is lost on me," said Brian Foley.

"The significance is," proffered Nick Marsden, "that your chum Father Sean Doyle was a double agent."

"I'm very much afraid that I think you're right, Nick," said Bill. "There's no other possible explanation. And it begins to look as if the red herring he spoke of in his letter was not the trail of child pornography which he had left, so much as his second, scribbled note, naming Alistair Vaughan."

"If that's true, then why, in heaven's name," asked Catherine, "did he give us that list of bank accounts? Surely, if he really was on their side after all, he would never have done that."

"Risky, I agree," said Marsden. "But he must have assumed that the list was useless to us, and that we would never have been able to do anything with it. In that," concluded Marsden, "he severely under-estimated the talents of our Major Bill Clayton."

"What's more to the point," said Bill, "he had obviously never heard of Jim Farlow."

Chapter Sixteen
ANOTHER LIFE

♦

It was a glorious September day, and was designed to be a glorious day in the history of Ireland, America and Great Britain. For once, Ireland's 'soft' weather had disappeared, and it wasn't raining. In fact, it was Battle of Britain day, but few who were present remembered that, or cared.

Many months of planning and preparation were reaching a grand finalé, a climax of pomp and circumstance and splendour and pageantry the like of which had never before been seen in what was about to become the new American State of Ireland. It was more than likely that nothing like it had been seen anywhere else before, either.

A pattern of events had led to this climax, a pattern that had been mirrored in all the nations directly involved in planning this momentous event. Debates had been debated, referenda had been held and won, votes had been taken, elections had been held, Parliamentary Bills had been tabled, amended and eventually passed, allies had been consulted, new treaties had been ratified and old ones re-drafted.

In Ireland itself, communities had united, graffiti had been removed, peace lines marking sectarian boundaries had been demolished, police stations had been made to look like police stations again rather than fortified barracks, new currencies had been printed and distributed, customs posts at borders removed, until all the trappings of a normal life had been restored. Then, at last, when there was final agreement that Ireland should form the 51st state of America, it had finally been possible to start transferring powers and responsibilities. For most of the people of Northern Ireland, another life altogether had already been started.

And so it was, on this glorious September day in Belfast, that the sovereignty of the Republic of Ireland and the United Kingdom Province of Northern Ireland, both now united, would finally be passed to the United States of America. Yesterday, a very similar set of ceremonies had been held in Dublin, which was to be the new state's capital. Everyone was there yesterday, and everyone would be in Belfast again today. His Majesty the King and seven other members of the Royal Family, as well as kings and queens from other countries around the world, would all be there. The presidents of the European Community member countries would be joining the presidents of other invited nations as guests of President Bill Minton and his co-hosts, the Taoiseach Michael O'Leary and the Prime Minister, Tony Weaver. There were diplomats and dignitaries beyond number, all assembled to witness what most regarded as the official end of 'the troubles' and the start of another life with the raising of the Stars and Stripes over Stormont Castle.

There would be no ceremonial lowering of any flag, though. Because limited dual nationality had been recommended and accepted for those north and south of the border who opted for it, in line with the proposals put forward in the final communiqué of the Constitutional Committee in Honolulu, the Stars and Stripes would be raised on a flagstaff placed between the Irish tricolour and the Union Jack. In this respect, the ceremony would be quite unlike that in Hong Kong, when Britain handed back the colony to China. In Ireland, both the tricolour and the Union Jacket would continue to fly together for some years to come.

The whole affair was to be a masterpiece of tact and diplomacy and, truth to tell, of compromise. The route lining party and the Guard of Honour would be jointly formed by men from the Household Brigade and the US Marine Corps. Music would be jointly provided by the Band of the Royal Marines and the US Marines. There would be two fly-pasts in salute, the first with the RAF aerobatic team, the Red Arrows, in the lead. Once the Stars and Stripes had been raised, so the British military contingent would take one step back, and the US soldiers one pace forward. The massed bands would, until that key moment, be led by the Royal Marines Director of Music, but he would then ceremoniously hand over the baton to his opposite number in the US Marines. The second fly past would be led by the US Air Force aerobatic team, the Blue Angels. And so on. Every sensitivity had been catered for.

After the handing-over ceremony at the seat of Northern Ireland's many and various forms of government, the meticulously planned motorcade would sweep down the long driveway from Stormont to the Newtownards Road, and cross the River Lagan at the Albert Bridge for a state drive through the streets of Belfast, past City Hall. It would then join the Westlink to the M1 motorway, to complete its 20-mile journey to Hillsborough Castle, the setting for a sumptuous banquet, jointly hosted by His Majesty the King and the President of the United States. The time it took to agree the seating plan for that beggars belief, but eventually all sides agreed that they had taken their proper place.

Everything had gone like clockwork in Dublin yesterday, and officials were determined that today would be as good, if not better. Every event had been practiced over and over again, to ensure that the timing was as perfect as possible, that every last detail was tuned to perfection, and that nothing had been left to chance. The flypasts, the arrival of the dignitaries, their drive up the long sweeping driveway to the elegant neo-classical mansion of Stormont, the motorcade through the streets of Belfast, lined by troops and police from all three countries, even the state banquet had been cooked, to be eaten by delighted civil servants chosen to act the part of great men and women.

Only the final act had not been rehearsed.

***

The evening sun was dropping below the sparkling Mediterranean horizon as the English couple finished their meal.

It was their favourite place. A table on the harbour wall, across the dusty road from the small bar run by Davros and Athena.

It reminded the man very much of the Old Harbour in Paphos, before it had been ruined by tourists. This tiny fishing village of Kopufano was not that far from Paphos, but far enough away to have escaped the attentions of tourists, and to remain unspoilt and undiscovered by the holiday trade. There weren't many places like Kopufano left in Cyprus these days. But because they lived on the island, the couple from England were able to explore the dusty tracks and rugged coastline away from the towering hotels with their sun beds and swimming pools.

Davros still went fishing from time to time in his battered launch, but no longer made his living from the sea. He caught enough to supply his small café bar across the road from the tiny harbour, and anything left was eagerly bought by friends and neighbours in the village. Davros spoke very little English, but his wife, Athena, had attended university in Cambridge many years ago, and still had a love of the place and of the English people. The couple at their table on the harbour wall were always welcome, as it gave her the chance to practice the language. They also contributed more to the bar's meagre income than the villagers could who chose to eat there. They were a nice couple, and Athena knew he worked somewhere high in the Troodos Mountains, but she could only guess what he did.

The English couple had finished their early supper. A simple meal of local fish caught by Davros, with a green salad and boiled potatoes. They were enjoying a glass of Keo brandy as the air cooled and the sun set.

The tranquillity was broken by Athena, rushing from the café.

"Come quickly, come quickly," she shouted waving her arms wildly. "Come quickly, and listen. Bad news from England."

They rushed across the road and into the tiny kitchen at the back of the bar, in time to hear the end of the BBC World Service news.

By all accounts, the explosion, or possibly a series of explosions, had been bigger than anything ever seen before in Northern Ireland, or on the mainland. Bigger than Omagh. Bigger than Canary Warf.

It was certain that many people had been killed from among the VIPs and dignitaries, and countless others injured, many seriously. It was too early to say who had died, but the news broadcast was immediately followed by solemn music.

The couple slowly retraced their steps to their table, and sat in silence for a few moments.

"Who the hell could have done that?" he asked, talking almost to himself as he looked out across the sea.

The girl shook her head.

"I doubt it was the Irish," he said.

She shook her head again. "I suppose that's a problem for the Americans, now," she said.

"We'll have to help them," he said. "It could just be al-Qa'Aeda, getting at us and the Americans at the same time. They've wanted to do that for years. We may even be able to pick something up from here."

"I suppose we might," she replied.

"We should have been there, you know," he said to her, quietly. "Today. We were invited."

"I know," she replied.

"If it hadn't been for you, we would probably have gone, too," he said. "In a strange sort of way, I quite wanted to go, really, although I wasn't entirely sure."

"I had a feeling we shouldn't," she replied.

"You always were a canny chap," he said.

"I just didn't want to go back, after all this time."

"Why?" he asked.

"We're so happy here," she said. "I didn't want to break the spell."

"You're right, of course," he said. "I had mixed feelings about it myself, to be honest. About meeting the old crowd again."

"We may never meet some of them again, after today."

"You always had a sort of sixth sense," he commented, "as well as nine lives. Catherine 'The Cat' has lost another one today. Do you realise that, Sergeant Wilson?"

"Mrs. Clayton, if you don't mind, Major," she replied, with a smile.

They reached across the table, and held hands.

"Take me home," she said.

They crossed the road to pay for their supper. Athena and Davros were in animated conversation.

"I'm so sorry," Athena said to the couple. "Terrible, terrible."

They nodded, and walked to the car, arm in arm.

Once again, neither of them noticed the two men on the motorbike.

Lightning Source UK Ltd.
Milton Keynes UK
13 January 2011
165690UK00001B/40/P